THE WAKING DREAMER

J. E. ALEXANDER

ISBN-13: 978-0-615-87651-1
ISBN-10: 061587651X

Printed in the United States of America. First printing, 2013.

For my mom, a fine skylark.

"Every night and every morn
Some to misery are born,
Every morn and every night
Some are born to sweet delight.

Some are born to sweet delight,
Some are born to endless night.

We are led to believe a lie
When we see not thro' the eye,
Which was born in a night to perish in a night,
When the soul slept in beams of light.

God appears, and God is light,
To those poor souls who dwell in night;
But does a human form display
To those who dwell in realms of day."

William Blake,
"Auguries of Innocence"

"I can't go back to yesterday because I was a different person then."

Lewis Carroll,
Alice in Wonderland

CHAPTER 1

Under a moonless sky distended with December rain, the well-dressed young couple passed boarded-up storefronts and broken windows; an amber-eyed little girl skipped between them, laughing gleefully at the serpent wrapped in her long hair. They passed drug dealers and their entourages, who said nothing, making no move to harass the white couple with the bronze-skinned girl. Those who hunted the streets knew to fear the strangers who had come to Detroit three days prior. The gangs of the Motor City had declared temporary truces to warn each other about the odd but lethal strangers.

Just leave 'em alone.

The message had not been heeded by all: one street boss, intent on establishing his presence in Detroit, disregarded it. Only a lone survivor fled to tell the story of the red-haired woman in the black satin dress and stiletto heels who had disarmed and broken all four limbs of the nine men found assaulting a homeless man. Her young male companion, in a tweed suit and bowtie and seemingly disinterested, had leaned against a nearby building while the red-haired woman easily dispatched the attackers. That the little girl, shoulders draped with the serpent, had sat and studiously watched the fight had only added to the mystery and terror the three now inspired in the city's ganglands.

They're looking for something.

That was the consensus, and the city's worst elements had agreed to leave them alone and let them look.

The trio wandered Detroit's most dangerous streets by night without any sign of concern. The couple showed no interest in displaying bravado or strength to those they passed, yet they did not fear their presence being known. Crack houses. Rundown buildings. Even sewers. Never finding what they sought.

Now the three walked down another unremarkable street, the abandoned, hollow buildings on either side offering silent testimony to a forgotten neighborhood. The homeless huddled in corners that held small fires burning in trash cans. Cars stripped of all value sat as rusted metal frames along the curbs. The lone remaining business, a liquor store with half-blinking neon signs, went dark as it closed for the night. The wheelchair-bound old man who slumped in front of the store wheezed into his hands before lighting another cigarette and coughing hysterically.

As he passed, the young man withdrew one hand from his tweed coat's interior pocket. He checked a silver pocket watch and smiled, returning both hands to his tailored slacks.

"Eleven o'clock. Another hour and it'll be Christmas," he said. His blue-eyed, dimpled countenance drew wide with a sparkling white smile as a gust of Lake St. Clair wind parted his short, black hair. "Are we certain we're in the correct part of the city, Rhiannon?"

The red-haired woman beside him nodded in affirmation, motioning for them to stop and turning toward the little girl. The woman's pale face was framed by a fiery waterfall of scarlet curls that cascaded down beyond her narrow shoulders. Her sparkling emerald-green eyes stared unblinkingly at her young friend.

"Amala," the red-haired woman said as she drew her lithe

frame down toward her knees so that she was eye-level with the child. Rhiannon pulled the folds of the satin dress and black overcoat inward against the bracing winter storm. "As Druids, we must come to understand when to let our Wisdoms guide us *and* when we must guide our Wisdoms." She motioned with her hand to the serpent. Seeing both effort and confusion in the girl's face, Rhiannon tilted her head to the side and caught the gaze of the thin serpent bobbing its head next to the girl's cheek.

"Your Wisdom experiences her surroundings in ways you cannot, but as Druids we may share in that experience with them. Yet, our Wisdoms would give in fully to their nature and inevitably lead us back, beyond civilization, if we did not provide them with the necessary focus."

Listening intently, the little girl's round face looked again to the serpent. The intensity of mastering a new skill twinkled in her amber eyes. There was silence, the woman and man watching wordlessly, the only noise the low howl of wind through the inner city's streets.

"She's in there," the girl finally said. The serpent's head had turned a moment before Amala's, and they both now stared in the same direction across the street to a ramshackle building.

"Excellent, Amala," the man said with a satisfied, approving smile, much like that a father bestows on his daughter when she learns to walk.

Rhiannon laid her hand on the child's head, stroking through the long tresses of rich chestnut hair. The girl's chest swelled with the comfort of a familiar touch, and as one, the trio began walking toward the new destination Amala had provided.

"Are you nervous, Amala?" the man asked as they walked.

The little girl shrugged. "Dunno. What's she like?"

"I wouldn't know. I've never met her. But I hear she's a fearsome terror to evil men everywhere. It is said she is as great as the endless oceans whose tides ebb and flow by only her whim. She is the fiercest Ovate in the world."

Amala's frightened expression earned Rhiannon's rebuke. "Stop that, Oliver."

"But I took too long to find her. Will she be mad at me?" Amala trembled.

Oliver's face brightened with a sincere smile. "No. She will positively adore you. Almost as much as I do. If that's even possible."

"I hope so," Amala said, relaxing at Oliver's words. "She does, too," she added, indicating her ophidian friend who raised its head to taste the night's air and watch behind them as they crossed the street.

A deep bellow rolled across the city as the engorged sky erupted in a torrent of rain, scattering the huddled homeless to the surrounding buildings. The sudden storm suffocated the noise of the falling footsteps and colorful exclamations. Still, the trio maintained an unhurried approach to their destination's entrance.

Rhiannon was the first to step through the broken door, gracefully contorting her supple frame over and underneath the splintered beams and jutting pipes on either side. Amala and Oliver followed. Together, the two Druids appraised the empty, low-ceilinged lobby of what appeared to be an abandoned hotel, their glittering eyes lighting the darkness. Broken furniture and debris littered the room, with only the faint sound of scattering rodents to accentuate the dull booming of thunder outside.

The serpent's head stared forward, flicking its tongue several times as it bobbed to the left and right. When it had swept the entire room, it returned to a resting position against Amala's cheek.

"Where is the Archivist, Amala?" Rhiannon asked, a teacher

patiently awaiting her pupil's answer. "Where is our Elder?"

Amala took a steadying breath and closed her eyes. The serpent responded, half of its body whipping around in the air, forked tongue extended.

"She doesn't know," said the girl with a voice that trembled despite her company and her own power.

"*She* doesn't know, or *you* don't know?" Rhiannon asked reprovingly.

Amala looked into the red-haired woman's eyes with the kind of hurt a child feels when they disappoint a parent. After a moment, she turned to face the young man. "Oliver?" she asked.

Oliver's face warmed as he knelt. "You cannot rely on your Bard Companion to tell you what waits in the darkness."

"That is why you must focus your Wisdom," Rhiannon added. "She may be distracted by the rats. You need to focus *through* her primal urges. Calm yourself. Druids and their Wisdoms share anxiety as well as thoughts. Fear is confusion and the hiding place of evil."

Rhiannon reached across to Amala's hand and grasped it firmly. "You have nothing to fear. The darkness hides no enemies your Wisdom cannot sense. Be still and listen as *she* listens, not as *you* would listen."

Nodding, the child closed her eyes again with a determined grimace on her smooth, round features. Even as she stroked a hand through the girl's hair, Rhiannon scanned the room for signs of movement.

Once more the thunder roared overhead, and the sound of pelting rain leaking through holes in the roof echoed sharply in the distance. Amala's serpent swayed, its tail slowly moving around the child's slender neck as it lengthened itself farther into the air.

"She senses someone else," Amala said. "But she ... I can't

tell ..." her voice trailed off, her eyes opening again and looking to Rhiannon for approval.

Rhiannon and Oliver shared a momentary look before he nodded and closed his eyes. Tilting his head, he was silent and still as the storm outside raged on. "Below us ... there is someone ... but ... they are ... *hidden*?" he said as his face registered confusion.

"Then we shall reveal what is hidden," Rhiannon said. Moving toward the broken door, Rhiannon reached one arm into the rain and waited. After only a moment, a rush of wind responded. Rhiannon retracted her arm to reveal a copper-headed hawk shedding its wings of water.

The hawk's narrow beak angled back and forth as its glowing eyes scanned the room. Amala's Wisdom buried itself tightly into the folds of her hair. Rhiannon waited as the hawk beat its wings once more before folding them inward and perching stoically on her shoulder.

"There *is* someone else here," Rhiannon finally said. "Possibly a third, but it's unclear."

Oliver reacted one moment before either Druid heard a muffled cry piercing the rhythm of the pattering rain. His head tilted to its other side, mouth slightly agape, and eyes closed.

"A woman ... mid-thirties ... pained with effort ..." he said.

"We cannot know how our Elder may test us. Always be cautious, Amala." Stepping forward, Rhiannon strode across the lobby toward a dilapidated staircase along the far wall, testing the rotting wood with one hand before motioning for Amala and Oliver to follow.

Into the darkness they descended. Rhiannon paused every few feet to listen silently to the urgings of her Wisdom and the continued screams that seemed to be increasing in both frequency and intensity somewhere below. Oliver frequently whispered confirmations of their direction. The stairwell continued deep beneath the hotel; the depth quieted the storm outside to reveal a woman crying out in agony.

The staircase opened at the end of a narrow hallway composed of moldy brick walls. The air was stale and damp, tasting of rodent feces. The group's slow steps echoed in the corridor along with the sound of glass and syringes cracking underneath Rhiannon's heels or Oliver's polished loafers.

None spoke as they negotiated the black. The Druids guided their hands against the narrowing confines of the brick walls to navigate, and the Bard intuitively followed the echoes and vibrations of the screams ahead. The hawk stared forward from Rhiannon's shoulder while the serpent's head emerged from Amala's hair, its infrared vision ready to be called upon.

"Twenty feet," Oliver whispered. "Ten feet ... five ..."

As they turned a corner, the contracting oppressiveness of the hallway suddenly gave way to an open boiler room. Several points of candlelight shone perched atop a crowded shopping cart of garbage, cans, and clothes, the light casting dancing shadows along the ceiling's rusted pipes. Splayed on the floor was a panting, sobbing woman with her legs spread before her. And kneeling there, coaxing the pained woman's swollen stomach with her aged, black hands, was an old woman layered in the rags and tattered clothes of a bag lady. A dozen green luna moths danced in the air above her head.

Without looking up, the old woman chuckled to herself. "And the three arrive at the moment they were meant to."

Amala saw confusion in Rhiannon's face as her mentor looked from the old woman to the pregnant one, and in her protector's confusion Amala suddenly was afraid.

"Hold the mother's head, Rhiannon. Comfort her," the old woman said without turning to look at them.

"Yes … Archivist," Rhiannon finally said after several breaths during which she looked again upon the pregnant woman. She then stepped forward and knelt down, lifting the woman's head into her lap and brushing the hair from her face.

Amala felt Oliver's hands reassuringly cradle her shoulders from behind. She watched mutely as the pregnant woman's frail, needle-ravaged legs bucked upward with each swelling contraction. She cried with the approaching birth, seeming desperate to free her body of the child within. Her sunken eyes searched the room through tears and sweat that beaded down her abscess-marked face.

She cried a desperate, hollow wail that begged for release. "Get out of me!" she growled as the next contraction's wave tore through her.

"Yes, he's almost here, child," the Archivist cooed, her wrinkled hands moving over her stomach. Thin black skin sagged on her homely face, layers of old scarves covering most of her features and holding back a mass of unkempt hair, in which the luna moths seemed to find refuge.

The woman's breathing grew shallow and forced, and with a body too weak to withstand the pain any longer, she found the strength to push one last time with every bit of rage and fear within her.

"Ah, here we are," the Archivist chuckled, withdrawing her hands from the woman's legs and cradling the newly emerged infant. The woman moaned once more and then went completely limp in Rhiannon's hands.

"Oh, yes, look at him. Wide-awake and a look of wit in his eyes," the Archivist whispered, staring down into the infant's face. Alert hazel eyes stared up, rolling around to the rhythm of a soft whimper. The infant squirmed a little, though entirely silent and transfixed by the old woman and the bright green wings that now fluttered around his face.

Rain was now falling through the broken ceiling, and the Archivist pulled one of her own scarves—a red one with gold-and-white five-petal flower patterns—from her head and wrapped the naked infant in it. She placed a single finger along the length of the umbilical chord. A blue arc of light passed underneath her finger, and the cord immediately fell away from the infant's body, bloodlessly severing the last connection to the mother.

"Elder," Rhiannon said as she looked with pain at the mother. "We brought Amala tonight as you instructed." She motioned to the girl, who stood uncomfortably still, her small hands fidgeting within the folds of her muted orange dress. "But what is—"

"The mother," the Archivist interrupted. "Poor thing will never fully recover. Find a hospital for her, Oliver. See that she remembers nothing of this or us."

Amala looked up at Oliver and saw him shaking his head at Rhiannon. "Of course, my Elder," he said slowly, as if unsure whether to obey or not.

"Amala and Rhiannon will stay with me. We have things to discuss. We will return to our Grove together," the Archivist said, not looking up from the infant still cradled in her arms.

Oliver looked like he was about to object when Rhiannon subtly shook her head. Still the Archivist did not turn to look at him as he sighed and stepped over the pool of birthing blood to kneel beside the mother.

Nine months of various abuses had robbed the mother of her natural beauty, transforming a once-petite face into a death mask with skin now stretched across a gaunt frame. Her long, dark hair was brittle and prematurely gray at the temples. As Rhiannon stroked the backside of her hand over the skeleton-like body, the mother roused and gripped the Druid's wrist.

"Get … it … away … from … me …," she slurred, eyes fluttering as the rise and fall of her chest waned dangerously.

Oliver bent and lifted the woman easily out of Rhiannon's hands. He pursed his lips and hummed a short series of tones softly into her ear. Her shivering body calmed immediately, responding to a wave of warm air.

"I don't know what's going on," Oliver whispered as Rhiannon stood. "Be careful, my morning flame. I couldn't bear the darkness without your light."

Amala recognized the tension release from Rhiannon whenever Oliver called her his morning flame. The two kissed before he winked at Amala. Bowing his head curtly at the Archivist's back, he carried the bloodied mother in his arms out of the boiler room.

With Oliver gone, Rhiannon turned to wait for their Elder's command. Amala's almond-shaped eyes locked onto the infant, and the serpent, too, craned its neck to see the newborn child. Amala's finger absently twirled around the serpent's tail in the same way other little girls twirl their hair. Her dazzling eyes were wide with interest in the baby, and she stood unmoving as the old woman, rocking the infant in her arms, began to slowly circle the room and whisper to him.

"Amala," Rhiannon said again with a lowered voice. "It is the highest honor of any Druid to serve their Grove's Elder. Ours is the oldest and most powerful of all the nine in the world. Obey her words and remember the lessons you learn tonight."

The little girl nodded quickly with a child's expression of awe, focusing her attention on her Elder.

"So, Amala," the old woman began as she finished circling the room and came to stand just before the child. "I suppose I should be asking you of your training, yes?"

"I'm learning how to listen to my Wisdom. I found you

tonight," Amala nodded before looking down at the ground. "But it took me three days. I'm sorry … I'll get better."

"You found me when it was time," the Archivist chuckled, crinkling her nose. "And what have you learned?"

Amala looked up as she began recounting. "Our Grove is called Silvan Dea, and you are our Elder, which means I do whatever you tell me."

The old woman seemed highly amused by this. "What else?"

"Well, 'Anna hasn't taught me the Dance yet. She said I have to learn how to listen to my Wisdom more." She looked to Rhiannon for approval, who beamed with pride. "But Oliver said he thought I was ready to learn to fight, and he tells me about the monsters I'll face. The *really* bad ones, too."

Again the Archivist tickled the infant's chin. "Oh, what of them?"

"The Underdwellers," Amala pronounced slowly, the word awkward in the mouth of a child. "And he told me about the Revenants, the Wights. And ghosts. And he even told me about the Shadowkind that you can only see out of the corner of your eye."

"Quite the education. Has he told you about the Old Ones?"

The girl shook her head.

"I see. You like Rhiannon and Oliver?"

"She's my best friend," the girl answered as Rhiannon looked down as if to weep. "And Oliver, too. I like him."

"And what do you think of the baby?" the old woman asked.

Amala stood unmoving, uncertain how properly to respond. "I don't know," she shrugged with a child's curious half-smile. "I don't know him. His mommy didn't like him."

"The child spent nine months whispering into her mind," she said, running a finger along the baby's lips and smiling with pleasure as he began to suckle. "We must pity those who are driven to madness, Amala. But of the baby, ask your Wisdom," she prompted.

As if in response, the serpent stretched forward. It tasted the air inches from the baby's face. The infant's eyes followed the serpent's bobbing movements, foregrounded by the green wings of the luna moths. The serpent finally brought its head back to Amala's and rested against her cheek.

"She likes him," Amala finally said, the serpent now disappearing back into the girl's thick hair. "So ... I like him, too," she said with a pleased expression on her round face.

"Good. A Druid must always trust her Wisdom," the Archivist said, kneeling again so that Amala and the infant were at eye-level. Amala caressed the baby's cheek with the back of her small hand as his hazel eyes slowly closed.

"He's tired," Amala nodded. "Babies need lots of sleep."

"Yes, Amala, they do. But you see, when *this* baby sleeps, he dreams, and when he dreams, he calls out into the darkness." The woman's expression grew distant suddenly, eyes narrowing as she looked down at the sleeping infant.

"Who does he call to?" Amala asked.

"That which does not sleep," the old woman answered.

Amala did not understand, yet she felt heaviness in the words. She saw Rhiannon's confused expression, too. "What does that mean?"

The Archivist shook her head silently.

"There are reasons why I wanted you here to greet this new life. I will tell you something, Amala—a secret. But you must promise me that you will tell no one. Not Rhiannon or Oliver. No one at Silvan Dea, nor any other Druid or Bard in any of the other eight Groves in the world. And most certainly not to your future Companion, however necessary it might seem. You will want to. You will feel that you need to. But you must not. Do I have your word?"

She nodded somewhat reluctantly. Rhiannon was friend, sister, and mother to her now; she did not know how she could keep anything from her. With Rhiannon nodding her approval at her, Amala knew that, above all else, to be a Druid meant to obey one's Elder.

The old woman leaned forward and whispered words into the little girl's ear, words not meant for Rhiannon, Oliver, or anyone else in all the world. Most of them made no sense to the child. One moment she almost giggled; another she grew quiet; and finally, she trembled with fear. After a few moments, the Archivist finished abruptly, looked over her shoulder at a dark corner of the boiler room, and turned again to the sleeping infant. "Ah, and so the battle for the Waking Dreamer begins."

The old woman's motions became quick and agile. She moved to the birthing area and bent down to drag a finger through a puddle of blood. She moved to a spot in the opposite corner and traced a small circle on the ground, edging the circle with various symbols. She hummed to herself, occasionally saying words that Amala did not recognize. Yet there was a charge building in the air as if the words spoken commanded their own energy. And Amala felt that energy, first in the fine hairs along her arms, and then through her Wisdom, who reemerged and excitedly tasted the air.

"Come, child, quickly," the old woman motioned, and Amala recognized the tone of adult urgency. Taking her Elder's outstretched hand, Amala followed and stepped into the bloody circle.

Rhiannon's posture tensed at their Elder's tone. "What is it, Elder?"

"Hold him like me," the Archivist said, ignoring Rhiannon and lowering the infant toward Amala.

The little girl shaped her small arms the same as the old woman's, and as she did the infant was placed into her care, still glossy with afterbirth and fast asleep.

Amala's Wisdom and Rhiannon's hawk both jerked toward the dark corner of the boiler room that the Archivist had examined. A sensation of the most primal, visceral panic shocked the child's small body. "'Anna!" she cried out instinctively, her arms trembling even as she held fast to the sleeping infant.

Rhiannon had already reacted, withdrawing the iron stave bound across her back and thrusting it defensively before her.

"It is not yet time for you to dream, child," the Archivist said as she ran a still-bloody finger in a strange pattern across the baby's forehead. "Not until Amala returns for you."

The old woman stepped outside the bloody circle, turning her back to stare into the dark corner. Thunder crashed again and again in an unending procession; lightning arced across the sky in web-like formations as rain poured into the room.

"Send word that we will arrive in the morning," she said aloud seemingly to herself, but as one, the mass of delicate moths turned in the darkness and flitted upward, disappearing through a gap in the roof.

Rhiannon's Wisdom had already taken flight up through the holes in the ceiling, perching itself in the rafters as the Druid spun her stave aloft over her head.

"Amala, take the baby and hide!" Rhiannon commanded.

"No," the Archivist corrected over her shoulder. "Remain silent and still, child. You and the infant are hidden within the circle. You are now responsible for his safety."

The serpent twisted in the air, growing more agitated. Rhiannon had told Amala about true darkness in the world—not the absence of light that came with the setting sun, but the absence of hope that gave space to invading despair. Oliver may have described the monsters, creatures of the night that masqueraded as humans or hid deep in the earth, but Rhiannon told her of the evil that festered in the hearts of the wicked. And Amala had always listened, secure with her mentors and yet fearing the day when she would finally see evil for herself.

The air around her grew heavy, immense; it tasted bitter, stinging the nose. The darkness intensified somehow, weighed down as if the shadows held form and mass. Amala felt pressure against the insides of her ears, and they popped so hard that she had to bite down on her own lip to stop herself from crying out. The infant now woke and gazed silently upward, unmoving in her arms even as she trembled in the cold downpour.

Amala's Elder stood yards away, staring fixedly at the dark corner of the ceiling. "Appear and be done with it," she said defiantly into the darkness.

She was answered by a bellowing sound that began like the rush of high tide. It grew quickly, becoming a mixture of roars and mocking laughter that caused Amala's serpent to contort tightly as she felt her knees grow weak with fear.

A figure emerged from the shadows of the corner. The figure was taller than the old woman and was concealed mostly in whirls of black, inky shadows that writhed in the air. Through the shadows, the figure's outline produced a pair of glowing, pupil-less red eyes devoid of white. It showed a wide, grinning mouth just beneath where a nose should have been. The mouth was set with two rows of unnaturally white teeth locked in a grin that mocked the innate and effortless softness of a genuine human smile. Yet a false smile could not hide the figure's capricious and unrelenting contempt for all.

Stave pointed forward as if she meant to skewer it, Rhiannon leapt at the figure with such speed even Amala's Druidic eyes could not follow her form. An invisible force met Rhiannon bluntly, effortlessly throwing her back against the wall. She groaned under the invisible pressure that pinned her upside down against the brick, blood seeping from her head, trickling down her fiery red hair. It was only her terror that kept Amala from screaming, never before knowing any man who could so harm the strongest and most powerful person she'd ever known.

Do you like my new monkey skin, Mother? I spent decades stretching it out. Don't you think it suits me?

The figure spoke into their minds, a chorus of murderers and sadists crying out as one. Amala shut her eyes but was unable to block out the figure's words.

Ah, it has been too long since I last saw you. Siddim, was it? Or Dachau, perhaps? No, no I remember now. It was Nyarubuye. Yes, hysterical weeping. The air tasted fetid and decadent. I saw you there prostrate on your knees, mourning the monkeys. It marred the moment's picturesque qualities.

The preternatural grin turned sideways as if an unseen nose were sniffing the air. *Where is the child? He called out for his Master. I can smell his mother's womb still fresh on his newborn skin. Where are you, little boy? I wish to know your untouched skin. Come out and let me taste your mommy's insides still wet on your pink flesh.*

The old woman sighed, looking directly into the red eyes. "It is not yet your time. Leave this place."

The shadows rolled down the walls like melting wax. They reached out like tendrils across the floor toward the old woman. The shadows entwined themselves like vines around her feet, climbing her body. With no change to her calm expression, she batted her hand backward as if repelling a mosquito, and the darkness recoiled immediately, retreating back into the corner.

If you're so powerful, why not banish me forever? Grant me a reprieve from the eons I have tolerated their ignorance and self-importance, their fawning and sycophantic ways. I long for the abyssal silence that once existed before the monkeys learned their grating speech.

"I do not claim such power," the Archivist said. "But the day *will* come when you and those like you are removed from this world. Soon."

Amala heard the figure laugh into their minds; she heard screaming children and weeping women in that laugh.

You know nothing. You're a meddler. The midwife to the bastard child. You covet power, hiding behind the throne. You will never wield true power. Power like that of the little boy's Master. Tremble before the Rugged Mountain, Mother.

"I fear nothing other than the great mysteries of the universe," the old woman chuckled.

Amala trembled, momentarily heartened by her Elder's seeming confidence yet terrified still that the red eyes would see her standing so plainly visible in the room.

Arrogance. The boy must be the Waking Dreamer. You know what he is meant for; what he will one day do. Bring him out of your hiding place and let him attend the world's burning.

At these words, something shifted in the old woman's expression. It was mercurial, both a fleeting smile and a worried grimace. Her hunched shoulders straightened then, and she turned her back abruptly to the red eyes wreathed in shadow. Amala watched as the Archivist closed her own heavy eyes and sighed deeply.

"The time will come, but it is not tonight. You attempt to force what is not yours to control. In this way, you have not changed. And you never will. I name you, Bezaliel. Leave this place, and do not return."

The whirling shadows reacted at her words, collapsing in on the red eyes and unnatural, grinning mouth. Amala felt the boiler room tremble, as if the entire building were being shaken. A low, rushing sound filled her ears as the shadows retreated into the far corner, distorting the figure's visage and melting its features into blackness until only the soft, flickering candlelight and rain remained.

The invisible force pinning Rhiannon to the wall suddenly released, and she fell several feet to the floor in a crumpled heap. Amala wanted to run to her protector but remained frozen where her Elder had commanded.

The Archivist took the infant from the terrified young Druid. Amala said nothing, petrified by the experience. Her serpent finally settled across her shoulder, but they both were still suffused with fear of the red eyes. Yet through it all, the newborn gazed upward, silent and seemingly contemplative.

"I am quite proud of you, Amala," she said, passing her hand over the girl's forehead as she looked upon Rhiannon. "Don't fear, child. Rhiannon will be fine. She's a Druid, made of things stronger than bones or skin. As are you. And you both will need it."

Amala wanted to cry, and yet her Elder's touch filled her with courage and hope. She continued to stare into the corner, waiting for the shadows to return.

"Elder ..." Amala began, suppressing tears.

"That was an Old One. He's known now in this age as The Grinning Man," she answered, her attention focused on the baby. "Most will never encounter an Old One in their lifetime, Amala. You, though, will encounter many. And I'm afraid you will face The Grinning Man again."

The girl's frightened amber eyes looked up at her Elder. "There is much still for you to learn. We have more to discuss tonight as well."

Amala nodded mutely, sensing her Wisdom's posture relaxing and feeling the onset of drowsiness that follows a moment of great effort and stress.

"Come, let us tend to Rhiannon and take you both away from here. We'll return to the Grove soon. First, though, we will take our young dreamer to his new home. There, you can say good-bye until it is time for you to hold Emmett Brennan in your arms again."

CHAPTER 2

Emmett Jonathan Brennan, turn that car around and get your skinny hipster ass back here now!

It was 7:36 AM when Nancy's first text came through. Emmett hadn't looked down to read it yet, Houston's speed-up-to-brake bumper-car traffic consuming his attention. A moment later the phone rang. Emmett may have been expecting the call, but he was still irritated by it. Nancy knew he didn't talk on the phone. Only text. When he didn't answer, he heard another text come through.

Pick. Up. Now.

Emmett was prepared for her reaction, convincing himself that skipping out in the pre-dawn hours was the best option. His *only* option. It was either a drawn-out good-bye like every melodrama film, or a pregnant woman's anger. And Emmett hated melodramas, so ...

He answered the phone.

"Good morning, Nantucket!" he chirped, his hands unconsciously bracing the steering wheel against his impending doom.

"No, no, no, no, you don't 'good morning' me, mister. No, a *good* morning would be waking up and finding I'd lost weight instead of gained it. A *good* morning would be finding a no-foam sugar-free latte awaiting me on my nightstand. A good morning is *not* waking up to find that the seventeen-year-old you told a court administrator you'd care for until he was eighteen has left and isn't coming back!"

"Mama Rose is mad, I get it." Emmett smirked, Nancy always oblivious to the *Rosemary's Baby* references he made.

"And why is she mad? Hmm, let's see. Did Emmett leave when he was a legal adult?"

"That's in less than two weeks," he said.

"Did Emmett have a plan for where he was going or how to provide for himself?"

"I can stand on a corner and spin signs," he replied.

"Did Emmett say good-bye to the woman who kept the bullies off him in high school? Who took him in so he could avoid another foster home shuffle?"

"Hey, I left you a note! With all the well-earned thank you's for everything you've done for me." It wasn't that Emmett wasn't grateful. He was. He just knew she'd never let him leave.

"A cryptic note riddled with quotes from movie sequences that took me nearly twenty minutes to decode. Here I am searching the Internet and thinking, okay, it's like your movie treasure hunt game you did for us with that DVD night of *Spirit's Away*—"

"*Spirited Away*," Emmett corrected under his breath, irked she couldn't remember such an important film.

"—only to finally figure out that you've left for Florida. Do you know how much I had to look up online to figure out half of these film references? And I don't even *know* who this 'Gull-ur-mow del Toro' even is!" she yelled, haltingly pronouncing the final words.

Emmett laughed and didn't bother to hide it from Nancy. "Oh, come on, you loved the note. Did you get *The City of Lost Children* reference? I put it in there for you. Plus ten points to you if you did."

"I hated that movie."

"Lies," Emmett cooed. "Big sis loves her some dark sci-fi and fantasy films, and she loves me more for exposing her to the best of them."

The two met when he was an outcast freshman and she a bored senior searching for a pet project. He became as much a fixture in her senior year as her makeup or smart phone—Emmett Brennan, the cute and lanky younger brother she'd never had. Two weeks after graduation she married a wealthy, hulking mass of a man named Gerry—a successful litigator who spent most of his time working in Dallas and who liked Emmett even less than Emmett liked him. Yet Nancy kept in contact, Emmett the welcome distraction for the young woman who already had everything.

When the latest nameless, faceless foster parent had died weeks ago—a woman Emmett was as unlikely to remember as she was to distinguish him from the dozen or so kids she already tended—Nancy had offered to take him in. Since then she'd spent long hours trying to guide him along the predictable path to the comfortable, if monotonous, life. School. Career. Marriage. Home. Fulfillment. She introduced him to her girlfriends, played hostess to double date nights everyone but Emmett seemed to know about. And though some girls had shown initial interest, the consensus was that, while intelligent and attractively aloof, Emmett Brennan could not be pinned down. Something else—or someone—called to him.

"What you're doing is crazy. I don't know what movie you think you're getting this idea from—"

"*Thelma & Louise* meets *Return to Oz* seems about right—" Emmett offered.

"—but you are turning that car around and coming back

here."

"Yeah. Not so much. Not happening."

She went silent. Emmett had to look away from the road to his phone to see if she'd disconnected or paused for dramatic effect. He saw she was still on the line, the picture attached to her contact information displayed still on his phone: Nancy and Emmett's zombified faces from last Halloween's horror marathon.

"Emmett, I'm going to assume that because of your age and inexperience you don't know when you've pushed a woman to her limit. So let me just tell you: you have pushed me to my limit!"

Traffic slammed to a vocal stop. Emmett strained against his seatbelt as he hit his own brakes an almost-half-second too late. Horns blared from angry motorists delayed to their destination. He appreciated the appropriateness of the moment.

"Okay, okay, enough with the character-defining banter! You want me to come back, but a couple more weeks won't make any difference. I'm not *happy*, Nancy. With any of it. The pre-planned life, the college courses, the environmentally responsible, pat-me-on-the-back-for-using-reusable-grocery-bags life. I get that it works for you, and I'm happy for you! But I need something different. Something … I don't know … something intrinsically … *alien*."

"Then watch *Star Wars!*"

He sighed and shook his head. Nancy knew him well, and yet she didn't know him at all. She continued admonishing him as he half-tuned her out, thankful even more now that he'd left before she awoke. She was warning him of being broke and stuck in the backwoods of some rundown trailer park, unable to find work, and trading on the generosity of people who would let a skinny, almost-eighteen year old stay in their home seemingly rent-free.

Emmett turned the phone's volume down, permitting himself a moment's reprieve. He breathed deeply, purposefully, and looked eastward at the dawn. Blinking, listless hazel eyes once again met the slow-rising sun ahead. He pushed his tousled, floppy black hair out of his face and tucked it back under his signature *Donnie Darko* hoodie. He pulled a pair of sunglasses from his glove compartment as the wide yawn of an insomniac racked his entire body.

He tried to shake off the miasma of post-sleep somnolence still clouding his mind. He'd slept terribly the night before his planned escape. It was always terrible, unfulfilling sleep, frustrating and featuring the same recurring dream: a dream about a painting and a woman. The dream painting was always *Belshazzar's Feast*, with the disembodied hand pointing at the words written in the air above the king's head. The woman, too, was always the same—an unknown, amber-eyed woman who danced with serpents.

With Nancy still lecturing, he took a sip from his morning hot chocolate—his signature drink no matter how many kids mocked him for it—released a tired yawn, and willed his half-lidded eyes to respond to the sugar.

Emmett turned his volume back up as he yawned again. Her maternal instinct overrode her sermon on the dangers young people, apparently, weren't prepared for out in the wide world. "I heard that yawn. Did you even get enough sleep to do this?"

"'When you have insomnia, you're never really asleep,'" Emmett quoted, "'and you're never really awake.' *Fight Club*. So much truth. But yes, Nancy, you needn't fear. By sugar and courage I drive forth into a new sunrise, with enough lens flare to make J. J. Abrams jealous."

"I have no idea what that means," she said.

"It means I'm wide-awake and so excited I could run to Florida," Emmett answered. "And YouTube the lens flare bit after I'm gone. Totally worth it. Just have sunglasses on so you aren't blinded."

"Em, that *car* won't make it to Florida."

He hated "Em." She knew it, and she said it when she had use for it. Nancy's older-sister role-playing usually meant he had to tolerate her sometimes-condescending comments. She cared; it was her way of caring. Though it grated on him, it was the closest thing an orphan who'd grown up in a dozen different foster homes had ever known.

The sea of red lights ahead winked out and traffic resumed forward en masse.

"A broken-down car is a road-trip movie staple, Nancy. And it's exactly what I need. Get thrown headfirst into adventure. Find allies in my quest. Learn something about myself and grow. I'm not going to get my hero's journey started in that condo of yours. So, Act One begins out here on the open road, Ridley Scott style."

"Let me see if I understand you. Because that's what you want from me, isn't it? To understand?" Emmett could picture her on the phone: arms crossed, nearly a foot shorter than him, pacing the hallway in front of Gerry's trophy case. It was the posture she took just before making what she felt was a logical and eloquent argument.

"Sure. Shoot away."

"You're leaving Houston, just getting into your car—a car so old it probably wouldn't make the drive—without a job or any money, and driving to Florida—a state you've never been to—with little money and no job or ability to get a job other than your high school diploma that isn't worth much, to find a birth mother you've never known and who's dead now, anyway, all because of Ridley Scott?"

This was the part when she raised an eyebrow, expectant of the imminent triumph. Too bad her logic always fell on deaf ears. Goes-with-his-gut ears.

"Hey! Ridley Scott can do no wrong. Well, maybe one recent wrong, but that wasn't his fault. He didn't write the screenplay."

Signs indicated the interstate was two miles ahead. Emmett checked over his shoulder and moved into the far-right lane as he heard Nancy's resigned sigh over the phone.

"I give up. You go ahead and leave because of a chick flick. And then you wonder why people gossiped about you in school."

Emmett rolled his eyes, irritated more that she'd call *Thelma & Louise* a chick flick than the fact that she was making a dig on his masculinity.

"Some guys want the damsel. I'll take Ellen Ripley. That Power Loader mech suit is so much sex."

"I'll buy you one then if you'll just stay through your eighteenth birthday. After New Year's you can head out. It can't be *that* bad here."

Traffic was thinning, Emmett increasing speed expectantly. He was close, and soon it would be an ending and beginning at the same time.

"Didn't you ever know that you didn't belong somewhere, Nancy? That you just needed to get away and try something different? Even if just to prove to yourself that you were fine right where you were in the first place?"

She went silent. Expecting she was preparing another counter-argument, another reason not to leave, Emmett was surprised by the quiet whisper that instead came through the phone.

"I never had to, Emmett. I got married," she whispered, and in her hushed tones permitted herself the momentary vulnerability she secreted away even from her husband—the vulnerability that, in rare, quiet moments when she thought no one was watching her, would lead her to look out the window at the people exploring life and long, too, for freedom.

He said nothing, for nothing else needed to be said. On some level, Emmett knew Nancy finally got it—more than just accepting, that she finally understood. Emmett was his own man. And he was leaving.

"So," she said finally, her tone curt and matter-of-fact. "How long's your drive?"

"I should get to Ormond Beach by tomorrow." The only thing Emmett had learned of his mother was that she was from that Floridian seaside town overlooking the gray Atlantic. It wasn't much information, but it was somewhere to start.

"Promise you'll call when you find what you're looking for."

He took a deep breath, willing the winter chill to steel his resolve. He would find a job. He could live in his car until he had the money to get his own place. Anything was better than what he had, floundering through purposeless days thirsting for some measure of truth in an otherwise unremarkable life.

"It wouldn't be an epilogue if I didn't," he answered, hanging up.

He checked the rearview mirror and saw the glass towers behind him silently awaiting his acknowledgement that he did not have the courage to leave. He pictured Nancy waving at him from the corner outside one of those towers, standing in the shadow of her comfortable, careful life, where the routine was exciting and the ordinary was comforting.

Emmett's foot reacted; the itching desperation to escape something that almost imprisoned him was quick to flare. He allowed one final moment's consideration for the commonplace life he was rejecting. Could he quench his desire for the exotic and the bizarre in the stylized suburban supermarkets and kitchen table fundraisers that subsumed Nancy's life?

Emmett released a heavy, deep breath of purpose. He needed to believe that life could be untamed, unbound from schedules. Life had to be about more than just existing. It had to be about *living*.

Edging forward in the congestion each time he saw a sign for the interstate, he had to constantly remind himself to slow down.

Five exits away.

His phone sounded from an incoming text from Nancy: *Not going to see u again?*

Three exits away.

Emmett did not respond. Only words on a screen, Emmett understood their underlying message. They were not accusatory but rather as a statement of fact, as if Nancy were finally accepting what she had not wanted to believe. And she was right. He had no intention of returning to Houston again. It was not his home.

The only place home exists is in your head, he quoted to himself. *Dark City* had it right.

Again, he fought the urge to push the car forward in traffic, feeling as if the city's skyscrapers were poised to reach from the heavens and bar his exit. He pictured the constructs of metal and glass wrapping their beams about his car, both embracing and strangling him all in one motion.

One exit away.

He was ready to leave it all behind in search of the adventure awaiting those seeking its fickle attentions. When he finally banked off onto Interstate 10 East, he jolted the car forward eagerly, reverently thankful to bleed the neon from his eyes as he sped toward the promise of an unknown, strange new day.

I'm ready. Let's do this.

CHAPTER 3

Morning soon became afternoon, and a sticky twilight descended over the Gulf Coast. Hours passed as the interstate proceeded southeast from the glass-topped skyline of Houston before turning north through the bustling port of Beaumont. Plumes of white smoke funneled up from massive refineries along the water's edge. Emmett felt his head lighten as he crossed a high, steel-framed bridge in Orange that led to Vinton. He focused his eyes straight ahead until he reached the other side. Perhaps it was his usual fear of heights or maybe it was a sense of foreboding as he left Texas behind, but whatever the cause, Emmett wiped his hands and urged the car forward with mixed anticipation and disquiet.

Seeing the sign welcoming him to Louisiana, he kissed his index finger and rapped his hand against the dashboard. "One down. Three to go."

Hundreds of miles of low-lying marshes escorted him on his journey. Navigating the knotted overpasses of Baton Rouge, Emmett bypassed New Orleans on Interstate 12 and took the shortcut toward Hammond and on to Slidell. The sun seemed to set almost as an afterthought along the horizon as he passed Gulfport and began to see highway markers for Pensacola, the first hint of his destination.

As the darkness heralded twilight, Emmett shook his head and stymied the first of several rolling yawns; his eyes felt as if they had swallowed too much light, but they finally adjusted to the approaching dusk.

The interstate grew sparse and unlit as he reached the Florida Panhandle. Void of landmarks or roadside diversions, mile markers ceased counting down. The fatigue of the previous weeks coupled with his usual insomnia finally caught up to him, and Emmett began to wonder if he could safely finish the long drive.

He considered stopping to sleep. The yawning had grown altogether irritating, as if reminding him that he had erred and not thoroughly planned the drive. He *had* researched it thoroughly, of course, ensuring that the roads he would take were all public and not under construction. He had budgeted enough money for gas and food, but an unplanned motel charge simply wasn't an option. Emmett resolved to finish the drive, somehow, on sugar and the promise of a sunrise over poetic unknown roads not yet traveled.

He rolled the radio knob searching for George Noory, finding only static-laden hissing in the deep wilderness. It was the perfect late-night hour for radio: conversations about monster hunters, wielders of dark magic, and people who dream of the future.

Without the radio to distract a mind that did not readily quiet on its own and his phone's battery long since drained, he tried having a conversation with himself but felt absurd for doing so. He quickly found himself passing the time by cataloguing the different rattles coming from the old car. It was all an effort to keep his mind occupied long enough to delay thoughts of money, job-seeking, and apartment-finding. When he was certain that he had nothing else to do but think on these things, he looked down and was oddly relieved to find the gas gauge's slightly shaking needle holding steady below *E*.

"Fail at math, Emmett," he said aloud.

Yet he felt thankful for something to focus his attention. The last interstate gas sign was at least twenty miles behind him. With so little gas left and the next major city, DeFuniak Springs, nearly forty miles away, Emmett decided it was prudent to pull off the interstate at the next exit.

When he reached the exit ramp, he shifted gears and coasted in neutral to save what little gas remained in the tank. The county road leading to the gas station quickly wound away from the highway and snaked deeper into the thick tree line. A sign marked the edge of Blackwater River State Forest, a vast stretch of feral wilderness that filled a huge swath of the northern Panhandle on Emmett's printed directions.

A small opening in a copse of towering evergreens revealed a makeshift gravel driveway that led down a slight incline to a rundown gas station; its sign along the road was unlit but the station windows still showed interior lights. Allowing inertia to carry the car the remainder of the way, he slowly pulled up to the only pump, idling for a moment before turning off the car. The gas pump sat under a handwritten sign: "CASH ONLY—PAY INSIDE." He pulled his hoodie over his head and, drawing its strings snug, braced for the brisk winter chill.

Emmett opened the car and stepped outside. He shook the fatigue from his limbs and stretched his legs to the sound of ach-ing creaks, rolled his head from side to side with an exaggerated moan, and forced the previous five hundred and ninety miles to shudder free from his limbs.

Then he looked around. He felt, for the first time since leav-ing Houston, complete isolation. Stepping out into Blackwater River State Forest's edge, the boy raised by concrete and steel felt suddenly able to breathe. Freedom tasted of silence, expansive space, and undisturbed pine. Emmett could not remember feeling drawn to nature before, and yet finally alone within it, he felt like he had finally returned home.

Soon, he had promised himself when leaving Houston for the unknown. For *this*. And though he was not quite yet *there*, he was *here* now.

"So ... when will *soon* be *now*?" he whispered to the night.

When no answer was returned, Emmett grinned and focused his attention on getting gas. Looking toward the gas station, Emmett saw that the store's interior lights were flickering on and off through heavily fogged windows.

He finished with the gas and stepped over a gravel embankment opposite the gas pump to walk the twenty or so paces to the store. The light inside still flashed off and on as he drew closer and reached for the door. Then he stopped.

The night's still silence was penetrated by an abrupt, loud snapping somewhere off in the distance beyond the tree line. The sound rebounded throughout the surrounding forest before dying away.

Probably an alligator. Or a bear. Does Florida even have bears? he joked to himself. But he wasn't laughing.

He blinked and looked around the clearing. As far as he could see in either direction there were no other cars, no other people anywhere near him. Then Emmett recognized how alone he was out in the middle of nowhere, though the thought did not comfort him as it had just moments earlier.

The boy who had grown accustomed to the vigilant neon of an unsleeping city found himself hesitating.

Too many hours on the road and epic quantities of sugar for the win, he told himself. Despite the unusual feeling in his stomach—fear perhaps, but somehow familiar—he had already pumped the gas. He couldn't begin his new life by stealing from countryside merchants.

He pushed open the door, feeling the immediate rush of dry, stale heat as it escaped into the winter air. A bell jingled on the handle, but other than that and the low hum of the refrigerators along the store's far walls, the store was unusually quiet. The overhead lights continued to flicker on and off and grew more erratic every second. In the alternating moments of darkness and light, accented only by the iridescent glow of the glass-paneled refrigerators, Emmett's eyes had trouble adjusting as he craned his neck to look around the aisles.

"Um, hello?" Emmett said hesitantly. An unsettling silence responded. "Hello?" he called out again. "Anyone there?"

Assuming that the station's employee simply couldn't hear him—perhaps he was in the restroom or in a rear stock room—Emmett cautiously approached the empty counter. He saw that the cash register was closed and the small security video screen behind it was flickering in sync with the lights.

A metallic crash like a trashcan being knocked over rang from outside. Emmett jumped around to face the door as his hand instinctively went over his chest as if to calm his racing pulse. Nothing.

Again with the bear-gator. Yet the fear was back, this time palpable in the flickering isolation. Again there was the oddly familiar sensation, as if some irretrievable memory were teasing him at the edge of his awareness.

Okay, what movie am I flashing back to?

He was quite certain he had never been to Florida before, and he had certainly never pulled off the interstate in the dead of night at a creepy gas station. Nevertheless, he felt the maddening awareness that comes with almost-captured recognition—just beyond the reach of his probing finger tips, but close enough to smell and even taste, its contents brimming with recollections awaiting remembrance.

Something isn't right, he admitted to himself as he quickly moved up the center aisle to the door. He felt an irrepressible urgency to leave—from what he could not remember, and yet dawning somewhere in his mind was a terrible memory. He shivered with a visceral sensation of panic, a deeply ingrained demand to take flight. It was the kind of panic that shockingly focuses all of the senses, so that a twig snapping in the distance becomes a violent crashing against the ears. Emmett reached for the door and pushed it open, cursing the bell that clanged into the empty night.

As the winter air assaulted his exposed face, he stepped outside and felt the door close behind him. He saw nothing unusual. His car was parked where he left it, and the light over the gas pump continued to flicker. Yet something felt very wrong.

This is the part in the movie when you are yelling at the idiot to run!

His body reacted strongly with sudden trembling; the hair along his skin raised with urgency. He felt like a prey animal being pursued unseen. He wanted to call out, but it felt like his throat was collapsing. His feet would not allow him to take another step forward. Waves of crippling anxiety washed over him, holding him in place. In his mind, he told himself to move.

Get back in the car!

He felt a rush of cold air drown his lungs as he tried to run. His body didn't budge. The fear became even more terrifying because he could do nothing but bear witness to whatever it wanted to show him.

And then fear, imageless and without context, suddenly took form. Ten or so paces away, standing between Emmett and his car, stood a shadow—no, darkness that separated from shadow. He had not seen it there a moment before; it had appeared during the time between the blinking of his eyes. Rising distinctly from the darkness, as if the form were crouched and was slowly beginning to rise, was an unnaturally pale, white nude form that was vaguely human in appearance, though scarred and riddled with bruises and tears in its skin. As its long, thin legs and arms stretched to the full extension of its body, it turned its shoulders upright to lift a pale, gaunt neckline. The last to come into view was its smooth, hairless skull crisscrossed with pulsing red veins that seemed to glow against the bone-white surface.

Black eyes on either side of a thin slit for a nose turned to look at him. The figure's face was scarred with a stretched, exaggerated expression that caused Emmett's stomach to lurch with rising bile. The figure hissed suddenly, flicking a long, coarse tongue out and between its thin, pale lips. Memory failed him, and his mind was at once both silent and screaming with every word for danger it knew.

Do something!

His body finally responded with an uncoordinated lurch forward. The figure lunged at that same moment like a pouncing predator, responding with a guttural, bestial mixture of growls and snarls. Emmett's legs tore into the ground as he wrenched his body away, flailing as much as running down the gravel road back toward the interstate.

Without chancing to look over his shoulder, he veered to his right by instinct, away from the road and back toward the gas station. His hands flailed open as his arms pumped, and a small part of his mind registered that he had dropped his keys in the confusion.

But fear was in control, and his instincts took him in an arch behind the rear of the gas station. The forest surrounding the station awaited him in the distance, and seeking suitable darkness to hide from … whatever it was that he was running from, Emmett pumped his legs with abandon. The grasses were ankle-high, the ground soft and yielding like slow-drying mud that seemed to conspire to slow him down. Thorns and thickets scathed against his jeans and his hoodie as he tore deep into the underbrush.

After several moments of running that felt like hours, he felt his limbs aching and his chest heaving with exhaustion. He could think of nothing else but to hide, and he bounded headfirst into a line of tall trees ahead of him, and with some measure of determination chanced a fleeting glance behind him.

In the inky blackness, he did not see his pursuer, and only by a narrowness in his eyes could he see the dark shape of the gas station behind him and the gravel road back to the interstate somewhere just beyond the store. He caught his breath with great effort and held it, listening in the night's silence for any notice of the figure that chased him. Only a single crow responded with a bleating caw, followed by a rustle of flapping wings as the bird took flight somewhere overhead.

What the hell am I going to do?

His mind raced, a thousand discordant possibilities and thoughts fighting for his focus. Emmett had no idea what that *thing* might have been, and yet maybe he should have known, should have remembered.

In the darkness, still and silent as the trees themselves, he saw the figure in the clearing moving toward him—a hundred or so yards away, nearly a third of the distance from the gas station to the edge of the tree line where Emmett hid.

The figure stared directly at him, and though concealed mostly by shadow and the darkness of a moonless sky, it had clearly targeted Emmett. It closed the distance in the breath of a moment, moving with an inhuman speed, all but flying across the ground. The rush of fear was so great that Emmett could taste the bile rising violently in his throat as he staggered in terror backward and lost all feeling in his extremities.

The figure drew to within an arm's length. It reached one hand to Emmett's face, a hand that narrowed with bent and gnarled fingers that looked more like misshapen claws. Emmett's mind pleaded for him to flee, and yet so stricken with terror, he could not will himself to move. The creature reached Emmett's throat immediately, suddenly, and, closing around the flesh with a choking grip, pulled Emmett close to it.

At once, the world around him—the mundane, listless world he had left behind and the unknown, new world he had just discovered—fell away, consumed by a torrent of agony. It was as if fire were feasting on his flesh. It was a pain of the most unnatural and unbearable kind, in which a human feels life being ripped away.

The creature tightened its grip on Emmett's neck. He struggled to breathe. The pain burned under the creature's grasp, and it didn't die away. It was seeping into his tissues and deeper into his muscles—first at the base of his neck and creeping outward toward his collarbone and abdomen. His body could not endure the violation, and every aspect of his mind still able to focus cried out for release … or a quick death.

He looked at the monster—it could be called nothing else. It spread its wide lips once again in a feral grin to reveal rows of jagged fangs. It seemed drunk on Emmett's fear and delighted that its prey finally looked upon it. Emmett willed his body to fight back, desperately urging his body to fight or to flee, but his limbs would not respond. He could do nothing but heave uncontrollably, swallowing the earthy, peat-like stench of decay that seemed to wreath the figure like a dense, unseen fog.

With a final choking breath, Emmett meant again to cry out for help, to scream for someone or something. When no words came and his body remained unresponsive, he allowed himself to look directly into the eyes of fear and terror, and in that moment a memory began to unfold somewhere in his mind.

... a river ... there were rivers ... and there was water. Vast, endless water. Skies pregnant and swollen with storm clouds that rained endlessly ... rained for so many days that the waters became endless as the darkness was endless ... as dark as the eyes that stared at him ... eyes that had seen the rain and the waters ... and pain, endless pain ... searing and ravaging and burning as the world was rent apart, and into the deepest fissures poured the many waters until nothing on the land remained but the wetness of the earth that had wept for far too long ...

Pain.

In the present, in the harsh winter cold, and in the shadow of the deeper forest, Emmett Brennan understood that he was dying. Whatever the creature was, it would penetrate every space within his body and suckle greedily on his very essence. And somehow, Emmett understood that it would not permit him the release of death. He would not die soon.

When will soon be now?

Emmett's eyes rolled sideways, and if not for the creature's claws around his throat, he might have shouted a warning to the bronze-skinned, amber-eyed woman he could now see across the field running toward them.

CHAPTER 4

Through his darkening vision, Emmett watched the amber-eyed woman leap through the air. The creature's grasp around his throat released suddenly, and as the creature spun around, Emmett fell backward. The woman landed on the soft grass only feet from the monster, twirling sideways out of reach of its claws. The creature and woman moved with such swiftness that both were a blur to Emmett's eyes; the monster brought its rending claws around toward the woman, who spun again in a complete circle, pirouetting out of reach with startling speed.

She was a young woman with dark, flawless skin, with long brown hair tied back behind her head and an athletic, toned body dressed in form-fitting black clothes that all but concealed her in shadow. Her glittering, round amber eyes lit up the night, meeting Emmett's for the briefest moment as if to confirm that he was still alive. She nodded at him once with a confident expression, seemingly unafraid of the monster she fought.

Emmett watched, transfixed as her arms, previously tucked close against her, suddenly sprang outward in a flurry of motion. Twin black serpents with glowing black eyes lashed out as she spun twice more away from the creature, striking the creature's skull with a cracking sound. In response, the creature reared to meet her change of direction. Still she managed to pirouette just outside the danger of its outstretched claws. Just as suddenly, her body contorted and the motion carried her backward again, forcing the creature to double back after her in a maelstrom of movement. Emmett had no time to think before reacting with a forced roll to avoid the creature's stampede.

Seeing Emmett cower on the ground, the monster turned on him only to have the woman step within reach, as if luring it back toward her. It responded with an anguished cry that mangled the air. The creature crouched low and swiped at her knees, but she easily stepped out of its reach, sweeping upward with a high kick. The creature pounced, sailing toward her, yet just as effortlessly, she thrust both arms outward, dove headfirst to the ground, and tumbled several feet from the monster before rolling onto her feet and continuing her seeming dance.

The woman would step in with a forward slashing motion, her arms whistling as her twin serpents sliced through the silent night's chill. With the same fluid motion, she would spin to the side with a backhand motion, striking at the creature's face while remaining just outside of its reach. Emmett could see that she was drawing the monster away. With every twirl, she lashed at the creature's eyes and face, and with each counter of its claw, she would dance back two or three paces.

There was a sudden explosion of sound somewhere in the forest, a low, booming roar that rocked the trees. The woman reacted first, turning toward Emmett as she lashed across the creature's face with both serpents.

"Stay down!" she yelled to him.

Another boom shook the earth, and there was yelling somewhere in the distance. A robed figure flew backward through the air out of the forest and crashed down on the ground near where the woman and the creature were still fighting. More screams erupted from the trees as another robed figure ran out and away from the fighting, pursued by a blond-haired man with an angular jaw whose open palms were pointed out before him.

The blond-haired man stopped and pointed one finger at the fleeing figure in the distance. Pursing his lips together, he produced a shrill, bleating whistle. A clear, rippling force rushed through the air and lifted the robed figure into the air and flung the figure twenty yards across the clearing.

The robed figure nearest the fighting managed to stand. His middle-aged, pockmarked face scowled at Emmett as he brought his hands up to his chest, motioning as if forming something in the air before him. He was chanting something, his discordant syllables tearing at the very air itself. Emmett watched with horror as the man's face began to contort, the features stretching as if made of hot wax. The man thrust his hands toward Emmett, and a globe of shadowy substance hurtled toward him.

Emmett had little time to react as the blond-haired man sprinted between Emmett and the oncoming darkness. Turning to face it with his raised palm before him, he released a single note of harmonious, pure sound that seemed to dissipate the shadows inches before they reached him. The robed figure had already renewed his chanting, but the blond-haired man raised his arms out and produced a reverberating, cavernous note that flung the robed figure high into the air. He fell to the ground again upside down, landing awkwardly on his neck.

The woman was still fighting with the creature. She bled in several places where its claws had torn across her tight black clothes. She spun back out of the creature's attack and brought both her serpents across its eyes, spraying what must have been its blood across the ground. The creature pitched forward and screamed, the sound nearly bursting Emmett's ears.

The woman spun around one final time, her serpents

wrapped around her arms as she grabbed something fastened to her back. Both hands swept upward holding a long staff that pierced through the creature's chest and out its back. Its claws grasped the shaft protruding from its chest, its mouth agape gurgling oily substances before collapsing forward to the ground.

His apparent saviors exchanged nods with each other as each surveyed the area. The woman knelt over the creature's rapidly decomposing body. A pervasive stench filled the clearing as the creature's form bubbled and dissolved into the ground.

Whether it was to run back to his car or to run into the forest, Emmett did not know. But he tried to stand and immediately felt an overwhelming wave of heavy nausea bear down through his head and pitch his body forward. His vision blurred as bile rose in his throat, and he felt the torrent of pain in his neck from where the creature had strangled him. He ground his teeth and willed himself to remain conscious.

"Hold on, mate," he heard a curiously accented voice say. The man was looking at him even as he was checking the nearest robed figure for a pulse. Emmett tried to focus through the pain by staring at his rescuer: effortless blond hair, clear green eyes, and the strong jaw and nose that gave one the appearance of having been lovingly chiseled from granite. Broader and taller than Emmett, he wore a well-fitted pinstripe shirt and slacks that were smudged with mud.

Emmett tried to breathe deeply and slowly through his mouth. He felt a sharp, biting pain in his chest as he did so and, after holding his breath, suddenly gasped for more air. Pulling down his hoodie's zipper, he saw his neck was covered in black, rotting gouges, tortured and disease-laden skin cracking off along its torn edges. It looked as if his neck had been burned severely and deeply, and that now the skin, still alive somehow, was dying anew from the sickest sort of infection.

"All right?" the blond-haired man asked as he crouched down in front of Emmett. "My name's Keiran. Is that your car at the station, then?"

Startled, Emmett looked back at the woman who had walked over to the other robed figure lying motionless further away.

"Huh? What?" he sputtered.

"Is that your car at the station?" the young man repeated, pointing in the direction of the gas station when Emmett did not respond.

Emmett mumbled something and stared blankly back at the man, feeling the pain coursing through his body. *I'm in shock. This is what shock feels like.*

The young man waited a moment before leaning toward him. "Is that your car, mate?" he asked more pointedly and slower, as if to focus Emmett only on his words.

The stranger's green eyes directly met Emmett's gaze, and in that brief moment Emmett saw a confidence in him, the same confidence he had seen in the woman.

My car. Low on gas. Emmett's mind began to regain its focus.

"Uh ... yeah, right," Emmett struggled.

"Good. Are you alone out here?"

Emmett was nodding, clenching his jaw from chills that wracked his body in the cold air. The blond-haired young man, Keiran, pursed his lips and whistled a sweet note that seemed to linger even after he had finished. Emmett felt a rush of warmth envelop him. The bitter December air felt immediately like Caribbean-kissed trade winds caressing his body.

"What the hell?" Emmett recoiled.

Silently, Keiran stood up with a Cheshire cat grin on his face. For some reason, in the midst of the bizarre and grotesque night, Emmett noted the young man's smile with a moment of clarity. It was a grin that signified a superior knowledge without being mocking, aloof without being apathetic. It did nothing to remove the horror of what had happened, and yet it calmed him somewhat from its effects.

The woman had returned to stand next to Keiran. Both serpents were coiled around her shoulders, both heads looking behind her into the darkness.

"The Underdweller's nearly gone. We'll need to bury the Revenants. Were there others?" she asked as she motioned to Emmett.

"He said he was alone. That's his car back there."

The pair turned to look at Emmett, who was only catching half of what they were saying to each other. His mind was racing with countless questions, things he wished to scream aloud even as he ran to his car. Yet when he tried to push himself up to stand again, he immediately fell forward. It was only the woman's swiftest movement that caught him. She gently lowered him down with her body so that he lay across her knees. Cradling his head in her hands, she ran a finger across his forehead and swept the sweaty mat of tousled black hair from his face so that her eyes looked down into his.

"I can slow it from spreading until we get him to the Grove," Keiran said standing over them. "But we'll need the Archivist to fully heal him."

Keiran's words were lost on Emmett as he stared silently into the woman's eyes. They sparkled as if a great swath of the sky had been drawn down into a crystal goblet. For the briefest moment as he looked up at her, his mind stirred once again with the odd feeling of familiarity.

"My name is Amala Amjadi," the woman said. "And this is my Companion, Keiran Glendower. We're going to help you. This will be difficult for you to believe, but that Underdweller— the creature that attacked you—has infected you."

Emmett wanted almost to laugh, to recognize verbally how ridiculous the situation was—the creature, his apparent saviors, each individual detail playing out in his mind like one of hundreds of films he had watched over the years. He needed for it to be a farce, unwilling to recognize how seemingly close he had come to death.

"Underdweller?" he scoffed. "So what're you two … monster hunters?" he mocked before coughing and wincing at the pain it caused.

Amala glanced up at Keiran. Emmett observed the deliberate sort of unspoken interplay between them, the look of closeness they shared.

Amala reached for Emmett's neck and traced her finger down the side of his cheek and toward the edge of his neckline just beneath his ear. Emmett's body reacted with a shock of pain that lanced through his body, causing his limbs to jerk out uncontrollably, his teeth to clench, and his voice to turn into agonizing moans.

"I'm sorry, but you're still in danger. That pain is from the Rot, an Underdweller's curse. It has marked you."

Needing to confirm the reality once more, Emmett touched the blackened skin himself and gasped at the pronounced pain, a pain that brought startling clarity.

"The Rot will consume your flesh first, and it will continue to grow more painful as it spreads into your chest. It will then fill your bloodstream and choke your organs. It's eating you alive, and if you do not come with us, you'll soon be dead."

"Come with you where?" Emmett asked hurriedly. "Who the hell are you two?"

Everything was changing so fast, details rushing at a mind already struggling to right itself. His mind wanted to deny it, yet already he could feel a restriction in his breathing, as if some unstoppable force were slowly closing his throat. Facing his own death for the second time that night, Emmett struggled to bring order to a chaos of wailing, conflicting voices, his thoughts racing too quickly.

Run away from them.

"I'm going to need you to trust us."

Find the nearest hospital and call the police.

Emmett again tried to stand, to walk on his own. The world turned upside down before he could stand. With a weakness crippling his entire body, he fell forward again.

Lie down and go to sleep. Hope that all of this is an elaborate nightmare.

Opening his eyes, he found himself in firm, strong hands that had kept him from harm. He was being lifted up by Keiran, his head pitched backward in a fight to stay conscious. His eyes rolled, half-open and unable to focus on the rapidly-changing world around him. A thousand thoughts flooded his mind as he struggled to mumble something, anything, to his two saviors, but he could only bite down against the discomfort and disorientation.

They were walking together back to his car at the gas station. Amala opened the rear door, and Keiran laid Emmett on the backseat. He stepped back as Amala swooped in behind him to hover briefly over Emmett, her hand gently caressing the side of his face as her starry eyes looked with disgust at the work of the Rot.

Emmett watched her movements slow as his vision seemed to blur. The pain was lessening somehow, and Emmett felt the immense weight of fatigue dragging him backward into sleep.

Go to sleep. It's just a nightmare … a dream … yes, it must be a dream. And the amber-eyed woman is here, too, just like all the dreams before.

As if hearing his thoughts, the woman's serpents suddenly spun around her neck and turned their glowing black eyes at Emmett. The woman's starry eyes registered momentary confusion, followed by wide-eyed shock.

"Emmett?" she whispered as his eyes finally closed.

Emmett knew he was dreaming. He'd had this dream countless times before.

He was standing in an apartment. It was the same apartment he had dreamed of throughout his life. He could hear the evening news anchor's polished enunciation from a television playing through the walls. There was a weather report of the northern storm blowing in from the Great Lakes. And there was an update on the mother and daughter who had been missing since the previous week.

The apartment was like a *Twilight Zone* curio cabinet. A seemingly endless collection of odd statutes lined shelves along the ceiling perimeter—hawks and other birds—with towers of unread old books stacked so precariously high that the slightest wind threatened to collapse them. Burgundy shawls doubled as lampshades, casting dim lighting over a pair of over-sized cream-colored ottomans in the room's center. A wooden table cracked down its length sat between the cushions, on which was a collection of nine Russian nesting dolls. The walls were covered in odd-shaped mirrors, shiny glassware, and hanging baubles that light and image bounced off. A hundred different reflections of Emmett bounded around the room as he tentatively moved through the living room. The fluttering color from the goldenrods and orange velvety wings of two Monarch butterflies sitting on the outside of the window's ledge registered in his periphery.

Hanging on the far wall beside the window was an unframed

oil painting of a group of people at a dinner table looking aghast at a disembodied hand in the air above them. There were five people sitting at a table set with food, each dressed in old period clothes. One of the men wore some kind of crown and, like the others, looked frightened by a hand above them pointing to words written on a hazy cloud-like backdrop. The letters were in a language that Emmett could not read.

"*Belshazzar's Feast,*" a voice said to Emmett. He turned to see a young woman standing behind him. It was always the same woman. Her face was concealed by the serpents coiled around her head except for the pair of amber eyes that stared at him.

"The Dutch painter Rembrandt created this portrait of the Babylonian King Belshazzar who, according to the biblical Book of Daniel, in drunken revelry blasphemed the sacred vessels taken from Solomon's Temple by the previous king," the woman continued as she always did. She stepped past Emmett to the painting and pointed up at it. "In response, the ghostly, disembodied fingers of a human hand appeared in the air and wrote on the wall words that the prophet Daniel interpreted as meaning that God had numbered the days of Belshazzar's kingdom, and that the Babylonian King had been weighed and been found wanting."

The woman lowered her hand and looked at Emmett. "The painting is currently on display at the National Gallery in London."

"Why is it here?" Emmett asked. He always asked the same question.

She always gave the same answer. "Do you know the words?"

"No."

The woman recited the words without having to read them from the painting. "'Look at the sky, how the orbits of the planets and stars never change, how they rise and fall according to their natural order. Look at the earth, how everything that takes place has their beginnings and their ends—summer and winter, and clouds and dews and rain. The trees appear to shed their leaves; the trees crown themselves in green leaves and fruit. All this from year to year forever and ever and ever like the bottomless sea and the endless rivers that lead to it.'"

"What does that mean?" Emmett asked, already knowing her answer.

The woman turned to Emmett and held one hand up with her palm facing him. She lowered the other hand, palm facing out and down. She always did this with a look in her amber eyes as if she were waiting for him to respond in kind. Yet he never did. And so the dream ended as it always did, the woman repeating the same seven words.

"One day, Emmett, you will save me."

CHAPTER 5

Emmett raised his eyelids with great effort, wading through murky, imageless darkness. As his eyes struggled to focus, so too did his mind. A formless memory surfaced, steeped in malevolence. He crushed his eyes closed against the torrent of returning images: trees and thorny bramble, a gravel road, a flashing overhead light. Then he remembered a crash. He had been running; his aching limbs told him so. He had fallen. He was attacked.

"Good afternoon," an accented voice greeted him. Emmett groaned in response, pushing his eyes open again to a whirl of unfocused shapes. As his vision sharpened, he could see he was lying on a plush bed in a massive room whose ceiling and walls were made of glass like an enormous greenhouse. He could see snow-crowned mountains carpeted in fields of thick evergreens filled the horizon. A stone walkway wound through the room whose floor was soft, red earth. Surrounding him were broad tufts of bamboo stalks, dark taro pads, and the soaring green and purple leaves of immense banana trees. Waist-high shrubs of wild, erratic palms and fragrant, feathery ginger blossoms lined a whispering creek encircling the bed. Several large, worn boulders accenting the path were home to heart-shaped fronds whose masses of twisting, exposed roots climbed the rocks, upon which sat several people in hushed conversation. And in the distance, Emmett saw a young woman in a diaphanous white gown and waist-length black hair dancing around by herself, her body encircled by a swarm of bees that seemed to elicit her gleeful smile.

Emmett tried to force himself up on his elbows, a dull tingling of a thousand pinpricks racing throughout his limbs. He felt an immense nausea in his stomach, wincing as his dry throat cried back at his own coughing. He forced himself to swallow what felt like broken glass.

"You'll want to take it a bit easy, then." Emmett saw a young man sitting relaxed in a chair opposite the bed with one leg crossed over the other, composed in his gray pinstripe slacks and fitted black turtleneck. His mind stumbled over the chaos of returning memories before registering the face.

"What the hell did you slip me?"

"I didn't slip you anything. Mind you, I kept you asleep for the last three days while we drove back, but Amala thought it would be easier. Here," he said, offering water.

Emmett felt too sick to protest, and he accepted it sitting back against the cushions. He groaned and squeezed his eyes shut as he drank and was rewarded with hysterical coughing.

"Three days?" Emmett asked, bracing against the discomfort. The coughing seemed to jar his memory, and tumbling out of the coalescing fog were dueling shadows: one of a white-skulled creature, the other a graceful woman who moved like flowing water.

"After this much time we'll obviously want to feed you. I'm feeling rather peckish myself. You might want to use the loo first, though." Keiran pointed at an open door behind Emmett where he could see a bathroom's sink and shower built from granite.

Emmett felt the telltale exigency and tumbled through the open door. It was a moment later when modesty resurfaced and he closed the door with the back of his foot, Keiran having turned away. When the door opened several minutes later revealing a beleaguered Emmett holding his stomach, Keiran stood up from his chair.

"I had your jumper washed," Keiran said, motioning to Emmett's hoodie, which was draped over the chair opposite the bed. "It is wicked cold here in Oregon," he added, handing Emmett a long, wooly scarf, which Emmett brought around the back of his neck but left untied in the front.

"Oregon?" Emmett scoffed, his mind still struggling to reconcile his surreal environment.

"Answers for all your questions. With food. Promise," Keiran smiled, motioning to another door at the end of the stone walkway. The door was built directly into a sheer wall of rock buttressing the glass walls, as if the structure were constructed alongside and within a mountain.

Keiran walked over and opened the door. Whether it was Emmett's hunger or confusion, he followed. They were in a smaller room. A central fireplace ensconced in tan-colored rock dominated the room, with a variety of floor rugs, thick body pillows of various colors, and low cushions surrounding it. Pottery as tall as Emmett featured wildly arranged and organically out-of-order floral arrangements. They were not the sort of trimmed bouquets found in a hospital, but rather were celebrations of living, unrestrained color.

"Who have we got here? An angel on the road, or a devil at the fireplace?" called out a baritone voice.

A pair of men entered the room from another door, walking as much as strutting. Not appearing much older than Keiran, they were deeply tanned identical twins with short brown hair and brown eyes, though one of the twin's eyes seemed to sparkle as if flecks of silver swirled in his irises. Like Amala's. And whereas Keiran was athletic and strongly built, the twins' wide barrel chests strained against their shirts.

"All right?" Keiran smiled, clapping each on the shoulder. "Emmett, this is Sebastian and Paulo Rodrigo." He gestured to each twin in turn.

Both nodded silently at the same time. The twin with the sparkling eyes narrowed them, staring at Emmett. "Interesting coloring," the twin said.

"How long with the Rot?" the second twin asked.

"Three nights ago in Florida."

"How unexpected," the twin with the strange eyes commented.

Emmett felt like a child being talked about by grown-ups at the dinner table.

"I never got to say good-bye after the aurora australis in the spring," Keiran said, ending the momentary uncomfortable silence.

"It's okay, we had to head back to Noronha early ..."

"Allessandro sends his regards..." the other twin added mid-sentence, to which Keiran smiled knowingly.

"So what brings you up here?" Keiran asked.

"*La Pastora* had us hunting the coast. We left Natal two weeks ago."

"Anything of interest?" Keiran asked.

"Rumors. An old man in Pureza said that several of the area's children had gone missing. The trafficking trade is too extensive to be certain what happened to them."

The other brother nodded. "There was talk of a disease spreading through an isolated village in Martins—odd muscle spasms, high fever, eventual death ... the typical thing you'd expect if they were active in the area and failing to cover their tracks …"

"… but since there was massive flooding in the area and the main roads were washed out, the villagers couldn't wait for officials to arrive. They burned the dead in case of malaria, leaving nothing left for us to check."

"So no evidence of Revenant activity?" Keiran asked.

"We followed a trail of similar signs north through the Amazon until we reached what we thought was a dead end in Veracruz. Then we started hearing talk of *el hombre de la bolsa* again …"

"… which we hadn't heard that far south of Monterrey before."

"The man of the sack?" Emmett finally interrupted. And though he'd heard of the foreign horror movie of the same name, he knew just enough Spanish to understand nothing of what was presently being discussed.

The twins turned and looked to Keiran as if it were his responsibility to explain. Emmett couldn't tell if they were being deferential to Keiran or were simply irritated.

"The Sack Man is a story parents in Latin America tell misbehaving children about an ugly old man who collects and eats bad children. Classic bogeyman story … except, of course, that it's not entirely untrue. Not when the bogeyman really *does* kidnap children and eat them, anyway," Keiran said.

Emmett's mind numbly absorbed Keiran's words as the twins resumed. "Honestly, brother, I wish we chased real shadows instead of our own. Some children went missing and some farm animals were slaughtered, but no Revenants."

"Since we were so close to the border, we caught a flight to rest and visit here. Paulo's got a crush on that widow who runs that restaurant you're so fond of."

The other twin—Paulo apparently, though Emmett was uncertain if he could ever tell them apart but for Paulo's unusual eyes—jabbed his brother before looking back at Keiran. "We were heading to say hi to Sophie. We'll let you get back to your tour."

Keiran clasped their hands individually before they left through the door Keiran and Emmett had just exited. Emmett watched them leave, noting that neither turned to say good-bye to him as they did so.

"Right, then," Keiran began before Emmett could ask anything else. "On to food."

Sure, we can just pretend I processed all of that.

They passed through a seeming labyrinth of hallways and passed at least a dozen or so people of various ages—usually in pairs, the woman always with glittering eyes—before reaching the rustic kitchen, its extensive deep cherry woodwork and granite facing an uncovered window looking out across a wide valley.

"Right. Have a seat, then," Keiran offered to Emmett, moving to the refrigerator. "The trick is always to find something that refreshes without being too objectionable."

Keiran withdrew a knife from a drawer and set to slicing various pieces of fruit. Emmett's eyes glanced sideways at the door, and in a moment he had decided that if he chose to run, short of throwing the knife at him, Keiran probably wouldn't be able to catch him.

Fine, genius, you run … and go where, exactly?

Keiran offered a kiwi wedge from his knife to Emmett. Emmett made no attempt to hide his leeriness as he regarded the extended knife or possibly drugged fruit. Keiran seemed comfortable with Emmett taking time to consider him as if he expected it.

Emmett finally accepted the offering with a loud rumbling of his stomach. He felt the first bodily objection as he hesitantly chewed, and tasting nothing immediately foul, swallowed it to quell his rising hunger.

"Mind that you don't drip juice on the floor, please," Keiran said, handing Emmett a napkin.

He took the napkin, prickling with irritation. Nancy's husband, Gerry, had done something similar once, too. By outward appearances, Keiran was not entirely unlike Gerry: tall, well built, and genetically blessed with the rugged good looks women bypassed lanky, boy-faced Emmett for. If that weren't enough reason to not like him, Keiran was a better dresser, too.

Hating the guy who rescued you isn't helpful, genius.

Unlike Gerry, though, Keiran exuded a relaxed manner. Emmett couldn't tell if it was because he was British or not, but when he spoke, Keiran seemed entirely comfortable in his own skin. To anyone else, that would engender an equally relaxed manner. To Emmett, though, it only served to remind him how uncomfortable he felt in his own skin—now even more with the Rot on his neck.

Emmett touched his jaw to test if it was still there, hissing at the pain.

"It'll hurt less if you don't poke at it," Keiran said.

No kidding.

A silver kettle whistled, and turning the stove off, Keiran poured steaming water into two ceramic mugs. He scooped heaping teaspoons of fresh leaves from a jar into a pair of silver strainers, releasing a heady, almost overwhelmingly sharp aroma. Keiran dropped a strainer into each mug, offering one to Emmett.

"Cream and sugar?"

Of course he drinks tea.

"No thanks."

"To rare joys," Keiran said, raising his mug. "Cherish life's simple pleasures wherever one might find them," he saluted.

Of course he's an optimist.

"I suppose you have lots of questions," Keiran said after setting his tea down.

"Nah, I enjoy being clueless," Emmett said. *That would have worked far better as inner monologue, Emmett. Go you.*

"Fair play," Keiran grinned. "I was cheeky the first time I arrived here, too."

"When was that?" Emmett asked, hoping to get information before he lost any pretense of patience.

"Seven years ago. I was seventeen and had come searching for answers. Like you, my life had been touched—or marred, rather—by the Underdwellers."

"Guess I have to ask, don't I?" Emmett snarked.

Keiran's expression was genuine confusion. In a way, Emmett regretted his sarcasm and was thankful Keiran didn't recognize it. "Sorry. What's an Underdweller?"

"Abominations that hide in the earth. Long-lived creatures that are wicked strong who exist only for the pleasure of devouring flesh."

The creature's jagged teeth and unnatural speed flashed in his mind. Silence passed between them as Emmett suppressed a shudder that was accompanied by a dull throb of discomfort along his neck.

No wonder I always preferred the George Romero lumbering dead type.

"What about the robed dudes with the face-melting?"

"Revenants. Their human worshippers. They practice what we call runic magicks, invoking ancient words of power to harm others. Ancient cults, secret societies, tyrants and sadists— Underdwellers have ruled entire kingdoms by proxy through their human Revenant cabals. Civil wars, human trafficking, slavery ... it's all their lot."

"So, soylent green really *is* people?"

Keiran raised an eyebrow in confusion.

"How'd you kill it?" Emmett asked. *Fewer movie references, snob.*

"Iron stave through its heart."

"Was kinda hoping for a more inventive trope there."

"Underdwellers avoid pure running water, and fortunately for us, they have lived underground for so long that their skin can't tolerate direct light. They only rise in full darkness when the moon is at its lowest apogee."

"You mean they don't rise under a *full* moon?" Emmett quipped.

"Silly superstitions," Keiran remarked more to himself than to Emmett. "The moon reflects the sun's light. The gift of light in the darkest hours of the night is associated with nonsense superstition. And the brightest reflection of light, a full moon, is viewed as an ill omen. You must appreciate the irony."

"Superstition makes for good storytelling. Can't have a horror movie without it."

Smiling, Keiran began clearing the countertop and rinsing the dishes. "Superstition is often a convenience for avoiding uncomfortable truths. A woman dares to live unmarried on the outskirts of town in the frontier, and rather than being a resourceful, capable woman who records weather patterns and uses medicinal herbs for various maladies—"

"She's a witch, and firewood is being handed out to the town's children as party favors," Emmett added as he saw Keiran already nodding.

"It's an unfortunate reality we contend with: this need to wrap the truth in fanciful stories, when the truth is so plainly evident," Keiran said.

"You say that like this wouldn't be all-new information to most people."

"If you know what you're looking for, it shouldn't be." Keiran set the knife down and sipped from his tea, his eyes dancing over the cup's rim. "You just don't know it."

Emmett shook his head dismissively. "Nah, I'm as tin-foil-hat as anyone else, but even I know you couldn't keep this off the Interwebs."

Keiran chuckled as if Emmett had just insisted that babies came from storks. "Do you watch the news? Even if you remove your everyday murders, kidnappings, and rapes—some of which *are* Revenant in origin, mind you—there are still other things."

"Such as?"

"Cattle killings, their sexual organs removed with surgical precision and all bodily fluids drained. Bodies left in unnatural positions with unknown odors and markings in the area. And normal scavengers refuse to approach the corpses?"

"Aliens, bro. Always always always aliens," Emmett snarked.

"Human combustion? People inexplicably incinerated from within with no evidence of chemicals or a source of ignition and their surroundings undamaged?"

"Not so much, no."

"You've never seen anything that you couldn't explain? Never experienced something that you wouldn't admit to others for fear they wouldn't believe you?"

"Any six-year-old with a phone and free app can turn you into a werewolf."

"Then look to stories and art. Human history is riddled with stories of Underdwellers, but—and this is critical, of course— you must know what it is you are looking for. Most fairy tales are based on some historical truth that people have otherwise forgotten."

"Straight-to-DVD films," Emmett dismissed.

"Haven't you ever wondered why in nearly every culture throughout human history, death is associated with a place *underground*? Why the bad people always go *down*?"

"You bury the dead so you don't have to deal with decomposition."

Keiran's eyes danced with enjoyment at their back-and-forth, irritating Emmett all the more. "Don't you wonder why most monsters fit what you have already seen of the Underdwellers? Rises from the earth, feasts on human flesh, impossibly strong with bone-white skin, and is destroyed by impalement or returns to the earth before sunrise? Cultures separated by languages and isolated by oceans all share the same common stories."

Emmett crossed his arms. "There's a reason most directors wisely edit info-dumps out of the first act, bro. Why? Because no matter how real this may all seem to you, no one else cares. No one *believes* anymore. Life shines with a green-screen glow."

A serious look passed between them, and without breaking eye contact, Keiran pointed over Emmett's shoulder toward a mirror hanging on the far wall behind him. Emmett hesitated for a moment before turning in his chair and, seeing his reflection, blanched noticeably in response.

In the natural sunlight pouring through the windows, the color of his skin along his neckline had darkened considerably around the Rot, as if it were already spreading. Emmett's eyes met his reflection, his floppy black hair matted with the greasiness of two days' worth of travel. But his hazel eyes staring back at him, fatigued from the travel, tired perhaps from too much sleep, looked insignificant and frightened by the diseased flesh around his neck. His mind fumbled with half-hearted assurances that if he could just get to a hospital, someone could fix him. Yet he knew that no story he could tell could do anything but have him, at best, humored by a disbelieving physician and sent home with some topical cream, or worse, committed to a psychiatric ward. No, he knew there was no other way.

"Doubt if it comforts you. But people who require evidence before believing are often disappointed in the answers they receive to their questions," Keiran said.

Emmett bristled at what at first felt like an empty platitude. He wanted to respond with something equally banal. Yet when he saw the Rot in his flesh, he realized that there was nothing he could do but trust people he did not know to help him.

Emmett recognized how small and helpless he truly was. It was a disconcerting, if humbling, realization.

"Okay," Emmett began. "Let's say I'm convinced. That still leaves the unanswered question."

"And that would be?"

"Who all of you are."

Keiran's only answer was his Cheshire cat grin.

Vagueness, much?

"Why don't we head outside where you can see the answer for yourself?"

CHAPTER 6

They exited through a series of hallways and oak doors out onto a sweeping mountain vista. The compound was built on the ridge of a high mountainside whose face featured a flat, wide ledge. Emmett stumbled as he struggled to take in the entire panorama, struck by the vista's scope and feeling dwarfed by the endless mountains. He was irritated by having to use Keiran's offered hand to balance himself, momentarily dizzy from the extreme heights.

Keiran took a satisfied breath. "Welcome to Silvan Dea, the Archivist's Grove."

Emmett kept his gaze aloft to steady himself. "Where are we?"

"About an hour outside Portland."

"I suppose I won't find a signal up here," he said, seeing no signs of development, power lines, or towers.

"Our Groves always intersect powerful telluric currents. Electronics never function well."

Emmett followed Keiran down a winding cobblestone path away from the compound. Ensconced in stacked rock and cut stone, the compound's central, circular tower raised high like a ziggurat. Its stone walls seemed to flow out of the rugged earth itself as if it were carved directly from the mountains, and over time, the fir trees and ambling paths simply grew around it.

"Silvan Dea, you said, right? How old is it?"

"It was built by our Elder, the Archivist, before the Spanish began exploring the region in the seventeenth century. Well, not built. *Grown*. Semantics."

Emmett's memory flashed with the name "Archivist," remembering what Keiran had said to Amala in Florida. "That's the person you said could heal the Rot, right? A librarian is going to heal this?"

"There are nine Elders worldwide, and the Archivist is the wisest and most powerful of them all."

"Elders of what, exactly? What do you people belong to?"

The cobblestone path they had followed along the hill dove into the ravine, ending at the darkened entrance to a cave. Keiran paused before the cave as if waiting for Emmett to enter.

Emmett shook his head with a nervous laugh. "Yeah right, not happening. I enjoy enclosed spaces even less than great heights. There's a reason *The Descent* is the only horror film to scare the piss out of me. No cave for Emmett. Thanks."

"Given everything that has happened to you, I can understand your doubting."

"I'm doubting you mean that," Emmett scoffed. "See what I did there?"

"This can all be too much to bear," Keiran said. He raised his arms out slightly with hands open at his sides, a gesture of openness offered with a smile. "For what it's worth, I am sorry."

Emmett wasn't sure if it was the lingering headache or the low pain in his neck, but hearing Keiran apologize was enough to ignite the frustration he had been withholding since waking.

"Then tell me who the hell you people are, John Steed. Try straight answers!"

"Welsh," he corrected.

Emmett blinked. "What?"

"Mr. Steed from *The Avengers*? He was English. I'm Welsh. And I don't fancy bowler hats."

Emmett lowered his head, succumbing to how overwhelmed he felt.

"Druids and Bards," a voice said.

Emmett looked up at the new voice. Feminine. Familiar. From Florida and so many countless dreams.

"I am a Druid, and Keiran is a Bard." Amala emerged from the shadows of the cave. Emmett could not hide the flush that reddened his face at seeing Amala's tapered, bronze-skinned form or his embarrassment at being disoriented and confused in front of her. "We are the Children of the Earth, servants of the Song of Creation."

Emmett rushed to hide his embarrassment. "If we're doing cosplay, I get to be the Pale Man from *Pan's Labyrinth*. Don't have the costume for it, but who cares?"

Amala's face was a blank, unreadable expression.

Always impressing the ladies, Emmett. Tell her about your favorite movies. Girls love it when you do that.

"We are the sentinels that defend the world from the darkness," Amala said.

Emmett had prepared himself for any kind of ridiculous or improbable explanation for the whole affair: a government conspiracy; a drug-induced hallucination; a medically induced coma. He thought he could tolerate any answer ... other than that.

"So where's your oaken staff? Or am I confusing you with wizards? I may not be up-to-date on current fashion trends in magic."

"Druid staves are crafted from iron, not wood," Keiran said.

"Iron drawn from the stars and shaped in cold waters beneath a full moon. We don't use staves. Bards, I mean."

"Oh, of course. Who needs a staff when you can whistle people into the air? Sorry. Stave. Not staff. Finally, a non-comic book convention setting where the staff-staffs-stave-staves debate can be settled. And linguists everywhere fist-bump the air."

Emmett looked away from them and out across the mountains. The sarcasm felt comfortable to him. Yet having said it, Emmett had to admit to himself that he had, in fact, seen Keiran do just that. Right before his eyes. And Amala had wielded twin serpents as she fought the Underdweller. Right after it had cursed him with the Rot.

He bit down on his lip, forcing himself to face the situation. He felt his knees grow weak with the inward acknowledgement. Silent and guarded, Emmett expected Amala or Keiran to say something. He was relieved when neither did, seemingly respecting the moment's acceptance with a reverence that comes from understanding the scope of the experience. Emmett felt himself recognizing the truth of everything and beginning the slow ascent toward belief. He was in *this* now: the grand compound, the stalking monsters, the silent guardians who stood against the encroaching darkness.

"Time is of the essence, Emmett. I am going to take you into the mountain to a place set aside for contacting the Archivist. Follow me," she said, turning her back to him and returning into the cave before he could protest.

Emmett stared dumbly after her, looking at Keiran, who only smiled. "I wouldn't make a habit of keeping her waiting. She doesn't fancy that. Believe you me."

Keiran had only made some sense of the situation for him. When Emmett looked at Amala, he was reminded again of a lifetime of dreams where a mysterious, dark-skinned woman with amber eyes explained the significance of a strange painting in a stranger apartment.

Fine. Red pill it is.

Reticently entering the cave, Emmett steadied himself with outstretched arms and permitted himself several moments for his eyes to adjust to the darkness. He felt the narrowness close around him. The crisp winter air was swallowed in a humid, sticky embrace the farther he walked in. Blind in the darkness, his ears sought sounds to guide him: whispers, faint yet persistent, echoing down long, unseen corridors.

His hands felt crumbling rock in front of him, and he turned to his right around a bend in the tunnel. He nearly cried out in panic, feeling the ground slope up underneath his feet just as his head grazed the ceiling overhead. But another wall ahead signaled a turn in the tunnel, and his path bent suddenly left.

Emmett's eyes quickly focused on soft light sources that gently eased him from the darkness. The tunnel had opened into a large cavern twenty feet high overhead and three times that size around. The cave walls were gray with visible veins of sparkling mineral. Water dripped somewhere in the distance, bounding along the echoing walls.

With a moment's worth of focus, he began to see obscure, foreign symbols and glyphs traced in dark colors along the uneven, hewn surfaces. Emmett ran a finger along the rough rock walls, tracing a symbol with his finger. He followed the symbols with his eyes as they traveled from the floor up to the ceiling, from which in the shadows stirred some motion. Emmett focused on the motion and finally saw the outlines of hundreds of dark shadows hanging, some crawling over each other. Bats. Hundreds of bats.

It would be bats.

"The Underdweller has marked you. The Rot will continue

spreading until it consumes you," Amala said. She wore a dark sleeveless shirt tucked into fitted black slacks. In the soft light from the candles strewn throughout the vault, Emmett could see that her waves of long brown hair were bound tightly back in several overlapping braids that draped down over a developed chest that slowly rose and fell.

In the darkness, her glowing eyes were like stardust. Emmett could not help but be mesmerized by how they drew any light around them and reflected it with an untamed brilliance. Just as they had in his dreams; a fact Emmett was uncertain if he had the energy left to attempt unraveling in his mind.

The woman of your dreams. Try not to make an ass of yourself.

Amala stepped down into the depression in the floor in the room's center.

"The Archivist is not like other Elders. She is often struck with wanderlust, traveling far outside her Grove and away from civilization for many years. She requires that we seek her out, proving ourselves capable in the search. We will make contact with her today, and when she responds, Keiran and I will escort you to her."

"I don't mean to offend you," Emmett began, glancing up once with frustration at the scratching sounds, "but there has to be a quicker method for dealing with this. I mean, what do you do with all of the people who must have this Rot?"

Amala stared directly at him without a hint of anything but total seriousness in her expression. "Most don't survive the initial attack, Emmett."

She knelt with a single, fluid motion at a point in the center of the chamber where nine irregular symbols danced around a ring of concentric circles. Placing the backs of her hands on each knee, she closed her eyes.

"Come and sit with me. This cave is a sacred place."

Of course it's a magic cave. He took a step forward and awkwardly knelt.

Emmett fell back onto the ground clumsily and crossed his legs. Compared to Amala's liquid movements, Emmett was aware of how ungainly his body was: tall, lanky, and often at odds with any center of gravity.

"Take my hands and close your eyes."

Embarrassed, he wiped his clammy hands on his jeans. Reluctantly, he took her delicate hands into his. They were soft and yielding to the touch, but held his own firmly with determination.

He sighed pointedly, bobbing his head. "What's next? Peyote and heavy sweating?"

"Close your eyes and focus on your breathing," she began with a measured tone, her volume lowered with each word. "Too often we focus on the external world, both hurried and harried outside of our core beings. The noise of living drowns our ears, and we grow deaf to silence."

There's truth in that.

"I want you to withdraw from the world and fold into your body. With each breath, exhale the world's noise. Release the chaos from your mind. Inhale the clarity that comes from the silence within."

His mind was pulled in a dozen directions, from the faint trickle of water to the itch along his arm. Yet with each breath, the sounds grew smaller, farther away. The sensations nagging at his consciousness quieted as if mollified solely by his breathing. Thoughts about his situation, the Rot, and each individual narrative withdrew until they were distant echoes. Without sensation or feeling, the world melted away around him.

"Our minds are letting go of the false world," Amala's soft voice began, seemingly timed to the rhythm of Emmett's breathing. "We give ourselves permission to leave everything behind and enter a quieter place. Call to her in the quiet place."

Emmett felt his lips murmur the name. His breathing slowed, drawing calm into his body and releasing disorder with each deliberate breath. He saw nothing in his mind's eye, felt no change in his presence, and so he called out to her again.

As his lips formed soundless words, he felt a hint of a breeze stroke the back of his neck. It was feathery like a whisper in his ear. In the darkness, his awareness focused on each individual hair that stood aloft along his arms, the tingling attentiveness of another presence near him.

He felt himself slipping back. It was the only way he could describe the sensation of leaving his body without having actually left it before. His consciousness eased out of his body and backward into a void empty of sensation. Emmett no longer felt Amala's hands, no longer heard her quiet yet persistent urgings. He did not feel the cave's warmth or closeness. Time passed without counting, and Emmett soon was unaware of his own limbs. His mind sharpened, focused without the burdens or boundaries of his body, concentrating on each minute detail as it manifested.

In the emptiness, Emmett did not have eyes, and yet his mind stretched beyond the limits of normal vision. Colors differentiated themselves from the blackness, birthing substance. Shapes took form. Sensation returned to his mind like tingling along the skin of his consciousness. Sound soon found ears that he no longer had.

An image of a woman took form, twice his age and petite with black hair. She held her hand underneath her stomach, the slight bump of pregnancy just beginning to appear on her small body. She exited from a bus onto a busy sidewalk and walked past a storefront owner unlocking his doors. Emmett felt the image expand into three dimensions, and he felt himself moving along the street behind her. He watched the images of cars and people pass, clouds sweeping across a bright sky in the early afternoon. The images gained depth and richness. He felt the brush of dry wind sweep through his being, heard the calls of children playing in the schoolyard she walked by.

The vision suddenly altered, the street and cars replaced by rows of books along high shelves. The sun's afternoon warmth became cool, and the dry breeze transformed into a stale, musty stillness. She was still walking, though her clothes had changed from a brown walking coat to a tweed sweater and dress. The silence of the surrounding library enveloped his senses, focused his awareness on her. She stopped to identify a book. When she would stop, Emmett's consciousness stopped as well, and when she would resume, he would feel himself drawn forward with her.

The scene morphed again, a wash of colors and senses rushing past and through his awareness. She was sitting in a corner chair in an apartment now, an apartment that was immediately familiar to Emmett. As fading sunlight filtered in through the drawn curtains of the lone window, she nodded to herself with a turn of the page of her art history book.

The familiar sights of his life's dreams filled his consciousness. The mirrors. The nesting dolls. The painting on the wall. Only this painting was absent the words above the king's head. Emmett looked deeply into the woman's eyes and saw her passion for the art she lovingly read. The baroque masters. The impressionists. The perfect swirls of oil on canvas.

The image of the apartment shifted again. The woman's pregnancy was more visible now. Her face was sunken and anxiety filled. She paced the apartment, weeping and shaking her head. She was begging someone to get out, yet there was no one else in the apartment with her. She was repeating the same words over and over, weeping as she did so. Gritting her teeth and covering her ears from some unseen noise, she finally grabbed a pen from the nightstand and began writing words onto her painting, words that Emmett immediately recognized.

Silence consumed the hollow sounds within the apartment, and once again the images merged and colors changed with the morphing of shapes and contours. Emmett felt a sharp, jolting rush of sensation as he was hurtled down a harsh, white hallway behind a rushing group of nurses and doctors.

Screaming pierced his consciousness. Hysterical, throttled fury. Amid the group of harried nurses, the woman strained vainly against her restraints, spitting and cursing. She frothed with rage. Large orderlies held her bucking fists and legs down as her mania stormed through her slim body.

Heavy perspiration matted her black hair to her face. Straining to hold her head up to see over the nurses, she looked directly at the dark corner in the room where two walls were joined. She wept hysterically. She gestured to the room's bare corner, pleading with the nurses to see what she saw. But they saw nothing, and in her despair she wailed. Emmett felt her sobbing tear into the depths of his soul.

The images shifted again. The room was empty now. The woman was lying in a hospital bed staring mutely into the dark corner of her room, her glassy eyes transfixed as if waiting for the shadows to stir into form. Her smooth face had sunken, and in her eyes it appeared that a lifetime had passed.

She felt her flat stomach, and looking down at where once a child grew within her, she wept. Taking a used, crumpled tissue from her lap and bringing it to her mouth, she heaved again, her curved, frail body retching forward with each gurgling cough.

Her breathing was increasingly labored. Her thin arms pushed herself up from her bed, and with effort she lurched forward with arms outstretched for balance. She reached for the call button on her nightstand, her coughing continuing with frightening intensity. Her face registered panic, her eyes welling with tears.

Emmett was filled with pain, as if his consciousness were being suffocated. He wanted to cry out, but he found that he had no mouth; he wanted to reach out for her, yet he found that he had no arms or body.

His awareness could not be changed, nor could his eyes be closed or turned away.

She fumbled with the call button, and a feeble, weak arm grabbed at her shoulder. The air was filled with the pungent odor of urine. She collapsed against the nightstand and off the bed, falling to the linoleum floor. With his acute awareness, Emmett could hear every grotesque, minute sound of her skull crashing against the edge of the nightstand. Crimson blood pooled beneath her head, her small body contorted in an unnatural posture.

When he thought his mind might shatter into a thousand discordant pieces, the images faded, each color returning to the empty void of his inner consciousness. Emmett felt his awareness returning to his body with the tingling of awakened limbs. He felt his essence drawn forward, anchored suddenly in substance. Emmett began to feel the fullness of his body—the contours of his limbs and the boundaries of his flesh.

"Everything that takes place has a beginning and an end," an ageless, genderless voice said. It was like a soft wind caressing the back of his neck.

"Summer and winter, clouds and dews and rain."

Beyond the voice, Emmett's awareness extended to a chorus of sounds that seemed to have been present the entire time, and yet only now with this voice did he become aware of them: a baby's joyous laughter; water splashing along river stones; the flutter of wings as a bird takes flight; the call of cicadas in the twilight; the roll of thunder across the edge of an approaching storm.

"The trees shed their leaves; the trees crown themselves in greenery and fruit."

There were millions of individual voices, calls, and sounds layered and woven into a brilliant, pure tapestry. They produced the most perfect, sustained melody Emmett had ever heard. It suffused his entire being, stretching every space within his mind.

"All this from year to year forever and ever and ever."

And with this pure sound of life and the voice that repeated the words on the mysterious painting, he heard another voice calling out to him. It continued to echo in his mind as the brilliant melody faded away to the periphery of his consciousness before it grew silent altogether, and only the insistent, repeating voice could be heard.

"Emmett, come back to me."

It was Amala.

"Emmett, come back to me."

Her voice was soft and delicate.

"Emmett, come back to me."

He realized that she was repeating herself, insistent and yet patient with a reverence for the experience.

Emmett could feel his body again, and with trepidation he opened his eyes, feeling the world rush in around him as if his head had just emerged from the fathomless ocean depths. The quiet trickling of water deep in the cave tunnels was thunderous. The warm, unmoving air in the room was sweltering. In the near-total darkness of the cave, Emmett's opened eyes felt blinded by what little light illuminated the surrounding area.

Amala was staring up. He lifted his neck, feeling his muscles respond to his command. Emmett gasped in wonder. A swarm of bats glided in a uniform flock above their heads, circling around the room with the natural grace borne of flight.

"Call to her," Amala instructed, this time with urgency in her voice.

"Archivist," Emmett said. He did not know if he felt foolish or afraid—perhaps both—but something felt too bare, too exposed. Had Amala seen what he had seen?

"Call out to her," Amala repeated.

"Archivist," Emmett said her name again. He felt his voice growing as Amala's grip tightened, urging him.

"Give her name meaning, Emmett. With faith that there is a release from the pain of this life, call out to her!"

Something in the pleading of her voice and the warmth of her hands told him that she needed him to *feel* the calling as much as say it. He had to bare himself even more—surrender to the experience and to the vision itself.

He saw the image again in his mind: the woman who had studied art history and smiled over the life growing inside her; the woman who wept for her missing child; the woman who collapsed and died alone with no one to love or comfort her. Emmett knew who that pregnant woman was. He knew who she wept for in the final moments of her life. He felt the agony rushing through him, coursing through every acute sense in his body, and centering in the dull ache where the Rot was consuming him.

"Archivist!" Emmett cried out, feeling tears he could not remember crying rolling down his cheeks. The air itself seemed to shift with an unseen energy, and the bats responded, turning as one with startling speed and diving down and through their arms. Amala held him firmly and unblinking, her amber eyes sparkling with the countless shapes thundering past her face.

Emmett watched with a mixture of wonder and terror as the swarm flew around and through them, tumbling and swirling over in a maelstrom of synchronized movement. He clung to Amala's hands, not wanting to ever let go.

Finally, the swarm shifted like a river tumbling over a waterfall. As one, the swarm of bats veered out the tunnel and into the world somewhere beyond.

After a moment's stunned silence, Emmett felt Amala releasing his hands. At first, he could not will himself to let go. Had she seen what he had seen?

Amala must have sensed Emmett's hesitation for she waited in the silence for him. He finally released her hands. The conflicting sensations and demands of the world returned as a flood into an already crowded mind.

"They will carry your message to the Archivist," Amala whispered.

Emmett's mind unfolded, his awareness focusing increasingly on his surroundings. "That was ..." *unworthy* of words? He ran a hand across his face to wipe away his tears, stifling a sniffle with an exaggerated cough. He felt embarrassed to be so exposed in front of Amala.

"Whatever vision the Archivist offered you, that is for you and you alone."

He felt immediately relieved to hear that the vision had been only his. When she stood, her soft manners were replaced with a brisk, practical expression void of closeness that Emmett felt jarring after the intimate encounter they seemed to share. She offered a hand to help him up, and he was surprised by her strength.

They were suddenly standing only an inch away from each other. Emmett was aware that he was holding his breath, and when finally he breathed, he tasted rose water and sweet cardamom in her presence. He could see Amala's eyes widening, and when he looked down at the curve of her neckline, he could see her heightened pulse beating visibly through her skin.

Emmett's lips slightly parted, and he knew he wanted to say something. Countless things ran through his mind.

He knew there was a reason Amala had been in his dreams. She was watching him, waiting for him to ask her.

The words began to form in the bottom of his throat. And just as Emmett summoned what courage he was certain he did not possess to utter them, a voice called down the cave's tunnel.

"Oi! You lot done in there? I'm famished!"

Amala blinked and stepped back from Emmett, turning her

head away for a moment. "Keiran will look after you while I attend to other matters," she said abruptly, her voice suddenly distant. "I will see you soon." And turning away from Emmett, Amala did not see the wounded, confused look in his eyes.

CHAPTER 7

"Record time, mate!" Keiran exclaimed, bounding excitedly up to meet Emmett as he emerged from the cave. His giddiness only added to Emmett's irritation with his interruption.

"Yeah, well, bats love me," Emmett shrugged, squinting in the sunlight.

"So we have time for a spot of lunch, then?" Keiran asked Amala.

"I cannot go, but I will see you both later."

"Right, well, let's get you sorted, Emmett!"

Amala turned without comment and walked off in the opposite direction. Watching her disappear into the tree line, he shook his head and followed Keiran.

"What, she just hangs out in the trees?"

"It's her way," Keiran answered with a knowing smile. "How are you?"

Emmett felt his heart surge into his throat. His expression must have registered some change, because Keiran looked away from him out of some shared recognition of the experience's intimacy.

"You don't need to tell me the particulars, mate. It's a private matter."

"I just don't know what to say." Emmett shoved his hands into his pockets and hunched his shoulders. "I'm somewhere between 'gonna need a bigger boat' and 'there is no spoon.'"

Keiran silently nodded.

Emmett looked back over his shoulder to where Amala disappeared in the trees.

"So, uh, Amala is your—"

"Companion?"

"Is that like wife or...?" he asked, trying not to give sound to the emptiness in his voice.

Keiran skipped up the steps to the front entrance, stopping to turn and face Emmett. Emmett found him intolerably bouncy. Combined with his good looks and dapper manner, Keiran Glendower was officially everything that Emmett was not. The cool accent only made it worse.

"Druids and Bards are joined together as Companions in their fight against the world's darkness. It's more intimate than marriage."

Emmett pulled his hoodie over his head, wishing he could disappear.

"Ever had a best mate that knows your darkest parts and accepts you exactly as you are? In life's bleakest moments, they are right there with you?"

Emmett shrugged, certain that if he spoke he would not be able to hide his conflicting emotions.

Keiran spoke as he slowly opened the door. "And they'd give their life for you. Not just once, but each moment of every day. Without hesitation."

Epically unattainable by me. Joy.

"As Companions, we come to hear the other person in our minds. Fleeting thoughts, of course—a word here, a memory's fragment there—and only during moments of heightened emotion."

It just gets better.

After navigating the labyrinth of Silvan Dea's many corridors, they soon entered a private room with shower and wardrobe. Keiran extracted several pairs of dark slacks and black wool sweaters. "Find a size that fits. I hope you won't mind if we dressed you in something more gentlemanly. A decent wardrobe does wonders for the spirit."

Emmett tried not to roll his eyes. Keiran's seeming genuineness only amplified his seeming perfection.

"Thanks."

Keiran turned to leave as Emmett looked through the available clothes.

"More answers with an early dinner, I promise." And with a parting grin that already was his defining characteristic, Keiran exited the room.

Emmett had relished the shower, washing away the stale odor of what he had accepted had been forty-eight hours of sleep. Hot water was immediate and plentiful, surprising Emmett since Silvan Dea was isolated atop a high mountain ridge. Emmett laid his head under the stream for a long time. The sting of the water against his neck was pronounced, but he gritted his teeth and hissed against the discomfort. It was brilliant like an explosion that leaves the vision spotted. Flakes of blackened skin fell from his neck, clouding the water at his feet. Yet even as it washed away, he found the same diseased skin underneath.

Emmett leaned against the porcelain basin, rubbing the fog from the mirror above with his towel. Worn hazel eyes stared back at him beneath errant curls of black, wavy hair. He traced the length of the rotting flesh on his neck down to his collarbone, horrified at how cold the decaying skin was compared to the supple flesh surrounding it.

Finding an assortment of the usual toiletries next to the sink, Emmett spent several minutes shaving his fine dusting of stubble and brushing his teeth, careful not to stare too long at the darkness crawling down his collarbone. He took a comb from the toiletry bag and began to run it through his tangled hair, not wanting Mr. Old Hollywood upstaging him.

Keiran returned to retrieve a dressed Emmett a short time later, escorting him to an adjoining garage where his car was parked between a pair of unremarkable vans. Expecting to see a cross-country swath of grime and insects splattered along the windshield, he found the car had been thoroughly washed and detailed—as much as a twelve-year-old car could be cleaned, he thought.

And Nancy thought the car would never make it out of Texas.

Impeccably dressed, Keiran wore gray slacks tailored perfectly above black loafers, and a pressed black shirt with a starched collar and silver cufflinks that perfectly framed his physique. He could walk into a room and draw everyone's attention with a handsomeness that was both intimidating and yet approachable. He was refined and confident, things Emmett, with his hoodie-and-jeans sensibility and predictable habit of stumbling over himself, lacked. Emmett knew he wasn't unattractive, but he lacked the athletic definition, stone-like jaw, and wavy blond hair that took away the breath of the people Keiran passed on the street.

It's obviously enough for Amala.

The drive into town took two hours, Keiran having insisted on Emmett driving. Much of this trip was spent negotiating a narrow dirt road that snaked down a hidden gorge behind the Grove, through crudely excavated tunnels in the mountainside, and finally out along the dark, barren countryside that sat shadowed at the base of the snow-capped mountains. Emmett cringed as he avoided potholes, mud pits, and the occasional tawny doe bounding through the snow.

Keiran peppered him with questions about driving manual downhill, as Keiran had apparently never done. Amala was the driver of the pair, he explained. Considering that Keiran could conceivably shatter glass with his voice or sheer a face of the mountainside with his outstretched palm, his inability to drive was odd. It was the sole thing thus far that Emmett possessed that Keiran did not.

Their road transformed into gravel, and then eventually dirt, before it blended into the winterscape next to a lone stretch of highway. Emmett could no longer see the stone compound in his rearview mirror. It was easy to see how the Grove could go unnoticed, safely perched on the hidden ledge within a tapered copse in the mountains.

Keiran asked if Emmett had family that should be contacted, but Emmett said no, quickly changing the subject back to how they had found him. Keiran shared how Amala and he had been tracking a Revenant's carnage through the Deep South for weeks. Details of the gruesome child killings left Emmett queasy as he navigated a series of roads into the outskirts of Portland.

Keiran guided him through several traffic lights and busy intersections. The downtown markets were a circus of activity in the late-afternoon hours. All manner of people perused stalls of live seafood and fresh, organic vegetables and fruits. The brisk air was tinged with the honey-infused aroma of freshly baked breads, and Emmett felt his stomach respond to the rich bouquet of tasty smells as they exited the parked car.

Keiran led him through an open marketplace busy with jostling shoppers and endless options. Chefs preparing their evening menus haggled over prices with shopkeepers offering samples of their wares with reckless abandon, calling out or shouting at passersby with their confectionary delights and lowest prices.

Emmett avoided a flying fish overhead with a careful duck and followed Keiran into a tiny shop with the name *Hiraeth* over the single, steamed window. The lettering pattern was of a sideways-facing, crimson-colored dragon with claws intertwined with the beginning and ending H.

The restaurant was little more than a wide counter with stools overlooking a cramped kitchen. It was comfortable in its uncomfortable size. Windows at their backs faced out onto the marketplace. Fryers filled the narrow restaurant with satisfying smells.

Keiran sidled up to the counter, motioning for Emmett to join him. A harried woman with flyaway hair hurried along the counter, shuttling hot plates of steaming food and manning the register. A dozen people lined the wall of windows awaiting their to-go orders.

"She serves breakfast all day. I love breakfast. Well, if the truth be told, I love all food." Keiran handed Emmett a paper menu from the metal prongs along the counter, pointing to several items of interest.

After finishing a transaction at the register and handing off two plates of food to another person along the counter, the woman finally hurried over to them. Her eyes and face brightened considerably with recognition.

"All right, love?" she asked.

"All right," Keiran answered with a wide smile. "Emmett, this is Mrs. Emaline Carmichael." Emmett nodded as she returned the greeting.

"I haven't seen you in months, my boy. I bin missin' you. I

was getting worried, but then I says to myself, I says, a strapping lad like that could well take care of himself."

"Ta. I only come back to Portland to visit you," Keiran flirted.

She waved a hand at him. "Oh, go on, then! I wouldn't reckon all the hearts you've broken! You sound just like my late Jack, God rest his soul. Always carrying on wit' the ladies."

Keiran leaned in with one elbow along the counter. "I'd fancy you even if you didn't cook for me," he deadpanned.

Emmett sat entranced by the conversation. Or, more accurately, by Keiran. Mrs. Carmichael seemed transformed just by his presence, and with each word she seemed to grow younger with energy.

Mrs. Carmichael looked at Emmett and leaned over the counter toward Keiran. "Is this another one of yours, then, love?"

"Aye."

Mrs. Carmichael and Keiran exchanged knowing glances, and she stepped back from the counter. "Crackin' lookin' boy, too. All right?"

Emmett had streamed enough BBC to understand. "Hello," he nodded.

"Yes, well, I promised my mate here the best meal in Portland, and I expect you will not make a liar of me," Keiran said as he clapped Emmett jovially on the shoulder.

"Well I should hope so, then! Look at you, Keiran! All skin and bones! I won't have any of it. What'll ya boys be having, then?"

"Emmett, may I order for you?"

"Sure."

"Fancy a proper Welsh breakfast. For two, please," Keiran said, handing the menu back to Mrs. Carmichael as she nodded and hurried off.

Emmett looked sideways at Keiran, and it was Emmett's turn

to grin.

"That accent of yours comes on a lot heavier when you're around others."

"What? Can't understand me accent?" Keiran asked with exaggeration.

"You'd be surprised how well versed I am with British television," Emmett said, excited he finally had something they could equally discuss.

"I actually never watched much telly growing up. Only knew of *The Avengers* from my best mate, Rory, when he dressed up one Halloween."

Emmett's shoulders sunk, deflated. *Of course. Because it wouldn't have been helpful to have at least* one *freakin' thing in common.*

Mrs. Carmichael returned with a plate of sliced breads and a smaller dish of jam. "Here you are now, lovelies, a plate of my homemade speckled bread, then—"

"It's sort of like raisin bread," Keiran whispered.

"—and a dollop of plum and elderberry jam. Now eat up, the both of you," she said sternly, pointing to Emmett. "This boy is too skinny, and a strappin' man like you needs a proper meal." Keiran beamed as she reached over and pinched his cheek.

Emmett found the bread's sticky moistness deliciously filling. They ate in silence for several moments, Keiran closing his eyes often with each rapturous bite, and Emmett equally comforted by the rich food.

Keiran raised his glass again and smiled when Mrs. Carmichael returned. Piled in heaping quantities were poached eggs, pork sausages and bacon, laverbread—a type of boiled seaweed mixed with bacon fat and rolled in oatmeal into a gooey paste—and fresh, steamed mussels, which Keiran indicated were a substitution because Mrs. Carmichael was never satisfied with the days-old cockles sold in the marketplace.

"Tuck in," Keiran said as he began to eat.

Emmett didn't hesitate, appreciating the tart, conflicting assortment of tastes and the satisfying fullness within his stomach.

Blissful expressions were exchanged as each enjoyed their meal. Emmett discovered that with a minimal amount of food already in his stomach, he was more ravenously hungry than before.

"How're you managing the laverbread?" Keiran asked.

"Could be worse," Emmett answered, covering his half-full mouth. "It's not monkey brains at Pankot Palace."

"Sorry?"

Emmett waved a hand as if batting a fly away. "Ignore me. It's my gimmick. Just tune me out like everyone else."

"And your gimmick would be?" Keiran asked, setting his knife and fork down and giving Emmett his full attention.

"Turn real life into a movie."

"Oh, well, I've seen fewer films than television shows. Not something we had much money for growing up, mind. But I think it could be quite fun being in a movie."

"Yeah, they'd love you, Marty Stu," Emmett said, wiping his mouth as he set his fork down. "They'd either cast an American to play you or an Australian soap star with a clunky American accent. No male leads with foreign accents. And definitely *not* a British accent. Brits can only play gay robots or villains. *Especially* villains. You can thank Alan Rickman for that. Everyone's still chasing the legacy of Hans Gruber."

Keiran looked genuinely conflicted. "I'm unsure how I'd feel about an American playing me. No offense."

"As opposed to a Welsh actor with an impossible-to-spell name? No offense."

"Ta."

Emmett took another bite, surprised by Keiran's interest in Emmett's safe conversation zone.

"So who would play you, Emmett? I assume you're in this movie, too, seeing as how you're the star of it at the moment."

Emmett hurriedly finished what he was chewing. "I've got this. I've thought about this for a long time. Casting an actor to play me in a movie based on my life. First, he'd have to be an edgy actor who hates the studio system but takes the occasional commercial role to pay the bills. He'll have done one really stand-out indie role the critics loved. Preferably a Jim Jarmusch movie so he can introduce me. The suits would object and say he couldn't carry the lead. And the nerds would rage on their vlogs about how miscast he was because, well, that's what we do."

"So who would this be?"

"I change every few months or so. Ezra Miller is my current pick, but my friend Nancy wants Dave Franco. Her obsession with those brothers is unsettling."

"You've certainly thought this through," Keiran said.

"Yeah, well, spoiler alert: I don't have much to talk about besides movies."

"You can catch me up on all I've been missing, then," Keiran replied. Had Emmett read those words by text message, he'd have read sarcasm in them. Keiran's face, however, was genuine warmth and sincerity.

When they finished eating a short time later, Emmett felt the drowsiness that comes from a full, satisfied stomach. Keiran reached into his pocket and withdrew a pair of twenty-dollar bills, and without waiting for the check, placed them down on the back of the counter.

"Thanks," Emmett said, to which Keiran clapped him again on the shoulder.

Seeing them rising from their chairs, Mrs. Carmichael hurried over and gathered Keiran into a great hug.

"Shall I wrap something up for you to take with, love?" she was asking Keiran as he held his own hands over his stomach in protest.

"I don't think I could manage another bite. Emmett?"

"No, thank you. It was really good."

"Well, all right then, you take care now, love," she said as she kissed Keiran on both cheeks. Mrs. Carmichael then leaned over and pulled Emmett into a similar embrace. She smelled sweet like gingerbread, and her roundness was comforting.

She whispered so close to his ear that he was certain no one else would hear them over the noise and bustle. "I know that shocked look in your eyes, love, like you're seeing the world for the first time. Pay no mind. Keep your heart open and don't lose sight of your friends." She kissed his cheek and released him, rushing off down the opposite side of the counter to a pair of waiting diners with bills to pay.

Emmett looked at Keiran, who was standing patiently waiting for him to exit. "And now fed, let us find Amala and what trouble we all might get into together."

CHAPTER 8

Emmett matched Keiran's leisurely pace heading to the car.

"So how much does Mrs. Carmichael know?"

"Her husband was killed several years ago by Revenants. She's intuitive enough to guess that there's more going on than what little we had told her. But she's a special person, and I like having her around."

"Does she know about your reworkin' *The Wicker Man*?" When Keiran's face registered confusion, Emmett quickly added: "The Druid and Bard stuff?"

"Ah, yes. Well, most families of Revenant victims don't really *want* to know the truth. It would drive them mad, or worse, into vigilantes. It's easier to think that it was the work of a serial rapist; anything to give them some sense of closure."

"Because serial rapists are better than monsters?"

"You can imprison serial rapists."

Emmett nodded at the logic. "If I were them, I probably wouldn't want to know."

"You wouldn't?"

He shook his head. "That the world was populated by unimaginable darkness? Unlikely. First rule of a David Fincher film: Don't ask what's in the box."

Emmett was certain by Keiran's face that he only understood part of that analogy.

"Some believe. Some can't. And some are unwilling to accept an obviously false explanation, but aren't quite ready to know everything," Keiran said.

"Like Mrs. Carmichael?"

"Like Mrs. Carmichael." Keiran nodded.

"Like me," Emmett chuckled.

"Don't discount your strength, Emmett. That you're alive is evidence of this." Keiran's face was uncharacteristically serious, and it looked as if he were wrestling with what to say next. "Emmett, have you ever heard voices?"

"Unexpected, much?" Emmett responded.

"Voices, Emmett. A voice in the wilderness leading you away from home, telling you to follow an animal. Or whispers in the sound of falling rain calling you back to the ocean?"

Emmett thought briefly of his life's dreams but shook his head. "I've never heard voices before," he answered truthfully, and it was a measure of Keiran's serious expression that Emmett responded without his usual snark. "Why?"

"The Children of the Earth are special, Emmett. Druids hear the call of animals, or Wisdoms, often when they venture closer to forests. Bards hear the Song in the rain and waters. It may happen at any age, though it is most common in adolescence. Because you had left Houston for Florida and resisted the Rot—something normally only a Druid or Bard could do—it seemed reasonable that you might have heard the Song and gone out in search of answers."

"No voices. I just needed to hit the reset button on life."

Emmett wondered if the entire trip away from Silvan Dea—the drive, the late lunch, and now the stroll—had just been an opportunity to ask the question in a neutral, non-mystical setting.

"Sorry to disappoint, but I'm not special."

Keiran shook his head. "No, you must be. Your coloring—your aura—is different. Amala said so. Even Paulo noticed it."

Emmett's heart dropped, and he was uncertain why. His face flushed as Keiran stared at him, and though he had to force himself not to look away, Emmett found neither jealousy nor competition in his expression. Only wonder. And confusion.

"As it is, the sun is setting, and we should be heading back soon. Have a seat and wait for me here. I'd like to speak to Mrs. Carmichael before we leave."

Emmett sat down and shook his head, the abruptness of Keiran's shift in conversation jarring. He watched Keiran disappear back inside *Hiraeth*. Whether it was the heavy meal or his physical exhaustion from the Rot, he could not help but yawn.

The horizon darkened with the setting sun. Fifteen minutes passed since Keiran had left. Emmett wondered if he had decided to leave him now that he had confirmed Emmett wasn't a fellow monster hunter.

Emmett nearly jumped with surprise when he turned his head and saw a child standing silently to his right. It was a little girl with light blond hair and blue eyes dressed in what looked like a Bugs Bunny costume and holding a basket with both hands.

"Oh, you scared me," Emmett smiled. He had no experience with kids and was never clear how to talk to them.

"Are you ready, E?" she tugged at his arm.

Emmett looked around for the child's parents and saw no one. The evening had grown bitterly cold and wet with a scattered drizzle. It was no place for a child alone.

Turning back to ask the girl her name, Emmett saw she had already run off. He could see the flopping ears bouncing on her head as she plunged in and out of darkness running underneath the few streetlamps.

"Wait!" he yelled, running after her.

"Come on!" she called out excitedly ahead.

The girl rounded the corner and disappeared. Only the rare beams of distant traffic reflected in closed storefront windows allowed Emmett to finally catch sight of her. He broke into a fast sprint, turning to follow her down a narrow one-way alley.

"Wait!" Emmett struggled to say, panting and shaking his head. He doubled over for a moment coughing, steadying himself against a trashcan.

The girl was standing at the far end of the alley, looking up at the tall brick buildings on three sides of her. Emmett caught his breath and began walking slowly toward her, hopeful the kid had calmed enough to allow him to lead her to an open store and call her parents or the police.

As Emmett drew close, the girl turned around and smiled wide at him. "I want to go trick-or-treating! You promised mom you'd take me!"

Emmett was about to sputter something when he heard a whistle behind him. Looking over his shoulder, he saw the shadows of several figures sauntering down the alleyway dressed in black with hoods covering their faces.

"Hey there, little lady," one of the figures leered. The others were fanning out to block the alley's exit.

Somewhere in Emmett's stomach, the bottom fell out. There were twelve figures total behind the lead. Emmett heard the urgent warnings from that quiet voice within each person. *Run!*

Emmett's hand instinctively went behind him, feeling the little girl draw close. He looked up either side of the alley, finding no doors or windows. The figures seemed to be laughing at his searching for escape, the lead one now drawing close enough that Emmett could see the wire-rimmed glasses he wore over passionless brown eyes.

"You wanna play tonight?" he taunted, eliciting more chuckles from those behind him. Emmett could smell the heavy alcohol and tobacco seeping through the man's pores. The man cocked his head to one side and appraised Emmett like an animal readied for slaughter.

"I thought we'd have to settle for a runaway," he slurred, licking his lips. "But fate gives us two well-fed beauties."

Emmett's body tensed as he prepared to lunge. But the lead man threw a heavy hook across his jaw, stars exploding in his vision as he painfully fell down to the ground. There was a muffled scream as the others swooped down upon the little girl, covering her mouth even as her costume was easily ripped from her body.

"Let the older one watch. Despair can be the most potent offering," the lead's voice drawled. Emmett tried to call out for help, his breath stolen by a chokehold from one of his captors. He struggled vainly against several strong hands that pulled him up and forced his head toward the alley's corner where two dainty legs trembled underneath a pack of feasting animals.

The lead man raised his hands and grunted guttural sounds. Over the rolling thunder, Emmett heard a low roar in his ears. He thought it was the adrenaline rushing through his body, but the roar grew so suddenly that he felt his ears popping from the pressure. His attackers seemed enraptured by the sound, their faces twisted in feral visages of exaggerated pleasure.

When Emmett thought his ears would bleed from the pressure, it suddenly receded, replaced with the attackers' labored breathing. The older man fell to his knees, his arms still held out wide as he lifted his head up toward a corner area where two of the buildings met in the rear of the alley.

A pair of red eyes appeared in the shadowy corner and

beneath the eyes an exaggerated grinning mouth. The eyes looked down at the unfolding horror, the adults excitedly ravaging the now-unmoving girl. The eyes then looked upon the kneeling man, who by now was offering whispered exaltations upon the shadowy presence.

Your obeisance is acknowledged. The voice was an explosion of disharmonious, conflicting sounds in Emmett's mind, and he buckled under its weight.

"We seek your favor, Old One," the kneeling man said with trembling hands raised above his head.

I require a living offering, the voice responded as its red eyes turned to the unmoving child who, even in apparent death, was still being violated.

"We have another!" the kneeling man proclaimed, pivoting on his knees to turn around and point at Emmett.

Emmett struggled again to free himself, but his captor's chokehold only tightened around his neck as the red eyes lingered on Emmett.

That is not ... wait ... let me see the eyes, the voice commanded.

Emmett felt the chokehold increase, and it was the loss of air that stopped him from moving. The red eyes bore down into his.

Mother will hide you, but I will always find you, the voice mocked.

"Is our sacrifice acceptable, Old One? Shall I shed blood for you?" the kneeling man asked. He removed a serrated knife from his back pocket and advanced toward Emmett.

The capricious, violent grin widened even greater than before as the red eyes narrowed. *There is only one thing you could ever do to truly appease me ... monkey.*

The kneeling man's expression registered confusion. He began to turn back toward the red eyes when a gloved hand appeared from the shadows beneath the mouth and made a backhand shooing gesture. As one, all of Emmett's attackers were lifted upward by some unseen force and violently thrown backward at the surrounding buildings, their heads twisted completely around.

Emmett felt the grip loosen around his neck. Crumpled bodies and pooling blood along the rain-soaked alleyway surrounded him. The red eyes and unnatural, wide grin stared back at him from the shadows.

Do you remember the unending rains that drove the Master's children underground?

The shadows unfurled around the red eyes and poured out across the alleyway, rolling over the unmoving bodies and toward Emmett. Thunder roared louder overhead as the red eyes drew closer.

Do you hear the call of your Master?

The shadows were upon Emmett, slithering up his body. The gloved hands reached out toward his face to touch him, and Emmett burst into a terrible scream so loud that he could wake the entire world from its slumber.

"Nooooooo!"

There was sudden and complete darkness.

A dull, dizzying thump against his head, followed by queasy uncertainty, and Emmett felt something—some*one*—gently caressing his face. He blinked the blurriness in his vision away, recoiling from a dark, featureless shape looming over him.

"Emmett, you're okay." The voice was familiar. It was Amala.

He blinked again, and the pier came into focus. In the soft glow of the slow-setting winter sun, he was sitting still on the bench where Keiran had left him. Families were passing him. Shops were still open. Amala was kneeling before him.

"Just breathe, Emmett."

His pulse was still racing. He felt as if he were just waking from a dream. Yet never before had he dreamt and not known that he was dreaming. He always knew.

He looked into Amala's eyes, and it was not the surreal expression from his dreams. Nor was it the intimate one in the cave. It was panic.

"Emmett, have the waking dreams begun yet? Have the red eyes returned?"

CHAPTER 9

Emmett looked out the window at the passing lights along the dark highway. He sat mutely stricken in the backseat, barely following the rapidly changing situation. Amala had been driving them back to Silvan Dea for nearly thirty minutes at speeds that teetered between dangerous and prosecutable, with Emmett managing to understand only half of what Amala and Keiran discussed.

Finding him apparently dreaming on the bench, Amala had drawn close to him and whispered into his ear: "Say nothing of this to anyone. Tell no one." He'd had no time to question her when Keiran had returned from *Hiraeth*, and it was a measure of Keiran's effortless calm that he had not questioned her when she'd told him that an attack against Silvan Dea was imminent and they must immediately return to their Grove.

They did not know Emmett, had no reason to care about or for him, and yet they faced danger beyond anything Emmett could conceptualize. Something in the dream with the red eyes and Amala's knowing he had been having a waking dream confirmed this. They faced this danger with a methodical, calculated preparation to protect him. He knew they would endanger their own lives to protect him. They had already done so in Florida, and Emmett sensed they would soon again.

Risking their lives to protect me. Words failed to affect Emmett more than that.

"Protecting Emmett until the Archivist makes contact is all that matters. If we do not reach her soon, he will die."

"I can go to warn the Grove while you take him away," Keiran offered as he continued to check the mirrors for what Emmett assumed was someone following them. "I can meet you both somewhere safe. Derrick's?"

"No, we cannot separate. Not yet. I have my reasons."

Keiran did not question this. Emmett wanted to interrupt, to somehow offer assistance in the face of danger. But he found only a litany of film clichés available to him and, feeling inadequate in the moment, retreated into silence.

"We have the river should retreat be necessary, Keiran. You understand what needs to be done if that occurs."

"Of course."

"And don't ever leave him again," Amala whispered, to which Keiran only looked down at his hands in his lap.

As the highway led toward the darkening curtain of rock from the mountains towering over them, Emmett began to feel his pulse quickening with anticipation. Amala began looking back and forth through all of the car's windows—her wide, searching eyes penetrating the darkness for any sign of movement. Keiran rolled his window down and allowed his head to lean slightly out into the cold, rushing wind. So far from the city, the car's lone headlights penetrated the night's blackness with great effort, and only the sound of the car's tires broke the forest's silence.

The paved asphalt of the highway soon gave way to gravel that spat out underneath their speeding tires as they turned off onto a series of winding roads. Every so often, the outline of a fleeing image would register in Emmett's peripheral vision. Always he would startle, his foot reflexively going down as if to tap the gas pedal harder to speed forward, and always he would look in vain for signs of the vanished something. The night seemed determined to torture him with hints of pursuit.

The enveloping silence of the dark night was maddening. Amala slowed to negotiate the narrow turns of the ascending path up and through the ravine to the Grove. Emmett's senses were exaggerated beyond comfort by the intensity of the drive. Plunged into total darkness and with only the span of the car's headlights to see, Amala seemed to jerk back and forth between the pressure to race back to the Grove and the care to not drive off of a cliff.

During the ascent, Keiran and Amala rapidly discussed details. Emmett's concentration was absorbed watching for unseen attackers, and thus he still could not follow what they were saying. Their planning was filled with names, places, and descriptions that he did not recognize. In fact, the only thing that he was certain of was that his safety was their top priority.

The road banked sharply to the right, and through the canopy of snow-tipped fir trees along the mountainside, the compound of living stone came suddenly into view. Both fell silent, searching in the darkness for signs of danger.

"No lights," Keiran said. "The great rooms' hearths always burn through the night, Emmett," he added.

"As with the moon, we are the light in the darkness," Amala said. She leaned forward over the steering wheel, indicating a point up ahead with an outstretched arm. "We'll stop right up there. We're going in the rest of the way on foot."

The car idled to a stop, and the three of them got out.

"Do we want to leave the car here?" Emmett wondered aloud, wanting to somehow contribute but feeling like the weak link in the proverbial chain.

Amala nodded, walking slowly past him as she scanned the road ahead. "I have a plan to escape if it comes to that, and it doesn't necessarily require the car," she whispered, turning to Emmett and holding a finger to her lips. "Keep him close to you." She nodded from Keiran to Emmett.

They wound up through the ravine toward the compound. Even with Keiran less than two paces behind him, Emmett suppressed a shudder from the feeling that he was being stalked. Trees and thick underbrush on either side of the road drew dark curtains around them, with the cold air swallowing any sound. The darkness, it seemed, jealously guarded its own secrets.

Amala veered off the path into the tree line. Emmett winced at the twigs snapping and snow crunching underfoot.

"Too much noise," he whispered. "Can't you walk *over* the snow?"

"Those are elves," Keiran responded equally quietly.

The moon's pale sliver overhead was a ribbon of gossamer in the sky. Flowing through the trees with a dusting of fine snow, the cold Northern winds howled as if the forest itself were weeping from some tragedy yet to be revealed.

Pausing next to a large copse of firs, Amala held up one hand. She craned her neck, and Emmett saw a dark shape slithering down through the trees and across her shoulders. A pair of long black serpents coiled around her neck, one sliding into her hand while the other turned its darkly glowing eyes to watch behind her.

With a gesture to follow, Amala began lightly stepping forward again toward the compound. Several more silent moments passed, and they soon were no more than twenty yards away from one of the meandering walkways circling back toward the Grove's rear.

Emmett felt it suddenly and without warning: a deep, tearing nausea that wrenched through his insides. He slumped against a tree, and as his insides heaved with protest, he vomited on the ground. He managed to gasp once for air before falling forward. Keiran's strong forearm swung around his waist and caught him, keeping him from falling into his own sick steaming in the snow.

Keiran carefully eased Emmett backward against a tree while cradling his head. He raised one hand to his lips and pled for silence. Emmett watched him crane his neck and lift his ear. He pointed up ahead on the path and mouthed words that set Amala's face rigid.

Emmett's face felt swollen and hot, spittle running down his chin. Keiran pulled close to him, whispering into his ear: "There are at least twenty Revenants ahead of us. The proximity of dark magiks will affect you because of the Rot."

Keiran's hold on him grew tighter, and he drew him so close to his body that he could feel his breathing on his neck. Keiran reached his other arm around him to encircle him, holding his neck in both of his hands. He made a deep, rolling sound in his throat that vibrated down Emmett's spine, a vibration that felt like cleansing water pouring over him. Within moments, his head felt light as his stomach settled.

A hawk with glowing eyes soared soundlessly down through the trees to land on Amala's shoulder. It made no noises except for the soft rush of fluttering wings in the darkness. Amala took a pebble from the hawk's mouth before it returned to the air.

Kneeling down to Emmett with Keiran behind her, she whispered into his ear. "Listen very carefully, Emmett. We need to reach the opposite side of the Grove. No matter what happens, do not allow yourself to be separated from Keiran."

Emmett nodded as Amala looked deeply into his eyes. Just like the first time he had seen her attack the Underdweller,

Emmett could see her concern for him.

"We're going to make it," she whispered.

"I can run," Emmett responded, looking between Amala and Keiran.

She held an arm out for him. He accepted and tried to stand, Keiran placing a leg behind him and catching him when he stumbled back. His head was still light and stomach mildly queasy, but he gave a nod of confidence after several steadying moments.

Amala whispered to Keiran. "Rhiannon has already engaged some south of us."

A preternatural scream penetrated the night, followed by the sounds of charging through the forest undergrowth. A dark figure appeared in the trees, leaping through the air toward Amala. She backflipped twice, bringing one leg up in a swift kick to the figure's head, the sound of bone crunching just as she danced back and brought her other leg around low in a swift undercut to its legs.

Another figure rushed from the trees with blades in both hands, a hood barely covering his pockmarked face. He raised a tapered blade in his hand and brought it down in a wide arch. Amala allowed the momentum of her low kick to fully twist her body around to avoid his swing. The Revenant turned as he missed her and brought his forearm around in a backward slash with his other blade, a serrated knife nearly as long as his forearm. Amala spun her arms with dizzying speed, her serpents whistling through the air and tearing deep gashes across his face and chest. Their fangs slashed across from one ear to the other with a brilliant spray of red on the snowy ground. He dropped his blades and crumbled in writhing agony, clutching futilely at his bleeding eye sockets.

Feeling the nausea welling up again, Emmett stumbled to sit upright. Amala stood rigidly over the two Revenants, now both dying or otherwise incapacitated. The hawk returned, crying into the night as it swept up higher overhead as if circling Amala, Keiran, and Emmett protectively. Through teary eyes, Emmett saw Amala taking a step toward him, chancing eye contact only for a moment to confirm he was unharmed.

"Focus through the discomfort," she whispered. Emmett nodded, clutching his stomach as he attempted again to stand.

Keiran came up behind them and put a hand behind Emmett's shoulders. He made a deep, purring sound at the base of his neck, the vibration from his lips brushing against his skin and traveling down Emmett's spine. Once again, Emmett felt the nausea wash away. He shook his light head, willing himself to concentrate.

"Thanks again."

Amala and Keiran had only a moment to look up as four more Revenants crashed loudly through the underbrush. Three of them raced for Amala, with the fourth swinging a large blade at Keiran's head just before Keiran pushed Emmett aside and rolled away from the blade's swing.

Amala was pirouetting in and out of her three attackers' swings as she wove her serpents through the air. Amala's spinning kicks would open holes in the Revenants' attacks, causing them to aim high or wide to parry her blows. Each time, a swing of one of her serpents would respond with bared fangs, tearing or gashing at exposed skin.

Keiran was back on his feet just as his attacker swung the serrated blade again at his head. The female Revenant was spitting words at him, incoherent, nonsensical words that seemed to scratch at the very air. From her incantation an undulating, inky darkness coalesced before Emmett. As she did so, Emmett saw her face stretch as her human features seemingly melted away.

With his hands held aloft toward Emmett, Keiran bellowed

a low note that caused the air before him to shimmer like a thick pane of glass, swelling into a sphere that seemed to contain the darkness before shrinking and collapsing the darkness into nothingness.

The female Revenant growled and swung her blade at Keiran's head. He easily dodged it, bringing his foot up in a high roundhouse kick toward her head. She turned in time and took a glancing blow to her shoulder before retreating two steps and returning with a direct thrust. As it whistled past his face just feet away, Emmett saw that the blade was covered in dripping runes and sigils along its length, and the very air surrounding it seemed to reek with decay.

Keiran ducked again, rolling on the ground once more away from Emmett and drawing the Revenant's attention toward him. He stood up quickly and raised an outstretched hand toward her, taking a breath and screaming out with a discordant, angry note whose concussive force clipped the side of her face, causing her to drop her blade and fall to the ground, grabbing both of her bleeding ears.

The two other Revenants continued to swing at Amala, their bloody, sigil-covered blades whistling in the cold air. Her movements were like water falling in sheets on rounded stones, flowing effortlessly with barely visible ripples. One of the Revenants seemed to stumble on an awkward swing, and Amala followed with a downward kick, her foot crunching the back of his neck. He fell under his own momentum, causing the other Revenant to stumble.

Amala drew back just as the hawk overhead rounded in the air and dove past her, its twin claws extending as they bit deeply into the soft, fleshy place underneath the Revenant's right ear. The eldritch words all but sizzling as they died on his quivering lips, the Revenant's face returned to normal as he limply fell to the ground.

"Come on," Amala called. They ran together, collecting Keiran up the road and closing the distance to the Grove. Crossing the long shelf, another figure came running from a hidden place behind a thicket of trees and underbrush. Amala sprinted ahead, easily dodging the clumsy swing of his blade and snapping his neck sideways with a backhand swing.

Several figures crashed through the underbrush and out onto the path, a mess of flailing limbs. A large bald man swung a meaty fist at a little girl he had pinned to the ground. She took a pair of punches directly to her small face before she raised an arm in Emmett's direction, as if pleading for help. Emmett began to run to her aid, but Keiran tackled him from his left side, sending him to the ground.

A feral snarl split the night as a massive mountain lion, composed of tense muscles sheathed in a majestic, tawny frame, charged from the shadows behind them. The great beast leapt over them and soared toward the Revenant. A wide claw took his head as the lion's massive body sailed overhead and landed just in front of the girl. Pushing the now-headless corpse off of her, the girl stood beside the lion.

"There are at least forty, sister, maybe more," her high-pitched voice recounted with great alarm to Amala, her small body still heaving for breath as she stroked the beast's heavily breathing flank. Emmett saw that her long, curly hair was matted with blood from cuts along her face, her clothes torn in places where her small body had been assaulted. At her full height, she barely stood taller than the mountain lion that was pacing next to her, the cat's golden eyes—preternaturally glowing as they were—watching behind her for attack.

"Lily, have you seen Rhiannon?"

Before the young girl could respond, glass shattered

somewhere overhead. Emmett jumped back instinctively, and at once they all looked up at the high stone walls of the structure to see someone flung awkwardly through an exploded window out into the air. Their eyes followed it in an arc as it landed on the ground near them with a sickening crunch.

A shadowed figure in the window's high frame leapt out with an overhead dive before landing effortlessly with a graceful roll on the ground next to the unmoving corpse. Dusting aside the gossamer threads of her dress, the woman Emmett recognized from earlier pulled herself up to full height as her naked feet padded soundlessly across the snowy ground.

"Defile *my* garden," she said bitterly as she spat at the headless corpse. "There are a dozen more inside the house. I was nearly overwhelmed."

"Sophie, did you see anyone else alive inside?" Amala asked.

As if in answer, a terrified woman screamed in the distance. From across the grounds they saw a pair running toward them. A young woman and man were both yelling for help as a dozen robed figures charged from the woods after them.

With reflexes of lightning alacrity, Lily sprinted toward the couple, hurling herself into the air while drawing her limbs to her chest. She sailed over the fleeing couple and released her legs into the neck of one of the pursuing Revenants with a sharp snap. The small child was deftly spinning through the combined attacks of ten or more armed Revenants as her mountain lion released a bellowing roar and leapt to defend her.

Sophie reacted almost as fast, her body convulsing as she flailed her arms out above her head. She pumped her arms in the air with a rhythmic drumming that Emmett heard soften under the din of an approaching roar. The forest nearly split apart as a torrential storm of wasps and hornets swarmed around the corner of the compound. The entire swarm sparkled iridescent in the night, its great mass hurtling together in a single, undulating cloud. The swarm raced around Sophie as she threw her arms to meet the oncoming rush of Revenants. The sickening impact sounds of millions of stinging and biting insects blunted the cries of the young couple as Keiran waved them to him.

"This way," Keiran called. Emmett did not recognize the young woman whose hair was matted to her face with rivulets of blood tearing down her skull. She clutched to the man, terror-stricken and consumed with panic.

"Help us!" he was screaming at Keiran.

"We're going to," Keiran was saying as he continued looking over his shoulder for signs of pursuit. "Who brought you to the Grove? Do you remember their names? Who were you with before the attack?" Emmett knew that the confusion was too great for them to make sense of Keiran's questions.

The young woman was sobbing, burying her face in the man's shoulder. He shook his head, panting with desperation. "You've got to help us! Please!"

Emmett felt it at that moment: that undeniable sense of panic. Battle sounds died away, and in their place, a small voice was distantly pleading with him to run. His muscles tensed even more than they already had, his pulse increased, and his brain sharpened on the pinpricks of ice creeping along the back of his neck. He could feel the approach of something that did not belong in his world … something *unnatural*.

Emmett saw more figures emerge from underneath the ridge along the outer shelf of the mountain across the grounds opposite them. They stalked the forest's edge, their long arms ending in slowly flexing claws. Even at a distance, Emmett recognized their jerky, forced movements as a voice within his mind cried out in alarm.

"Underdwellers. At least ten with more in the distance,"

Keiran gasped.

"Keiran," Amala urgently whispered. Emmett saw Keiran turn toward her, and with an expression born of both tension and calm, he nodded at something Emmett could not see on Amala's face. Keiran raised his right hand with his palm facing her. Amala did the same, touching her open palm to his, and then lowering her left hand and crossing just underneath their joined arms, Keiran soon doing the same with his own. Emmett had little time to process the image's familiarity before they separated.

"No matter what happens," she whispered as they released their hands.

"I will," Keiran promised.

Amala turned to Emmett and drew her lips to his ears. "I will come back for you, Emmett … like the bottomless sea and the endless rivers that lead to it."

Before Emmett could respond, Amala leapt away and rushed to meet their attackers.

CHAPTER 10

Amala called out loudly for all to hear. "Sisters! To me!"

The Revenants sprinted toward the three Druids like starving predators. Amala's sideways charge broke their dash as she dove directly into their path, spinning herself wildly in an attack that seemed intended to distract more than harm. The Underdwellers responded with equal speed, slashing their long claws at and just missing her midsection as she leapt over them with a swinging kick.

The sound of running footsteps caused Emmett to turn with a start even as Keiran was already reaching his arms out to meet whatever force was approaching. A feeling of relief spread over Emmett as he saw the twins Paulo and Sebastian emerging from the eastern side of the compound. As Sebastian ran toward Keiran, Paulo sprinted toward the Druids and crashed headlong into the melee, bringing his iron stave down into an Underdweller's chest as it twisted to avoid a high, powerful kick from Sophie.

"Keiran," Sebastian coughed as he collapsed into him.

"Did you see anyone else alive?"

Sebastian quickly shook his head, holding one hand to his stomach to control the bleeding from a vicious tear to his midsection that had torn away most of his shirt. "No, brother, we just returned to Silvan Dea when they attacked."

Keiran gingerly pulled Sebastian's hand away and, seeing a dangerous gash from which blood continued to pour, shook his head with a curse. Sebastian hissed at the pain of the cold winter air against his deep wound, his face clenched tightly as he held his hand against the unstaunched bleeding.

"Do you have anything left?"

"I was saving it in case Paulo needed it," Sebastian shuddered. "There are more Revenants. A lot more," he said through gritted teeth.

Keiran's expression grew dim, and he was obviously considering this news carefully as he looked from Emmett to the two strangers who huddled in fear near them.

Amala's movements were a blur in the darkness, and Sophie and Paulo's both seemed equally timed with Amala's, as if they all fought together as an extension of each other; one swinging high as the other swung low, one pushing forward as the other guarded their rear. Sophie's legs and Paulo's arms both pumped through the air as Amala's serpents and the hawk overhead wove through the fray, claws and fangs in an aerial ballet of blurred motion as they maneuvered the narrow spaces between bodies and creatures.

A vicious attack by one of the Underdwellers caught Sophie along the midsection, and she seemed to freeze mid-swing, hands clutching feebly to her stomach to hold her insides from spilling out. As she fell lifeless to the ground, the glow of the remaining swarm all but winked out in the darkness, and somehow lessened lacking precision or coordination, the cloud of insects quickly dispersed with a swipe of one of the Underdweller's claws at the air.

Even as Sophie fell, Amala and Paulo lost none of their focus, their movements so fast that their figures were blurred by the night's shadows. One of the Underdwellers was retreating as Amala rained down repeated slashes, her arms pumping in the air at such dizzying speed that the eyes could not even follow them. The other Underdwellers continued to attack Paulo with rending slashes, which Paulo narrowly avoided, tumbling sideways and rolling away just as he raised an arm toward the forest as if silently calling out. A pack of snarling wolves charged from the trees after the Underdwellers.

Another group of Underdwellers emerged from the forest. The tallest creature, its skull of unnatural white visible even in the darkness, raised its clawed hands aloft as the other Underdwellers fanned out behind it in an equal physical display. The wind carried whispers of something terrible like the low roar of an approaching storm sounding in the distance. Emmett saw darkness blacker than the night's shadows billow and swarm around the Underdwellers and suddenly wash forward across the mountainside like a tsunami crashing down from the sky overhead.

"Dark Fire!" Keiran yelled, and Emmett saw that Amala turned for a split second before having to lunge away from an Underdweller's downward slash that, without her lightning reflexes, would have easily torn her arm from her shoulder.

The inky blackness roared along the ground at startling speed in an undulating wave, and in its wake it left scarred and pitted earth that smoldered and trees whose limbs and trunks were burned down to cindering stumps. The wave swept out over the edge of the cliff and careened over boulders that cracked in the night. Lily and her mountain lion were too slow in jumping away. The Dark Fire rolled over them, melting their skin and exposing their now-lifeless insides.

Amala and Paulo leapt away from the Dark Fire. It left a

great tear in the ground that still burned, separating Keiran and Emmett from them at a distance. Keiran looked back at the Underdweller as it was already repositioning itself in a straight line toward the compound.

"We have to go. Now!" Keiran exclaimed.

Emmett saw across and through the burning ground that Amala and Paulo were suddenly flanked by an emerging group of Revenants whose facial features were already melting away, spitting overwhelming and inexpressible words of dark power at them. Distracted by their new attackers, Paulo stumbled backward and did not see the Underdweller behind him. His back arched as the Underdweller's claw ripped out the front of his chest, his wolves falling to the ground with yelps of pain. Paulo was rigidly fused with the creature's claw penetrating the front of his broad barrel chest. With a gurgling sound that could be heard even over the great noise of battle, his head finally slumped forward never to move again.

"You bastards!" Sebastian wailed with grief as he fought uselessly to stand. "I'll kill you all!"

Paulo's death distracted the Underdwellers, and Amala, who had not stopped in her deft weaving through their attacks, seized the moment and somersaulted through the air, landing several yards away. Through the Dark Fire, she turned toward Keiran and nodded wordlessly before sprinting away, drawing her attackers with her.

"Come on!" Keiran commanded Sebastian through gritted teeth as he slipped his neck around Sebastian's arm and hoisted him upright with a yell of pain. Sebastian's massive frame still fought with what little strength he had, but Keiran took hold firmly of Sebastian's weight as he pointed at a place up ahead along the side of the compound.

"I'll hunt you all down!" Sebastian screamed, hurling curses at them.

"That way!" Keiran said to Emmett, pointing to a spot up the embankment.

Emmett tugged at the couple to follow. Keiran strained under the weight of Sebastian's muscular frame, continually turning his neck to look behind them. Even through the smoldering Dark Fire, the second group in the distance could be seen preparing to conjure another wave.

They followed the building's edge and turned at its eastern corner. Keiran finally stopped at a particularly large boulder cut for the compound's foundation and lifted Sebastian's arm to lean him against the structure's exterior. Out of view, Keiran placed his hand against the boulder's center and pushed. With some effort, the boulder fell into the wall, and within moments a dark tunnel appeared into which Keiran immediately crawled. After a moment's silence, he returned to the opening with a match strike, a lantern held aloft with his other hand.

"Emmett first. Hurry," Keiran said, motioning quickly for him. Emmett knelt and crawled through the opening on what felt like a stone floor. Keiran handed the lantern to him and jumped back outside, urging the couple in.

Emmett reached out a hand and helped the young woman stand up just as the other young man crawled through. She was shorter than Emmett and probably in her early twenties. Her eyes were swollen red with crying, her pale complexion and button nose framed by medium-length blonde hair. She continued to sniffle, rubbing her nose as tears tumbled down her cheeks. The young man put a comforting arm around her, slightly taller than her with a similar complexion and his hair cut short across his forehead.

"Some help, please," Keiran said through gritted teeth. Emmett handed the lantern to the young woman and reached an arm out to Sebastian, who Keiran was easing in through the low entrance with great effort. Sebastian cried out in pain, finally letting go of Keiran and collapsing against Emmett. Keiran quickly slid through and pushed back the boulder, returning it to its place.

By the lantern's light, Emmett could see a deep tunnel bored into the earth. Structural beams framed the entry, and sconces along the tunnel wall held unlit torches. A wet, refreshingly clean wind blew out from the tunnel with the vaguest hint of falling water somewhere in the distance.

"In we go."

Still supporting a labored-breathing Sebastian, Emmett looked at Keiran with incredulity. Even with the shock of the attack on Silvan Dea and the deaths he had already witnessed, he could not help but stare into the darkness with dread.

Oh, joy. More cave.

Keiran surveyed the room, resting his eyes on the young couple that stood holding each other. "May I have that, please?" Keiran asked the young woman, pointing at the lantern.

She nodded numbly, handing it to him. "Cheers," he said with a forced smile, beads of sweat following down his angular cheeks. Even in this moment of great flight and despair, Emmett found Keiran's presence a momentary comfort.

"What are your names?" Keiran asked with a deliberate, if forced, tone of reassurance in his voice.

The young woman said nothing, her eyes staring at the ground. The man looked up from her to Keiran, his expression a mixture of terror for himself and fear for the woman.

"Troy," he mumbled. "This is my baby sister, Ellie."

"It's nice to meet you, Troy and Ellie. I promise we'll get out of here."

Keiran turned and opened the lantern window, withdrawing

the wick with some effort and holding the flame aloft. Guarding the flame with his other cupped hand, he leaned against one of the walls. A brilliant flame emerged like a phoenix, streaking into the cave down a narrow aqueduct-like channel carved high along the wall. After a moment, the flame returned, streaking down the opposite wall.

Keiran blew out the flame in his hand and dropped the spent wick. He walked to Emmett and nodded at Sebastian, lowering his neck so Sebastian could reach an arm around.

"Come on, mate, not much farther," Keiran whispered, Sebastian clutching still at the wound that freely bled through his soiled fingers. Perhaps the pain of his wounds cut through the despair of watching his twin die, for he was quiet and still now but for the hissing gasp with each movement.

"Just leave me. I can hold them off."

"Keep it up and I bloody will," Keiran gritted as he lifted Sebastian forward. "Emmett, come on, mate. Lead!"

"Uh, right, come on," Emmett said to the couple. Swallowing his own claustrophobia, he led them down into the tunnel. The thin line of fire illuminated the corridor with soft, dancing light. He looked behind him to see that the young couple tentatively followed, the man wrapping his arm around the trembling woman.

"The tunnel bends to the right, Emmett, and crosses over a river."

"Got it," Emmett answered, continuing down the earthen corridor. After several yards, the corridor did bear right, its floor descending with a mild grade. With the turn, the wind grew colder, wetter, and the dull, hollow sound became rushing water. The floor curved up in a low arch like a bridge. On either side were wide openings in the floor, through which Emmett could see a river as clear as an untouched spring rushing underneath.

"I see the river," Emmett called out over the loud noise of the rushing waters, finding that after he passed over the tunnel abruptly ended.

Keiran turned the corner still supporting Sebastian's weight.

"Now what?" Troy asked, staring down into the river.

Keiran extracted himself from underneath Sebastian, leaning him gingerly against the wall. He looked down into the water and began removing his shoes.

Emmett's eyes widened. "You're kidding, right?" he asked skeptically, watching Keiran throw his shoes against the wall.

"We can't go down that!" Troy yelled.

Sebastian coughed, his voice rasping. "Either you hold your breath or wait for the Revenants to find you."

Ellie wept loudly, Troy in a state of complete shock. Emmett had already seen more than he could have believed possible and, understanding what their pursuers were capable of, recognized his only option.

"The water is like ice this time of year, but I can sort us on the other end," Keiran said.

Troy let go of Ellie, who held onto herself and leaned against the wall. An expression passed between them as if they knew they had no other choice but to comply. He tentatively inched forward, leaning over to look into the wide openings in the floor. With one hand against the tunnel wall, Troy leaned down to run his hand in the rushing river, its churning spraying a fine mist of cool water up through the openings.

"It's cold," Troy said, turning to look back at Ellie. "But I think we can do it." She whimpered, hiding her face in her small hands.

Keiran stepped around the couple, leaning in close to Emmett and motioning for Sebastian to join them. "All right?" he whispered, gripping Emmett's shoulder.

Emmett nodded knowingly, their eyes exchanging unspoken fears. He watched Sebastian hobble along the wall to them in the corner, hissing sharply as he cradled his arm against the gash in his chest.

"Can you do this?" Keiran asked.

Sebastian clenched his jaw. "I'm going to lose a lot of blood in there if you don't seal it up."

Keiran pushed Sebastian's hand away and forced his own against the wound, the dark blood seeping out between his fingers. "Emmett, help me hold Sebastian up."

"I hate this part," Sebastian growled as Emmett swung Sebastian's other arm around his neck. Feeling as if he were being embraced by a silverback gorilla, Emmett prepared for the unknowable worst.

Keiran closed his eyes and intoned something low. Almost immediately, the awful smell of burning flesh suffused the area as a hissing sound filled the room. Sebastian gasped, his wide frame jerking against the pain as Emmett struggled to hold him despite his growing nausea. He held his mouth shut to keep himself from yelling, though as the hissing sound continued, his muffled cry soon grew as shrill as a child's.

It eventually ended, Sebastian's bucking frame going limp. His breathing was labored as he tried to settle himself. Keiran withdrew his hand tentatively, and Emmett was startled to see the wide, gaping wound had been cauterized completely underneath a painfully long scar.

Emmett looked at Keiran, who looked at him with resolution. "We need to leave now."

"And Amala? We just leave her?"

Keiran's green eyes became glassy, withdrawn, and to Emmett it seemed that some measure of strength had drained out of his face with the effort of healing Sebastian's wound. He bit his quivering bottom lip and looked away, tilting his head closer to Emmett to whisper in his ear. "She'll find us when it is safe to do so."

"No!" Ellie screamed hysterically, a wrenching, painful screech that echoed down the corridor. Keiran and Emmett looked up in time to see a robed figure turn the corner swinging a wickedly curved blade. Troy threw an arm up to shield himself from the blow, but the blade sliced through his arm and into his neck.

Keiran leapt in front of Emmett and Sebastian, raising an open palm toward the Revenant. He cried out a loud, discordant note. The man was hurled violently back against the tunnel wall. The limp body slipped to the ground, a swath of blood smeared along the wall.

Ellie screamed, nearly collapsing against Sebastian, who reached up through his own overwhelming pain and tried to hold fast to her. She flailed madly, screaming hysterically for her brother, whose mangled body fell forward, detached mostly from his head, and disappeared into the rushing water.

With his arm still outstretched, Keiran collapsed backward. He steadied himself against the cavern wall, and Emmett could see that Keiran was terribly drained. His unfocused eyes and slack jaw took several moments to return, during which time his body jerked spasmodically.

"Keiran! Are you okay?" Emmett shook him.

Keiran finally responded with a loud cough, rolling forward and heaving deeply as he lowered his head over his knees to steady his breathing "No more time," he croaked.

Ellie was alternating between fits of hysteria and catatonia, and Sebastian's trembling body had drained away most of the color from his dark features. Emmett stepped over Keiran and lifted Ellie off the ground. She kicked and screamed incoherently, but Emmett persisted and raised her over the floor opening. He had no way of knowing if she would live or die. But an icy prickling was already crawling up his spine. He knew what was coming, understanding the approaching paralysis and dread and seeing that neither of the Bards with him had much strength left.

"Take a deep breath," he said to her as he lowered and released her into the rushing river. Her screams died away just as she disappeared in the torrent of water.

His muscles began to constrict, his movements slowing. Sebastian and Keiran were barely moving. There would be no help arriving, no special powers to protect him from the approaching Underdweller.

He grabbed Sebastian by the arm and heaved him over to the floor openings. He nodded to Emmett, drawing a deep breath just as Emmett pushed him headfirst into the river. Emmett then put his arm around Keiran's waist and pulled him up. "Come on," he struggled, lifting him to the water. Keiran was trying to speak over his continued coughing, but Emmett pushed him headfirst into the river.

Emmett took a step forward just as the Underdweller rounded the corner. He felt his body become rigid, his mind screaming against muscles that refused to comply. Drawing a deep breath, Emmett fell into the floor opening, his frozen form engulfed by the icy-cold waters rushing around him. Within moments the world was dark again, his body hurtling face-first down a smooth, wide tunnel.

CHAPTER 11

As Emmett was swept away, the distance from the Underdweller somehow returned some control over his body. He struggled to roll onto his back, gasping for air in the exposed tunnel. The water careened sharply to the right and then to the left before straightening downward. Emmett had no conception of the river's direction or the distance he had traveled.

His descent slowed as the tunnel floor leveled off, emerging into a waist-deep riverbed. Gasping for air, he felt a strong hand grab onto his arm and pull him from the water until he was sitting upright on a sloping, muddy bank. "Up you go, mate."

Emmett saw that they were in a heavily wooded inlet with a wide embankment and thick evergreen canopy on both sides. They stood at the base of a towering mountain range, at the bottom of which was located a large hole that water steadily poured from. Beside the river was a small cove. Sebastian was resting against a large boulder, his skin so pale that Emmett feared he might soon die. Ellie was huddled against the wall with her knees drawn up to her cradling arms as she rocked rhythmically in mute terror.

Keiran hobbled past Emmett into the cove, opening a crate seated inside underneath a pile of dead shrubs. He pulled two lanterns and matches out, lighting each and setting them down. "I've got enough left in me to sort Sebastian," Keiran said, returning from the crate with bundles of towels and clothes. "There's a small boat with a motor kept here. The Columbia River is downstream. We'll use the boat to put a safe distance between the Revenants and us."

"Where are we going?" Emmett stuttered through chattering teeth.

"Somewhere safe."

"Okay," Emmett accepted, noting how Keiran deliberately looked away and said nothing else. "What do you need me to do?"

Keiran turned to him with a smile, pained though it was by the obvious weakness in his face. It was an expression not only of confidence but appreciation. "Get Ellie to dry herself off, and then come help me with Sebastian."

As Emmett turned his head and followed Keiran's sideways glance, he saw for the first time what was floating in the water in front of Ellie. Emmett's stomach turned inside out at the sight of the headless corpse, the surrounding water muddied with the blood and insides that radiated outward from the body.

Emmett barely breathed as he looked to Keiran. "Shouldn't we do something with his body?"

"I don't want to be caught defenseless while digging a grave."

"But Keiran," Emmett said as he lowered his voice.

Keiran glanced at Ellie once before looking solemnly into Emmett's eyes. "Life is for the living, Emmett. We have to be getting on."

Emmett finally nodded, taking the towels and clothes and walking to Ellie. Her hair hung dripping against her face, her tiny body trembling under heavy, soaked clothes.

"Ellie?" he whispered, kneeling down to eye level. "We need to get you out of those wet clothes. Can you stand up?" Her stare was unresponsive. Emmett followed her eyes to her brother's remains. She nodded vacantly as she slowly stood.

Emmett considered the awkwardness of the situation and placed the clothes on the ground, unfolding the towel in front of her. Looking away from her, he said, "I'm going to hold this up while you change, okay?" Emmett turned his head and watched Keiran whispering to Sebastian, cradling his limp neck in one hand as his other passed over his midsection. Keiran was singing a low melody.

Sebastian gasped aloud, his body buckling. Keiran continued his song, closing his eyes and straining to hold Sebastian's body. Sebastian kicked his feet and coughed founts of blood into the air, his arms continuing to thrash in Keiran's strong embrace.

After several moments, Sebastian's body fell limp. Keiran's melody waned until Emmett heard only the nocturnal movements of the forest. He cleared his throat, chancing a glance down to see if Ellie's exposed legs were covered yet. He felt the towel taken from his hands, and he finally looked to see Ellie wrapping it around her hair, wringing the water out with a lifeless expression.

He stepped back to Keiran, who sat with his back to the cove wall with Sebastian in his arms. Keiran's face was unrecognizably tired. At Emmett's approach, Keiran looked up to see Ellie drying herself off, wearing the overalls provided.

"I managed to pull out the poison that was on the blade that cut him. Help me get him changed."

Keiran lifted Sebastian's massive torso, and Emmett helped remove his torn clothes. His arms were both encircled in thick, tribal tattoos beginning at the wrist and wrapping all the way up past his shoulder and around his neck. Their patterns were varied and complex. Blood stained a torso crisscrossed in slashes—some new, others old and already scarred over. The tears along his midsection were closed underneath a layer of scarred, burnt skin reaching from his navel down his pelvis.

"I wish I could have done more, but I've expended too much energy tonight. He'll have to mind the scars," Keiran said, motioning to Sebastian's stomach. Emmett thought of the deeper scar, of Sebastian losing his twin, the man who finished his thoughts with words that flowed in tandem with his own.

As they dressed Sebastian, Ellie returned to an upright fetal position against the cove's far wall, staring blankly out into the forest with unfocused, lamenting eyes. Keiran laid Sebastian down on the ground as he slept.

Keiran stepped behind Emmett and quickly pulled his pinstripe slacks off. Emmett held a towel up, averting his eyes out of modesty. Keiran stretched his back with an audible sigh before shaking his head and running his hands through his wet hair. As Keiran pulled an identical coverall over his body, Emmett caught a fleeting image of similar tattoos—deep, tribal patterns swirling in dark inks—around and contrasted against Keiran's athletic, if pale-skinned frame.

"I'm going to get the boat ready and put Sebastian inside. There are dry socks and shoes in the trunk."

Emmett waited until Keiran had left before changing, his skinny body feeling overly exposed in front of so many strangers. He changed quickly, drying his floppy hair. He found several pairs of soft shoes of various sizes with wool socks. Once dressed, he put his wallet into his back pocket and grimaced as he pocketed his soaked phone.

"One last thing," Keiran said, stepping over to the crate and withdrawing a phone from it. "I hate these bloody things," he mumbled, turning the phone on and taking pictures of each of them.

"What are you doing?"

"We need identifications," Keiran said, squinting his eyes as he scrolled through the phone's menu. "Ah, here we are, then," he said, pressing a button and waiting a moment before bending down and smashing the phone onto a rock.

"Let's get moving."

Keiran navigated their boat along the shallows with a single oar for twenty minutes, the river eventually deepening enough that he could use the motor. Lying between Keiran and Emmett, Sebastian slept with effort, the occasional moan escaping his lips. Ellie hunched at the bow, staring blankly out at the passing trees before also falling into a coma-like sleep. Emmett's mind numbly recounted the evening's events as a silent, black and white picture show in his mind. He glanced at each person in turn, feeling selfish that his mind rebounded back on the direness of his own situation.

"How are you holding up?" Keiran whispered.

Emmett looked at his hands and cleared his throat, wiping his eyes and pushing his hair out of his face in one motion. "No idea."

Keiran drew a hand through the gentle current and refreshed his face with the cold water. There was exhaustion evident in his eyes, green eyes that had until now brightened with the promise of adventure but had been dulled by the darkness they had witnessed.

"We'll reach Portland by sunrise."

"And then what?" Emmett asked.

"Amala wanted you hidden somewhere safe."

"But shouldn't we go back for her?" he asked, concerned that his almost pleading sounded accusatory.

He watched a dark shadow pass over Keiran's face.

"My word means everything, and I gave my word to Amala that I would protect you. Even if it meant abandoning her. And she knew that it might be so."

If it weren't for me, you would have stayed to fight with her. Closing his eyes, Emmett lowered his chin to his chest.

Though he had said nothing aloud, he felt somehow that Keiran's silence confirmed what he was thinking. Emmett laid his head in his hand, feeling the approaching emotion. In the encompassing silence, he swallowed his own guilt and found the taste bitter in his uneasy stomach.

You wanted an intrinsically alien life.

He'd gone searching for answers about his mother, for meaning in a journey he'd seen in countless films. What he'd found, though, were people acting of their own interests, interests he did not know and whose outcomes he could not fast-forward to the end to determine.

With all that he had already learned, and with so little he was certain that he yet knew, Emmett wondered how the Children of the Earth did what they did ... when even he, with so little to offer the world, found himself lacking any belief that he could make a difference.

Emmett shook his head as he looked down at his hands, willing the nihilism to leave his thoughts. He needed to be strong. *Now is not the time. Not now.*

His inner reflection was punctuated by raindrops, as if the sky were tapping him on the head to distract him from contemplation. The raindrops fell heavier and more frequent. He looked upward. The night was still relatively clear above, and farther down the river he saw no significant storm clouds, either.

"What the hell?" Emmett began, turning his head around to look to Keiran and gasping as his eyes grew wide with the sight forming behind them.

Directly above the mountain's pinnacle, a swirling mass of turbulent clouds as black as an oil slick spiraled inward toward a central point. It was as if a great titan in the heavens were drawing the whole of the sky to it. Lightning sparkled across the edges of the storm as the spiral grew, winds seeming to pull the trees from the ground and fling them into the air. As Emmett stared at it, he felt once again small and insignificant, dwarfed by a raw power that was greater than anything he had experienced before.

"It looks like a hurricane," he said, his eyes unable to steal away from the terrifying scene. Wind churned the river around them, and Keiran rotated his hand on the motor to the highest setting.

"It's the fulmination of the Dark Fire. It is not of this world, and so when it is conjured, it consumes itself in a storm like that."

Lightning strikes fired down as if the angered heavens meant to rend the mountain in two. The earth growled in response, and with a heavy grumble that seemed to upend the world around them, a sheer face of the mountainside separated and raced downward in a landslide of rocks, trees, and snow.

Emmett felt like he might vomit, watching the rock rain down the mountainside. He watched in mute horror as the clouds loosened, slowed, and suddenly dispersed. As the mountainside still heaved with falling debris from the landslide, the storm overhead disappeared into the otherwise clear, starry winter night.

He felt numbness, a total lack of any semblance of feeling. Not only from the bitter chill on the air and the smattering of rain but also from the awareness of wholesale destruction witnessed. No film, no matter how grotesque or violent, could ever match the reality of what had just occurred. Never again.

Emmett wondered if Amala had been trapped in the landslide, yet even before he could acknowledge the wrenching horror of losing her, he dismissed the thought entirely from his mind.

Only the untold death of so many nameless faces remained in his thoughts, chilling as much as the Oregon winter air. Emmett's fatigued body drew another long yawn and shuddered with the discomfort of the Rot, the danger of their predicament and uncertainty of their destination accentuating both the pain and loss.

CHAPTER 12

Sebastian awoke soon after Ellie, the color having returned to his face. Her continued incoherent whimpering echoed in the otherwise empty morning twilight. Though Emmett had little success in quelling her with comforting words, Sebastian's imposing physicality seemed to reassure her, Sebastian holding Ellie's shuddering shoulders as she cried into the space between his pronounced shoulder and bicep.

The river's current quickened as they approached the Columbia River. Emmett heard the hollow rush of wind as a timber-rich breeze touched the edges of his chattering teeth. As the river bent around a copse of trees, the Columbia finally came into sight. Keiran guided the boat toward the muddy banks, and as they neared, he motioned for Emmett to jump out and help pull it up onto the river's edge.

Sebastian lifted Ellie's small frame effortlessly in his thick arms as she nestled against his chest. Keiran stepped out after Sebastian and, knee-deep in the river, led the rowboat back out into the channel. Emmett watched as the Columbia's faster-moving current caught hold of the bow and claimed it for its own.

Keiran submerged his head under the river's waves for several moments before returning to the shore. Chattering, too, as

Emmett did from the icy water, Keiran stepped next to Emmett so that their feet were touching. He released a single note from his lips that blew a rush of hot air down their bodies, quickly drying their wet clothes.

"Did you send the warning out to the other Groves?" Sebastian asked.

Keiran nodded. "I could hear a pod of Pacific grays just off the coast migrating south. But I don't know if my song reached them. Too many bloody dams."

A rustle of feathers sounded in the distance. It was barely audible to Emmett and yet obviously heard by the two Bards who both turned their heads at once in its direction. A single brown-feathered hawk circled overhead, making several narrow passes before gliding down silently and landing directly in front of Keiran. Its brown wings were accented with layers of copper and snow white, its alert, glowing eyes regarding Keiran and Emmett as it looked between them. Lowering its head to the ground and opening its beak for only a moment, the hawk released something before crying loudly and sweeping back up into the night.

At Keiran's feet, a pair of white pebbles had been left, and he bent down and ran his finger over them as he closed his eyes and nodded. He said nothing, but already Emmett could connect what the message was likely to mean.

"Do we wait for her?" Sebastian asked.

"No. They'll lead them away so we can escape."

Sebastian stiffened his shoulders. "Escape to where?"

"The Portland train station. They won't attack us in a public setting." Keiran looked up at the stars and turned around twice on his spot before settling on a specific direction. "The highway should be in this direction by several miles where we can get a ride. Let us be moving quickly."

Keiran led the weary group through the forest, and after several hours of numbing darkness, reached a long stretch of empty highway. Sebastian seemed content to carry Ellie, who remained silently tucked in his arms. Emmett found the exertion focusing on his mind. Despite a silence that normally would have felt maddening, the forest's chilled air combined with the panting of his own breath as he trekked over uneven terrain kept Emmett's mind blessedly occupied. That the Rot was aching and his body groaning under the weight of its own fatigue made Emmett long for a warm bed far from forests, rivers, and the shadows of pursuing Underdwellers.

The first big rig truck to pass pulled tentatively onto the shoulder as Keiran waved it down, the other three remaining behind a growth of shrubs at Keiran's behest. Rolling his window down only partially, the driver maintained a safe distance as he called out from the cab of his vehicle and asked Keiran if he needed help. A moment later, the driver opened his door and waved for them to get into the truck.

Emmett climbed into the rear of the truck, helping guide Ellie in and followed by Sebastian then Keiran. The truck driver was a burly man in his mid-forties with a mane of reddish-brown grizzled hair that covered most of his face. Keiran settled Ellie into the passenger seat up ahead of them. The three men adjusted themselves to the narrow space between the packaged freight in the cargo hold.

"Should we leave Ellie alone up there?" Emmett asked.

"The driver won't do anything to her, and he won't remember anything of us, anyway," Keiran said. "Bardic persuasion. It's forbidden to use it except in the most dire of circumstances. This would qualify."

"She can get some sleep in the front. She needs the rest more than we do," Sebastian said to Keiran as he attempted to find a tolerable position. Whereas Emmett's lanky frame easily folded itself up to sit down and Keiran's athletic frame had to make some adjustments to the confining, limited space, Sebastian's wide shoulders barely fit even as he sat at an angle.

"And how is she, then?" Keiran asked as he, too, stretched his neck sideways and rolled his shoulders forward and downward in a shrug that released an audible pop from his obviously fatigued muscles.

"What we would expect," Sebastian answered, and the three in turn put their hands on the floor to steady themselves as the truck lurched forward.

"Do we know who brought her to Silvan Dea? In the confusion of the attack, I don't believe that was ascertained."

Sebastian struggled to stretch the length of his thick arms above his head. "I don't think she even remembers. Shock will do that."

"Aye," Keiran nodded as he looked to Emmett, as if to confirm Emmett's own condition relative to what Ellie was experiencing. Shock was accurate if blunt, Emmett thought, and yet he could not help but feel a measure of strength in Keiran's concern, and he did not want to be a further burden than he already was.

"She'll survive, and one day she'll be okay," Emmett said plainly, wishing to indicate that the same was true for him— even if he did not presently know how that might be possible for either of them.

The expression on Keiran's face told him that he understood what Emmett was attempting to communicate, and he reached his hand out and clapped Emmett's shoulder in response. "Indeed."

Emmett yawned again, though this time it felt fuller and lasted so long that he had to shake his head once and blink heavily afterward to focus a tired mind. As the truck gained speed underneath and set the cabin to a gentle sway, Sebastian whistled softly and filled the narrow space between them with a warm, tropical breeze. Emmett's cold skin relaxed as he felt himself slip down the steep slope into the dark ravine of unconsciousness. He felt nothing in his fatigued body or in the discomfort caused by the Rot as his mind released its ever-loosening grasp on wakefulness and submitted to the immobility of sleep.

Somewhere in the periphery beyond the murky somnolence of half-sleep, Emmett heard a pair of voices in heated argument.

"I simply refuse to believe that," one of the voices said. It was Keiran. "The difference is that we have choices. The freedom to choose defines us."

"I don't share your faith in humanity, brother."

"I place my faith in individuals, Sebastian, like you."

Through the haze of half-sleep, Emmett could hear Sebastian scoffing. "And where does one find faith in our world? That the things we fight for are even *worth* fighting for anymore?"

"Oh, Sebastian, how do I return you your faith?"

"You can't. And I don't blame you, brother. It's not your fault that Paulo is dead. It's theirs. I understand this." Sebastian was clearing his throat, and Emmett sensed movement as if he were repositioning his body. "But it's all of our faults, too. All the Children. And our Elders. We deny ourselves the right to seek them. Revenants kidnap, rape, torture, and murder. We tell ourselves that not doing more is for the greater good. That to act in a way like them is to somehow *become* them?"

"Is there any point in our arguing the Great Preclusion?"

"I *am* going to *him*," Sebastian said as if in answer. "Today. You can come with me or not," and this last word's emphasis felt almost accusatory.

"I'm not certain what benefit there is," Keiran replied. Even in his murky half state of sleep, Emmett heard the anguish in his voice, a tone suffused of the despair one feels without hope for reconciliation. "I have always been patient in listening to your feelings on this matter over the years, more so than your own brother."

"We cannot reach Belladonna without travel by air, which we could never accomplish with Emmett's Rot. There is only one Grove we could reach by land. *His*."

"I would not turn to *him* unless I had no other choice or was a bloody fool. His help does not come without a price," Keiran said with seriousness in his voice that caught Emmett completely off guard.

"You would call me a fool after the number of times I have saved your life?"

"And I couldn't say the same? No, Dr. Hazrat is *not* the answer to your grief. It is not my place to speak for Ellie, but Emmett is not going to him. He has been called by the Archivist herself, and he will be afforded that opportunity."

Emmett's mind lifted itself fully into wakefulness, his eyes still closed and body unmoving.

"That's a decision for Emmett to make, Keiran. You know the rules we live by."

"What value is there in a decision if not made in the proper context and with a complete understanding of what is at stake?"

"Choice defines us, Keiran."

"How does one quote *ikkibu*—the affirmation of choice and free will—only moments after quoting Omar Hazrat—a man who openly defies it? One might say you were trying to have it both ways."

There was a sudden rush in Sebastian's breathing that was audible even over the low roar of the truck's many tires along the highway. It was the heavy pattern of someone overcome by an excitement that felt intrusive and aggressive. "We all have choices, Keiran. I've always believed in that."

"And yet you question the Great Preclusion, Sebastian?" Keiran pleaded.

"I advocate balance. I don't blindly adhere to dogma for the sake of dogma. You may laud the free will of the ignorant, but choice isn't noble if people choose the wrong thing," Sebastian said bitterly.

"There are moments that define our lives. Rarely they are grand; often they are small. In my world, there is hope; hope that each moment gives life to another opportunity to make the *right* choice. I cannot resolve a world where we punish those for actions they have yet to take."

"Empty words," Sebastian cut.

"I believe, perhaps desperately and even a bit foolishly, that there exists some small measure of opportunity—finite and small, yes, but an opportunity nonetheless, that something could intersect in the normal trajectory of a person's life—some*one* could intercede knowingly or unknowingly, causing that individual to make the *right* choice."

"Your optimism is blind," Sebastian said.

"Perhaps, but it is my hope. It sustains me as the Song sustains me, and from my admittedly limited experience of life's mysteries, they are one and the same. Which is why this conversation always pains me—that there is no room for hope in your world."

Keiran fell silent, and with the silence there was emptiness where the words and emotions behind the words hung still in the unmoving air. Emmett heard desperation in Keiran's words, and yet an acceptance that whatever he was saying, he doubted would make any difference. Emmett understood this somehow, and in doing so wondered if Keiran was saying all of this for Sebastian's benefit or his own.

"They make their choices," Sebastian growled, and Emmett was certain that their discussion was finally drawing to its own bitter, disparate end. "Humans covet the darkness. What else is there to say? Philosophy is only convenient until you have to bury the corpses of your fallen. All I want is to use whatever means we can to punish them for those choices! How can you not understand this? Even with everything you have seen?" Sebastian nearly yelled.

Emmett felt his own pace surging. Even without knowledge of their argument, he understood by their voices that their disagreement had reached a climax from which a physical confrontation might be the eventual conclusion.

"My brother, please," Keiran said in a calm, measured voice. Even for Emmett, who was not involved in the conversation, Keiran's lower tone had a calming effect. "Regardless of our disagreements, Sebastian, I wish no ill will between us. We should be close to the train station, and now that Emmett is fully awake, we can make final preparations to depart."

Emmett wanted to sigh with exasperation. Feeling foolish with his eyes closed, he opened them to see that both Bards were staring directly at him.

"Your breathing and pulse had changed," Keiran said without prompting, raising one finger to the side of his head and tapping his right ear. "How are you feeling?"

Stretching his neck, he pushed himself upright to a full sitting position, cramped by the freight surrounding them.

"Fine," he said as he adjusted his shoulder and felt the raw soreness of the Rot. "What did I miss?" he asked, not wanting to directly confront Keiran on what Sebastian and he had been discussing. He was not so arrogant to believe that the conversation was entirely about him, and yet he understood that in some way Sebastian wanted Emmett to make a choice that Keiran did not believe him capable of making.

"We were deciding on our destination. Strategy would dictate that we separate—Sebastian with Ellie, and you with me, Emmett—and reconnect at an agreed-upon location. Circumstances being what they are, however, require consideration."

"We are in agreement that neither of us benefits from separating from the other Bard. A full attack by an armed Revenant group would prove difficult to defend against in our weakened states," Sebastian said.

"And Emmett awaits contact from the Archivist," Keiran added.

"Then what remains is for us to escort Emmett to a location safe from further Revenant attacks until the Archivist makes contact," Sebastian concluded. "A Grove that can protect him—"

"And *that* is your only reason for wanting to go there, then, is it? *Emmett's* safety? It's for *him*?" Keiran interrupted with an uncharacteristically and surprisingly heated tone.

Emmett could see that Sebastian's earlier anger was tempered now by a profound expression of pain that Emmett did not know was possible in a man of such imposing—and at times, threatening—physicality.

"You would question the integrity of the man who saved your life in Kanchenjunga? Who carried you across the Himalayas to Nepal? Even when you'd given up, when you begged for me to leave you behind to frozen sleep, I never abandoned you. With the Shadowkind in pursuit the entire way until we reached Titan Arum. I told no one in that Grove what you did—not even Amala. You know the Children of Titan Arum would have called for the Tribunal had they known. Do you know what they call the Tribunal there, Keiran? The Unknowable Pain."

Emmett could not believe that Keiran's face had blanched so noticeably.

"The Abbess herself questioned me that first night when we arrived. She suspected what you'd done—was looking for any reason for the Tribunal. In the Lady Lysianne's Grove, right within the very walls of Titan Arum itself, I lied to an Elder. I even lied to Amala; the Unknowable Pain wouldn't compare to what Amala would do to you if she knew. And you lecture *me* on choice, question *my* honor?"

Emmett's eyes darted to Keiran, fearing that either Bard might soon explode. Yet Keiran was more statue than human. He was staring unblinkingly at Sebastian with a face that, though it had recovered, was now so unreadable and guarded that Emmett was certain that its taut, angular features might shatter from the stiffness they maintained.

When Keiran spoke, it was with a voice that was unrecognizably quiet and devoid of the emotion he so freely expressed in his mannerisms since meeting Emmett. "We will go to the Lighthouse, then, Sebastian. When the Archivist makes contact, you and I should have sufficiently recovered our strength to part company. And we will never speak of this again."

The way Keiran said this final statement, Emmett wondered if Keiran meant something had just transpired between them that finally ended their friendship. Piecing the two conversations together, the first on the boat fleeing Silvan Dea and now in the truck on the way into Portland, Emmett knew that whatever or wherever the Lighthouse was, Keiran did not want to go there.

Yet the reminder of whatever had once transpired between Sebastian and Keiran in the Himalayas was enough to cause Keiran to change his mind. Emmett could only begin to imagine its implications. He felt almost dizzy from the effort, so drained as he already was from the experiences hours before.

If Sebastian believed this was their friendship's ending, he did not show it. "We are in agreement."

Keiran and Sebastian both turned their heads up as if listening to something that Emmett could not hear. A moment later, Emmett felt the truck slowing.

As Sebastian began to adjust his massive frame wedged between the freight, Emmett saw Keiran turn to look at him with an expression of significant reservation. If Emmett had not believed Keiran one of the bravest people he had ever met, he would have thought that Keiran was afraid.

With a sense of foreboding and the uncertainty of their movements, a deep shudder ran down the length of Emmett's back. He listened to the truck's tires lurch underneath and turn into a quiet, still winter morning beyond. He knew neither the Lighthouse nor Omar Hazrat, but he did feel that he had enough of a measure of Keiran Glendower to believe him that going there was not their best option.

CHAPTER 13

The sun was hinting at its eastern rise when the truck crossed the distinctive red steel of the Broadway Bridge over the Willamette River. Heading into the Portland train station, the truck followed the road around to the high clock tower, its ornate green awning framing the main colonnade for Union Station's front entrance.

Thanking the driver for his help, Keiran added another hundred-dollar bill and suggested it best that the driver forgot that he had ever met the four of them. The man stared at Keiran soundlessly with a dazed look in his otherwise glassy eyes. The driver got back into his truck and turned toward the lofty Portland skyline, leaving them standing on the curb, Ellie mutely huddled in Sebastian's embrace.

"I still think a private car service might be more sensible, Keiran. Or even a chartered plane."

"Yes, but anonymity is far easier to maintain in a large sea of faces than when you are easily identified in the backseat of a rented sedan. And I don't want to be defending a Revenant assault thousands of feet in the air."

The four travelers proceeded cautiously into the terminal with a shared tension born of the very real possibility of their being pursued. Emmett remained with Sebastian and Ellie inside the main concourse while Keiran went to purchase tickets. The terminal was still empty, several janitors moving slowly through the terminal with carts in tow. The glossy marble floor was reflective beige with maroon squares, and the soaring coffered ceiling featured classical woodcarvings and polished copper light fixtures framed by a bank of large open windows facing the horizon.

Keiran returned several minutes later with four tickets. Emmett accepted it and looked it over. "Thanks. My first train ride." He read the ticket. "Nova Scotia?"

"The Lighthouse is located in Peggy's Cove, just outside of Halifax." Keiran handed Sebastian his and Ellie's tickets and folded bills. "Shops should open soon. Why don't we purchase some new clothes and freshen up before we board."

"Agreed."

"If you will keep Ellie, I will take Emmett. They will be looking for four dirty travelers. Let us reduce the likelihood of being identified."

Sebastian put a wide arm around Ellie. "Come, little sister, let's get you something pretty to wear."

The sun soon rose over a crisp, wintry morning. The station's first trains lumbered to life with the hustle of commuting traffic. Families arrived in throngs to see people off or greet new arrivals as Emmett and Keiran wound through the steadily busier terminal. Keiran ducked into a restroom stall and emerged with an envelope containing four identifications with their faces and names on them.

"Always maintain one person in each major city who is sufficiently disgruntled with their low-paying government job to produce identifications when needed," Keiran said as he handed Emmett his new card. Emmett found his face, wet and shocked, from moments after emerging from the river staring up at him.

The shops lining the station were aglow with twinkling Christmas tree lights in holiday-themed windows dressed in seasonal red and green tinsel. The comforting timbre of Bing Crosby's "Do You Hear What I Hear?" rolled along the bustling corridors.

Outfitted in new clothes that allowed them to blend with the throngs of winter travelers, Keiran led Emmett to a small eatery for breakfast just as Emmett's stomach audibly rumbled, a sheepish grin on his face.

Relaxing on his stool with tea in hand, Keiran now wore a fresh taupe linen suit of low-rise slacks and a two-button, double-vent jacket framing an open-collared, carrot-colored shirt. He was a striking image to the passersby that chanced a second glance at him, which was too many people to not make Emmett feel that much less significant in the physicality of his obviously handsome wake.

Yet when he spoke to Emmett, when his green eyes alit with joy whenever he responded to something said with a smile of genuine mirth, it was with an unpretentious air. He either had no idea or no care for how striking he was to those who passed. Emmett could only note inwardly how unremarkable he was when standing in the shadow of Keiran Glendower.

Emmett ate his muffin, watching Keiran's face. He scratched at the turtleneck sweater and shifted uncomfortably in the khaki pants Keiran had purchased. He longed for a well-worn pair of jeans and a comfortably familiar T-shirt.

"So, the bird, the rock," Emmett began as he cleared his throat. "I'm guessing that meant that Amala is okay, right?"

Keiran nodded as he took another sip from his tea and patted his mouth gently, returning his napkin to one leg as he crossed it over another. Even with the fatigue of fight and flight, his new clothes seemed to invigorate him.

"The message was only intended to let me know that she had escaped the Grove with another Druid, Rhiannon. They will take a route away from us to draw them from you," he answered as he placed his steaming tea down and took knife and fork properly in hand to eat from his plate of scrambled eggs and sausage.

Emmett watched Keiran set his utensils down and take a careful bite from his croissant. He marveled at the Bard's composure even while discussing the likelihood that dozens of Revenants were chasing his Companion.

His Companion. Yeah.

"If she thinks she's being tracked by Revenants, she'll do her best to lead them away. Keep them distracted long enough for us to disappear."

"What? As in GPS-tags-underneath-your-car tracking?" he remarked dryly.

"You watch too much telly, mate. Revenants are too intoxicated with the dark powers to bother with such things. The few that wield such implements find themselves at something of a disadvantage since any Bard can produce a shrill whistle that can superheat the circuitry and disable it. Assuming it even works in proximity to our Groves or their dark magiks."

"That's convenient."

"Even a gun is rather pointless for them. I can detonate the bullet while it's still inside the barrel, after all. The cruder instruments—the blades, machetes, knives—those are far deadlier and often inscribed with their own curses."

Emmett thought back to the attack and recognized what had been obvious and yet not noted as relevant in his mind before: that all of the Revenants had attacked with simple weapons, often wickedly curved or serrated and covered in runes or sigils.

Keiran looked over his shoulder and scanned the milling

crowds of the terminal, the ever-present drone of peripheral noise as travelers hurried along to their morning commute. A noticeable wince marred his otherwise smooth, cultured countenance as he brought one hand up to rub his closed eyes.

"What's wrong?"

Keiran leaned closer to Emmett as he shook his head as if to clear it from some kind of pain. "Pay no mind, Emmett. It's the bloody noise. The artificial signals. Even with our meditations, the Children can only tolerate urban centers for so long."

"Sorry."

Keiran straightened his back in his chair and took another long drink from his tea, as if to will the discomfort away. "We must focus through the discomfort for peace."

Emmett took a bite from his plate. "You're the picture of calm, K." Emmett tried to hide his own surprise at having given Keiran a nickname.

Emmett was thankful for a recorded voice announcing another scheduled departure to break their conversation. Hearing Keiran speak of Amala turned his stomach over on itself. Yet despite what he felt and the questions remaining, the past several hours and the attack on Silvan Dea had left Emmett with an appreciation for the young man. And neither jealousy nor envy felt appropriate.

Keiran made to stand from the table and looked at the clock.

"Listen, I've been meaning to say something," Emmett said as he caught Keiran's arm with his hand before he could stand. "I need to say thank you."

There was so much more that Emmett wanted to say, things he understood that he could not even say to himself yet. His mind was racing too fast to maintain a semblance of order over his own thoughts, and through the chaos were the hundreds of new questions that he had: of Keiran and Sebastian's time in the

Himalayas, of this Omar Hazrat and the Lighthouse, of the Dark Fire and the power of the Revenants to move against and ultimately destroy the Grove of the world's most powerful, if absent, Elder. Despite it all, he recognized the simple truth that he would have died many times over if it had not been for Keiran and, sensing that he was still in danger, knew that he could not survive without him.

"You'll repay the debt before our time together is through, to be certain," Keiran said as he folded his napkin and rose from the table.

Emmett doubted that he could ever deserve what had already been done for him by a stranger who had no reason to so willingly and joyously protect his life.

"Right, sure," Emmett scoffed. "I will save *you*." Emmett snickered at the ridiculousness of this thought when he caught Keiran staring oddly at him.

"What?" Emmett asked. Keiran just stared at him as if he were a stranger passing on the street and Keiran was struggling to remember where he knew him from.

"Nothing. Sorry, too much on my mind. Come on, then," Keiran recovered, shaking his head as he led Emmett out.

They exited the café and strolled through the terminal appearing casual and yet both feeling the cautiousness one feels when he believes he is being followed. Business commuter traffic had steadily increased. They ambled along the south end of the terminal, wandering down long corridors featuring rows of queue lines for waiting trains.

At one point, Emmett saw Sebastian approaching them. Keiran made a quick gesture that he interpreted to mean that he should look away. Out of the corner of his eye, Emmett saw Sebastian brush up against Keiran as he passed him, continuing to walk on with Ellie huddled beside him. Though Keiran did not say, Emmett guessed that he had given them their identifications.

Throngs of bustling commuters hurried past them, the collective clamor of hundreds of conversations over mobile phones swirling together to form a porridge of noise that often caused Keiran to wince with a twitch of his head. There was the odd tick or motion that Emmett caught each time out of the corner of his eye as he pretended not to be watching Keiran's every movement, if only so Keiran would not feel self-conscious, but also because Emmett was beginning to understand what kind of sacrifice Keiran made protecting him.

Staring into storefront windows at the myriad of holiday offerings, Emmett paused in front of an electronics boutique whose flat-panel monitors near the front door played the morning cable news.

"At least twenty students remain unaccounted for who were trapped in the college's dormitories at the time of the fire. A press release from the board of regents states that University President Kellner expressed, 'profound sadness at the tragedy,' as well as a commitment of full cooperation with state and local officials investigating the fire's cause. Already, unconfirmed sources have reported several lightning strikes ..."

Emmett half-watched the well-manicured woman recounting the previous night's tragic fire. Cell phone videos flashed onto the screen picture-within-picture as computer reenactments crafted only hours after the event replayed the frightening last moments of the students' lives. The ticker along the bottom of the screen catalogued the weekend box office grosses.

His attention noticeably perked when the news anchor, with an explosion of new graphics on-screen and oddly themed introduction music, transitioned into a story with obvious meaning.

"In related weather news, forestry officials say that containment is underway for a series of landslides in the Cascade Range east of Portland. There is no word yet on the extent of the damage, though the area is uninhabited."

Um, what the hell?

"Coming up after the break, we have updates on the Gulf Coast child murders; highlights from the weekends' games; and America's favorite actress stops by to talk about her new reality show project!"

Emmett tugged on Keiran's arm and motioned toward the monitor as an image of Mount Hood played over the anchor's words. "Are they talking about what I think they're talking about?" he whispered.

"They're covering their tracks. They pay handsomely to plant fictitious stories in the media. People don't want to *know* the true world, Emmett. It is the ally to darkness."

Looking into his eyes, Emmett expected to see a countenance of mourning on Keiran's face. Yet for the destruction of the Grove he belonged to and the loss of life at the hands of the Revenants and the Underdwellers, Keiran was the picture of detached calm.

Nodding, Keiran looked down as if to acknowledge this to Emmett. "It was just a building. Stone, brick, and mortar. The walls do not breathe as we do. Buildings can be rebuilt. Do not mourn for *things*, Emmett."

"And for people?" Emmett asked, not accusatorily and yet wondering how he could not be affected by the deaths of so many people. Emmett may only have known Keiran, legitimately, for a couple of days, but he sensed that he was not the uncaring and unconcerned person that would not think twice about the loss of life.

Keiran's face at once registered the emotional balance of his words, both the profound sadness and the basic acceptance of them. "Mourn only the living, Emmett. The Archivist teaches us this: let the dead *remain* dead." Keiran patted him firmly on the shoulder.

Images of unspeakable evil and forgotten death flashed through Emmett's mind timed to the Christmas music playing through the terminal.

Emmett numbly watched the news fade into commercials. So much unknown death.

"'Fiery the angels fell; deep thunder rolled around their shores; burning with the fires of Orc,'" Emmett said quietly, turning away from the television monitors.

"William Blake?" Keiran asked.

"*Blade Runner*," Emmett flatly responded. "Let's get out of here."

Keiran and Emmett's fake identifications passed inspection as they queued for their train. Keiran kept Emmett close to him and continued to scan the crowd.

"Won't we know if one of them is close? It's hard not to notice that I'm convulsing on the ground, you know."

"They are likely to use initiates who have not performed those things which make you ill," Keiran quietly said. "Poor fools who are trying to prove their worth who otherwise know nothing of what they're involved in. We have a term for them: cannon fodder."

Emmett checked their tickets as they exited one passenger car and entered the next, negotiating the narrow walkways and regretting the claustrophobic space. Checking his ticket again, he nodded at the door in front of them.

"Seat number 237. That's oddly fitting."

"How so?"

"Room 237? *The Shining*?" Keiran's blank face caused Emmett to sigh. "Getting the supernatural STD off my neck is priority number one. Amala, number two. Catching you up on basic pop culture is a very close third."

Sebastian and Ellie were already sitting in the compartment. Keiran nodded at them, guiding Emmett quickly into the compartment before casting one final glance down the corridor and closing the door.

"Hey," Emmett said. He saw that Ellie had purchased a plain yellow dress and white cardigan sweater, and she had combed her soft hair back out of her eyes to reveal a clean, if mournful, face. Sebastian wore dark mushroom-colored slacks with a black polo shirt, his heavily inked arms tensing underneath a coat draped over his lap.

"All right?" Keiran nodded, noticing Sebastian's rapidly tapping foot.

"We were followed," Sebastian said coldly, not taking his eyes from the window.

"How do you know?" Keiran asked.

"I just do."

"Did they see you board the train?"

Sebastian shook his head. "I don't think so. Ellie and I used a crowd of tourists to hide in. We purchased two sets of clothes and changed after we were seen. There was a short, older man with a pencil-thin mustache, and a tall, thin woman with a high nose."

"I don't remember seeing either of them. What about you, Emmett?"

Emmett shook his head. "Nope. Sorry."

"Then it is just as likely that we have eluded them."

"Except that they'll notify others."

"We will take turns searching the train. If they are on board, we will exit at the next station. Agreed?"

Sebastian nodded reluctantly, continuing to stare out the

window.

The morning passed uneventfully, and shortly after the train began its journey, Keiran left to tour the other cars. Emmett was thankful for Ellie's presence, as he was uncertain whether Sebastian would want to engage him in conversation about what had been discussed. Yet his attentions were focused exclusively on caring for Ellie, touching her arm often in a reassuring way or whispering words asking how she was doing. Throughout their time, she alternated between a mute, catatonic glaze of an expression and rare moments where she took notice of Sebastian with a slight movement of her eyes across his chest. This did not go unnoticed by Emmett, who had to reassure himself that not every attractive woman was so entranced by muscles.

I'm witty. Girls like snark and an encyclopedic film knowledge to rival IMDB.

When Keiran returned, Sebastian left to do the same, careful first to don his sport coat and cover his broad, tattooed arms. Whether it was being on the train heading toward the Lighthouse or his time spent caring for Ellie, his singular focus was on protecting them from the people that he believed were following them. It was something of a game to intrude into other private compartments, and the two Bards told Emmett of how they had to find increasingly elaborate reasons to explain to the surprised passengers within.

With Sebastian gone, Ellie sat mutely on the opposite side of the compartment, spending long stretches of time silently staring out at the passing countryside. Unlike Sebastian, Keiran seemed content to allow her the private space, looking introspective in the empty silence.

Stifling increasing yawns with his hand, Emmett rested along one of the benches in their compartment, eventually tiring of watching her lifeless eyes stare unblinkingly out the window, and finally succumbing to a long nap. It was a restless nap, disjointed by the tumbling thoughts in his mind and interrupted frequently by errant bumps of the train. Upon finally waking, he felt as restless as before.

Within a few hours of their departure, the coastal mountains and thick forests receded to vast, open plains. Emmett continued to drift in and out of a bored half sleep as the afternoon rolled along with little notice given to the passage of time.

By the approach of the first evening, Emmett was growing restive with boredom. It appeared they had achieved a relative safety aboard the train, which permitted his mind to dive into various images and thoughts of the preceding days that he understood could only be quieted with distracting activity.

"I'm going to see what I can get to eat," he said after suppressing a rumble of his stomach. "And I seriously need to stretch my legs. Anybody want to come?"

"Are you hungry, little sister?" Sebastian asked, looking first to Ellie. When she shook her head and stared out the window, Sebastian declined the invitation.

"Keiran?"

Rubbing his bleary eyes, he straightened and ran his hands through his hair. "Of course. Cheers." He stood up with another yawn, and after a moment of disorientation that he cleared with a shaking of his head, preceded Emmett out of the compartment.

CHAPTER 14

Keiran and Emmett walked down through the aisles into an empty dining car. Each table featured a miniature rosemary bush pruned to resemble a tiny Christmas tree wrapped in silver taffeta tied neatly into a ribbon.

Emmett stared at the menu while Keiran stretched again, staring mutely out the dark windows at the passing countryside. "You reckon there's anything worth having?"

"That depends," Emmett said, flipping the laminated placard over.

"On what?"

"On how picky you are."

When the server greeted them, Emmett ordered sandwiches for both of them and a hot chocolate for himself.

"I'll have a coffee, please. Black," Keiran said.

She reached for the pot on the counter and poured Keiran a cup.

"Cheers," Keiran thanked the server, taking a long draw and permitting himself a grimace only after the server was gone. "Can't imagine that coffee would be to anyone's taste."

Emmett thanked the server when she returned with his hot chocolate. With the past few days' chaos, it was the simple things that brought comfort.

Emmett absently twirled the Christmas ribbon on their table. "Death, darkness, and Christmas. How Kubrickian."

"Christmas makes me miss home," Keiran said.

"How'd you celebrate?" Emmett asked.

"My family would drive north to Tenbury Wells for the annual mistletoe auction. Mum would select cut holly for all of us to fashion wreaths out of. And you had your traditional music, immense sweets, and Christmas crackers for everyone. Just wonderful memories, really."

Keiran watched him patiently, and in the silence Emmett realized that he had not spoken. "I had a different foster home practically every year. Never really celebrated."

"Sorry," Keiran offered.

"Nah, it's cool. I'm not humbug on it. No need to go sending Dickens's ghosts after me."

Keiran sipped his coffee. "Wouldn't accomplish much, mate. They're not much for haunting."

"What? Ghosts?"

"Aye."

"Oh, I need to hear this. Details, please." Emmett sat up noticeably.

"They're like images superimposed onto a photograph. They don't interact, really—just sort of *fill* the empty spaces with their memories."

"So no chairs stacked on kitchen tables?"

"Afraid not."

"That's disappointing."

"I can show you sometime if you like."

"Pass. I have enough difficulty dealing with the living. And things that apparently like to *eat* the living."

"Fair play."

Emmett motioned with his hand for more. "What else is real?"

Keiran blew out a long sigh. "There are more things that go bump in the night than I could likely recount for you here. Some are quite harmless creatures that disappear with deforestation.

"Dude, I'm a sci-fi and fantasy nerd. Cumbersome world-building is my crack. Educate me!"

"You've heard of fairies, yes? Nymphs, tree spirits, and tall, hairy beasts like that are found in some places left in the world. More often the forest creatures are Druids who have been sub-sumed by their Wisdoms and abandoned civilization. You find the same thing with Bards who embrace the Song at the sacrifice of their lives in tales of lake monsters, sirens, and merfolk."

"Delicious. I love it. So Champy and Bigfoot are you all running around going *Where The Wild Things Are* on us?"

Keiran chuckled. "Not everything is so blessedly simple. There are the darker creatures, the rarer ones that still live in remote places; the sort of powerful beings that inspire a degree of terror in those who are unlucky enough to come across them."

"Like Revenants?"

"Older. If such a thing is even possible."

The server returned with a tray of sandwiches that Keiran and Emmett set into. Watching the first orange patterns wash the horizon in the pre-dusk hues of a setting sun, Emmett turned and put his back against the wall, laying one leg across the bench. Both ate in silence, enjoying the reassuring motion of the train. For Emmett, it was the simple task of eating that felt somehow grounding to the earth against the whirlwind of thoughts that seemed determined to keep him aloft high in the air overhead.

"I'm absolutely shattered," Keiran finally yawned.

"You said it would be some time before you were recharged."

"A full night's sleep should do the trick, but this has me

halfway there. You?"

Emmett ran a hand along his covered neck. "I checked in the bathroom earlier. It's down below my collarbone already."

"And the pain?"

"I sometimes get this shooting pain in my chest, but it's gone before I can think about it. It's just ridiculously sore, like I've been punched too many times."

"You seem to be managing."

"Yeah, but the same can't be said for Ellie. I don't think I've heard her say more than a few words since last night."

"I'm not certain there's anything I can do for her at this point other than to keep her physically safe. The tragedy of losing a loved one is compounded by witnessing death's senselessness firsthand."

"So what are you going to do with her?"

"Until she recovers, I have no way of knowing where she is from or where she should go to next," Keiran said, sipping his coffee.

"What about Dr. Hazrat? Can he care for her?"

"Barring other circumstances, that is the safest course of action. I'd wager the Lighthouse would relish the opportunity to provide safety to her after the Archivist seemingly failed to do so."

Emmett deliberately paused, considering his next words. Omar Hazrat had finally been breached in the conversation. Alone from the others and seemingly safe from Revenant attack, he felt like he had the first true opportunity to extract from Keiran answers to so many questions swirling in his mind.

"Keiran, about what you and Sebastian were talking about in the truck."

Keiran placed the coffee mug down on the table and clasped his hands in front of him. "Yes, let us discuss that."

Feeling his back straighten, Emmett sat up and tried to appear calm despite the urgency he felt toward the conversation. He waited silently for Keiran to begin.

"As it goes, there are things I might choose not to discuss with you at this moment. Such as my time in the Himalayas. That is something I cannot share with you. I ask for your confidence. Do I have it?"

Emmett had not forgotten that Sebastian pointedly said that the events had been kept from Amala. Considering this, Emmett remembered that Amala had instructed him to keep his unusual waking dream secret, too.

What other secrets do you people keep from each other?

"Of course," Emmett answered. "We'll just hang a lantern on that."

"As to Omar Hazrat and his Grove, the Lighthouse, it's important that you understand that like any group, the Children face their own internal disagreements. The Great Preclusion would be an example."

"So what is it?"

"Once every several generations, one of the Children is born with a special power to see into the hearts of men and predict their futures. We call them the Mara. Or the Dreamers. There is no foundation for the gift anywhere in *ikkibu*, which is the name we give to a collection of stories, traditions, and the taboos we maintain over forbidden things."

"So where's the problem?"

"*Ikkibu* holds that all humans have choice. There is nothing more sacred to the Children."

"Okay," Emmett nodded.

"The Mara claimed to divine the actions of men before they made the choice to act. The Mara punished people for crimes they had not yet committed—oftentimes years or even decades before the supposed future act."

Keiran paused to thank the server who had returned to fill his coffee.

"Brutal civil wars were fought, one Grove defending their Mara from the other. It was bloody chaos, Emmett. Dark times. Eventually, the nine Elders—led by the Archivist herself—gathered at the ruins of one of the oldest Groves in the world, off Yonaguni Island. There they issued the Great Preclusion, forbidding all recognition and legitimacy of the Mara."

"I'm not connecting this with what seemed to be the earlier disagreement."

"Darkness is a euphemism. Because most need to deny its existence, darkness has spread now unabated."

"No doubt it's Zombie Apocalypse time out there," Emmett said.

"Which is why Children are now openly questioning the Great Preclusion and whether we should reclaim the gift of the Mara."

"So what you're saying is that some people want to use the Mara to predict who may kill or hurt others and stop them before they do so?" Emmett asked plainly.

"In a matter, yes. The Archivist still teaches against it, as does Sebastian's Elder, *La Pastora de la Isla*, the Lady Karina of the Grove Belladonna off the coast of Brazil. But the voices of opposition grow with every tragedy."

"So I'm guessing that this Elder, Omar Hazrat, isn't playing on the same team?"

"Omar Hazrat claims to *be* a Mara, Emmett."

"Whoa, points for a well-paced reveal," Emmett breathed. "At least that explains the cage match."

Sighing with his eyes closed and straight back against the bench, Keiran took a deep breath. "Underdwellers are unable to rise to the surface unless they are called by their human follow-ers—an act that requires both power and resources, but also sig-nificant bloodshed and suffering. Without their cabalists to sum-mon them, the Underdwellers would essentially be trapped in the earth."

Emmett didn't understand where Keiran was going. "So?"

"If the Revenants were wiped out, we could effectively elimi-nate their darkness once and for all from the world. It would not remove the threat of other fell creatures, but one cannot underes-timate the extent of Underdweller damage to our world."

Emmett finally understood the conflict. "No offense, K, but I'm waiting to hear something unreasonable. I mean, what's the problem? I thought hunting down Revenants was what you did."

"Humans who follow dark paths—yes, we locate and elimi-nate them. The Great Preclusion forbids us from condemning someone for an act they have not yet committed."

Emmett's mind raced through the discussion and tried to empathize with what Keiran was saying. Yet with the soreness from the Rot in his neck, he found himself struggling to not agree with the sentiments expressed by Sebastian.

Keiran seemed to see this, and he leaned forward across the table toward him as he spoke. "We're talking about an ability that is considered suspect even among those who advocate its use. It is erratic, unpredictable, and prone to manipulation if not out-right error. What if an innocent person was convicted of a crime they had no intention of committing?"

"Couldn't you just put tails on everyone you suspect could be a Revenant?"

"We'd bloody-well spy on every human being, then. Consider how that could be used against our own people. How could their visions be verified? It's the word of the Mara only that you have as to the truth, and even if you were right nine times, what if the tenth person accused were innocent?"

"You speak dismissively of the other nine that were evil as if their actions mean nothing," a baritone voice sounded behind them. So focused on Keiran, Emmett all but jumped as Sebastian entered the room. He sat down beside him on the bench, setting his massive arms on the edge of the table. His jacket was off, and the scrolling artwork of ink around his arms caught the eye of the server who stared longingly at him.

Keiran simply nodded. "All right?"

"Ellie asked me to get her something to eat. She's not feeling well enough to leave her bunk."

"They have sandwiches," Keiran observed nonchalantly as the server stood silently awaiting his order. Scanning the menu quickly, Sebastian pointed to a pair of items and asked for them to be wrapped to take back to his compartment.

"So, we're introducing Emmett to the great, wide world, are we?"

Emmett saw instantly in Keiran's eyes that he did not want to continue the conversation with Sebastian present. Emmett made to say something to change the conversation, but Sebastian interrupted him before he could speak.

"It's not my place to intrude in that, brother. That is for you, and I still respect our people's ways. Let me say at least that in the past few centuries, darkness has spread farther than at any other point in human history. This dismissive attitude on the part of mankind is precisely the reason for it."

Sebastian shifted his considerable size on the narrow bench to look squarely at Emmett. "Have they told you what the first ritual of an Underdweller summoning is?"

"We've only just eaten, brother."

"No, they haven't," Emmett answered. He wanted to support Keiran, and he knew Keiran did not want to have the conversation with Sebastian present. Yet images from the Silvan Dea attack still drifted through his mind in the silent moments when no one was speaking to him. Emmett could not bear it any longer, hoping some kind of meaning would give him closure.

"An infant's blood. If I told you the manner in which it was collected, you'd beg me to tell you it was a lie."

"Oh, do we have to do this tonight? Honestly," Keiran sighed.

"But it isn't a lie, and it's done worldwide. There are twelve other rituals—thirteen acts so foul, so unnatural, that you couldn't bear knowing."

"Is there a point to this?" Keiran asked, watching Emmett's face twist in disgust.

"Not acting leads to countless deaths."

"And you believe that it's our fault, then? That we are to blame?"

"'To her is given the Dance, and to him is given the Voice, and by the Song they guide and comfort the Children in Darkness and Light,'" Sebastian recited.

Keiran's shaking head hung low in his hands. "The Song is lost when we abandon our beliefs, Sebastian. 'Life is a tapestry woven by hands we cannot see and composed of notes that we cannot create.' See? I can quote *ikkibu* just like you. It is the first of our teachings that we cannot force that which we do not control."

"You believe that with complete certainty?" Sebastian dismissed.

"Faith does not require that I understand. Only that I believe."

"At what cost do you pay for the comfort that comes with blind obedience?"

"A high cost, to be certain. But one I am prepared to pay, for the alternative is one I could not afford."

"You're not the one who pays it," Sebastian said. "Ellie and Emmett do. And Paulo. Show me how your faith will bring him back." With these words, Sebastian's expression solidified the pure essence of their disagreement.

Emmett was afraid the tension would boil over if Sebastian's posture was any indication. The first mention of the Great Preclusion brought the anger right to the surface. His brother's death seemed to serve as a catalyst for everything he must have already been feeling. Without a target he could channel his anger toward, Keiran had become a viable option by default.

Keiran lowered his voice and looked on his friend with a calm expression. "I will not presume to understand what the loss of your brother is, Sebastian. I will not abandon my beliefs. You will not abandon yours. That is why we always reach a stalemate when we have this discussion."

Emmett was certain that Sebastian was preparing to say something more, perhaps some kind of statement that, though well-intentioned in Sebastian's mind to win over Keiran or even Emmett to his beliefs, would bring him into further conflict with Keiran. He knew that he had to do or say something.

"How long before we reach the Lighthouse?" Emmett offered, hoping to avert their attention.

It was only the reappearance of the server pausing one foot from the table with a tray of wrapped food that caused them to relent.

"The evening after next, I would say," Keiran finally answered, deliberately looking up at the server as if to force Sebastian to as well.

"Thank you. My friend here will pay for the food," Sebastian said without breaking eye contact with Keiran. The server set the food down and hurried away.

"The sandwiches look good," Emmett observed, trying to find some way to bring the abruptness of the moment to a softening close.

"Indeed. I should think that Ellie is waiting for her food, yes?"

"Yes," Sebastian said slowly. He grabbed the food in one hand and stood, never breaking eye contact with Keiran. Emmett held his breath, half-expecting that the two Bards would break into a physical exchange if any other words were spoken.

"Enjoy your conversation. I trust you will guide Emmett with the same honesty and truth as when you were guided by Oliver," he said, finally turning away without saying good-bye to either of them as he walked out of the dining car.

Only after the door closed behind him did Keiran blink, and Emmett felt the apprehension straining through his body relax with an audible sigh. A moment's pause revealed a wounded expression, as if Sebastian had just said something that was more personally hurtful than any other words could be.

"Yeah, that *just* happened," Emmett quipped, trying to lighten the moment with humor. "This thing between you guys has *got* to stop."

The rigidity in Keiran's countenance did not lessen, though Emmett could see he made a considerable effort to refocus his attention on Emmett. "It's a sign of my exhaustion that I didn't hear his approach. Heaven knows the man has an audible walk."

"Did his brother feel the same way?" Emmett asked. "Paulo? Did he question the Great Preclusion, too? Or is it possible there was disagreement between them as there is between you two?"

"Honestly, I couldn't tell you. I didn't know Paulo as well as Sebastian. And again, I love Sebastian as my brother. However, if you asked me if I trusted his judgment in this matter, if I would place my own faith in Dr. Hazrat's teachings, I would say a resounding no. And Sebastian knows that."

"And that's why he's so angry. Because he thinks he's earned your trust."

"Yes."

Because he lied for you to protect you in the Himalayas.

Emmett drew a long breath, considering the weight of Keiran's words. "I guess that explains why you were so hesitant to go to the Lighthouse in the first place."

"I can't guarantee that we're not escaping one bad situation and entering another *trying* one," he said with a raised eyebrow.

"But it's not like we're in any actual danger going there, right?"

Keiran shook his head. "These are the Children after all, and if any were more zealous in their hatred of dark magiks, it is those at the Lighthouse. Silvan Dea was a place for contemplation and recuperation. Dr. Hazrat minds his Grove like a bloody fortress."

"How comforting," Emmett remarked, an image of a lone prison built on a craggy island conjured unbidden in his mind.

"Anyway, a few hours of sleep would do us all good, I think. But there is one more important thing I must say to you before we return, Emmett."

Emmett finished his hot chocolate and nodded. "Shoot."

"Amala would normally guide you through this process, but seeing as how she is not here, you are left with my rather fumbling ministrations."

"No idea what you're talking about, K."

"When the Archivist contacts you, she may take one of many different forms: a whisper on the wind, words in the clouds; that sort of thing. Remember everything that you experience, and no matter what happens, tell no one. Not even Sebastian or Ellie."

"Got it."

You people with your secrets.

Keiran extracted cash from his pocket and left it for their server before they returned to their compartment. Emmett saw the look of relief on Keiran's face when they found Sebastian and Ellie already fast asleep in their separate bunks.

"Sleep well," Keiran said.

"Yeah, you too," Emmett said, feeling a detached sense of foreboding as he watched Keiran wedge a block under the door handle.

CHAPTER 15

Keiran had waited for Emmett to close the curtain to his narrow bunk before turning in. Only when he allowed himself to peek from behind the corner of the shade did Emmett see that Keiran had left his halfway open, his eyes mostly closed with his face turned toward him.

Emmett rested on his back with his legs crossed and hands behind his head. The low ceiling of the cubby did nothing to alleviate his claustrophobia, but he closed his eyes with several steadying breaths. He spent several minutes sleepless on his back, several more on his side, finally turning onto his stomach with his face buried in his pillow.

Just relax already. His thoughts were a swirl of images and questions, the low background hum of the moving train spreading a great canvas before him as he wrestled to gain control of the orchestra and bring silence to his mind's coliseum.

As he struggled to *not* struggle with sleep, he continued to catalogue sounds: wheels turning on the tracks; low, rhythmic breathing of deep sleep; soft, patterned snoring; creaking floorboards as someone walked outside their compartment.

After some time—how long he did not know—Emmett felt the watery curtain of unconsciousness slipping over him. An aspect of his mind felt uncomfortably anchored high above him, still counting each revolution of the train's wheels along the tracks and still tumbling through images of Druids and Bards locked in deadly combat with Underdwellers and Revenants in a world he no longer recognized.

First time on a train. I might as well enjoy it.

Sighing with frustration, he rubbed his eyes and quietly got up. He slowly drew the door open, stepping out into the corridor and closing the door behind him.

Emmett walked down the train corridor, pausing as he felt a prickling feeling on the back of his neck. His mind registered that something odd had passed him in the window. When he turned and looked, he saw nothing but darkness.

What was that? Taking a tentative step, he leaned into the row of empty seats and brought his face within several feet of the window.

Was that a face?

He saw it again in the corner of his eye, a muted image in the window. He recoiled, banging his head against the seat. He forced himself to look, and then he saw it: a face staring back at him.

What the hell?

He saw blue eyes and blond hair staring mutely back at him in the window. A petite, pretty face. Ellie's face. Her reflection moved with him, her hand brushing against her cheeks as he raised his hand to his face; her lips agape as Emmett stared back at his reflection.

The floor lurched forward, and Emmett fell on the ground. He opened his eyes to darkness. Urgency sounded in his mind. He wasn't breathing. He couldn't see. Survival overrode his confusion, and his eyes pushed open as his mouth tried to gasp for air. In the moment's chaos, his brain quickly identified a hand firmly covering his mouth.

They found me! They're trying to kill me!

Instinct brought his hands and legs up, but something stronger held his body down. Another pair of hands grasped his shoulders. Restraint. Firm, yet not painful. He tried biting down, but the hand moved underneath his chin and cupped his jaw, closing his mouth.

As his eyes moved wildly around the room, irises engorged, an explosion of what little light was available flooded his vision. Focusing, he saw two figures hunched over him: a deeply tanned, hulking man, and a second, fair-skinned younger man whose green eyes were staring directly into his.

"Bloody calm down," Keiran hissed as Sebastian wrested control of his body. Only now could Emmett see him in the semi-darkness enough to see he was back in their private compartment. He ceased struggling, and Keiran and Sebastian immediately released him.

The emergency red lights along the floor suddenly alit, casting the Bards in a foreboding glow. They held their heads aloft with closed eyes, listening acutely to the growing commotion within the train. Then both Bards opened their eyes.

Sebastian held three fingers up.

Keiran shook his head, holding five fingers up.

"She may not be," Sebastian said cryptically, to which Keiran shook his head.

Emmett made an exaggerated waving motion. "What's going on?"

"The train stopped," Keiran whispered. "You fell out of your bunk making strange noises. We couldn't wake you."

I was dreaming. Without remembering falling asleep. Again?

"Revenants," Sebastian whispered. "And Ellie's gone." Sebastian drew himself to his full height in the small compartment. "I will draw them away to the west. Take Emmett east to the Lighthouse."

"No! We go together," Keiran corrected.

"I won't run," Sebastian said, and even Emmett saw the grave look on his face. "Not this time, Keiran. Not again."

Keiran looked down at the floor with an expression of acceptance before standing and rolling up his sleeve to reveal his heavily inked forearm as Sebastian did the same. Together, each grasped the other by their forearm, the tattoos' patterns seemingly joined together.

"The Song lifts us," Keiran whispered.

"And guides the Children home," Sebastian responded with equal reverence.

They released each other's arms, and Sebastian nodded once at Emmett before turning and opening the compartment door. Stepping out into the corridor, he looked down each direction before disappearing.

Emmett felt nauseous, not from Revenant proximity, but the hollowness one felt knowing someone was going out to meet death on his behalf. The burden left him sick.

Keiran reached underneath his bunk's covers, withdrawing a blunt pipe the length of his forearm. "You may have to defend yourself," he said, pushing it into Emmett's shaking hands.

"You're kidding, right?"

"It's from a storm drain back at the Portland train station. It's pure iron."

Emmett stared dumbly as he looked back and forth between Keiran and the pipe in his hands, feeling both inept and absurd. Keiran grabbed his elbow and drew him to his body, leading him out the compartment into a rush of confused, rising voices.

A tremendous scream pierced the train. Keiran's head turned down the opposite corridor just as the crashing sound of running passengers thundered through the train.

"They'll kill everyone on the train. We have to get off right now!"

"What about the passengers?"

"You are my only priority!" Keiran yelled back as he winced in obvious discomfort.

A blaring emergency siren exploded in their ears, and down the corridor Emmett heard the wail of passengers as confusion gave way to chaos.

The corridors swelled with frightened, half-awake passengers. Keiran pushed past them, dragging Emmett along. An explosion rocked through the train, followed by the gnawing sound of metal grating against metal. The floor shook violently, toppling passengers over each other.

"Fire!" a woman screamed.

Keiran and Emmett turned to see the orange glow of flames outside of the train's windows. Passengers trampled over others. Keiran pushed Emmett against the wall, using his body to shield him from the stampede.

Emmett's ears filled with the wailing cries of children and terrified adults. They had no way of knowing what was coming for them.

"Keiran, we've got to do something!"

"I gave Amala my word. I can't save everyone!"

Another explosion rocked stopped the car, nearly knocking it off the tracks. An unsettling howl bayed into the night, followed by another dark call that rose above the screaming passengers and twisting flames crackling outside.

The exit was several feet from them, but with so many people trampling over each another, Emmett knew they could not reach it. Keiran put his open palm against a window and, growling, shattered the glass outward in a fine, powdery dust.

Abandoning any attempts at remaining hidden, Keiran stuck his head outside before turning around to grab Emmett by his shoulder. He pushed Emmett out as other passengers fought toward the window. Falling several feet to the wet grass below, Keiran landed beside Emmett and pulled him to his feet.

Chaos reigned as screaming passengers poured from the burning train. Emmett could see that the rear car's explosion had heaved it clear off of the track and left it skewed along the ground in a path of burning wreckage and warped metal.

A woman pleaded in the distance for her lost child as another man pulled an older passenger limply from the wreckage. Two men huddled over a collapsed pregnant woman whose hysterical sobbing could not be controlled. Passengers in states of visible shock limped away nursing injuries. Someone was crying as they tried to call on a phone that wouldn't work for them; another absently stood with a blank face, trying and seemingly unable to take pictures with their cell phone of a collapsed, bleeding passenger who moaned on the ground.

"My God," Emmett whispered, horrified by the chaos.

"It's not sodding over," Keiran said hastily, scanning the crowds of people.

Emmett's head turned with Keiran's as another howl sounded far in the distance, a preternatural, tearing sound that pierced the crackling sounds of flame and cries of wounded and frightened passengers. An older gentleman sitting mutely on the ground near them holding his hand to the side of his bleeding face did not even move or take notice as the animal's wail sounded again.

A shrieking cry drew everyone's attention as someone staggered from the back of the wreckage. Someone was limping, cradling their opposite arm, and calling out for help. Several passengers responded and began running toward the figure, including the older gentleman sitting near Emmett.

"No," Keiran said as his hand shot out to stop the man.

Another passenger reached the flailing victim first. With an arm outstretched to help them, the victim responded with a lunge and snarl toward their rescuer, the cradled arm arcing in a backward slash with a long machete that glinted in the surrounding fire's glow. The sickening sound of severed flesh rent the air as the rescuer fell backward with a gurgling plea for help.

A moment of stunned silence was drowned in pandemonium as fear gripped the frightened passengers. The robed figure cried out as he sliced downward with a vicious hacking of his machete on his fallen victim, his face sprayed with a sheet of brilliant red as the nauseating sound of metal on bone tore the air.

Emmett felt the urgency of rising bile in his throat, and a thousand aching voices exploded in his mind. Shuddering against the convulsion, Emmett's arm shot out to steady himself against Keiran, who, seeing him, reacted immediately with a deep note.

"We need to head east and try to outrun them," Keiran pointed.

The robed Revenant was joined by two more stepping from the train, both covered in a smattering of blood soaking through their black robes. One dragged a screaming Ellie by her hair along the ground.

"Help me!" Ellie screamed.

Emmett tore away before Keiran's hand could stop him. He saw Amala and the other Druids fighting at Silvan Dea, and Paulo's body arc rigidly as the Underdweller plunged its claws into and through his chest. He saw Troy's headless corpse floating in the river. Keiran would have them flee again, leaving others to die for him. But Emmett was too angry to run.

Adrenaline propelled Emmett's narrow frame the hundred or so yards between them, his heart pounding in his chest as he ran with the pipe held high above his head.

"Emmett, no! Stop!" Keiran called out behind him.

The female released Ellie and snarled. The other two raised their machetes and ran at Emmett. Bounding over twisted wreckage and burning grass, Emmett charged one of the men, swinging his pipe awkwardly. He dodged Emmett's clumsy attack, and it was only Emmett's tripping awkwardly to the ground that saved him from a vicious sideways swing of their machetes.

He rolled onto his back, preparing to block their inevitable killing blow. A clarion, deep sound called in the distance, and Emmett felt a wave of heat rush over him. Two of his attackers were slammed back by an unseen force.

Sebastian hurtled toward him, his wide frame visible in the dancing flames of the train's wreckage. He brought one foot against the nearest attacker, kicking with such strength that Emmett heard bones crack. The other man redoubled his machete swing, recovering from the blast with an upward attack that forced Sebastian to leap back.

The woman was hissing sibilant, scathing words into the air. Emmett raised his pipe and lunged at her. Her incantation interrupted, the woman raised a long, sigil-covered knife and jabbed at Emmett. She moved faster than him, sidestepping his ill-timed swings and slicing him along the length of his arm, causing him to yell as he dropped the pipe.

Sebastian jumped back as the man slashed the air with his bloody machete, their eyes focused on each other. Hearing Emmett's cry, Sebastian feigned a forward attack and spun away from him, stepping into the space between Emmett and the woman in time to block her knife with his own body.

In a single moment that felt to Emmett as if it could last forever, the woman reached a hand up to stroke Sebastian's trembling features before spitting into his eyes. Obscene laughter erupted as she dropped him to the ground with her wicked knife still protruding from his chest. Emmett's throat seized with an agonizing scream as he watched Sebastian fall into a heap on the ground. His lips twitched as blood trickled from the sides of his mouth.

The woman was suddenly clipped by a concussive force that blew over Emmett's head and sent her tumbling through the air. She landed in the burning wreckage, skewered by jagged metal. A second force hit the remaining man in his head, snapping his neck sideways and sending his seizing body to the ground.

Keiran ran to Emmett and pulled him up. Feeling the blood pouring down his arm, Keiran closed his eyes and hummed a low note, running his hand along Emmett's arm. His touch became a searing heat, and Emmett gasped as the wound closed.

Ellie's crying drew their attention, the young woman pulling herself toward Sebastian. Keiran's firm grip held Emmett steady, and Emmett saw a flash of warning as Keiran stared past him.

Ellie's crying grew softer as her lithe form hunched over Sebastian. Keiran stepped in front of Emmett and inched closer to Ellie with his open palm held before him.

She suddenly lunged up and swung with a fierce slash, her hand drawing the knife out of Sebastian's body with a spray of blood. She snarled, jabbing at Keiran. He began to form a melody, but she kicked dirt and pitch at him, his concentration broken as he shielded his head with his hands.

She slashed the knife and caught the edge of Keiran's shoulder. Hissing through clenched teeth, Keiran brought his other leg around in a wide kick that met her other arm, pushing her back several paces.

Screams rang out near the front of the train. Gurgling sounds assaulted the night, followed by people begging for mercy from some unknown attacker.

A wide grin snaked across Ellie's face. "Silvan Dea falls tonight," she said knowingly. More frantic screams erupted, and Emmett strained in the darkness to see figures chasing other figures. Grotesque cheers called into the night as Revenant worshippers fell onto their victims, bludgeoning, slashing, or hacking at fallen passengers in a mass of flailing limbs and helpless, unanswered pleas.

"Flesh given for power!" she cried, bringing her knife down directly toward Keiran's heart. "For Bezal—"

Emmett swung his recovered pipe directly at her face, connecting with bone before she could drive her knife into Keiran's chest. She obviously had never considered Emmett as he struggled to position himself, never saw him as any threat to her. His vicious blow wrenched her petite frame backward with all the righteous anger he did not know he could possess.

Her head unnaturally snapped to the side, Ellie crumpled motionless in the grass. Her glossy, unfocused eyes stared blankly with her mouth slightly open. With the knife lying at her side, her body resembled a rag doll tossed unused into the corner of a child's room, her legs folded awkwardly underneath her.

Emmett dropped the pipe, collapsing onto his knees with the shudder of the blow. His arms vibrated as the feeling of broken bone traveled up the length of his arms and throughout his body. The rage burning in him was suddenly extinguished, and the cold night assaulted his lungs as he struggled to heave air into a nauseated stomach. Fighting lightheadedness that blurred his vision, he focused on Keiran's face.

"Emmett?" Keiran asked tentatively, reaching one hand out toward him.

Continued screams demanded the focusing of his consciousness, and Emmett willed himself to concentrate. He nodded at Keiran, standing upright as Keiran did so.

"I'm ... I'm okay," he stumbled. He knew he wasn't. He had never hit another person. Never *hurt* someone. Never *death*.

I may never be okay again.

But there was no time for it.

Keiran watched him for a moment and seemed to recognize the shift in him before examining his own shoulder. Satisfied that the cut was not too deep, he scanned the area for others converging on them. Dark, cloaked figures ran about the area chasing passengers, but none seemed to be moving toward them.

"I can't fight all of them. We can use the cover of darkness to run."

"You knew, didn't you?" Emmett stared down at Ellie's limp form.

"I didn't know for certain," Keiran said as he knelt down and held a pair of fingers to Sebastian's neck. "His pulse is nearly gone." Keiran lowered his head over Sebastian and whispered something into his ear. Standing quickly just as another great howl sounded again in the distance, he grabbed Emmett's arm with an urgency that communicated more than any words could hope to.

"Do exactly as I say; in a moment, things are going to get much, much worse."

How worse could things get?

"What about Sebastian? We can't leave him!"

"He'd only slow us down," Keiran said unemotionally.

They hurried past the rear car and out into the empty fields beyond. They had run several hundred yards as another howl sounded. It was so close that Emmett felt the edges of his skin clamber, and he recoiled from something hot breathing against his neck.

Keiran abruptly stopped, holding Emmett fast to him in the darkness.

"Show yourself," Keiran commanded firmly to the unresponsive night.

When nothing happened, Keiran tensed his shoulders and pushed his chest out. When he spoke again, it was with a voice filled with both courage and terror.

"I name you, Baraqiel. Reveal yourself."

From coalescing shadows directly before them, the outline of a stooped figure suddenly appeared. Keiran whispered something soft and a halo of fireflies rose from the surrounding grasses, their dancing lights casting the figure in an ambient glow.

An old, haggard woman covered in a tattered robe leaned with great effort against a gnarled wooden staff nearly twice her height. She took a labored step toward them, and as she did so, the prairie grasses wilted in a wide swath before her.

Keiran held his open palm outstretched as his other arm pushed Emmett behind him. "I have named you. Do not approach us."

The heavy folds underneath her swollen, pupil-less eyes contorted as a wicked, toothless smile spread across her pockmarked face. A dry wheeze followed a rasping chuckle that passed with effort over her cracked lips.

"The sad, sad boy who cried atop the snowy mountain," she rasped in a high, keening voice. "He knows the name the Elders fear to share with the Children."

Keiran released a tempered note from his lips, which the old woman laughed at, waving a crooked hand at him. "Children fumbling in the dark, make-believe and feeble art," she dismissed in a singsong tone.

"Who is that?" Emmett whispered.

"Not a *who* but a *what*. An Old One known as the Hag. She minds the Black Hounds," Keiran said, motioning toward

Emmett's left. Emmett's eyes followed, and he recoiled. A pack of large black mastiffs the size of horses appeared seemingly out of the darkness, their fierce, glowing red eyes staring at him. Their deep panting exhaled a thick, rolling mist in the night's cold air.

"Mother's beauties," she rasped, her haggard stare lovingly draped over the waiting hounds. "They are hungry for a hunt."

"We are warded," Keiran said confidently, holding his exposed forearm up. "I command you to leave."

The Hag raised a crooked finger and wagged it at Keiran with mock consternation. "Perhaps you, weeping Bard. But this one," she said, indicating Emmett with her finger, "this one has not yet been Born to the Song. Even now, Death pursues him. My babies smell it. Salty pores drawn down-down-down to the lowest moors."

The hounds took a collective step forward, the grass before them wilting beneath their massive paws. Keiran maneuvered himself between them and Emmett just as the Hag looked at Emmett. "You are familiar to me, little orphan."

"Do not look at her," Keiran snapped. "Close your eyes, Emmett! Now!"

Emmett shut his eyes as he cowered behind Keiran.

"He is under the protection of the Archivist!"

The Hag released a throaty laugh that chilled Emmett's soul. "You presume to speak for her, false witness? You who lied to your Elders through tears for your lost love? Weep and wail, cry to the storm's northern gale."

"The Archivist has called him to her!" Keiran defiantly proclaimed with pride that bolstered Emmett's frightened spirit.

"Her Grove has fallen. All the way down the mountain, tumble-tumble and rumble all the way," she cackled.

Emmett wanted to believe that Keiran could command the Hag away, that his authority was greater than whatever power she commanded. So hopeful was he that he opened his eyes and looked to Keiran.

"Born under the Light of Arthur, yes? An only child? Did you know what your mommy endured for you? What awaited her in the corner's shadows long after the meddler stole you away?" the Hag intoned as her pupil-less eyes found Emmett's.

"Damn it, Emmett! Close your eyes!"

Emmett nearly tore away in his own terror, closing his eyes tight and pulling his hands over them, as if to keep anything from entering them. There was silence but for his own breathing, Keiran's labored breathing, and the heavy panting of the Black Hounds.

The Hag finally spoke. "The Old Ones do not suffer the little Children, weeping liar. Give me Emmett Jonathan Brennan, and I will leave. Let me spare you the suffering that awaits those who harbor him. You who have already seen so much of Death and found you had not the taste to endure it."

She knows my name!

Emmett felt Keiran's grip tighten as if he were steeling his resolve.

"Buildings may burn or crumble, but we survive. If no other Druids or Bards live, I still do! The Archivist's Grove survives because Silvan Dea lives in me! Emmett belongs to us! I have named you, Baraqiel, and commanded you leave!" he shouted.

Emmett felt the palpable silence as the Hag apparently considered her response. Finally he heard something rustle in the grasses and, hearing Keiran release a long-held breath, chanced an open eye to see that the Black Hounds had bounded off for the train.

"Cower in fear all you wish, only child. But I *know* you now. The meddler may hide you, but I will see you again."

The howling called again in the distance, and the echoing

screams quickly died out, replaced by the baying of the Hounds. Where once there had been audible chaos, now only the crackling flames could be heard. The Hag pushed her staff forward, taking a step seemingly into shadow and vanishing into the cold night.

She knew me. She knows me.

Emmett could not bring himself to utter another word. The shocking, icy air blew through limbs that were engorged with adrenaline, and his body was trembling, too, with a fear of new, unimagined horrors that would be forever burned into his mind.

Keiran shook him by his arm as he forced his face directly into Emmett's field of vision. "I need you to focus, mate. You trust me, yes?"

Emmett nodded dumbly, unblinking.

"Then run!"

They abandoned any semblance of cover and broke into a long, unending run out into the empty plains, hundreds of miles from help and lost in the wintry darkness.

CHAPTER 16

They ran for hours through waving prairie grasses before reaching a farm just before dawn. Keiran said nothing as they ran and Emmett dared not speak for fear he would have to slow down to do so. When Emmett could run no longer, Keiran hummed a melody that suffused his limbs with an uncomfortable urgency that helped him continue.

Collapsing underneath an oak tree behind the farm's home, the effects of Keiran's melody melted from Emmett's limbs. They wobbled as if feeling had only just returned to them after years of disuse, and he quickly floundered as he tried to hold himself upright.

"Careful. Just keep rubbing them. Keep the blood moving down there."

Keiran looked exhausted. His head seemed to sag under its own weight, and when he spoke, it was devoid of his usual cadence.

"Normally, my Bardic hearing would allow me to know if we had been followed on foot. But I am so drained that all I hear is a distant ringing. The Revenant worshippers need only follow our trail through the grass to find us."

"How long do you think we have?"

"Hours. They'll need to dispose of any evidence. Bold though their move against us was, I can't believe they've surrendered their need for secrecy."

"So what now?" Emmett coughed.

"We'll change into these clothes," Keiran said, motioning to a clothesline near them. "I've enough in me to *persuade* whoever lives here to drive us to the nearest town."

As Keiran stood, Emmett readied to ask the hundreds of questions tumbling through his mind: Sebastian, Ellie, the passengers, the Hag and her Black Hounds …

Keiran seemed to sense this and held his hand up. "Not now, Emmett. Please, I need to get us away from here first," he said, turning away and walking to the home.

As Keiran was knocking on the door, Emmett struggled to stand. He headed for the hanging clothesline just as a solitary light over the front door turned on above Keiran's head.

Keiran returned as Emmett was changing, having procured for them a ride from the farmer and his wife to a larger town thirty miles away. Riding in the backseat of their pickup truck, Emmett collapsed from the strain of the journey. Keiran, too, surrendered to his own exhaustion, his eyes closed and head tilted forward with his neck against his chin. Emmett jumped each time he thought he heard an animal in the distance, hoping that Amala had finally come for them.

When they reached the larger town, Keiran used his remaining few hundred dollars to pay the farmer and purchase a pair of bus tickets. The previous hours had passed in silence, Emmett holding himself upright and trying to appear as calm and centered as Keiran had always been for his sake. If Keiran noticed this, he gave no indication, though he rarely looked at Emmett directly. Keiran never stopped looking around them, no longer bothering to hide his suspicions from Emmett. If a person stared too long in their direction or walked too close to them, Keiran would move them somewhere else with a constant glance over his own shoulder for any signs of pursuit.

Waiting for their departing bus, Keiran produced a whistle that caused the vending machine to short-circuit. He appeared with various snacks as he led Emmett to a secluded area of the bus depot, leaving the other passengers at a comfortable distance.

"Eat as much sugar as you can," Keiran said as he pushed a pair of candy bars and a fruit juice can into his hands. "Your body will go into shock soon if you don't eat enough. It's not proper nutrition, but in extreme situations, survival is our first priority."

When Emmett began eating, he found his greedy appetite could not be sated. He tore open the can and drank with loud gulps, ignoring an obnoxious belch that he pushed through so he could continue drinking the sweet, sugary carbonation.

"That's not a song we often use given the resulting hunger and thirst ... and belching," Keiran offered with a half-grin, though over his candy bar Emmett did not see the usual Cheshire cat twinkle in his eyes.

Both ate ravenously. Keiran grinned sheepishly over his own burp.

"I won't tell anyone," Emmett said groggily. Having eaten his fourth candy bar, he could feel the resulting sluggishness as the sugar coursed through his blood and submersed his aching muscles.

"Want to talk about it?" Keiran asked.

Emmett stared out over Keiran's shoulder at the long stretch of highway beyond the bus terminal. He wanted to be anywhere but here where the mundane elements of a lost life surrounded him: scattered people texting, children playing with each other, and piles of candy bar wrappers. In another place and time for any other person, these would have been simpler things.

Never again.

"I had to see a social worker once when I was fourteen. Lucy Janus was her name. Her office had this black and white photo of some urban skyline with a lemon-yellow sunrise overhead. I don't know why I remember that—I couldn't even tell you what the woman looked like now. Except that she had a stack of folders and my life was in one of them. She never made eye contact with me, just flipped through my folder while talking. And I kept my eyes fixed on that sunrise, wanting to be anywhere else but there."

Keiran only nodded as he looked down at the table, not making eye contact with Emmett, who stared blankly at his own hands.

"She asked me all these questions. What I do for fun, what do I think of my teachers, do I hurt small animals, blah, blah, blah. And on and on she drones about movies—do I prefer them violent, do I know they aren't real, do I think I'm a character *in* a movie. Anyway, I play along and answer her questions. After about ten minutes, she tells me we're done, that I suffer from derealization, and to start taking the cocktail of pills she was recommending the nurse prescribe."

"What's derealization?"

"It basically means you're disconnected from the world. You look out and see things and they don't seem real to you. Perception is altered and everything feels separated from you."

"What did you say?"

Emmett laughed bitterly and shook his head. "I should have just walked out. But I don't know why—maybe it was just wanting to stay a while longer and stare at that lemon-yellow sun— but I told her she was wrong. So wrong. I told her that Jean-Luc Godard was right: truth really *is* found at twenty-four frames per second. Characters act according to their archetypes, and there's always some kind of resolution in the end through which the protagonist finds meaning and experiences growth. Just because I preferred the consistency in film didn't mean that I didn't know the difference between make-believe and the real world."

"You said all of this at fourteen?"

"It probably wasn't worded as eloquently, and I may have said 'like' every four words. I can't complain too much, because three years of selling those pills bought me my car. So, whatever," Emmett snarked.

He felt the bitterness of grief in the back of his throat, somewhere between his tongue and soul. "You know, Keiran, everyone who's ever taken care of me has died. My birth mom. My foster parents. Every group home I've lived in was run by someone too sick or too old not to suffer a heart attack or die of an overdose. My life began with death, and it's been death ever since. So this idiot social worker says it's not healthy for me to relate so closely with movies. And all I thought was, either everyone dies and nothing means anything, or everything's a lie and there's meaning in the farce."

Keiran kept his eyes down, continuing to offer a quiet nod every so often.

"So you ask if I want to talk about it, and I appreciate it. But I don't know what to say, man. Everyone always seems to die around me. I don't know why when I met you and Amala I thought it would somehow be different."

Keiran cupped his head with his hands. He cradled himself for a moment with a heavy sigh, pushing his hair back and stretching his arms in a fluid motion.

"The first time I killed someone, I told myself the feeling would go away. That the face would stop haunting me whenever I closed my eyes. That I would reconcile what I'd done and find a way to settle the matter within myself."

"How long did it take?" Emmett asked.

"It hasn't," Keiran answered

"Well shit, thanks, K."

"I see his face every time I close my eyes to sleep. It never recedes, Emmett. It always hurts. And it bloody well *should*. That's why we're the good guys. When you finally feel it, it remains with you forever. That's how you know that you're still human … and not a monster."

Emmett felt a pinprick of emotion within him as Keiran said this, but he shook his head as if to will any thought of it from his mind. *Not now. Not yet. It's too soon.*

"So what about all of those people on the train?" Emmett asked, quickly finding something to change the subject to. "Do you think any of them made it out alive?"

"Unlikely. I would suspect that the Revenants boarded at some point, overwhelmed the train's crew, and when we were far from any major areas and it was dark enough to provide them sufficient cover, began their rampage. Chasing passengers into fires or slowly cutting people reaps the suffering they covet and use to appease their Underdweller masters."

Emmett sighed under the weight of the unknown world he was now part of. He considered the middle-aged couple seated on the other side of the terminal, watching them talk. What would they say to the nightmares Emmett had witnessed? Even if Emmett told them everything, given them proof, could they even believe their world was more illusion than reality?

That Emmett still found himself in moments of wishing it were all fantasy told him otherwise. Watching how the husband doted on his wife while she smiled at him made Emmett think of the other helpless passengers aboard the train, running on instinct from an unseen attacker, pleading for mercy they would never find at the end of a cruel blade. They could never know the darkness that stalked the world.

The darkness that seemed to breathe; shadows that concealed unimagined cruelties. Ellie's dead, listless face melted away in his mind, replaced by a face so burdened by heavy wrinkles that it looked like an expression had been carved into a candle and then a flame lit atop its wick, sending melting wax down all sides. The Hag formed in his mind, and Emmett shuddered so visibly that Keiran noticed it, too.

Perhaps understanding Emmett's disquieted expression, Keiran shook his head quite suddenly. "No, Emmett. Don't speak of her, lest you invite her attention to you."

"Can I even ask questions?"

"You're wanting to know what she is, I suspect," Keiran said.

"Death? You know, with a capital D."

Keiran shook his head. "No. Death isn't a person; it's the inevitable end of life. Personifying death gives you the ability to negotiate with it. But you can't bargain with death. It is the end of your existence. It's neither good nor evil. It just *is*."

"So what is *she*?"

"Every culture has stories about her. Some say she greets the dead; others believe she's a harbinger of disease; others that she's a wandering spirit visiting places of great battle. But she is none of those things. She and her Black Hounds feast on the despair of the dying."

"An Old One," Emmett said.

"Yes. The normal conveyances of existence hold no interest for them. They are so old that creation holds little fascination for them. Immortal and thus removed from the moralities and ethics that bind all life, their motives are alien to us. They cannot be destroyed, and their powers are beyond ours. We avoid them at all costs."

Checking around him to be certain no one was watching in their direction, Keiran pulled his plaid sleeve back and leaned forward across the bench. "The Children are warded," he said. Revealing his tattooed arm, he turned it around so Emmett could see the back of his tricep. Tracing one finger along the unusual markings running its length, he settled on a particular ring of swirling lines that entwined several runes Emmett did not recognize.

"I am all but invisible to the Black Hounds, and only because I confronted and named her did the Hag deign to take notice of me." He pulled his sleeve back down and settled back. "Naming an Old One is a matter for another time, Emmett. Trust me when I ask you to forget you heard it and never tell anyone that I spoke it."

"Keiran, what she said about me—"

"Old Ones speak in unintelligible riddles, and they do so for reasons known only to them. Perhaps they have lived so long that what some would call prophecies are simply patterns to them. Who can say?"

"She knew things about me," Emmett pressed. "When I opened my eyes, she knew I was an only child. Hell, she knew my full name!"

"The eyes are a conduit for many beings. She knows you now, and whatever that should mean for your life, we will simply have to face it as it occurs. But talking of her more than necessary is just an invitation for her renewed attention, and I daresay you would benefit from less of it," Keiran said with finality.

Emmett understood Keiran's gentle admonishment, and though he wanted to ask more, he stopped when he saw the bus pulling up to the terminal.

Keiran motioned to Emmett. "Time can offer us distance. Let us hope for a quiet journey to the Lighthouse, yes?"

Emmett stood from the bench. "Hey, just one more question, okay?"

Keiran nodded. "Of course."

"These Old Ones ... you said that they couldn't see you. But one of them knows me now. If she comes back for me, can I be warded, too?"

Keiran did not respond with words but a firm grasp of Emmett's shoulder, nudging him toward the line forming to get onto their bus. "Pay no mind to what she said, mate. Not to deflate your ego, but the Old Ones have no interest in people, Emmett. Why expect that it would ever happen to you again?"

Emmett did not respond to Keiran's smile as they boarded the train, though something in his statement tugged at the back of his memory, leaving him feeling disquieted and apprehensive. For some reason, Emmett felt like that was not the case.

CHAPTER 17

A s the bus drove east to Chicago, Emmett tried to sort through everything, reproving his guilt. Ellie had all but killed Sebastian and had tried to kill Keiran, two Bards who had saved Emmett several times over. Killing her, however tragic, was necessary to save his own life and someone he cared about. But then his mind would argue back: *Couldn't you have disabled her without killing her? Why didn't you swing at her arm instead of her head? If you had to hit her, why do it so hard?*

When his mind challenged him, he burned with anger over those who had fallen trying to protect him and the innocent people who were unlucky enough to board his train. The image of Ellie's face staring lifelessly at him would morph in his mind into the ashen, flat reflection in the window in his dream.

Emmett had not shared the dream with Keiran. It lacked the gossamer surrealism of his life's dreams—dreams of Amala, which he dared not share with Keiran, either. No, the dream felt *too* real. Sounds and smells were appropriately specific; the air itself held suitable weight; and when he looked at what should have been his own reflection, he saw Ellie's face staring back at him as if he were looking through her own eyes at himself. It was just like the waking dream Amala had woken him from in

Portland and promptly told him never to tell anyone of. What that ultimately meant, he could not say.

He eventually grew exhausted thinking of Ellie and the train. He thought of Amala, feeling her holding his hands in the cave beneath Silvan Dea. And he thought of *Belshazzar's Feast*, and Amala's recitation of the words in the air above the king.

Only a few days ago, Emmett had been preparing for a fateful drive through the cold interior of the Florida Panhandle. The words had always been there, seemingly meaningless and yet suddenly now one piece of a greater mystery. As if seeking some affirmation for his decision to abandon his Houstonian *unlife*, he had left seeking purpose in the promise of the open, unending road.

Seated now on a bus driving through the Midwest and seeking sanctuary until he could be cured of a preternatural disease that would likely kill him, Emmett wondered if he had become Belshazzar.

Will I be weighed and found wanting?

The remainder of the bus ride was fortunately uneventful. With nothing to discuss of importance that couldn't also be overheard, Keiran eventually kept Emmett distracted by talking endlessly about soccer. This had the added problem of confusing Emmett, who required a fair amount of education on how the sport worked and the basic politics of football clubs throughout the United Kingdom. Otherwise, the hours of Keiran discussing the particularities of the Dragons' current roster held little attention for him other than it distracted him until their bus pulled onto the traffic-laden Chicago roadways.

"Before we head to Nova Scotia, I'm going to need some more money. I have no way of knowing if the Revenants discovered information on our accounts," Keiran told Emmett as they exited the bus. "An unattached financial source and full night's sleep would both be ideal. Amala and I have a contact here in Chicago who can help us."

The Chicago skyline's glimmering walls of glass that rose in every direction held a commanding, austere beauty to them. With their few remaining dollars, they caught a cab to Keiran's contact. Between towering skyscrapers defiantly stood a run-down, two-story home with a poorly patched, slanting roof, boarded windows, and bricks littered with graffiti.

Emmett raised an eyebrow at Keiran as he walked past him up the short steps to the front door. Keiran knocked three times before taking a single step back and brushing his hair aside, stiff-ening his shoulders straight and confident.

"We're closed," a gruff voice barked from the other side of the door. "Can't you read the sign?"

Though Keiran did not look, Emmett did, and he saw a white board hanging from the side of the house. He could barely make out the words Food Pantry 10 AM through a swirling mess of gang characters layered over the sign.

"I have not come for food, brother, but rather to be fed," Keiran said simply. Something clicked from the other side of the door, locks tumbling and bolt after bolt unfastening. Finally, the heavy, burnished door swung inward to reveal an older gentle-man stooped in its frame.

Keiran held his arm straight down in front of him, and with a slow movement so as not to frighten the old man, pulled his sleeve up past his elbow. Emmett could not see the details of the man's features, but after only a moment he seemed to step back from the doorway. Keiran turned and quickly motioned for Emmett.

The door closed behind them, the old man's hands turning many locks as he secured the door. A black gentleman in his fif-ties, he stood slightly shorter than Emmett and was round at his center with a balding, gray pate and brown eyes that squinted behind a pair of bifocal lenses. He turned to regard the two of them, his bristly moustache filling out his weathered face.

Straightening his navy-blue cardigan pullover, he nodded and made approving sounds, stepping around each of them and examining them from all angles. He adjusted his glasses twice before dropping them to hang from a chain fastened to each end.

When at last it seemed that his appraisal was finished, the old man's face warmed considerably, and he held his arms open to Keiran. "I almost didn't recognize you, boy! You keep getting bigger on me each time I see you!"

The two embraced in the narrow hallway, and Emmett finally began to look around the home that they had stepped into. Nondescript but otherwise pleasant, the home had low ceilings and old wood floors. Framed portraits of an old woman and young girl lined the walls, neither of whom Emmett recognized.

"The examination was a bit much, don't you think?"

The old man waved a hand at him. "This old man's eyes had to be sure, the way they play tricks on me nowadays."

"Emmett, this is Mr. Derrick Williams."

Emmett held a hand out and nodded. "It's nice to meet you, sir."

"Call me Derrick, son. 'Sir' was my father."

"I'm glad to see the house is still standing, albeit in some state of disrepair. Why don't you let us pay for a renovation?"

"Ah, don't you start with me. You just walked in. Everything's new nowadays. Developers would rip this place right out from under me if I weren't serving meals here five times a week. Vultures," he cursed before motioning for them to follow.

They stepped into a small kitchen not much wider than their train compartment. A metal table with a pair of folding chairs was cluttered with unopened mail and clipped coupons. Stacked along the walls were tall piles of boxed canned goods and bags of rice, some standing higher than Emmett. As Emmett leaned back and looked down the hallway, he saw cases of dry goods all around the living room between rows of standing racks where all manner of clothes hung.

Derrick motioned for them to sit down as he busied himself in the old refrigerator next to the sink underneath the lone, barred window that looked out on a skyscraper.

"How are you, Keiran?" Derrick asked as he returned with a pair of glasses and a tall glass carafe of milk.

"I am well, Derrick. Very well."

"And Amala? How's my beauty doing? I do miss that beautiful smile of hers."

"She is well, too, Derrick. I'm certain that she misses you."

Derrick poured each of them a tall glass of milk and prodded them. "Growing boys need their calcium. Drink up!"

Keiran and Emmett both smiled and obliged, and it was Emmett's rumbling stomach that made him sheepishly mumble an apology.

"We were passing through the area, Derrick, and we're in need of your help."

"You name it, and it's yours."

"We need to leave Chicago and need money and a place to rest tonight. Five thousand should be sufficient, I'd say."

Emmett had to hide his blanching face. Making little more than the minimum wage he could earn working at the local drive-in during the sweltering Gulf Coast summers, his discomfort with asking for money—particularly in amounts so large—made him squirm enough that he wanted to stand up and walk out of the room.

"Done," Derrick said simply, and noticing Emmett's poorly hidden shock, he smiled in return. "The special account Annie set up for me just before she left still has thirty thousand or more sitting in it accruing interest every year. The bank is always calling me trying to sell me this or that, but I tell them to leave that money right where it is. You know I won't touch it, but whatever you need from it, it's yours."

"That's brilliant, Derrick. Thank you."

"We can buy you airline tickets tomorrow morning after you get some sleep, and we'll get you on the first flight out of O'Hare. Where are you boys heading?"

"For your own safety, Derrick, it's best that you didn't know." Keiran looked to Emmett in return. "Go ahead and show him."

Understanding as Keiran pointed to his neck, Emmett nodded and pulled the collar of his shirt down enough to expose the rotting flesh underneath. Derrick made a hissing sound and shook his head.

"No amount of convincing on your part would get you past a row of pat-downs at the airport, not with that growing down your neck. Annie had several old cars in a storage facility. All of the registrations and plates are fake. I assume you're being followed."

"Possibly," Keiran confirmed.

"How long have you had it, son?" Derrick asked, turning to Emmett. "The Rot?"

Emmett felt at a loss for words suddenly, fumbling each time he met a new person and forgetting that they understood his situation better than he did. "Uh, almost a week now."

"The last new moon?" he asked knowingly just as Keiran nodded. "Cursed things. There's already too much evil in this world without those horrible creatures running around in it. It must be getting bad by now."

Emmett shifted in the chair, as talking about the Rot often caused him to become more aware of its gnawing discomfort.

"Derrick's daughter was a Druid of Silvan Dea. He knows something of what you are going through right now with the Rot and the rather sudden acclimation to the hidden world."

Emmett stared in mute surprise at Derrick as the words settled in. Keiran had not told him where or who they were going to, specifically, and when he had looked around the aging home, he had assumed that Derrick was nothing more than a kind, old man. That his daughter was a Druid, that he understood firsthand the strange and surreal world Emmett had been plunged into, and that perhaps his perspective was one that Emmett could relate to since he was on the outside looking in, was enough to flood Emmett's mind with a thousand questions to ask.

"The finest Druid in the world, excluding Miss Amala, of course," Derrick said, almost privately to himself. Standing, he looked down at the floor and closed his eyes, whispering something too soft for Emmett to hear. Keiran lowered his eyes respectfully as well, and aware that something reverential was passing between them for his daughter, Emmett, too, lowered his head.

"I thank the Good Lord that her mother never lived to see her death," he said quietly, lifting his head. "Why don't the two of you follow me downstairs and we'll see about getting you set up. I just finished with dinner, but there are plenty of leftovers. I hope you like your food deep fried, Emmett."

Nodding, Emmett allowed his rumbling stomach to answer for him.

Though the surface level and upstairs of the home were in a state of disrepair, Derrick's basement was almost cozy, with simple, thin carpeting over a concrete floor and new wood paneling on its four walls. A large bed with a lamp and dresser sat in the far corner of the long room, along with a simple sofa, an old television that seemed capable of receiving two, grainy channels, and a kitchenette next to a small table that could comfortably seat the three of them.

"After Mabel passed away, I didn't have much else to do but sit around the house feeling sorry for myself," Derrick said from the kitchenette as he looked over his shoulder at Emmett. Unwrapping several containers of food, Derrick set different bowls out on the table for them.

"With Annie running around, the house just got too lonely. I started tinkering down here, making up all sorts of excuses to fix things that weren't broken. But I didn't have enough light, so I brought some lamps down. Then the arthritis started acting up, so I had a kitchen and bathroom installed. I was spending so much time down here that it made sense to have a bed delivered."

"Cheers, Derrick," Keiran said as he was handed another plate of food. "These are the nicest accommodations we've seen in the last two days!" Emmett abandoned all pretenses at refinement and dove hungrily into a plate of fried shrimp, okra, and sweet potato casserole.

"Well goodness, have you been starving this boy all week?" Derrick chuckled.

"Sorry," Emmett managed with a half-full mouth.

"We ate a bit at a bus terminal yesterday."

"Vending machines don't count," Emmett garbled as he ate.

"And you've been on the road for how long, exactly?" Derrick asked.

Keiran feigned a tired expression. "Days that feel like weeks, honestly. I tell you, I can't remember the last time my face touched a pillow."

"The linens are always clean here, son," he said, motioning to the bed against the far wall. "It's not much to look at, and there's not a lot of privacy."

"It's brilliant, Derrick, really."

Derrick shifted in his chair and watched Emmett hungrily eating with a satisfied smile on his face. "If Mabel were here, she'd keep you fed for days! It was all my wife could do to cook for hungry kids. The soup kitchen was her idea."

"Best meal in a long time, thank you," Emmett said as he wiped his face. "I haven't eaten real food since the train station."

"Train?" Derrick asked Keiran, and immediately Emmett regretted saying anything. "Were you boys on a train within the last few days?"

Keiran looked at Derrick as a dark, knowing expression passed between them.

Derrick's head lowered as his aged hands passed over his face. Turning around in his chair, he stood up and walked to the counter to grab a newspaper on the stove. He handed it to Keiran, who unfolded it on the table for Emmett to see as well.

The sooty black and white cover page featured the same litany of days-old news: orange juice futures affected by the heavy frost moving through Florida; a pair of double homicides in Fuller Park; the controversy surrounding a contentious call made during last weekend's sports game that had most of the nation still arguing and two famous radio commentators calling on Congress for legislative action; and a small, bleak photograph of a wreck of charred metal hiding in the small bottom-right corner of the page.

Emmett flipped through the pages to B-15 to read the story, as there simply had been no room on the front page for the story itself.

"I saw it on the news earlier but didn't think twice about it. That business with the train catching on fire and all of the people killed. That was *them*, wasn't it?"

"Yes," Keiran said as Emmett found the page and ran his

finger over the article.

The article was less than a narrow, three-inch strip of emotionless data: the date of the accident, the number of people dead, the lack of survivors, and the controversy surrounding the politicians who had taken up the cause of the train explosion to push for additional industry oversight.

"You go for months without hearing anything and start to believe that maybe they don't exist," Derrick was saying as Emmett stared at the article in an obvious state of disbelief. "Then something like this happens, and you remember how the Revenants killed your wife and daughter. All they said was that it looked like a short in one of the electrical wires, but that it would be months before they knew for certain."

"Unfortunately, Revenant cabals cover their tracks rather well," Keiran sighed. "And in several weeks, everyone will have forgotten."

"There's nothing here," Emmett mumbled as he pushed the newspaper away in disgust. "Nothing. No hint that anything out of the ordinary happened. They couldn't even be bothered to write two paragraphs. They expect people to believe this? No wonder print is dead."

"There was barely a mention of it on the network news, Emmett. Everyone is talking about last weekend's game," Derrick said as he looked down at his own hands and shook his head.

Emmett couldn't stop staring at the article, noting how small it was compared to the full-page ad opposite it advertising next month's concert. "It's not even about who's *behind* the curtain. It's like no one realizes there even *is* a curtain! Status quo and we're good to go!" Emmett cleared his throat, fixing his attention on the wall behind Derrick's head. Too much had happened for him to let go of his carefully maintained control over himself.

Not now.

"I know that look in your eyes, son. I see it in the mirror everyday. People just don't *want* to know the truth. Then one day someone they love dies, and they wake up."

Derrick pushed himself away from the table and rounded back to the kitchenette, his fists clenched tightly at his sides. Emmett felt his face flush with frustration, and yet his words were mute in his mouth when he reminded himself that while his anger was on behalf of people he did not know, Derrick's was understandably justified by his wife and daughter's deaths.

Perhaps to comfort Derrick by sharing in his anger, Emmett wanted to say something. But he saw Keiran shaking his head silently at him with a small gesture of his hand to remain silent.

"I'm getting too old, Keiran," Derrick said heavily, keeping his back to them as he gripped the counter in front of him. "You could be killed in broad daylight, and people walking by couldn't be bothered to notice except to take a picture. Babies go missing, children are sold around the world, and people just sit at home and watch it all on television like it's a movie of the week."

"There are bright spots," Keiran offered tentatively with a soft voice. Emmett watched the expression Keiran tried to affect: that calm, hopeful understanding he offered people who just needed to tell someone that they had had enough. It was an expression that Emmett knew well.

That's Keiran, Emmett realized.

Derrick turned around with an anguished look tearing at his face. "Oh, really? What would those be?"

"People like you, Derrick," Keiran smiled warmly as if he were telling a worried parent that their sick child was going to recover. "You're so devastated by your loss that you've built a new living area underneath your home so you can avoid disturbing the memories that you have above you. Your life was robbed from you, and the people responsible are still free, likely hurting others the same way that they hurt you. You have no way to ever have justice or experience some semblance of closure."

"What's your point, son?" Derrick asked, resignation in his voice.

"Yet here you are, fighting the only monsters that you can: hunger, poverty, hopelessness. You're using what I happen to know is a meager monthly benefits stipend to feed people the world has forgotten, never once touching the money your daughter left because of the honor you have for her memory. That makes you the bravest man I know, Derrick. If I came here for no other reason than this, it was to remind myself why I fight."

Derrick's anger seemed to diffuse as he collapsed back into his chair. He cast his eyes down with the look of a man who had bore too heavy a weight for too long. Keiran made no move to speak further, but he gripped Derrick by the shoulder firmly for several silent moments.

"I can still remember Mabel's funeral. It was a Sunday morning in February. She'd always wanted to be buried in her Sunday best. No one here knew what had happened to her, and we couldn't have an open casket." Derrick turned away for a moment with his hand to his mouth, but clearing his throat he continued.

"My goodness, it was a beautiful service. Emmett, I don't know how many funerals you've been to, but this one was the finest, with flowers from all over the city. She was loved by so many people. We had the service at her family's old church across town, and then we all left for the cemetery to see her buried. I'll never forget it: the weather was rainy and the funeral home had brought a tent out. They had those awful metal folding chairs next to the site. Nothing you could sit on for more than a few minutes without feeling sore."

Emmett sat rapt, reminding himself to blink even as he watched Derrick's eyes.

"The minister came over and said a final prayer when they walked the casket down. They began lowering her into the ground, and I'm sitting there holding my little girl, Annie, holding onto her so tight with all the strength I could, because she was the only reason I had left to live. And this sweet melody just appeared then in the air. The sweetest, most beautiful singing you've ever heard."

Derrick shifted in his chair to look at Emmett with directness that he was surprised did not make him uncomfortable. Not knowing Derrick, something of his despair rang so true for Emmett that he felt like he knew the man almost as well as he knew Keiran. Perhaps, in some ways, even more.

"You see, Emmett, I didn't know it at the time, but the Druid and Bard who had saved Annie, and who had tried but were unable to save Mabel, had come to her funeral. They had been there all along, way in the back by the trees. The Bard was this handsome young man." Saying this, Derrick looked at Keiran like an admiring father, and as Keiran nodded respectfully, Emmett realized who that Druid and Bard were.

"He was singing the most beautiful song for my Mabel. A paean, Annie later told me. A song praising Mabel's life and the lives that she touched. There were no words. None that I recognized, anyway. And just as the casket was lowered into the earth, a flock of snow-white doves—Mabel loved doves—flew from the trees, over her grave, and into the sky."

Derrick was weeping, smiling at Emmett with eyes filled with appreciation. "They came to honor her, Emmett. They didn't have to, but they did. In their own way."

Emmett was not certain if Derrick was reliving the memories for Emmett's sake or if he believed that Emmett needed to understand that the emotions he was experiencing were valid and true. Or, Emmett wondered, perhaps Derrick was unable to live without those memories anymore.

"Two days later, Annie left with them to learn what she needed to. I don't think I had any choice in the matter, and for years after I asked myself if I made the wrong decision in letting her go. But she needed to do it. She saw for herself what those things did to her mother, and she couldn't live not being part of it. She was always special, talking to animals even as a girl. But she never left her mama's side until they took her from her. I close my eyes at night and see her face crying over Mabel's grave. Then I hear that beautiful song they sang for Mabel, and I know Annie is with her right now."

Derrick saw the confusion in Emmett's face. "I don't think Annie could ever let go of Mabel's death. She was supposed to let go of it all when she became a Druid, and even though she hid it from all of us, I know she never did. About a year later, Annie came to me to tell me that she was certain that she knew who had killed her mother. She had that same look in her eye when we buried Mabel, that same mixture of anguish and revenge. She said she was going to finish it, track them down and bring an end to those who were responsible for so much death.

"I would have gone with her, but I was too old and worth nothing to her. These old knees can barely walk up and down those stairs anymore," he said, wiping the tears out of his eyes. "I tried everything I could to stop her. I tried to reach Amala and Keiran but couldn't find them. Annie said good-bye, and I never saw her again. A few weeks later, Amala came to see me. She had found my baby," Derrick's voice broke.

Emmett felt Derrick's pain as brilliantly as if it were his own. He saw the faces of the doomed train's passengers in Derrick's eyes. He saw the Druids and Bards who had risen to defend

Silvan Dea. He promised himself they would never leave his mind's eye. He saw in Derrick's eyes his own broken reflection, and the guilt that he was certain he could never fully let go of.

For perhaps the first time in his life, Emmett's mind was entirely silent as he spoke from his heart. "Your daughter would be proud of you. You help people now, honoring her life. Others would give up, but you live for them." And as Emmett said this, he looked from Derrick to Keiran and understood he was speaking more to himself than to either of them.

Derrick nodded. "I try my best. I don't know if it's good enough, but it's all I can do. Someday soon, I'll be going home to be with my wife and daughter, and if I can measure up halfway to the lives they led, I'll feel okay about standing in their shadow."

Emmett didn't know how to respond. Keiran, of course, allowed silence to convey his respect, and so they sat quietly as Derrick wept.

"Thank you, son," he said, putting a hand on Keiran's shoulder after several moments of silence had passed. "Thank you both for listening to an old man who can't quite manage to let go," he said as he patted Emmett's hand with his own.

Emmett did not wish to burden the man with the horror he had seen, for he knew that Derrick was someone like Emmett who would be too wounded to know how evil was continuing to infect so many people's lives. Emmett wished he could tell Derrick what his words meant to him and how they had given him the freedom—the distance, as Keiran said at the bus depot—from things he had struggled to reconcile in his mind.

"Each of us must find our own way. Some lead, others fight, or heal, or even comfort. The only crime is to know and do nothing," Keiran said.

"Emmett, hear these words from an old man who has seen

enough in this world to know what he's saying. These are good people. Don't ever lose them."

Thinking of Mrs. Carmichael, Emmett nodded and said goodnight to Derrick. Steadying himself, arthritis in his knees, the widower began the slow walk up the stairs to the bedroom he had once shared with his wife.

CHAPTER 18

With a comfortable bed and Keiran's repeated assurances that they were safe from immediate danger, Emmett permitted himself to succumb fully to his own fatigue. He welcomed the opportunity to not dwell on the murders aboard the train as the heavy dinner slowly settled in his stomach, bringing with it the blissful dreariness of approaching sleep.

Keiran had bathed first, admitting to Emmett that the strain of the past day had been the lack of clean clothes. A wardrobe along the far wall was filled with several suitable outfits, all of which Keiran said that he and Amala kept at Derrick's should they ever have need.

"I'll tell you this much, there's nothing that can raise one's spirits more perfectly than a well-tailored outfit," Keiran had admitted to Emmett. Emmett lay on the bed watching with heavy eyes as Keiran pulled various clothes from the wardrobe for the two of them, nodding occasionally or absently mumbling agreement to something Keiran would say as he felt himself giving over to a deep sleep.

At some point between Keiran matching pants to socks and billowing steam pouring from the bathroom's slightly ajar door, Emmett's eyes closed. Too often restless when his body was tired, his mind acquiesced to a swollen presence of silence and quieted itself for sleep. As the previous day's events effortlessly fell away, Emmett rolled onto his side and tucked one hand underneath his head. He relaxed as Keiran disappeared behind the bathroom door.

Some time passed as Emmett relaxed, the room dark save for a narrow beam of light coming from the slightly ajar bathroom door. The room was empty, and assuming Keiran had gone upstairs for something, Emmett rose for his turn in the bathroom. He sighed with a long stretch, pushing himself upright and plodding across the room.

His eyes narrowed even to the small blue nightlight behind a fake clamshell on the bathroom's sole outlet. It was just enough light to see the tiny white square tiles along the floor. He felt a prickling all along his skin, a reminder of how horribly filthy the past two days had been and everything he had experienced.

Closing the bathroom door, he peeled his clothes off into a pile at his feet and turned the shower knob. The shower responded soon with warm water. Stepping in and closing the beige curtain, he allowed himself the simple luxury of water pouring down and over his face, slowly washing away the layers of blood and gore that, though long since gone, he felt still coating his skin.

Emmett stood leaning against the wall for some time, his mind drawing blissfully blank as he rinsed his hair and body clean. When at last he finally turned the water off and drew the shower liner back, he smiled when he saw a pair of thick towels sitting atop a stack of fresh pajamas laid along the rim of the sink.

They're still warm from the dryer, he thought, feeling the thick towels in his hands. He loved the feeling of a heated towel after stepping from a shower into the chilling cold of a home in winter.

The thought formed somewhere distant and unbidden in his mind as he ran the warm towel over his face. *He's going to spoil me.*

After drying himself off, he pulled a pair of comfortable wool pajama bottoms on and snaked himself into a long thermal shirt that snugly clung to his lanky frame. He ran his towel over his floppy hair again, wringing out the moisture before draping the towel over the sink. Lifting one edge up, he wiped a broad swath of fog from the mirror and looking up felt his mind jump with such a start that he thought he might scream.

A pale, narrow face framed by wet, blond hair stared back at him from the mirror. It was Ellie's face: flush with life and blinking as if seeing her reflection for the first time. He looked down at himself, feeling with his hands his own skin. He saw his own naked body beneath him, the Rot spreading across the white flesh of his chest, the small birthmark just above his hipbone. It was a young man's body. It was *his* body.

He looked again into the mirror, and the billowing steam had clouded its image once again. Drawing the towel across the mirror—slower and more deliberate this time, as if hesitant yet curious of the reveal—he saw Ellie's face staring back at him with an expression he knew could only be his ... with eyes of both horror and wonder and lips that barely moved as he slowly mouthed words of confusion.

What the hell? Am I dreaming?

Emmett looked around the bathroom and pushed himself into the acuteness of his own senses. It couldn't possibly be a dream, he kept telling himself. His dreams were always the same: a young woman who he now knew had been Amala speaking to him of a portrait he now knew had once hung in his mother's apartment.

This moment, though, was contiguous. Grounded. Emmett felt the steam from the shower still moistening his skin; he heard the faintest buzz from the nightlight as its bulb struggled not to burn out; even in the air he breathed, he tasted the soap that remained on his lips; and he felt his own presence within his body, conscious of his own physicality and the boundaries of his arms, hands, and even fingers.

This is not a dream.

Someone coughed loudly, and Emmett jumped with a start. The bathroom door swung open, and Emmett recoiled with a start as he lifted his hand to defend himself.

"What's the matter with you?" an unfamiliar voice said to him.

Over his raised fist and tense, half-closed eyes, Emmett saw a young man standing framed in the doorway, a curious expression on his face. He was probably several years older than Emmett, with short golden-brown hair that was flattened along his forehead over a pair of dark eyes. He stood naked, casual, and with a playful grin raised both hands up above his head.

"I'm unarmed," he laughed as he put his hands back down. "I just came in to get a glass," he said as he pointed first and then picked up a small glass on the sink.

With alarming recognition, Emmett imagined clothes covering his athletic, nude form, and with suddenness he recognized Troy Brooks, Ellie's brother, standing in front of him.

When Emmett did not immediately lower his fist, the young man narrowed his eyes with a grin and tilted his head. "You still on edge, Elle?" he motioned with a hand at Emmett's raised fist, and with a gentle motion lowered Emmett's hand with his own. Emmett felt his body refusing to relax, though there was unmistakable softness in the young man's touch.

My God, what the hell is going on? Emmett screamed into his mind.

When Emmett said nothing, the young man stepped closer into the space separating them. Immediately, Emmett recoiled from their naked awkwardness and, casting a glance in the mirror, saw Ellie's nude form folding itself inward as her arm came over to cover the front of her body.

The young man stopped within inches of him and placed his hand on the back of his neck. It was an intimate expression that set the hairs along his arms on edge. There was unsettling closeness between their bodies, and Emmett wasn't certain what he found more troubling: that two siblings embraced naked, or that each time he looked in the mirror he saw Ellie's reflection as his own.

"Hey, we don't have to do this, okay? If you don't want to, we can walk away. We're only here right now because *you* wanted to be here. But we can leave. If that's what you're afraid of, don't be."

Without realizing that it was happening, Emmett felt words form in his mind as if a separate consciousness shared the space with him. The words came fully formed and unbidden as if an aspect of himself were conversing wholly and separately apart from him, yet using his body to do so.

"What about Kellner?" he heard himself ask in response with a feminine voice that he immediately realized was not his own. "We need his resources." It was Ellie's voice, though it sounded so unlike what Emmett had heard before, with a calm, straightforward manner.

"To hell with him, okay?" Troy said as he reached his other arm around and tried to pull them together in embrace. "He's a fool. He doesn't have your ambitions. Just kill Kellner and take his place. No one has the power to challenge you. And you've got me."

Ellie pushed away and took another step back as Emmett's mind raced with confusion, this time his heels touching against the shower stall.

"Fine, whatever," Troy said with frustration. "I don't get you sometimes. You're afraid of Kellner, yet you're the one who was saying just two days ago how you were going to kill him and take control! So which is it with you?" Troy's body tensed noticeably as his hands motioned in the air with his raised voice.

The firm seat of Emmett's mind felt only confusion and an overwhelming need to run, yet that second aspect within his mind, the odd, separate consciousness that seemed to speak on its own with Ellie's voice, suddenly felt a hot flush of anger. Pure, raw anger.

"Shut up!" she spat as she stepped forward. His hand—Ellie's hand—flew out with a stinging, loud slap across Troy's face. "He'll never let us in if he knew what I had planned! He'd never allow us to move against the Children!"

When the second awareness within his mind spoke and acted, it did so independently as if Emmett were in the audience of a theatrical production, both watching as a scene played out before him yet feeling the full emotion of the experience from the actors' performances.

"We proceed as planned," Ellie said through his gritted teeth, as if to quell the racing pulse that pounded within his chest. "We need Kellner. For now. Once our contact within the Grove is secure, we move against Silvan Dea. And I won't hear of your fear again."

Emmett watched as Troy's face changed from frustration to bitterness. The slap had done nothing to his jaw, yet his eyes seemed to glass over with a wounded expression. Perhaps not that the slap itself hurt, but rather what it had symbolized. Emmett had not sensed fear in him when he had been speaking, but instead some kind of concern and a willingness to abandon their plans for Ellie's sake.

"Fine," he said heavily, turning away and walking out of the bathroom.

Emmett allowed himself to catch his own breath as his mind reeled: What was Ellie's relationship to Troy? Who was this Kellner? They spoke of him as if he was the leader of the Revenant sect. And their plans to attack Silvan Dea—did that mean he was watching something from the past play out before him? Some kind of vision of what preceded the attack?

Then Ellie's words resounded again in his mind. *Once our contact within the Grove is secure, we move against Silvan Dea.* The words echoed with shocking clarity, and Emmett stared back at the sullen face in the mirror.

Who the hell are you?

"Emmett?" a distant, hazy voice called out. Turning his head toward the door, he felt a wave of disorientation as the bathroom shifted around him, jerking itself in strange contortions as his vision blurred.

"Emmett?" Again, a voice called out his name. It was closer now and warmly familiar. It was Keiran. In the darkness, he heard Keiran calling his name. His consciousness—alone again without the second aspect—emerged from beneath the gelatinous surface of sleep and opened his eyes, light and sound rushing in all at once.

"All right, seven sleeper? Time for a spot of breakfast, then," Keiran's voice sounded as Emmett struggled to open his eyes. The room was fully awash in light, and Emmett squinted against the spots in his vision.

"Bright," he felt himself croaking with a dry mouth, recognizing through his own muddled senses that he spoke once again with his own voice.

"Aye, apologies," he heard Keiran saying as he switched off the overhead lights above the bed. "I've been trying to wake you for several minutes now, actually. I never knew you were such a heavy sleeper. Sleep through the end of the world, I daresay."

"I'm not," Emmett said, licking his lips and swallowing as he struggled to wake.

"Could have fooled me, mate," Keiran responded. "It's half past seven. I'd like to get on the road within the hour. There are towels and toiletries on the sink, and I hung the clothes I thought might fit you on the right side of the wardrobe. I have some things to discuss with Derrick upstairs, so take your time. But let's try to get a move on," Keiran said just before leaving the room, his voice bouncing with an irritating cheeriness that Emmett found ill-suited for the early morning.

In his grogginess, Emmett rolled over onto his stomach and buried his face in his pillow. Already, his mind was attempting to make sense of his dream. It was, indeed, a dream, Emmett reasoned.

What about anything that happens to me is normal?

Peeling his shirt off in the bathroom, he winced as the fabric tugged at the Rot. He traced his finger around its perimeter, which was now crawling down toward his abdomen. Turning around, he looked back over his shoulder and found that the Rot was spreading along his back, too, at an alarming rate.

For only the briefest moment, he wondered if he was still dreaming. That his dream had seemed so convincingly real earlier made him second-guess himself now. Yet Keiran had spoken to him as Emmett, and staring into the mirror now, he saw his tousled, floppy black hair and the decaying stretch of the Rot crawling down his body.

Showering was both uncomfortable and dully painful. He attempted hot water, which produced throbbing discomfort deep in his chest; cooler water sent shocks of brittleness along the edges of the Rot. No matter what he did, the pain was becoming increasingly unavoidable, and though he showered for ten minutes, the pain itself never grew tolerable. It was all he could do to grind his teeth against the soreness as he rinsed and then carefully toweled himself dry.

Ascending the stairs a short time later, he followed the distant sound of discussion back to the upstairs kitchen.

"Good morning, son," Derrick said brightly as he motioned for Emmett to join them at the small table. "Coffee?"

"No, thank you," Emmett said as he sat down.

Keiran sat in the chair next to him, obviously refreshed from a full sleep and impeccably dressed once again. His face was cleanly groomed, and he was wearing a pair of gray, tailored pants with a well-fitted, long-sleeve dress shirt the color of soft pink tulips tucked in underneath a black belt whose flat silver buckle matched his diamond-shaped silver cufflinks.

You would never know what he's been through in the past forty-eight hours.

"All right?" Keiran said as he counted through a wad of money in his hands.

Derrick returned from the stove holding a bowl of steaming oatmeal and sliced peaches dusted lightly in cinnamon that bobbed along in the center of the oatmeal. Into this he poured a generous helping of fresh cream as he placed the bowl down in front of Emmett. Setting a napkin and spoon down, Derrick returned to his conversation with Keiran.

"When you boys are ready, we'll go get the car."

"And then you *are* going to leave, yes?" Keiran asked, and it was obvious to Emmett that they had already discussed this because Derrick sat back in his chair and made a dismissive gesture with his hand.

"I have never run from these people, and I don't intend to start doing it now."

"This isn't like last time. I cannot guarantee that they won't track our movements here to Chicago, and if they do, you're in danger. You must disappear for a while."

Derrick was still shaking his head. "I won't run from them. Even after they killed Annie, I've always been safe here."

"That's because Amala and I lived across the street for three months," Keiran added, and Emmett saw the look of surprise on Derrick's face at the revelation. "Yes, Derrick, we relocated to Chicago. Amala didn't want to tell you because she knew how crushed you were by losing Annie. The last thing she wanted was for you to live in fear of your own life, as well."

"I didn't have much to live for, anyway," Derrick admitted.

"Annie would never have wanted you to be murdered as her mother was," Keiran added. Personalizing the issue with the memory of his daughter seemed to work as Derrick finally nodded in agreement.

"I've been meaning to visit my cousins down south, anyway."

"A proper holiday," Keiran offered with a smile, patting his hand on Derrick's arm. "When we are confident of your safety, we'll contact you."

Emmett saw a look of regret in Keiran's face, and he felt the same regret acutely, too. Once again, someone's life was affected by his presence, that perhaps even death was a risk.

"The weather report said they're expecting a snow flurry from up north. I don't have it left in my back to shovel out there. So at least I get to avoid that," Derrick said with forced humor.

"Best you tuck in and eat before we get on the road," Keiran said to Emmett.

The morning remained uneventful. Derrick took twenty minutes to pack several suitcases while they waited. Keiran seemed preoccupied, often staring off at pictures of Annie along the walls. Not wanting to add to an already complicated situation, Emmett said nothing of his dream.

When Derrick was ready, he looked around the house once and shook his head, having each of the boys carry a suitcase for him as he locked several external bolts on the front door. Derrick drove them in his station wagon along the congested arteries of suburban Chicago, taking Lake Shore Drive north as it wound through the harbor district and hugged the Lake Michigan coastline.

When they finally reached a storage center on the outskirts of the city, Derrick handed Keiran a set of keys to the locked garage he had parked directly in front of. Several minutes later, Emmett and Keiran had rolled the unassuming car out of the opened garage and, filling it with a portable tank of gas Derrick had purchased earlier, tested the engine with a satisfying rumble.

"Thank you, Derrick, for everything," Keiran said as they embraced.

"Oh, it's nothing, son," he said as he stepped back and turned to Emmett. "You take care of each other," Derrick said as he extended his hand to shake Emmett's. "I want you to come visit me in July for my slow-cooked ribs. Put some meat on those skinny bones of yours."

"Thanks, Derrick."

"And the same goes for you, Keiran," he continued, looking at Keiran. "Bring Amala with you, understand? Tell her I miss that gorgeous smile of hers."

"Aye. Travel safe, my friend."

"I'll be thinking about all three of you," Derrick said finally and, rolling his window up, backed his car up and turned out to exit the storage center.

Keiran smiled and motioned to the rumbling car. "You drive. I'll navigate."

"Road trip incoming," Emmett said excitedly as he jumped into the driver's seat.

Under the crowded Chicago skyline, they pulled out of the storage center, turning right where Derrick had turned left. Answering the call of the endless road, they headed northeast toward the Canadian border and the Grove of Dr. Omar Hazrat.

CHAPTER 19

Keiran's piping-hot tea and Emmett's appropriately themed holiday mint cocoa exhaled billowing steam in their cup holders as the two continued on their journey. They filled the passing hours with absentminded discussion about random things, never tiring of talking or laughing. Keiran shared his love of opera, of Renata Tebaldi and Maria Callas's performance of "Ave Maria," in particular, and his love of jazz. Emmett, in turn, named his favorite indie bands and bemoaned his broken phone and lack of music for the ride. When Keiran said "hipster music" was something he hadn't heard of, Emmett roared with laughter at Keiran's confused expression.

Hours of in-depth film deconstruction consumed the long drive, Keiran obliging Emmett's passion with countless questions. At one point, Emmett insisted they pull off the highway so he could use both hands to perform a particular scene. When driving resumed, Keiran asked him the relatively simple question of what his favorite movie was. This lead to a day-long treatise of Emmett cataloguing the films of the "twin Davids of Truth"—David Cronenberg and David Lynch—and how every element of life could be traced back to a scene in one of their movies. And through it all, mind-bendingly complex as it was, Keiran listened with rapt attention.

Keiran also talked of his childhood, painting a windswept vista of coastlines and rolling hills of South Wales. He described summers spent along the River Tawe. He spoke of a youth consumed with the Eisteddfod, the nine-hundred-year-old Welsh festival celebrating his people's language, coastal-inspired food, romantic literature, and the songs, poetry, and theatre of the bardic tradition—the bards of *known* history, not the Bards of seeming fantasy that had come alive for Emmett.

When talk turned to Amala, Keiran hesitated. Emmett could see his worry, and as much as Emmett longed to hear about her past, he saw how difficult it was for Keiran to talk about her without worrying over her safety. Seeing this and recognizing the connection they shared as Companions only made Emmett feel low himself, conflicted as he was by his feelings for her and his value of Keiran's sincere friendship.

Taking no chances that their movements could be traced, they crossed the border into Canada using fake names without corresponding photo identification. This proved simple enough with Keiran's money and Bardic powers. They abandoned the car once inside Canada; Keiran was concerned that logging of their license plates could prove problematic if Derrick had stubbornly returned home and was captured.

They paid cash for another bus from a small town to Halifax. A commercial truck towing fish cargo from upstate New York was happy to give them a lift into town, where they finally exited and began the long walk toward Dr. Hazrat's isolated Grove. It was much colder than Chicago, something the boy from the humid South could not begin to imagine was even possible.

As the city disappeared and ceded to the woodlands beyond, Emmett felt as if he were entering a place hidden behind the veil of the modern world. Against the midday sun, storm clouds encroached from the north, the sky bruised with swirls of black and purple overhead. The long, narrow road wound through the forest, providing no markers to indicate where they were going.

As the road turned at a break in the tree line, Emmett could see the first hints of the Lighthouse. He had half-expected an actual lighthouse poised over a cliff, and though he could hear the distant crashing of ocean waves and tasted the Atlantic's salty spray on the wind, Emmett was surprised instead by the awesome presence that Omar Hazrat's Grove commanded.

It was an elegant, architectural expression of a New England colonial mansion, with its wide stone foundation and tiled roofline. Its Dutch Gothic-style red brick walls and gray corner-stones framed a towering inspiration of English Tudor design, with irregular chimneys and large waterspouts lining the roof-top. Strong, vertical lines of masonry ran up lofty spires crowned by stone animal statutes that rode along curved brick arches. The elegant columns were four stories high with rows of spires and parapets lining the roofline rising at least another fifteen feet. Keiran explained that whereas Silvan Dea was grown from living rock, the Lighthouse was built brick by brick by its members.

The iron gates featured heavy bars topped with intricate leafy designs. At its center conjoining the two gates, metal was shaped into a massive crest of a lion's head, its gaping maw biting down on a twisting, writhing form that Emmett immediately recognized as a Revenant.

"That's your one-sheet teaser right there," Emmett snarked.

Keiran reached for a large chain that hung off of a lattice protruding from one of the gate's pillars and pulled down, releasing finally after feeling tension.

"Let me do the talking," Keiran whispered, to which Emmett nodded.

Creaking, the iron gates soon swung in toward the grounds.

Unlike Silvan Dea, the Lighthouse sat coldly within a bevy of bare, craggy trees washed in the salty ocean winds. A stone path wound through what Emmett quickly realized was a cemetery, with impressive stone mausoleums and markers arranged along the grounds. Stacked rock walls capped with stone statuary accented by dense ivy growth snaked through the grounds.

"The honored dead," Keiran said, his disagreement evident on his face. "They do not forget their fallen."

"What's wrong with that?"

"A lot of bad decisions get made in honoring the memory of others."

Emmett saw Keiran staring behind Emmett. Emmett knowingly followed his stare as he turned around and tried to hide his own startled jump. Standing about fifty feet away from them next to one of the mausoleums, a pair of figures stood silently as they watched them. Emmett could not see their faces, for they were bundled in large jackets whose fur-lined collars sat just above their ears.

"Patrols," Keiran remarked. "Come on."

"We aren't the droids you're looking for," Emmett said back and wondered if Bardic ears would hear him over the howling coastal wind.

They soon reached the manor entrance as both doors swung soundlessly open. In their shadow stood a young, fair-skinned boy appearing no older than fifteen, medium height and thin in a pressed black suit and starched white shirt, with a matching vest across which hung a silver chain, and tucked underneath was a bold, blood-red silk tie.

"*Bienvenue, mes frères,*" the young boy said with a high voice, his curly blond hair falling forward into the soft lines of his cherubic face as he lowered his blue eyes reverently and bowed low before them.

When Keiran remained still, Emmett did not bow in response.

"Thank you, Eitan," Keiran said. "I have come to seek sanctuary from…"

" … *oui*, your intentions are known to the Ovate," he said, his English weighted with his French-Canadian accent. His long eyelashes blinked several times as he moved a manicured hand forward across his face to brush the long, blond curls from his eyes.

After a moment of silence where Keiran only stared at the boy without a readable expression on his face, Eitan turned in place on finely polished black dress shoes, motioning with a small hand for the pair to enter.

Emmett felt the cold exterior winds drawn behind him as the large doors closed. Folded within his heavy coat, he felt the draft from the towering ceilings above him. His eyes adjusted to the large shadows covering entire swaths of the foyer, seeing that the marble entrance rose nearly thirty feet overhead to a circular dome of thick glass, at the center of which hung a large chandelier whose hundred or so candles cast the trio in a soft glow.

Eitan stepped in front of them with his hands folded neatly behind his back. He swiftly escorted them down the narrow corridor that lead underneath a sweeping stairwell, the corridor lined with oil paintings of men Emmett did not recognize, gilded mirrors, and wall sconces holding candles. Its narrow width was eclipsed by its greater height, its arched ceilings ending in a curved point that ran its full length. Whereas Silvan Dea felt like a flowing stream of earth, the Lighthouse was a testament to a grand, cold European estate.

The corridor ended at a pair of wooden panels that opened into a small velvet-lined compartment the three entered. The floor immediately lurched underfoot, and Emmett heard the whirring motors of an old elevator churn for several minutes as he felt the car steadily lowering them deep underground. It was all he could do to focus on staring at the back of Keiran's neck to remain focused, the looming feeling of the enclosed space all around him.

The silence made the space feel even more confined. Eventually, the elevator halted to a stop, and the panels slid open. They exited and continued down a winding corridor until the hallway turned and emptied into a massive great room carved seemingly from the deep earth itself.

The room rose nearly four stories high to a grand ceiling whose intricate carvings and detail Emmett could barely see at such a distance. Long tasseled tapestries of deep burgundy hung on the earthen walls between large fireplaces carved fifteen feet wide out of solid rock.

At the opposite end stood the most impressive feature: a sheer wall of immeasurable blue, swirling with eddies that flashed streaks of brilliant silver and yellow. Noting the fish and shadow of lumbering giants floating just beyond the blue wall, Emmett realized it was the ocean itself—seemingly held at bay by some invisible force. A length of water extended outward like a lava tube, and at its end it fanned out like a shell. The water's currents undulated in the air, and in its magnificence, it appeared as if the ocean itself had grown an arm and reached out into the cavernous room.

"Seriously. Hashtag more cave," Emmett mumbled under his breath, awed as he was by the spectacle.

Framed in the shell-like shape of water sat a single, high-backed chair. Seated comfortably in it was a lone gentleman. The young boy quickly walked the length of the great room and turned to stand just to the side of and behind the gentleman. Emmett looked to Keiran, who took one step in front of him and inclined his head in a small bow.

"Ovate of the Lighthouse, Elder of the Children, Guardian of the Song. May it please the Turk of the Northern Storm, I present our brother from Silvan Dea, Keiran Glendower," the young boy intoned formally with a squeaking voice that echoed through the cavernous room.

"Dr. Hazrat, I humbly request sanctuary."

Dr. Hazrat rose from his chair and glided across the room, closing the distance within moments. He commanded an impressive height and strong frame, his black hair and thin beard trimmed short and neat along his powerfully built jawline with flecks of silver accenting his gray eyes and hair. He wore a finely tailored suit with a bold yellow tie over which draped a charcoal-colored, double-breasted frock coat with peaked lapels, fitted sleeves tapering the full length of his long arms.

"My young brother, it pleases me that you have returned to us," Dr. Hazrat said with a deep, richly baritone voice that hinted at an almost-velvety purr.

Keiran motioned to Emmett. "Emmett Brennan, an Underdweller survivor."

Dr. Hazrat turned to Emmett, the fine lines of his face belying a gentle age of tempered wisdom. "Welcome to the Lighthouse, Mr. Brennan. As my guest, you enjoy both the comforts and protection of my Grove," he said with an extended hand.

Emmett felt the lyrical quality of his voice as if the finest silk were lightly draped over his ears, and almost immediately Emmett felt himself swept up in the power of his countenance. Dr. Hazrat was the first Elder he had met, and his was the poise that comes to those who command immeasurable strength. Emmett felt both lightheaded and breathlessly without words as his gray eyes moved across his face.

Emmett thanked him with a nod, unsure what to say. His eyes felt drawn by a dark shadow over Dr. Hazrat's shoulder, seeing something large churn in the deep blue waters beyond the great wall.

"I apologize that you have been waiting this long for treatment for the Rot," Dr. Hazrat said plainly, his eyes looking at Emmett's covered neck. At that mention, Emmett blinked, his attention returning to the Elder.

"Thank you."

Dr. Hazrat took a step back, spreading his arms in an open gesture. "As you have already been called by the Archivist, my power would not heal you."

Emmett fought the urge to look accusingly at Keiran. In the maelstrom of the week's events, Emmett had not stopped to ask why another Elder could not heal him. He felt flush with questions whose possible answers could have left him angry.

"We still have another week," Keiran said with a clipped tone to his voice that seemed to suggest he wished to redirect the subject. "Until then, we needed to find refuge from Revenants still pursuing us."

Dr. Hazrat bent his arms behind his back, turning to look upon the great wall of deep-blue water before him. Emmett saw another dark shape glide through the waters.

"Revenants would not dare attack the Lighthouse. Their futile attempts to garner the necessary strength within one hundred miles of us do not go unnoticed by me. It is troubling that after so many centuries of Revenants avoiding direct confrontation they choose this moment right now to act so *openly*."

Keiran remained silent, Emmett following his lead.

"I was, of course, quite disturbed to hear of your message of Silvan Dea's loss. And the recent train attack by the same force. All passengers dead by fire except *certain* passengers under aliases unaccounted for. I have already made the necessary arrangements for the security footage to conveniently disappear.

We would not want Mr. Brennan to become a wanted man, would we?" he asked.

After a moment's silence, Dr. Hazrat returned to his chair. Smoothing the fans of his frock coat, Dr. Hazrat turned and sat down upon his throne, holding sovereignty over the room and everyone within.

"The attack on Silvan Dea was not isolated. The embers still burn at our southern Grove in Brazil, apparently attacked at the same time as yours."

Keiran could not hide his shock. "Did anyone survive?"

"I have not heard from *La Pastora* or her Attendant, Allessandro. I have already sent Druids to *Arquipélago de Fernando de Noronha*. If it were not for our routine purging of this area, I would assume an attack against us was imminent."

Dr. Hazrat paused as his words traversed the length of Keiran's drawn face.

"Necessity has nonetheless dictated our security be increased."

"I know. I saw them trailing us from the city's limits," Keiran said.

"Indeed. Oliver has always considered you the observant tactician."

Emmett could sense Keiran's tension. Not following all being discussed, he understood that what was happening was greater than even he and his connection to the Archivist.

The interplay that passed between Dr. Hazrat and Keiran was unquestionably tense. Though Emmett felt himself bursting with questions, Keiran's repeated warnings held his tongue.

When neither spoke, Dr. Hazrat finally broke the stalemate. "Keiran, this attack against Silvan Dea surprises you? That the *daoi-syth* followers openly attack our Groves?" Emmett heard a gentle urging in his words like a patient father nudging his child along toward a conclusion or understanding the child had yet to learn.

"They did in the past when the dark magiks were openly practiced," Keiran said. "All nine Groves have been rebuilt within the last millennia. The Lighthouse was moved to the New World shortly after the attack against it in the village of Eyam in 1665, was it not?"

"Indeed, you know your history well," Dr. Hazrat said, a smile playing across his face as if the child approached the end of his lesson. "But in an age of sophisticated computers, would it not be foolish to openly attack us? Even now, the American government is investigating every tiny particle from the train, every scrap of metal touched. How could such carelessness not lead to the Revenants' exposure, and thus to their destruction?"

"Theirs or ours? We would have more to lose if knowledge of us were publicly accepted."

Dr. Hazrat only nodded, though, never breaking eye contact with Keiran. Emmett assumed a man as poised and articulate as he must have understood the intimation, as respectfully as it might have been made. If he did, he gave no indication of any slight.

"We all have much to lose from Revenant activity. Consider Mr. Brennan here, his life nearly taken. He is why we must vigilantly seek these monsters."

With the mention of Emmett, Keiran allowed his eyes to glance sideways at him momentarily, and though he said nothing, Emmett could see that Keiran was affected by the thought.

"I confess my interest is piqued considering the risk they took in attacking that train. It would require enormous resources, suggesting both deliberateness and methodology that is not common, in my experience, of most Revenant cabals who are too often murdering each other to gain station with their

Underdweller lords. One must inevitably ask what makes Mr. Brennan so important."

Keiran quickly responded. "If their goal was to destroy Silvan Dea, that would mean they were coming for me, its lone remaining Bard."

"I see," Dr. Hazrat said, still watching Emmett. "And the attack in Noronha?"

"It is known to all Children that the Lady Karina is a close confidant of the Archivist. That would likely be known to Revenants of some power, as well, making *La Pastora's* Grove a target."

"Perhaps," Dr. Hazrat said as he slowly nodded his head, still watching Emmett's face for reaction. "I wonder, though, if there could not be another explanation, something that might not seem important to either of you." At these words, he shifted the direction of his body toward Emmett to match eyes that stared fixedly at him. "Tell me, Mr. Brennan, was there anything else that you saw during the incident with the train attack? Anything that, in retrospect, might seem important?"

Though he did not dare break eye contact with Dr. Hazrat, Emmett was certain that Keiran was watching him out of the corner of his eye. He remembered Keiran's admonishments, but now they echoed in a different way as Emmett realized how the conversation, with its engendering of trust, had subtly shifted.

What if he can tell that I'm lying?

"I don't think there's anything normal about what happened on that train," Emmett said, thankful something deft had actually come to him that didn't require a movie quotation no one but he would have understood.

Dr. Hazrat turned his gaze to Keiran. "And you? What did your powerful Bardic hearing gather that night?"

"The horror of dying passengers," Keiran said flatly.

Dr. Hazrat only nodded. "I suppose there is nothing else beyond that."

"Yes."

"Then you would agree with me, son, that something definitive must be done to confront the Revenant threat? Something more than what we do even now?" he asked, shifting his eyes between Keiran and Emmett to see any sign of reaction.

Emmett knew that, standing in his Grove and having offered his protection and sanctuary over them, Dr. Hazrat was asking Keiran where his allegiance to the Great Preclusion stood, and perhaps even which Elder's interpretation of it he held allegiance to.

Keiran must have been prepared for this, because his answer came without pause. "I do agree that everything must be done to combat darkness, and I have been sworn to do everything within *ikkibu* to fulfill my oath."

Dr. Hazrat seemed to weigh these words before responding. "Indeed," he finally said with an approving nod. "You would both benefit from a brief respite before dinner. My Attendant, Eitan, will show you to adjoining guest rooms."

Keiran bowed his head. "Thank you."

Emmett felt himself releasing the tension around his neck as their meeting drew to an abrupt close. No other words were spoken by Dr. Hazrat as he rose from his chair and, with his hands clasped behind his back, walked back to the high wall and stared silently at the churning waters beyond.

As Eitan led them out of the grand room, Emmett chanced one final look over his shoulder and thought he saw Dr. Hazrat raising a hand up to the blue as if to trace the movement of a dark shadow that swam through the water. Something Emmett had all but forgotten since the Revenant's attack tickled the back of his mind: memories of oceans, and the rain, and the deep places that humans are not meant to traverse.

Just as quickly as he remembered it, Emmett realized that Keiran and Eitan were rounding a corner of the long hallway, and he hurried to catch up.

CHAPTER 20

Emmett felt lost traveling the labyrinthine corridors of the Lighthouse. Young Eitan led them from Dr. Hazrat's reception room to the elevator and, after ascending several floors, down a series of winding hallways to a suite of connected rooms on the compound's eastern side.

Comfortably plush interiors and tasseled nineteenth-century European furnishings greeted them, their rooms facing out over the high, seaside cliff. Thick, mullioned windows barely muffled the roar of the stormy Atlantic bellowing in the distance.

A single door joined the two rooms, and after thanking young Eitan, Emmett turned the lock on his exterior door and quickly opened the door connecting to Keiran's suite.

"Is it safe to talk in here?" Emmett asked, looking around the room. "Or is yaoi boy out there going to hear us from down the hall?" he motioned to where Eitan had just departed.

"Despite our disagreements, spying would seem undignified to members of the Lighthouse," Keiran answered, opening the rosewood bureau to find a selection of fresh attire within.

"Suit yourself, but I'm watching the paintings for eyes that move."

Keiran sat down on his four-poster bed. He rubbed his

forehead and sighed before lying back with his hands tucked behind his head.

"Best you wash up before dinner."

"I'd rather skip it," Emmett said. "I'm down for New England-y, atmospheric-dread-lovin' castles just like the next cinephile, but this place exceeds the trope, K. Even for me."

Keiran shook his head. "No, they will consider it an affront if we do not show."

"I don't know if I'm up for much more of this," Emmett confessed. Seeing Keiran's exhaustion, Emmett nodded and headed back toward his suite. "Fine. I'll play along and go get cleaned up. A good carb-out at dinner might actually lead to sleep for a change."

Keiran managed a partial smile as the adjoining door closed.

Having showered and found an assortment of clothes, Emmett dressed and joined Keiran just as Eitan returned. They followed him down the stretching hallways to the grand staircase. A sorrowful chorus of mourning a cappella voices joined together within the high, echoing coffered ceilings to produce an almost hypnotic lament. Young, tender voices harmonized tenor, alto, and soprano ranges into a sustained alloy, which was contrasted by deep, repetitive baritones that added an almost tribal undertone. The effect was both resonant and profound.

"Since the founding of the Lighthouse, they have always maintained a group to sustain this song. It's the Children's paean, the song for the dead," Keiran said.

The dining room was larger than any reception hall Emmett had ever seen, with its coffered ceiling nearly three stories high above with a glass-domed rotunda open to the night's rainy sky. A long table stretched from one end to the other with seats for more than one hundred visitors. At each end of the dining hall stood massive, roaring fireplaces that cast dancing shadows against the far walls.

A crowd of Children milled about the dining room, some talking to each other in hushed tones, others standing idly. Emmett saw men and women of many ages, all healthy and strong like Keiran.

Several people were waving to Keiran, some raising their glasses in toast. Keiran smiled and gestured to them as they followed Eitan across the dining room. Emmett watched as conversations ended abruptly. As usual, Keiran never evidenced the slightest notice that he captivated so many people.

Eitan guided them through the throng, approaching the long table on the far side to stand against the far wall. A young girl walked immediately up to them holding a tray with tall-stemmed glasses filled with a dark, amber liquid. Bowing, she handed a drink to each of them in turn before retreating.

Emmett looked at the drink, sipping it cautiously at first and finding that he enjoyed the hot, buttery cider as it warmed his insides.

A man in his thirties with hands resting in his pockets stepped away from his group and walked over to them. He was broadly shouldered like Keiran, with impossibly high cheekbones featuring pronounced dimples when he smiled. His honey tweed suit accented his wavy jet-black hair and starkly blue eyes.

"Keiran Glendower," he said warmly, clasping him on the shoulder. "I'd heard you were here. How long has it been, brother?"

"Too long," Keiran answered. There was a moment of surprise on his face before he quickly recovered. "This is Emmett."

"I'm Oliver Gray," he said as he shook Emmett's hand.

Oliver turned his attention back to Keiran. "How have you

been?"

Keiran casually bobbed his head, a guarded, non-committal expression compared to what Emmett had come to expect from him. "I'm not one to complain."

"I've been meaning to contact you for quite a while. Since you're here, we can finally sit down. Can we talk tomorrow?"

"Oliver?" a sultry voice sounded behind them.

As one, they turned to see a lithe statue of exotic beauty. She was likely Amala's age, with a flawless complexion and almond-shaped black eyes that sparkled so brilliantly that Emmett thought he would be blinded by them. Her thin, high shoulders were framed in a full-length blue silk dress, and braided in her long black hair was a wreath of creamy white flowers whose intoxicating scents hinted of vanilla and honey from far-off islands.

"My midnight flower," Oliver said with the longing in his voice one hears from a lover. "Keiran, this is my Companion, 'Anoi Pua Haukea."

"It is almost time for our shared meal," she all but purred.

Oliver nodded. "Of course. We'll talk later, Keiran. Glad to see you!"

The Druid stepped between Keiran and Emmett and took Oliver's arm in her hands, guiding him away. Emmett casually shifted his weight from one foot to the other, catching Keiran's eye with his own arched eyebrow.

Keiran took another sip of his drink. "Remind me later." Keiran motioned with his head, and Emmett looked up to see Dr. Hazrat descending the stairs.

With hands folded behind his back, he maintained a confident posture, gazing out at the crowded room as all turned at his approach. He reached the bottom of the stairs and walked toward the head of the dining table, shaking hands with and nodding to different Children. The room quickly organized itself as everyone took their seats. Eitan guided Emmett and Keiran to a pair of chairs before excusing himself and joining Dr. Hazrat at the front of the table.

All fell silent looking to their Elder. Raising his arms, Dr. Hazrat slowly stood and gestured wide to those assembled. "My brothers and sisters," he began with a cavernous voice that projected down and throughout the gathering. "It is our tradition that we share one meal each day. It reminds us not only of who we are and where we come from, but of who we are meant to be and where we are going. People who cannot appreciate this are destined to wither and perish in the passing of ages."

Dr. Hazrat stepped out from his chair and, with his hands folded behind his back, slowly began to circle the table. Emmett noted the rapturous, expectant stares awaiting his next words.

"Silvan Dea and Belladonna were recently destroyed by Underdwellers and Revenants, with Dark Fire that has not been conjured in the new world in nearly a century. It is believed that even the Old Ones attended their destruction."

He paused for several moments, allowing the gasps of disbelief to pervade the room.

"This exceeds our worst fears, my Children. No word has returned from Belladonna, and as always the Archivist's whereabouts are unknown. We must assume these two Groves lost. What is to prevent more Revenants from learning of this and assaulting the remaining seven? How far will we permit darkness to pervert our world?"

Heads nodded in agreement. Continuing his circling, Dr. Hazrat continued. "Some would call us revolutionaries, even blasphemers," he chuckled, allowing others to laugh derisively. "But how can we allow evil to ravage our world, all for one group's interpretation of thousands-years-old oral traditions?

What is more important to us: dogmatism or salvation?"

Many rapped their knuckles against the table in agreement. Emmett watched their engaged expressions with rapt amazement.

"When will we command the courage to stand up and fight for what is right?" Dr. Hazrat continued, raising his powerful voice over the din of approval. "When will we possess the temerity of purpose and the boldness of character to seize our rightful destiny as defenders of all that is good, decent, and pure in our world?"

Thunderous applause responded to his call, and Dr. Hazrat stood back with an expression of satisfaction. He continued circling the table, finally stopping behind Keiran. With a raised hand, those gathered in attendance fell silent once again.

"My sons and daughters, for over three hundred years, our forbearers gathered at this very table to break bread. In this very hall, the sounds of their beautiful voices raised in chorus memorializing the honored dead. They guarded the Song of Creation, the great and varied ballad that binds all life together. Since this Grove was built here on this coast, your Elder has stood resolute in defense of our homes from all dark followers of the Leviathan."

Dr. Hazrat paused to look around the table and then continued back toward his seat. "I have asked you to heed my word, to have faith in my teachings. I ask that you continue to believe. In the coming days, we will hold fast to our faith. In this gathering, here in this home. Remember that we are the Children of the Earth, and as witnesses to the vast mysteries of creation, we broker timidity and fear for evil no longer!"

At once, all those seated around the long table stood and cheered. The excitement was such that even Emmett found himself applauding with greater feeling than he would have consciously realized he felt for Dr. Hazrat's words. Keiran applauded with a guarded expression, though, and Emmett saw that he was careful to nod whenever Dr. Hazrat was looking in their general direction.

After several minutes of exultation, Dr. Hazrat finally motioned for them to sit as he retook his chair. Servants appeared carrying large silver serving plates of hot food. Keiran and Emmett set to selecting from platters of roasted meats and fishes with large bowls of yams and bright-yellow or deep-green squash. Fresh, cracked loaves of bread still warm from the oven were placed on wooden boards with bowls of freshly churned salted butter and ceramic pots of scented honey. Last were delivered dishes of cinnamon-dusted fruit cobblers with sweet icing drizzled over doughy lattices.

"This is what I call a meal," Emmett said as he dug in, giving himself permission to overlook the surreal experience of the pre-meal speech and simply enjoy the large feast before him.

Keiran nodded as he arranged several items on his own plate. The people around the table ate largely without speaking, several conferring quietly, but otherwise observing a silence that was accentuated by the continued melodies in the distance.

"Emmett Brennan," Dr. Hazrat called from down at the end of the table. Any lingering discussions suddenly stopped, and all in attendance turned as one to look at him. Even the clattering of utensils grew silent, and Emmett felt everyone's eyes focused intently on him.

FFS, he thought as the bottom of his stomach fell out.

He felt Keiran's hand pat the side of his leg, to which he relaxed somewhat.

"Sir?" Emmett responded, wiping his mouth with his napkin.

"You are our newest guest at our table, and yet we know so little about you. Would you tell us where you come from?" Dr. Hazrat cocked an elbow up on one of the arms of his chair.

"Well, uh, I'm from Texas."

"Family?"

Emmett felt himself flush. He knew things would be simpler if he simply said none. Yet he had his experience with beings that could see into the truth of his soul through his eyes, and the last thing he wanted was for Dr. Hazrat to call him a liar in front of Keiran and the Lighthouse.

"Foster care," Emmett answered truthfully. "I have no one else."

Emmett felt Keiran pat him reassuringly on the leg at this.

Dr. Hazrat drank from his glass and then set it down. "Do you know of your parents?"

Again, Emmett felt heat rise in his face as all Druids and Bards at the table looked to him for his response. "I don't know who my father was. I only know my mom died after having me." He looked down, conscious that his stumbling was more pronounced than anything he could possibly say. He already wished he had said nothing.

"Fascinating," Dr. Hazrat said from behind his steepled fingers. "Fascinating. You can see it in his eyes even now, can't you?" he asked to no one in particular.

Emmett's eyes flashed upward noticeably with Dr. Hazrat's choice of words.

"Please do not mistake my comment for a sign of disrespect of your upbringing," he said soothingly as he motioned with a hand around the table. "You need not feel shame among others who share in your pain, your brothers and sisters."

Dr. Hazrat then leaned toward his Attendant. "Take Eitan here, an orphan in Saint-Philippe, Quebec, fleeing the abusive home he had once been a prisoner in to the false promise of comfort offered by the streets of Montreal. Homeless, starving, and relying on the generosity of strangers, which does not come without its own price. But that was before I found him and gave him a home and a family."

Emmett saw that most of the Lighthouse members nodded at this statement, and out of the corner of his eye he saw Keiran cast his eyes down at the table.

"Look at Eitan now: a respectable young man with a future of his own making and a family to support him on each step of his journey." Dr. Hazrat passed an extended arm over the entire table. "All of this is possible because of our Grove. You'll find a similar story with every Druid or Bard that you meet here."

Emmett felt the burden of the continuing stares from the other Children, and as Dr. Hazrat fell silent and looked at him, he felt that he had to say something.

"Why is that?" Emmett asked with feigned curiosity, wanting only to leave. "Why the same story?"

"Most never ask the 'what' of a situation, fewer ask the 'how,' and the fewest ask the 'why.' I commend you," he smiled without a hint of condescension, toasting Emmett with his glass.

"But that is the question, isn't it? Why? I, of course, have a theory, one which you will never hear uttered within another Grove."

He inclined his head as if to further impress upon Emmett the full measure of his words. "Would you like me to share this secret with you, Mr. Brennan?"

Emmett felt Keiran's foot pushing against his underneath the table but was uncertain what he could do to end the conversation. "Yes."

"Would it surprise you if I told you that the attack against you by the Underdweller was *not* by random occurrence?"

"Are you saying that they chose me?"

"If by 'they' you refer to the Underdwellers and Revenants, the answer is no, I do not mean them. I believe we are touched by destiny; a touch of grace for some and misery for others, but such is the fickle nature of destiny. I believe that the concept of randomness—that each of our free, individual choices leads to random and unpredictable outcomes—is ultimately meaningless. The truth of creation is that we are all on predetermined paths that, no matter what choices we make, we still eventually arrive at."

"I don't understand. How would my past have anything to do with my attack? You said that we all had that in common."

Dr. Hazrat nodded. "Yes, and this is my best evidence of my belief." He motioned for a server to refill his glass from the silver decanter seated directly in front of him. He permitted himself to enjoy a long, leisurely sip before continuing.

"All the Children come from broken homes or have suffered great loss. Neglected, abandoned, abused, and yet they hear the clarion call of the Wisdoms and of the Song."

Emmett sat stiffly without comment. *Where the hell is this going?*

"Why is this? I know you must wonder this. All who come before me ask the same question. Why? Why those gifted with the strength to resist and defeat darkness share a common, universal origin of despair. Some believe that even as children, we are uniquely responsible for the things that have happened to us because of the decisions that we and others around us have made. Now, Mr. Brennan, I am sure you will conclude from my expression that I do not share in this belief."

Several Druids around the table chuckled at this while other Bards nodded with expressions of condemnation, and even Dr. Hazrat suppressed a laugh of near-condescension.

"With all that I have seen and experienced, I cannot escape the conclusion that there is and always will be a definable purpose guiding our every movement. I believe in destiny that sets our feet before us, guides our hearts, and fuels the dreams by which we dare to imagine the unknown. If existence is defined by a limitless collection of random occurrences in this world, what purpose would any of us have for doing what we do to defend it?"

Several Druids and Bards across the table from Emmett were nodding in agreement. "So," Dr. Hazrat concluded, "where does that leave us? If you believe as we do that destiny exists in our lives, and that all of us share in this common story, then one must inevitably arrive at the most frightening question of all."

As before when Keiran and he first met Dr. Hazrat, their conversation had begun as a sort of nebulous cloud. Before his eyes, it had drawn itself inward, redirected, and taken a different form. Now when Emmett looked plainly at the conversation's direction, it was so clear that he couldn't imagine why he hadn't seen it before.

"Were we always destined to experience the pain that we suffered as children?" Emmett said before he realized that he had spoken aloud.

Several members of the Lighthouse beamed at Emmett. Oliver was nodding enthusiastically at him. Even Eitan's face was filled with seeming ecstasy. Dr. Hazrat clenched his fist and shook it with an expression of rapture.

"Exactly, my son! Bravo!" he exclaimed triumphantly, pointing at Emmett, and several people applauded him. "Yes, you have named it precisely! The question establishes a sense of providence; the inevitable answer brings us greater sorrow, but only if we do not act upon it!"

Emmett looked down at his plate, finding that he no longer was hungry. He could feel that nearly all of those around the table were still watching him, though by the sounds of silverware to plates, many had returned to finishing their meals once they saw that Dr. Hazrat had finished his thoughts.

Underneath the table, he felt Keiran's hand pat his knee reassuringly again, though for whatever reassurance Keiran could offer, Emmett felt only a sense of hollowness and great exhaustion. Perhaps most of all, Emmett once again understood why Keiran had not wanted to come to the Lighthouse.

"Dr. Hazrat, may I ask a question?" Keiran asked, drawing attention from the obviously stricken look on Emmett's face.

"By all means, son," Dr. Hazrat responded.

"If destiny rules our lives and all is predetermined, then who decides that fate?"

"Has your Elder not instructed you in this?" Dr. Hazrat asked with a slight leer.

"I've never met the Archivist," Keiran answered, and Emmett did not hide his surprise at hearing this. "So I wouldn't know."

Dr. Hazrat's unreadable face eventually warmed with a grin, though its exact meaning was unknown to everyone at the table. "Let us ask Eitan what he knows of our history, and see if a boy under the tutelage of the Lighthouse has not received a better education in three months than a man who has spent years in the trees of Silvan Dea," he said with a stinging rebuke that Keiran accepted without reaction.

The young boy stood immediately from his chair, his tumbles of blond curls falling into his face. He nervously pushed them back with trembling hands. Clearing his throat, his soft, almost feminine features drew quickly into a determined expression, his shaking hands moving quickly to button his black, double-breasted jacket over his red silk tie as he nervously cleared his throat again.

"At the beginning of creation, the Composer sang a Song that pierced the void and divided it into two halves: one of pure light and the other of total darkness. Both were given equality in the composition of our experience, and with the formation of our world, the influence of light and dark waxed and waned predictably throughout the ages. Both pursued each other in an endless dance of ascent and descent, progression and regression." His high voice stopped as he looked to Dr. Hazrat for approval, for which he was rewarded glowingly.

Eitan looked out across the table. "To this earth where the first life was born, the Composer sent the Children to watch over the balance. Across and over the many waters, we found solace in the Song. Wicked though the world may be, we remain its only sentinels."

With an approving nod, Eitan quietly sat down. "It is my belief that the Composer gifted us with the Song and the hidden voices of the Wisdoms for one purpose: to provide a resolute and unfaltering presence for good in a world that is plagued by such unrepentant and wicked evil. That our lives all share a common thread and that we all can empathize with similar pains and challenges confirms this belief for me. As it should for you."

Keiran nodded silently, allowing his face to convey an expression of acceptance. Emmett saw that without exception, every other Druid and Bard around the table joined in their appreciation for Dr. Hazrat's words. Though this was the first Elder Emmett had met, he had to wonder if the passion of their reactions was uniform in other Groves.

Clapping his hands together loudly, Dr. Hazrat stood up from the table. At once, all in attendance joined him. Emmett and Keiran followed their lead.

"As always, I have enjoyed our time together. The responsibilities of my position dictate that other issues await my attention. Be of good temperance and cheer, and fear nothing that lurks in shadow. May the Song lift you all."

All in attendance except Keiran and Emmett responded:

"And guide us all home."

Those around the table sat as Dr. Hazrat exited the dining hall with his Attendant, Eitan, in step behind him. Emmett looked at Keiran, who made the briefest shake of his head before continuing with his meal.

After a comfortable amount of time had passed and few remained, servers began to clear the tables away. Keiran signaled to Emmett and they withdrew quietly from the table, returning to the grand staircase leading to the upper halls.

"All right?" Keiran asked when they were alone.

"T.M.I. on an epic scale. If ever there were a lesson in the value of not asking questions, that was it," Emmett said as they ascended the stairs.

"How so?"

"Remember what I told you, K? First rule of a David Fincher film: Don't ask what's in the box."

CHAPTER 21

They returned to Keiran's room, Keiran lying down across his bed and rubbing his temples. Emmett paced before him, barely contained energy bounding around in his mind as he replayed the dinner over and over.

"I've visited two Groves so far, and no offense, Keiran, but you people are trying even *my* affinity for the 'strange and unusual.' And that's not an easy thing to do."

"They are both extremes, Emmett. The Archivist guides through wisdom that is expressed in self-discovered truths. Dr. Hazrat does not hesitate to teach you what *he* thinks you should know. It's not my place to judge, and the concept of choice is something I value. It frees me to believe my life is anything I make of it."

"It's just been a 'My God, it's full of stars' sequence of moments since we arrived," Emmett admitted. "First there's the throne room where, funnily enough, a river *actually* runs through it. What is it with you people and caves, anyway? And then there's the creepy boy Attendant who'd keep slash-fic writers busy for the next decade. Oh, and then that speech of Hazrat's? It was legit *ridiculous*. Like, 'Hitler Reacts to Omar Hazrat Speech' YouTube-video-worthy ridiculous."

"Emmett," Keiran began slowly, clearly exhausted and struggling to keep up with him. "Until this moment, I have been circumspect with you. Not because I believed you couldn't handle what I had to tell you, but rather because I felt like it needed its proper context."

"And now?" Emmett asked.

Keiran looked down at his own hands. "I think we are beyond the need for withholding. Despite the death you've seen, you approach the world with new wonder and something that I believe is hope. To me, that is enough and everything at the same time."

Emmett was at an immediate loss for words, and despite his tumbling thoughts, a part of him felt something resembling pride. "Coming from you, that means a lot." Emmett was as surprised at those words as Keiran obviously was to hear them. Uncomfortable, Emmett busied himself with taking off his shoes.

"Yes, well, as I said before, the Lighthouse promises to be a trying experience. It is ironic that in our coming here you will likely learn more about the nature of evil than anywhere else."

"Why?"

"Because it's so important to them. It defines them. It's not enough to defeat evil; they have to understand the nature of it. The struggle."

"And you don't agree," Emmett said.

"As it is, there is already enough mystery in this world for me to spend a lifetime trying to understand. Some people focus their lives on knowing the motives of evil. I have no need to understand it; only to defeat it."

"No offense, but that almost sounds like something Dr. Hazrat would say."

"The truth, Emmett, is that there is much to agree with Dr. Hazrat on. Yes, there is great evil in this world. Given the destruction that is bore by innocent people like you, Derrick, and Emaline, I would of course give anything to destroy it once and for all."

"Yet you support the Great Preclusion?"

"Evil cannot *be* wholly destroyed. It's a concept, not an entity. A promise of power that tempts those who are weak of spirit. Which is why it does not merit exploration."

"For what it's worth, I'll take your word on it over anyone else's."

Keiran looked at Emmett with his mouth slightly ajar as if uncertain what to say. It was an expression Emmett was not accustomed to seeing on Keiran's face, and it was the second time in one evening Emmett had complimented him.

"Thank you."

Emmett fidgeted again with his shoes. Only days before, Emmett had found Keiran irritatingly perfect, his Companion the woman of his dreams. But he had saved his life twice already, and Emmett knew that at his core, Keiran Glendower was a decent guy.

Keiran yawned, and seeing how tired he was, Emmett began to feel guilty for keeping him awake.

Let him sleep. He's earned it already. Exposition can wait.

"Okay, Atreyu, it's time for some epic sleep. The Nothing can wait for tomorrow. BT Dubbs, in this analogy, I'm Bastion and not Artax."

As always, Keiran understood none of what Emmett said but saw him heading for his own room. "I don't want you sitting awake worrying needlessly."

"Nah, I'm good, K. Serious. Creepy dinner, but I'll live. I'll shut up about movies long enough so you can get some sleep. We'll talk tomorrow morning."

Keiran nodded as he began to unbutton his shirt. "Leave the

door unlocked. In case you need something."

In his suite's darkness, a sliver of moonlight breeched the diaphanous curtains bound to the windows. His mind groped through the terrified faces he had passed on the train. With a prescient shudder of discomfort traveling down the length of his chest, he admitted to himself that he could not recall the features of a single, doomed person.

The onset of sleep, of course, never came. Emmett was aware of his frequent tossing and turning, and with each repositioning, he felt more awake than before. He stared at the ornate clock hanging on the opposite wall, its constant ticking with each swing of its long hand seemingly timed with the crackling of the logs slowly burning in the fireplace.

As the early morning hours before dawn began to draw close, he finally threw the thick down comforter back and stretched. He swung his legs over the side of the bed and stood up, ambling across the room. When all else failed, walking could offer the kind of distraction that would lead to a quiet mind. Or the sun would rise and a new day could begin.

Slipping a pair of house slippers over his feet, he opened his door and stepped out into the dimly lit hallway. He turned right for the stairs, a window at the opposite end behind him flashing with an arc of brilliant white as lightning lit the pounding rain.

Ambling quietly down the hallway, he passed many closed doors before reaching a stairwell. Gripping the banister, he padded down the carpeted steps and emerged on a lower landing that opened out into a larger foyer where divans surrounded a small piano.

The Steinway grand piano was polished perfectly along its maple and spruce lines, the rosy sheen almost glowing along its smooth surfaces. The piano lid was propped open, and as Emmett allowed himself to sit on the bench in front of it, he looked in and saw that the strings had all been dusted recently, the tightly wound copper dully reflective.

Emmett was startled by the shadow of someone standing across from him in the corner of the foyer.

"What can you play?" an aged voice asked. Emmett had not seen the figure before and did not recognize the face as a man stepped into a path of light.

It was an older gentleman in his seventies, thin and medium height with white hair combed directly back over his scalp. The gentleman's focused green eyes betrayed the appearance of his age and stooping posture with an alertness that was clear even in the darkness.

He straightened himself with an air of dignity as he walked around the piano to join Emmett on the bench. He wore a pressed black suit and simple black tie, and he walked with the support of a long cane atop which he held a silver knob.

"Please do not stop on my account," he said, Emmett noting his German accent. "I'm afraid I don't get to hear much in the way of performance with this as often as I would like."

"I don't really play."

The man rested his cane against the Steinway and stretched his hands across the keys, his mottled skin juxtaposed by finely manicured nails that hinted at wealth.

He launched into a sweeping arc across the piano. The rich notes imbued the foyer with a haunting elegance that was magnified by the dapple of moonlight filtering through the inky darkness of the stormy night outside. The Steinway was obviously positioned at a perfect angle within the foyer, for the sounds echoed so perfectly that each note played at precisely the right moment along the edges of Emmett's ears just as another note replaced it.

"It's beautiful."

"It is Chopin's Nocturne, ninth opus, number two. I have spent several years attempting to master its intonation." Emmett could not tell if he had, indeed, mastered it, but he found himself overwhelmed by the mastery with which the man performed the piece.

"We have not met. It is my custom to greet new students upon arrival. You, however, did not travel by plane with the other girls."

"By train," he said, and in Emmett's mind the images of Ellie walking the lone car in his vision aboard the train with Keiran and Sebastian appeared. "It was my first time."

"My name is Charles Kellner," the gentleman said, the music coming to an abrupt halt as he extended his hand.

Emmett's mind reeled, and it was all he could to not jump back from the piano. Then he felt the exertion of another consciousness again, the sense that two minds shared the same private space, as that second mind came forward to speak.

"Ellie," she said, taking the gentleman's hand lightly in her own.

"How do you like the school?"

"I never thought I could afford it. Thank you for your scholarship."

Oh my God, how could I have forgotten?

"I have had my eye on you for some time. I am glad you were able to attend."

"There are hundreds of other girls who would have paid for my place," Ellie said.

"Vast financial success is one of only many methods for attaining power, and it is of no use if it is not wielded. Power, you see, is something that everyone seeks. What kind of power do you want?"

Emmett felt the unsettling disconnect as emotions he did not recognize as his own flooded through him. Anger. Bitterness. Pain that Ellie had tried to quell with all manner of encounters. A wash of images flooded through his mind: drugs, anonymous sexual encounters, and increasingly dangerous adventures delving deeper into more sinister realms of physical experience. All to deaden the pain.

Yet the hunger was never sated. The pain was never healed.

"Raw power," she answered.

"Power requires a focal point. Absent, it burns through you and leaves you an empty husk. What is it that you want to wield this power for?"

A pair of red eyes and a preternatural grinning mouth wreathed in shadow hovering over a pair of unmoving limbs appeared in Emmett's mind.

"Revenge," she breathed deeply, and Kellner only nodded.

"Your rage can be poured into a deserving vessel if you commit yourself."

"How?"

"Come to a dinner I am hosting tomorrow night, and I will show you," he answered. Reaching for his cane, he slowly stood from the bench. "I have an apprenticeship open in my private group."

"What would I need to do?"

"Come with an open mind," Kellner said. "I have another young man attending for his first time. Troy. A nice gentleman."

The thrill of success surged through Ellie, mixed with a lustful desire at the mention of Troy's name.

"I will see you at ten o'clock."

Before Ellie could respond through Emmett, he felt a sudden jerk along his shoulder, a forceful tug that nearly toppled him backward over the bench. The foyer dissolved in a haze of darkness.

Emmett felt himself flailing. A hand held his wrist down as he opened his eyes against the assault of sunlight. Through spots in his own vision, he saw Keiran standing over him with a worried look on his face.

"Emmett? Emmett! Wake up!"

After several disorienting moments, Emmett realized that he had awakened on the ground. He pulled himself upright and propped his back against one of the bed's legs while Keiran went to get a glass of water from the bathroom.

His eyes were open fully now with the bright flood of daylight. He drew in a long breath as if he had been underwater for several minutes, and his throat was filled with the dry, cold air of the suite, the fire in the fireplace having burnt out hours before. Where moments before the classical piano feathered his ears, now there was only the hollow sound of the distant ocean waves crashing against the cliffs below.

He tried to catch his breath. He paused and willed his pace to slow. The Rot demanded his attention, shooting pain slicing across his chest. He hissed, clenching down with his jaw as he looked down. The decaying patch of dead flesh had already snaked down past his stomach and was winding toward his navel.

"You want to tell me what that was all about?" Keiran asked, kneeling beside him.

Keiran explained how he had awoken after sunrise and heard Emmett talking in his room. After knocking on Emmett's door and hearing only Emmett talking, he came in and found Emmett lying on the ground mumbling in his sleep and twitching his limbs various directions. Concern ceded to panic when Keiran was unable to wake him, shaking him for several minutes before

Emmett finally awoke with a start.

His black, floppy hair matted to his sweaty face, Emmett looked down and saw that he was still in his white boxer shorts, just what he was wearing when he remembered getting into bed.

As Emmett accepted the glass of water, Keiran stood up and hurried back into his room, returning a moment later pulling a shirt over his torso.

"I guess I can't complain about not getting any sleep," Emmett said.

"How much pain are you in?" Keiran asked as he took the glass away from Emmett and looked at the spreading patch of blackened skin down Emmett's torso.

Emmett cursed as another cough sent wrenching pain into his chest. "I'm nauseous when I move. I can't catch my breath. And my skin's flaking off. Basically, I'm the Fly, but without swag hair." Keiran traced his finger around the perimeter of the Rot just above the skin, careful not to touch it for apparent fear it would cause Emmett further pain. To Emmett, it seemed as if Keiran were estimating how much larger the Rot had grown.

"Yeah. This thing is really starting to annoy me. I may have to see someone about having it removed," he snickered.

"It looks like it's at least tripled in size. It'll be in your blood soon, too."

"Lovely."

"Have you seen anything that might have been a sign or contact from the Archivist? Have you heard anything unusual like a voice in your mind or whispers that you did not know where they came from?"

Emmett had no way of knowing if the dreams were contact from the Archivist. Amala had been explicit that he tell no one of his waking dream in Portland. But it was clear that his dreams were more like memories of things that had happened to Ellie and seen through her eyes. That he was, in some way, within Ellie's body and seeing things from her perspective.

Amala told you not to tell anyone.

But Emmett would be dead within a week. He could not afford to waste time in assumptions that could be wrong. Amala still had not come. He was on his own with Keiran. Time was something that he had little of remaining.

"Emmett, what aren't you telling me, mate?"

He knows something's up. This is it.

"Keiran," Emmett began slowly as he sighed and looked into his eyes. "Could you hand me my shirt? We need to talk."

And for the first time since he'd tumbled down the proverbial rabbit hole, Emmett found himself in the rather unusual position of having to pace himself as he explained things to Keiran and tried to answer his many questions.

CHAPTER 22

"That's about it, I guess. I woke up with you standing over me, and that brings us up to the present."

"That *is* everything, yes?" Keiran confirmed.

"Yep." *Except about how Amala told me not to tell anyone of what she called the "waking dreams" or the dreams I had every night of Amala before meeting her.* He accepted Keiran's sincerity and had no need to create problems between Keiran and Amala. No matter how much he may have wished for her to be free of him.

"You were not asleep," Keiran said. He was sitting across from Emmett along the edge of the bed as Emmett sat upright propped against a hedge of pillows. He still sat in his white T-shirt and shorts, his heavily inked left arm lying across his lap.

Emmett felt a rush of relief from the certainty with which Keiran spoke. He would know what was going on; he had to. He would know what to do.

"If it were a dream, it would be constructed from your own memories, not Ellie's. They are most certainly visions."

"I could have just heard Kellner's name on the news broadcast in Portland."

"He is how I am certain. Charles Kellner is a Professor of Anthropology and President of a small private college for women in northern California. He is also an accomplished pianist. His 1923 Steinway is something of an affectation of his. I do not recall that detail being mentioned in the news report."

"I don't know, K. Seems like a stretch to me."

"There is The Grinning Man, the red eyes you saw."

"That's real, too?" Emmett asked exasperated.

"He is an Old One, Emmett, like the Hag. It is not possible that you could have described him as you did unless you had encountered him. Or rather, Ellie encountered him."

Emmett rocked back with the implications. Even as he retold the entire story to Keiran, pouring over every detail that he could remember, his mind had begun to rationalize away everything he had experienced as nothing more than fanciful dreams induced by fatigue, insomnia, and shock. It had made it easier to tell Keiran what had happened when he assumed there was a sensible explanation. He *needed* it to be rational, if only to tell himself that he was not going crazy.

He stumbled for words. "This is *real*?"

"Kellner's parents were wealthy industrialists who were executed for selling munitions to the French Resistance during World War II. His uncle, a mid-level bureaucrat within the National Socialist Party, adopted him. Kellner used the money his family had laundered and established a private college. His occult research required our investigation of him."

"So he *is* the Revenant leader? Not Ellie?" Emmett asked.

"Druids were sent to pose as students, and when nothing was discovered, he was classified as a harmless, if eccentric, collector. Wealth often leads to boredom, and it was determined that Kellner's interest was purely academic."

"You said it would take a powerful leader to launch that attack."

"And this could not have been Ellie?" Keiran asked.

"My Rot never had me doubling over on the ground near her."

"That only proves that she did not have contact with Underdwellers or Revenant magiks for a period of time. It would have been necessary for her to be clean due to the possibility that someone would sense it in her presence when she was planted at the Grove."

The mention of Ellie being planted reminded Emmett of the most salient and problematic revelation if these were, as Keiran was certain, Ellie's memories as visions. "Keiran, she said she had a spy at Silvan Dea."

"As difficult as it might be for me to accept that such a thing was possible, I cannot discount that."

Emmett ran through the faces of those he had met at Silvan Dea. "If I have another vision, perhaps I'll see who the spy was."

"No, that would prove nothing," he said curtly.

Keiran saw the confused expression on Emmett's face. "Emmett, don't you understand what is happening? What you're experiencing is not contact from the Archivist. You are seeing through *another* person's life. Regardless of how or why, there is no doubt in my mind that you've been touched with the gift of the Mara. You're a Dreamer."

At first, Emmett felt only confusion, and in his mind he all but laughed at the absurdity of it. *The Mara? Only the Children are born with that gift!*

"That's not possible, is it?" he shakily laughed.

"Perhaps your contact with the Archivist unlocked something; the visions could just as likely end when you finally reach her and are cured of the Rot. I do not know. You are quite literally seeing *into* and *through* another person."

Emmett found that he had stopped breathing, and he had to tell himself to resume. *Breathe. Breathe. Breathe.* There was numbness in his limbs, and he looked down as he told his toes to wiggle. *Move.* He felt detached from his body, as if listening to their conversation from a great distance away. It was shock, of course, and an inability or perhaps unwillingness to accept what Keiran was saying.

"What are you going to do to me?" Emmett asked in almost a whisper, his eyes staring down at his own hands folded in his lap. He could not bring himself to look up. He was manifesting something that was forbidden by most of Keiran's people. Would he have to seek sanctuary with the Lighthouse? Would the Archivist refuse to heal the Rot if he did?

"Emmett, listen to me." Keiran put his hand over Emmett's and leaned forward so that Emmett had to look up into his face. It was a gesture of friendship, solidarity, and of something Emmett had not experienced before: brotherhood.

"The Archivist will heal the Rot, and then we will determine *together* what will be done. You must promise me, however, that you will tell no one of these visions, particularly here."

More secrets. Just like Amala.

"Yeah, okay."

"If the visions progress as they have, we need to be mindful that you are entering this state without realizing it. I'll need to stay in your room to keep an eye on you."

"I don't want this to turn into a thing," Emmett said sheepishly. "I'm fine. Really. I'm not gonna go all *Memento* on you and start marking myself up."

"I'm not going to take any chances. When you have another vision, at the first opportunity when no one else is around, I want you to tell me. As soon as you are able, yes? No matter what you see, I want you to tell me everything."

"Sure. No more holding back."

"And Emmett, the gift of the Mara is a fickle thing. Lacking perspective, you are experiencing one side of a story as remembered by someone who is now dead. You must appreciate why drawing conclusions from that could be problematic."

Though the argument between Keiran and Sebastian over the Great Preclusion had meant little to him at the time they had it in Portland, Emmett had understood that anyone with a precognitive gift would obviously be an asset against Revenants. Keiran's opinions to the contrary had seemed unfounded until now as Emmett's mind sifted through the images and struggled to apply much-needed context to them.

"Come on. Let's wash up and go down. Breakfast and fresh air should help."

Emmett only nodded, allowing Keiran to help him get dressed and head downstairs.

It was sitting at the table eating that he first noticed the trembling, his spoon shaking in his hands as he tried to eat his fresh muesli. Keiran only patted his shoulder, telling him it was the inevitable consequence of the Rot's continued penetration of his body.

Eitan entered the dining hall and greeted them just as they were finishing breakfast.

"*Mon frère,*" Eitan said in his high voice as he addressed Keiran with a low bow. "Dr. Hazrat has requested both your company in his private study."

Exchanging knowing looks, Keiran nodded and followed with Emmett behind him. They passed several flights of winding stairs and hallways before they reached a circular room with high walls lined floor to ceiling with ornate wooden bookshelves and a gold rail from which a ladder on wheels rolled around the circumference of the room. A multi-tier chandelier hung down at its center, and spread among several large burgundy chairs and tasseled area rugs stood several wrought-iron floor lamps.

Dr. Hazrat sat in one of the chairs with an open leather-bound tome. He had eschewed his frock coat for an evening jacket, though it was scarcely late morning, and his polished black loafers for comfortable down-lined slippers. He sipped from a crystal glass and nodded at Eitan with a whispered thank you before Eitan closed the double doors behind him as he exited.

"Please, join me," Dr. Hazrat gestured to a pair of chairs opposite him.

"Thank you," Keiran said as he sat down beside Emmett.

"I trust that your accommodations have been sufficient for your needs?" he asked, setting his drink and book down on an end table next to his chair that sat before a large, roaring fireplace that crackled with the sweet smell of pine.

"Yes, thank you, sir."

Several moments of silence passed, and Emmett was unsure what Dr. Hazrat must have been expecting them to say or do. Then the door opened again and Oliver Gray strolled in just before Eitan bowed a second time and closed the door.

"Ah, yes, Oliver. Do join us," Dr. Hazrat said.

"Thank you," Oliver nodded. Emmett studied him fully for perhaps the first time. He was obviously American by his accent, and his square jaw and athletic features reminded him of Keiran. He also wore his black hair in the same casual, unassuming manner, the style for those whose attractiveness was as effortless as the color of their eyes. Oliver's were crystal blue and perfectly complimented the amaranth-colored long-sleeve shirt with silver cufflinks that he wore tucked into tailored, fitted slacks.

Dr. Hazrat unfolded his hands and placed them on the arms of his chair. "Earlier this morning, I was gifted with a disturbing vision."

Emmett allowed his eyes to glance over at Keiran, and though he wanted to ask the obvious question, he wisely remained silent. Keiran was guarded in his own expression, not filled with the indulgent look in Oliver's eyes.

"May I ask you your vision, Elder?"

"You may," Dr. Hazrat said, as if he were waiting for the request before proceeding. "It was a vision of the three of you," He paused, either to ascertain that each was listening or just to increase the dramatic effect of his words.

"Those with the gift of visions are known as the Dreamers, Mr. Brennan, or the Mara in the old tongue," Dr. Hazrat began as he leaned toward Emmett. "The Dreamers were chosen by the Composer to guide the Children."

"What were we doing, Elder?" Oliver asked.

"Fighting to save Amala Amjadi."

"If she is in danger, we must leave at once!" Oliver said hurriedly as he made to stand from his chair. Dr. Hazrat shook his head ever so slightly, and the subtle movement was not lost on Oliver, for as quickly as he had reacted, he sat back down.

In the ensuing silence, Oliver stared at Dr. Hazrat, who stared at Keiran, who was trying not to stare at either of them. All of them were watching one another for some kind of reaction to indicate what they were truly thinking.

Dr. Hazrat steepled his fingers together, tapping them silently as he regarded Keiran. The surreal exchange was broken only when Keiran finally nodded and leaned forward in his chair.

"Can you tell us anything about where we were so we can find her?"

This seemed to appease Dr. Hazrat, Emmett saw, as the briefest smile escaped his jaw. "I saw two street signs. Considering the weather overhead and the surrounding landscape, I have determined the location for you. Here," he said, withdrawing a slip of folded paper from within his jacket pocket.

"It occurs within this week, as Mr. Brennan was still infected with the Rot. That the address is less than a half-day's drive, coupled with the position of the moon overhead, indicates that this event occurs late tonight or early tomorrow," Dr. Hazrat said as he gave Keiran the paper.

"I'll have one of our unmarked vehicles brought around so we can leave," Oliver said.

Keiran's eyes betrayed hesitation as clearly as Oliver's eyes showed eagerness. Dr. Hazrat had been watching Keiran this entire time and noticed it, too, with a slight uptick of his eyebrow.

"You do not wish to bring Oliver with you, brother?"

"Amala is my Companion. I would never ask another Bard to risk his life."

"She was my charge long before you, Keiran. I love her, too." Oliver looked wounded by Keiran's exclusion. "I would never allow her or you to stand in danger alone."

"It is not in question that Oliver will be with you, as I have already seen it in my vision. It has already happened and also must still happen yet. What remains is not to debate its existence, but rather to experience it directly. There also remains the continued threat of Revenants apparently pursuing Keiran." On Keiran's name, Dr. Hazrat notably looked at Emmett. "Though no word has reached me of any within the area, there may be spies who would signal their comrades and descend upon him as he is traveling. I could not permit such a risk to be taken. The three of you will go together."

Keiran showed no additional objection in his face as he looked to Oliver. "Then we leave at once."

"Together, again," Oliver beamed. "Like old times."

Emmett stood as well and stepped behind them toward the door, Keiran turning to follow him just as Dr. Hazrat cleared his throat.

"I should mention one additional thing," Dr. Hazrat said, pausing once again for both their attention and the effect that his words caused.

"There was a presence of *another*, a being of such power that its own energy obscured it from any meaningful recognition. I cannot say what it was, but I can tell you that powers such as those do not come to the young. They are harvested only by those of great age; the very, very *old*. I should think you would value Oliver's presence."

Emmett understood enough to know what Dr. Hazrat was implying. An Old One.

"We will find Amala and prevail, and return immediately to the Lighthouse," Oliver said confidently to Dr. Hazrat.

"I wish you safe journeys, gentlemen. May you break the silence of despair and bring the light of truth to the darkness that births deception and lies. May the Song lift you."

"And guide us home," Oliver responded.

When Keiran, Oliver, and Emmett emerged in the hallway, Eitan was awaiting them, holding three long coats.

"The car is properly stocked with essentials for a journey of at least a week in length, if not more. Clothes, dry food, water, and a billfold with American and Canadian currency, should you have need of either. Directions are included with maps, as well."

"Excellent, Eitan, thank you," Oliver nodded.

"What's our route like?" Keiran asked.

"Northeast back through Halifax until Northumberland Strait. Follow the coastline around New Brunswick and across the Confederation Bridge into Prince Edward Island at Port Borden," Eitan said.

"I know that area," Oliver nodded.

"Where is Seacow Pond?" Keiran asked, unfolding the slip of

paper.

"The northernmost tip on the Gulf of Saint Lawrence," Eitan answered. "A six- or seven-hour drive depending on the weather."

Opening the massive doors to a gust of bitterly cold winter wind, Eitan handed a pair of keys to Oliver with a low bow. They followed Eitan down across the grounds, and when they reached the walls surrounding the Grove's perimeter, Emmett saw a black four-door sedan waiting for them, its engine idling warmly and what was likely its heater fogging its windows.

Oliver and Eitan exchanged bows, Keiran following with a short nod. Emmett, for his part, had grown weary of the ceremony involved in parting company with any member of the Lighthouse.

As the trio loaded into the sedan, a hawk screeched in the distant line of snow-capped trees, piercing the silence of the mist-shrouded afternoon. Oliver immediately took to the driver's seat, and when Emmett looked at Keiran and saw him stepping into the passenger front seat, he suppressed a moment's irritation before getting into the backseat himself. The sedan's interior was both roomy and toasty, enough so that he pulled himself back out of his coat before buckling his seat belt.

Emmett looked up at the grand face of the Lighthouse as he felt Oliver urging the car forward, the two silent in the front seat as he watched the Grove's stone walls fade in the distance.

This is going to be a long ride, Emmett sighed as the sedan pulled out onto the road, and quickly gaining speed, it hurtled toward another Old One and to rescue the woman of Emmett's dreams.

CHAPTER 23

They rode through Halifax, passing seaside cottages lined by high snow banks of powdery white. They took Highway 102 north into Truro, where Oliver turned onto Highway 104 and followed it to the Trans-Canada Highway.

For two with an apparently shared history, Oliver and Keiran were entirely too quiet throughout the trip for Emmett not to notice. The tension could have been due to Amala, Emmett thought, and he had to remind himself that he was not Keiran's sole focus. Keiran tried to hide the look of longing in his eyes, but Emmett saw it. And his heart raced knowing that they sped toward her.

The Rot was outright painful now even during moments when he remained still. Any movement felt like nails against sunburnt skin, and he was unable to fully catch his own breath. Even lying motionless in the backseat as the sedan crossed the long bridge over the turbulent winter whitecaps of Northumberland Strait to Prince Edward Island, Emmett felt the Rot draining his life.

Despite the evening's gray gloom and approaching storm front low across the horizon, Emmett saw enough of the island's rolling hills and coastal red cliffs to appreciate what green beauty must exist under the layered banks of winter snow. As the sun set in the west, Oliver drove north toward Seacow Pond.

They arrived in the seaside village after nightfall. Keiran and Oliver had disagreed for the previous hour about the wisest course of action: to drive directly to the location or approach indirectly to identify potential threats.

What surprised Emmett, though, was which side each took. Oliver's faith in Hazrat was such that he advocated an immediate arrival. Keiran, though, approached the situation with greater pragmatism and emotional detachment. He could not permit them to plunge headlong into a situation that could be an ambush; or, as he offered when Oliver seemed to take offense at the suggestion that Dr. Hazrat could be wrong, an unknown situation where the Revenants' strengths were not yet measured.

Despite being older, Oliver treated Keiran as his equal. He listened and often nodded when Keiran made a valid point. Only when the legitimacy of the Mara was intimated did he express anything other than his high opinion for Keiran.

For his part, Keiran showed Oliver equal respect. Keiran weighed his words carefully. Remembering back to Portland when Keiran said that Sebastian and he had spent long nights arguing over the Great Preclusion, Emmett understood now how someone who believed so strongly in something could still be so close with someone like Keiran, who believed quite the opposite.

When they finally pulled into the village's empty streets, the two Bards had at last settled on a compromise. They would stop several blocks from the address and spend time watching for signs of Revenant activity. If they found nothing, they would move quickly to the appointed destination and await the unknown hour when their paths would apparently cross Amala's.

In the December darkness, the arctic northern winds howled

across the coastline with an unrelenting freeze that even Bardic song could not fully protect Emmett from. They parked and observed for over an hour, Keiran and Oliver rolling the windows down so they could listen fully to the night. Bundled in his heavy jacket, Emmett sat shivering in the backseat, his teeth chattering so loudly that he shrugged sheepishly at Keiran when he turned around to check that Emmett was okay.

"Sorry," Emmett managed to say as he pulled his arms tighter across his chest for warmth and clenched down at the pain the movement brought.

"I have heard nothing since we arrived," Oliver said to Keiran, whose face was clearly concerned for Emmett but eventually turned back to Oliver.

"Neither have I," Keiran confirmed.

"Are you ready?" Oliver asked, looking first to Keiran and then to Emmett.

"I'm ready for warmer weather," Emmett chattered.

"My mind has not changed. Emmett should not be going with us, Oliver. With the spread of the Rot, he is absolutely in no condition to defend himself."

"Regardless of whether you believe in Dr. Hazrat's vision, it is tactically a mistake to leave Emmett alone. He is far safer with us."

Not again, Emmett thought as he remembered Keiran's eyes when they drifted down the river from Silvan Dea. *You would have gone back for her if it weren't for me.*

"I'll be fine," Emmett managed to sigh, summoning fortitude within him that he was uncertain even existed and willing it to exert control over his shaking body. "Let's go get Amala," he said as he opened the door before Keiran could protest.

The northern winds' full onslaught was unbearable. Emmett bit down on his lip and pulled the hood over his head, tucking his hands into the coat's lined pockets. The address was the juncture of two roads that ended at an aging dock where several small boats were moored for the winter. Metal buildings lined the water's edge, and even in the howling winds of the approaching storm, Emmett could hear the clinking of the floating docks rolling up and down with the squally tide.

Oliver stepped around to Emmett and Keiran's side of the sedan as he zipped his coat up and surveyed the area. "Anything?" he asked.

"If they are here, they're not close enough to hear them," Keiran said.

Keiran looked to Emmett. "Have you felt anything?"

"No stomach-churning goodness," Emmett managed to say.

They crossed the street, Keiran following behind Emmett as Oliver led. There was no sign of another person in the sleepy coastal town. With the approaching storm looming dangerously like a kraken along the watery horizon, no fishermen were returning to the dock that night.

With some trepidation, Oliver craned his neck to look into the building through the boarded windows' partially broken slants. Seeing nothing before turning to Keiran one final time, he carefully pulled on one of the boards and, finding the wood heavy with moisture and all but rotted to a pulpy mess in his hands, easily separated it from the frame enough that they could enter one at a time.

"It's clear in here," Oliver finally called out over the torrent of wind. He reached a hand through the opening and helped Emmett step through the frame and into the dark warehouse and finally Keiran. With only the dim streetlights that dotted the road outside, Emmett's eyes had already begun to acclimate. The warehouse featured no unobstructed windows. The warehouse was unremarkable with tarp-covered stacks of crates and wooden pallets. Only Bardic hearing could assure them that they were alone.

Stepping toward the open center of the room, Oliver turned around in slow, wide motions, watching for any signs of disturbance as Keiran guarded their rear. Narrow, poor light breached the slats of the boarded windows. As his eyes poured over the unmoving dark patches in the far, unseen corners, Emmett wished Amala's glowing amber eyes were with them.

"*Willkommen*," a deep voice echoed. Oliver and Keiran reacted with the first ringing syllable. Oliver's arms sprang outward in a display of preparation just as Keiran sprinted forward and all but tackled Emmett in his arms.

"I will not attack you unless to defend myself," the refined voice said.

"Kellner?" Emmett whispered aloud with recognition. Oliver cast him a confused look as he felt Keiran's rebuking grip on his arm to silence him.

"Yes," the voice answered, and with that the icy warehouse was flooded with a flash of hot air like the opening of a mighty, burning furnace. The darkness seemed to ripple as if being torn apart, and from the nothingness stepped forth an old, impeccably dressed gentleman in a black suit whose determined expression and distinguished appearance Emmett immediately recognized.

"Charles Kellner," the old man said as he stepped toward them with the dull, echoing clicking of his cane along the concrete floor. He had manifested on the opposite side of the factory more than a dozen yards from Oliver at a distance that caused Oliver to step back with hesitation upon his sudden appearance.

"How the hell did—" Oliver began, looking back over his shoulder at Emmett.

"I do not have much time, so let us dispense with the usual pleasantries."

"We determined that you *weren't* a Revenant!" Oliver shot back with disbelief. "I was there when Rhiannon reported her findings!"

"And she was correct."

"You invoke dark magiks," Oliver pointed at him accusingly.

"If I was a Revenant, your young friend here would be suffering quite a bit more than he already is," Kellner said, motioning with one hand at Emmett, who was in generalized pain from the Rot but otherwise not nauseous with convulsions.

"Then what *are* you, Kellner?" Keiran asked, releasing Emmett and taking one step in front of him to physically separate Kellner from Emmett.

"There are *other* powers in this world besides the *daoi-syth*. *Older* powers."

"The Wights," Oliver said, and he made no effort to hide his disgust.

"I will thank you to offer some measure of respect."

Oliver dismissed him with a sneer. "Wealth has made you delusional."

Emmett had no idea what they were discussing, and though he dared not speak, he was grateful when Keiran spoke up as if to translate for him. "Kellner, the Wights disappeared when most of their believers in the *Schutzstaffel* were executed for crimes against humanity. I can't believe that you would resurrect their worship in the Old Ones given what the Nazis did to your parents."

"It's ridiculous, anyway," Oliver scorned. "The Old Ones take no interest in humans. Wights that invoke the Old Ones are usually slaughtered by the summoning for their affront."

Kellner did not react to Keiran's words but looked instead to Oliver. "I have not come here to discuss dogma. I arranged our meeting tonight at personal expense. As my time is short, I wish to conduct my business and depart."

"Assuming I would let you to leave," Oliver threatened.

"The Children can claim no action against me. My order does not engage in the practices of the Revenant cultists, nor do we summon the *daoi-syth*," Kellner said in a tone of seeming academic debate and not with the defensiveness of someone who fears for their life.

"Wights kill, Kellner. The summoning rituals require it," Keiran said.

"*My* order only kills *evil* men. A Bard should appreciate the distinction."

"I sure as hell don't," Oliver said as he took a testing step forward.

Kellner lifted his hand and snapped his fingers, and at once the warehouse was filled with an explosion of bright, orange light. A trail of fire burst to life in a single line that encircled Kellner, the flames uniformly as tall as their knees but dancing with red flames whose cores were streaked with an unnatural blue and purple darkness.

"I do not wish a fight," Kellner said.

Oliver's posture remained offensively threatening. "Then what do you want?"

"To tell you that I did not order nor aid the attack on your Groves."

"Who said you did?" Oliver asked.

"It will, of course, become known soon that the attack was led by a former protégé of mine. I did not know that she was using my resources to build a secret Revenant force to attack Silvan Dea. That is, of course, until it was too late."

"Or she *was* and this is intended as misdirection," Oliver accused.

"I would have nothing to gain from attacking the Children.

Her sect attacked my school attempting to murder me, as well. I only narrowly escaped."

The Bards said nothing as Kellner continued. "I wish no war with the Children and did not support what was done. You will tell your Elders this. If they wish proof, tell them it was I who summoned the Hag to dispose of Ellie and her minions."

Emmett saw Keiran look briefly at him before speaking. "So that's the reason why you arranged for us to come? To tell us you didn't do it?"

"Yes. Though the Children have no direct claim against me, I would nonetheless be foolish to submit myself directly to your Groves for the delivering of such information. Or my servants ... assuming I had any remaining."

"How *did* you arrange this?" Oliver asked pointedly.

"I knew that you would come only if your Companions were in danger," Kellner said looking between them, and despite Emmett's discomfort he noted the plural designation and how Oliver turned his head slightly to look at Keiran.

"So I arranged for them to be followed for the last several days and attacked tonight by another Revenant sect unconnected to Ellie. Their numbers are small, but the threat had to be sufficient for the Turk of the Northern Storm to see it."

"Why us?" Oliver questioned.

"You both come from the Grove that kept watch over me, adding credibility to your voices when you return with an accounting of my words."

"Amala *is* here?" Keiran asked.

"She will be."

"So you're the old power Dr. Hazrat sensed," Oliver reasoned.

Kellner's head lifted slightly with this information, and Emmett knew that Oliver must have regretted revealing it. It was obvious in Kellner's expression that he did not know of this.

"As flattered as I am by the comparison, I am afraid it is not me. Though I am not surprised to hear that such a power is *present* in these affairs."

"What do you mean?" Keiran spoke before Oliver could.

"Only that I knew Ellie. I mentored her in the ways of the Wights. I am quite powerful, but not as powerful as Ellie became. She could not hold that kind of power; not as someone so young and so angry."

"So who was it?" Oliver asked.

Through the continuing pain in his head, Emmett squinted against the glow of the dancing flames surrounding Kellner and saw an odd look in his eyes. "I doubt very much if it was a *who* so much as a *what*. A patron more powerful than me, to be certain."

Emmett felt the air rushing past his ears as if it were being sucked from the surrounding area. The darkness surrounding Kellner seemed to ripple. Shadows separated as Kellner stepped back with his cane clicking along the concrete floor. He disappeared into wavering shadow, the flames encircling him burning out with not even a wisp of smoke or wreath of heat remaining.

Oliver bounded forward to the place where Kellner had once stood and spun around several times before cursing.

"If this is the location of Dr. Hazrat's vision, and Kellner confirmed that he had arranged the attack, then where is she?" Oliver demanded.

Keiran and Oliver both heard it at the same moment: a distant shuffling of feet along the docks. Emmett lurched forward to the ground as his hands shot out to break his fall. He vomited a hot torrent of bile. Both his vision and hearing were awash with competing stimuli as his mind tumbled, the familiar wrenching sickness clashing with the persistent pain of the Rot.

Oliver jumped with such sudden speed over Emmett's prone figure that he was almost a blur, bounding toward the nearest boarded window and extending his open palm outward. He wailed a screeching keen that blasted the boards away. Again, Emmett pitched his head forward, nearly falling into the steaming pile of his sick as Keiran wrapped a firm arm around one side of his neck and lifted him with his other arm underneath his opposite shoulder.

Keiran whispered a calming melody into Emmett's ear, and Emmett felt the familiar rush of hot water being poured over his head. He quickly regained his composure and nodded, forcing himself upright to hurry behind Keiran as they followed Oliver.

The deserted waterfront was shrouded in a wet fog that hung low to the water. The roiling winter storm raged farther east out to sea as rain lashed down on them. Emmett barely heard or saw the first wave of the attack. Two bellowing clouds of darkness hurtled through the night, and as Oliver sprinted forward toward their unseen attackers, Keiran lunged sideways, knocking Emmett to the ground. The warehouse wall exploded with another massive hole where the darkness collided with it.

Oliver called out with a tenor note into the roar of the storm, and as if in response, Emmett heard the high-pitched screech of a hawk overhead. His eyes met Keiran's at once, and the wash of relief and worry in Keiran's eyes confirmed what he knew.

Amala was close.

"Come on," Keiran said as he pulled Emmett up, breaking into a full run.

Oliver turned down the road between a pair of buildings just as three figures dashed toward Keiran from a hidden alleyway. Twisting mid-run, Keiran spun to meet his attackers with a forceful note that blasted into two of them just as the third spun out of the way and headed for Emmett.

Determined to fight through the numbing cold that was enclosing his lungs, Emmett brought his fists up, prepared to fight. The Revenant worshipper raised high a curved blade stained with bloody runes.

Keiran reacted with another wail, producing a wall of sound that hurtled a shimmering force toward the attacker. The assailant reacted quickly and slashed his blade downward, slicing Keiran's force in two with a shrill sort of whine. Doubling back, he brought the force of his blade fully at Emmett's head, and Keiran's defeated attack bought Emmett just enough time to duck out of the swing.

Emmett stumbled back as his attacker swung downward with a heave that could have easily sliced though him had he not ducked away. The blade whistled through the air just as Keiran leapt into the man from the side and knocked him to the ground, falling into a tangled heap of kicks and punches. Emmett looked for some kind of weapon. He heard Keiran suck in a heavy breath just as a swift knee was brought to his chest. Winded, Keiran did not react in time to another series of punches to his face.

The Revenant raised his blade high over Keiran's head. Emmett prepared to jump on him just as a hawk dove through the air, striking the attacker's face and spraying a plume of blood across the ground. He dropped his blade and clutched at the eyeballs dangling from his emptied sockets.

Emmett saw a woman's figure standing over Keiran's body before he heard her. Her scarlet red dress and black crushed velvet overcoat fell down to her black heels. Her green eyes twinkled like polished emeralds, and her impossibly long neck was framed in a mass of red curls that tumbled down the length of her narrow back, the pounding winds tossing it into the air as if it were living fire.

Emmett saw the hawk wrestle its wings in the wind and land atop her shoulder.

"Amala's engaging the bulk of their force over there," the

woman said to Keiran.

"Come on," Keiran said to Emmett as the woman sprinted off.

They ran together, turning down the same alley Oliver had. As they burst from the narrow passage to an empty parking lot, Emmett gasped and struggled to concentrate as another wave of nausea rippled through him.

The parking lot was a mess of bodies. Only a pair of street lamps cast any light on the fighting. Emmett could see that Amala and Oliver were openly fighting at least four attackers, with several more lying motionless on the ground around them. Amala's arms pumped in the air with such speed that her twin serpents were a blur in what was quickly becoming a downpour of ice.

Oliver was managing to buffet the scratching, dark words they spat at Amala as they summoned wretched globes of inky darkness. He met their attacks with his own songs of force, shielding either Amala or himself from their power with walls of invisible energy that either absorbed or reflected the darkness.

The red-haired woman dove into the fray with twirling abandon, her arms flailing out in wide sweeps as her hawk took flight again. The bird circled once overhead before diving down and clawing the eyes of one of her attackers. Emmett all but collapsed on the ground as Keiran released him at the edge of the fighting, raising his hand high into the air and calling down a bellowing force of invisible energy that toppled one of the attackers with a sickening crunch.

Neither Amala nor Oliver gave notice of them, yet Emmett saw their movements flow as one, the others' arms and legs an extension of their own body. The woman pirouetted between Amala's arms as she feigned an attack at the Revenants. Oliver ducked through the twisting serpents then and bellowed a powerful note of force that picked their attacker several feet off the ground, where the hawk's razor talons connected with yielding flesh and neck.

Emmett's body was racked by the spreading chill of the storm's onslaught overhead. Though the nausea was subsiding with the final dead attacker, he was aware of the dizzying pain the Rot and the arctic winds were sending through his body.

Over the howling wind and rain, Emmett thought he could hear something else. Distant and vague. He could not tell if the sound was real or imagined, but as he focused, he felt an unusual sensation run up the length of his back as something brushed against his ear like a whisper.

Far across the opposite end of the parking lot, a swirling, coalescing mass of undulating darkness swam through the air toward them. The falling rain parted in wide sheets like drawn curtains. The massive shadow twisted high in the air, floating along on currents that bore it aloft high above the surrounding buildings in the distance.

As it crossed over the mass of fallen bodies, the two flickering street lamps exploded violently in a shower of sparks. The area plunged into darkness, pierced only by the hint of lightning arcs crackling across the stormy horizon.

Emmett saw the darkness contort, jerking in the air and racing suddenly right for him. He saw Keiran lunging toward him with a raised hand as he sang a high-pitched, almost screeching note whose volume was swallowed by a deafening bellow of thunder above. The darkness swirled and parted for the invisible force that hurtled toward it, reforming a moment later and tearing through the stormy night at Emmett.

Again, Keiran lifted both arms wide and growled an angry note that was heavy with desperation. It was a low, throaty rumble that formed deep within his body and produced a brassy tone of anguish pouring out at the darkness. With startling speed, the darkness swirled in the downpour, undulating in a sort of hypnotic dance. Yet Keiran persisted, holding his low voice with great effort. As waves of baritone notes resounded, the darkness seemed to twist back in on itself in the air, unable to descend upon Emmett.

The dark mass was only feet from Emmett now. He saw Keiran straining to hold his note that seemed to be barring the darkness. Emmett registered confusion in some distant part of his mind—a part not already subsumed by the pain—when he saw Amala and the other woman jumping after Keiran.

Amala and the other woman grabbed at Keiran's arms and pulled him out of his song. As they did, the darkness swirled in the air. Suddenly free, it plunged through the rain in a whirlpool of shadows, hurtling toward him just as he closed his eyes shut and braced for the impact.

In a distant corner of his mind that could concentrate over the unendurable pain and coldness, Emmett wondered if Death—or just death—had finally caught him.

Emmett screamed as the swarm swallowed him. He raised his arms to cover his eyes, and as his hands brushed up into the shadow mass, he reeled with fear as he felt a thousand different things crawling over his hand.

Another roar of thunder sounded as the sky broke apart and opened with a streak of lightning flashing through the air, the sizzle of ozone pungent in the rainy night. In the blur of light and darkness, Emmett's heart raced with hope as he saw someone standing only feet away from him.

Help me! Emmett's mind screamed.

The darkness of the swarm suddenly parted, and Emmett saw a figure approach. Her dark hair was matted to her face, her glittering eyes searching his for recognition. Her beautiful face was marred by an expression of profound fatigue, her dark features glowing, though, from the brilliant arc of lighting overhead.

Delirious with cold and pain, Emmett recoiled as he felt something brush against his cheek that was soft and comforting. A hand that had been held before him in his dreams stroked his face now with delicate care, sweeping across his forehead to push his wet, tousled hair from his eyes.

"Emmett, don't be afraid. The Archivist is trying to speak to you."

CHAPTER 24

The world was spinning.

Emmett struggled to focus through the alternating patches of light and darkness clouding the edges of his vision. The edges of his extremities had ceased sending signals of feeling to his brain. He struggled to breathe, painful though it was to expand his chest and even more painful to inhale the biting frozen air. He was dying. Though gradual, the pain was such that he was uncertain if he even cared.

"I can't," Emmett stammered. He didn't know what he meant to say as he felt Amala's hand stroking his face. Her touch was comforting, what little of it he could still feel.

She laid him down on the ground, the writhing cloud still enclosing the two of them in a cocoon free from the rain.

"Listen to me, Emmett. You need to focus. Look at me," she said, one hand holding his face as the other grabbed his hand. Even as his awareness was dimming, Emmett could see the same confidence and poise as when he had last seen her.

He blinked cold tears out of his eyes as he focused, gripping her hand feebly with his own.

Not dead yet, he told his slowing mind.

"That's right, Emmett, just focus on me. I am right here with you," Amala said, returning Emmett's grip with her own reassuring one. "Steady your breathing just as we did last time, remember? You can do this," she said, mimicking the same deep breath that he forced himself to draw.

He wretched and heaved, feeling the Rot constricting his lungs tighter even as he struggled to draw air. He shook his head as he returned to the shallow, rapid breathing that he was able to manage, desperate to fill his lungs.

"Keiran, Oliver, Rhiannon, I need you!" Amala called out. Emmett could see through his cloudy vision that the swarm parted again as the two Bards and the red-haired woman appeared. Oliver and the woman were on opposite sides of him as Keiran crouched down directly behind Emmett's head and, lifting it tenderly, laid it over his knees as he looked down into Emmett's eyes.

Emmett squeezed Amala's hand again as he blinked another pair of tears down the sides of his face, his body violently trembling.

"I'm sorry. I can't," Emmett managed through his trembling mouth.

"It's the fever," the red-haired woman said.

Oliver stared into Emmett's pale features. "The Rot has seized onto it."

"We need to slow it down," Amala said, and though Emmett's fading mind barely registered the words, he still possessed enough awareness to hear the urgency in her voice.

They know I'm going to die.

Keiran was cradling Emmett's head in his hands, and Emmett could feel Keiran begin singing. His song translated as vibrations that coursed throughout his body. It was low and deep, and he poured the song out as his green eyes remained fixed on Emmett's.

"Oliver, assist him," Amala said. He felt his other hand suddenly grasped by Oliver, who placed his free hand on Emmett's chest and fixed his eyes on him. Emmett felt the throbbing sensation moving down Oliver's limbs and through both of his hands: a cavernous, yawning feeling that seemed to join and amplify Keiran's song.

"Slower," the red-haired woman urged as she tilted her head and watched Emmett, her hand brushing his floppy hair away from his eyes. "Much *slower*," she repeated, and Emmett found that her words seemed to stretch unnaturally as all other sounds lengthened, too.

The howling winds grew quiet, and the thundering storm faded into the periphery of his awareness.

"That's it, Emmett," he heard Amala slowly say. He saw that her mouth was moving just as slowly. His eyes rolled between Oliver and the red-haired woman, and he saw that the pattern of the rising and falling of their chests was slower, their eyelashes brushing closed in unhurried blinks.

The world around him was slowing down. The Rot's stranglehold lessened and he breathed easier for the first time in days.

"Focus on the swarm," Amala's voice was saying somewhere in the distance. Emmett could see her kneeling directly over his body, and yet the slowing sensation seemed to affect the presence of sounds such that someone who was next to him seemed many yards away.

"Hear the pattern of their sounds. Let them carry you backward."

Emmett's eyes met Keiran's again, and he saw that he was holding the note with great effort. Oliver looked the same, too. A thin line of blood was slowly seeping out of their noses.

They can't do this forever. It's going to kill them to keep this up.

Out on the northern tip of an island in the coldest ocean, high above the rest of the unknowing world, Emmett took a steadying breath and closed his eyes with purposeful exhalation.

Focus on the swarm.

And when he did, everything happened at once.

He heard it without hearing it. He knew it without knowing it. The flaps of tiny wings fell away individually until there was only one. Then Emmett heard each of those sounds returning. He could hear a chorus of sound that was vibrant and alive, each sound divergent and distinct. It was not an unruly mass or chaotic swarm; it was a tapestry of sound and life that moved with purpose, with a beginning and an ending, like a masterfully arranged song composed of thousands of perfectly tuned yet individually unique instruments.

It's the Song, Emmett believed.

As he said this to himself, he found that his awareness was slipping backward, focusing his consciousness toward that peaceful, quiet place within himself. The world receded and fell away. His world coalesced with a swirl of merging colors and shifting images, shapes soon taking form along the periphery of his mind. All the while, the Song swirled around him.

"Emmett Brennan," he heard an ageless, genderless voice say.

In the nothingness, Emmett felt himself reach out to the voice with his own awareness. "I'm here, Archivist."

"Still with a look of wit. Your journey is not over. Seek me. Open your eyes."

Emmett felt himself rushing backward, the world coalescing again as the bitter cold assaulted his skin. Emmett's awareness quickly stretched throughout his limbs, and with some effort, his mind returned fully to his body, feeling the tingling awareness in his restored limbs.

"Archivist," Emmett whispered as he opened his eyes. At once, he felt Keiran and Oliver's hands pull off of his body, and the low, throbbing sound they had enveloped him in disappeared. The world violently rushed in around him as the deadening constriction of the Rot seized his chest greedily with claws that tore into his muscles and organs.

Even with the shocking return of all the pain in his body, Emmett could not help but gasp in wonder as he looked up and saw that the dark, writhing swarm had taken shape and color. A glowing luminescence glimmered in millions of eyes as countless butterflies and moths hovered in the air around them, forming a brilliant canvas of color upon which was painted a forest he had never seen.

Amala and the red-haired woman both raised their eyes upward, looking around with their own unhidden awe. Each insect held its position perfectly despite the pelting rain overhead. As one would fall away in the wind and rain, another would quickly rise to assume its place, drawing in the air a vivid, ever-shifting panoramic canvas of lifelike color and depth around them.

"Praise her," the red-haired woman breathed as she gazed around in wonder.

Amala stood slowly as if not to disturb the swarm, turning with deliberate care in a circle as she looked upon the living canvas. Emmett watched her move thoughtfully as Keiran and Oliver struggled to lift their heads from the exhaustion their shivering, wet bodies were obviously burdened with.

"Amala," Rhiannon whispered, "is this—"

"Yes," Amala nodded. "Is this where the Archivist is, Emmett?"

"She said 'seek me.'"

A bellow of thunder resounded in the stormy night as Amala lifted her two hands before her, palms facing out away from her. "We come soon," Amala said to the swarm with a hushed whisper. A ripple shuddered through the mass of color, and with a strike of lightning that arced across the sky, the swarm disbanded in a flurry of motion and disappeared into the shadowy night.

The roaring storm returned. A screech sounded over the howling night, and a rustle of flapping wings followed a copper-feathered hawk that swooped down and came to rest on the red-haired woman's shoulder as if it had been circling overhead the entire time.

Emmett managed to lift his head enough to see that Oliver was doubled-over. Keiran, too, was slumped, though he had managed to keep Emmett's head cradled in his knees even as his torso and drooping head threatened to collapse. Emmett could see that his eyes were half-closed and his mouth slightly ajar as the pouring rain mixed with the nosebleed to mat his white skin with red lines.

Amala moved swiftly and grabbed Keiran's shoulders. "Help me get them into the van," she said as she wrested Keiran sideways along the wet ground.

Rhiannon easily lifted Keiran up as Amala bent over Emmett. Her wide eyes twinkled in the darkness as her hand delicately brushed against his pale, cold cheeks.

"Hold on, Emmett. I won't ever let you die," she whispered before lifting one arm underneath his legs and the other under his shoulders and cradling him in her arms.

Emmett felt delirious with pain from the movement, only distantly aware that Amala was carrying him. He soon felt dryness and warmth before he moaned heavily and rocked to one side on a hard, metal floor.

His final image of semi-wakefulness was of Keiran's form lying next to his, and his glassy green eyes staring catatonically at him, dazed and unfocused, beneath wafts of wet, matted blond hair.

Then Emmett felt movement and heard the sound of tires rolling along over gravel. Then there was only blissful, silent darkness.

CHAPTER 25

When Emmett opened his eyes, he felt no pain in his body. He felt whole and fully healed. That was the exact moment when he realized that he was dreaming.

He was seated now at the end of a wooden pew in a small, empty church. Emmett did not recognize where he was but recognized the startling clarity of his senses: how the light reflected off of the silver candelabras on the table at the front of the church; the smell of wood polish along the rows of pews; the fragrant incense that wafted along the quiet, unassuming air; Ellie's face reflected in the colored panes of the stained-glass windows.

Not a dream.

"I did not think you would come," a voice said behind him, and Emmett turned to see a middle-aged man in the black shirt and white collar of a priest. His face was plain and unremarkable, neither handsome nor ugly, neither skinny nor overweight, and with ordinary brown hair and common brown eyes. Had he not been wearing the outfit of a priest, Emmett thought, he would be lost and forgotten in any room full of people without a second thought paid to him.

"All is ready?" To this question, Emmett felt a reaction in his mind as if a second awareness was present, and he felt her nodding in answer. Somewhere within was a building sense of anticipation, as if Ellie were excited about her acceptance of the priest's offer, an excitement that felt colored somehow by a latent, primal emotion. Fear?

Emmett tried to concentrate on the priest and found that his mind seemed unable to retain the memories of his face or sound of his voice. The priest folded his hands behind his back and paced the length of the church, stopping before the altar with his back to Emmett.

"Kellner suspects nothing?"

"He is powerful but easily fooled."

"Anyone can attain power. Few can wield it. Always remember to whom you owe your loyalty."

A patron more powerful than me, to be certain, Emmett remembered Kellner saying.

"What do I have to do?" Ellie asked.

"Our contact within Silvan Dea is ready. You attack tomorrow night."

"I'm going to destroy Silvan Dea," Ellie breathed.

"*I* destroy it. And the whoring meddler hiding behind the throne," the priest growled, his skin rupturing as bones protruded violently from his neck.

The priest lowered his head as if in great discomfort, and Emmett watched as the walls shuddered. A rippling coursed visibly through the priest's body as if power would riven the flesh and bones and explode forth. He raised his head again and the bone quickly receded, the flesh immediately mending itself as the walls grew motionless.

"So your promise remains? I serve you and am rewarded?"

"You would doubt me?"

"I doubt everything," Ellie responded.

The priest tilted his head to one side as if he considered the crucifix hanging on the wall above him. "It is the irony of your finite existence. You were created with the inherent wonder of one who need not struggle to believe. Yet you squander your pitiful lives doubting everything."

The priest fell silent, nodding eventually to himself. "You will obey and not question me again, and I will grant you your desire."

"You will destroy him," Ellie said. In Emmett's mind, he saw the image form: Ellie collapsed beside a little unmoving girl, pleading with her to move, screaming for the world to hear the pain that would never fully go away.

"There is only one person who can destroy The Grinning Man, Ellie. If you do as I say, that person *will* destroy The Grinning Man, giving you your revenge."

"Not by you? Who then?"

"A boy."

"A boy?" she scoffed. "Kellner said the Old Ones are immortal; they cannot be destroyed by mortals!"

The priest snickered. "Monkeys fumbling in the dark for knowledge they could not possibly comprehend. You would be driven mad and your soul wrenched from your body if you but dipped your toe in the yawning maw that is the infinite and starry ocean of my greatness. Only *I* possess the knowledge you seek."

"How? The Wights believe that nothing is greater than an Old One."

"All beings serve a master," the priest answered. "Even the Old Ones."

"You would destroy something that serves you?"

The priest ran his hands over the table, and Emmett saw each item melt under his touch. Again, Emmett felt the rush of excitement and fear from Ellie.

"If it suits me," the priest answered, turning now to face Ellie.

Something shifted in his expression as he looked at Ellie. As a sinister grin spread across his unremarkable face, his brown eyes suddenly turned black.

When the priest spoke now, his voice felt colder and more brittle. "Oh, now this is quite interesting? Spying into the … future, perhaps? No, no, it's your past, isn't it? You have taken a new form again; I did not recognize you. And though I have missed our conversations, I see you are still not ready for your Master. You will leave now, Waking Dreamer. For all your untapped power, you are, in fact, entirely powerless to stop me killing all those you hold dear. Go and gestate in life's womb some more, never forgetting from whom your power emanates. And to whom you will one day serve."

Without preamble, the priest waved his hand dismissively, and Emmett felt himself violently ripped from Ellie's body and sent careening backward into a bottomless void where the terrified screams of his plummeting consciousness echoed unanswered.

CHAPTER 26

Emmett sat upright with such sudden force that it was only Amala's lightning-fast reflexes and, apparently, the fact that she was beside him, that kept him from toppling over.

"Easy, Emmett."

The deep, resounding soreness in his chest stretched through him with an explosion of pain, and Emmett nodded as he ground his teeth and managed to steady his labored breathing.

He saw that he was still in back of the van. Keiran and Oliver lay beside him, their faces cleaned now but seemingly asleep. Rhiannon was driving the van.

"How long?" Emmett croaked.

"We've been driving for an entire day. We're on our way to the Archivist."

"You people and your cross-country drives," Emmett said. He tried to laugh and choked, bringing his hand up to his chest.

"The Rot has consumed more than half of your body. The fever seems to have worsened it. But we are almost to the Archivist. She will heal you and guide us on the next steps of our journey."

"How are you?" Emmett asked, feeling lost in her eyes and unsure where to begin with all he wanted to say to her.

"Rhiannon and I have been tracking you both since you left Chicago. We only made it to the Lighthouse as you were leaving, and with a Revenant sect following us, had no time to stop you."

Emmett nodded, trying to sit up and feeling Amala's steadying hand behind him. "Is Keiran okay?" he asked, and it was a measure of how much Keiran's friendship meant to him that he did not flinch at the expression Amala's face undertook when she looked at him.

"He'll be fine, Emmett. They need their rest, but they should be awake soon."

Emmett saw that her other hand was resting on his leg, and he stared dumbly at it for what felt like an eternity. It was a woman he hardly knew, and yet had spent each night with throughout his life. The adventure he faced may have been precipitated by the Revenant's attack, but it was with Amala that it had begun.

Emmett looked into her eyes and made to whisper to her. She leaned in close enough that her ear was to his lips, sending a shudder through his body even as he tasted the air around her. "Amala, what is the Waking Dreamer?"

For as long as Emmett lived, he would never be able to adequately describe the expression that night on Amala's face. It was a countenance possessed of so many conflicting emotions that he doubted even she could acknowledge them: understanding and confusion; confidence and concern; resolution and doubt. It was like everything in all her life and in all the world finally made sense and was, at the same time, thrown into upheaval and chaos. She was reassured and yet still questioning. She seemed to see Emmett for who he was, and yet it was if she had never known Emmett before now.

She blinked. Once. Twice. Three times. Then drawing a steadying breath, she whispered back.

"You are."

"Hold on!" Rhiannon screamed. The van's brakes cried with anguish as the van careened off the road. Oliver and Keiran flew forward, and Amala braced herself against the wall as she held Emmett to her.

There was momentary confusion as the van skidded to a stop. Oliver and Keiran both were shaking their heads, waking from their deep sleep as Amala set Emmett down and jumped forward to the passenger seat.

"What could be causing that?" Amala exclaimed.

"What happened?" Oliver demanded, pushing himself up.

"What the sodding hell is going on?" Keiran called out, looking first for Emmett and, seeing he was okay, trying to stand and look up front.

The two Bards craned their necks to see out over the dashboard. Emmett, who was still lying down, struggled to prop himself upright but hissed as the Rot squeezed the air from his lungs.

"I've only ever *heard* of such a thing before. Never have I seen it," Oliver said with a voice that alternated between awe and horror.

"Where are we?" Keiran asked.

"Blue Ridge Mountains in the Appalachians," Amala answered. "Where the Archivist told Emmett she would be waiting for him."

Emmett saw Oliver and Rhiannon exchange knowing looks.

"Could she be causing this?" Keiran pointed.

"Would someone tell me what the crap is going on?" Emmett yelled.

"I'm going out there," Oliver said.

"You will not."

"Try and stop me, Amala." He dove past Emmett and threw the back doors open.

"Go with him, Keiran," Amala said.

"Stay here, mate," Keiran said as he passed.

"Would either of you tell me *something*?" Emmett pleaded.

Rhiannon was still staring out the window at something that she could not take her eyes from. Amala turned back and looked at Emmett. "We're approaching the place that the Archivist showed you. But there's something going on."

"Amala? I need you!" Keiran called out from outside the van. Amala turned and launched out the door without another word to Emmett. Before he could turn to Rhiannon, she, too, burst through her door and sprinted after Amala.

"Oh, you have got to be kidding me!" Emmett exclaimed angrily as he cursed several times and was rewarded with a slice of pain from the exertion. He had come too far to not know. With great effort, he willed himself upright and swung his legs out and slid out of the back of the van.

Life as a Druid or Bard must have been one of sensory overload, Emmett thought. His surroundings and environment had already changed more times in the past week than they ever had in his whole life. Once again, he found himself in an alien world. With the damp mud beneath his feet, Emmett looked out on the thick, unbroken wilderness. The soft rustling of falling nettles and whistling of owls were carried on a chilled air that was heavy with the natural scent of raw pine.

The van was parked on the shoulder of a gravel road that extended in either direction to points unseen in the darkness. A hawk's long cries careened through the silent night's emptiness as one glided past him and swung low overhead before circling back out over the surrounding forest.

Walking around to the front of the van, he saw the four standing together a dozen or so yards ahead at a point where the headlights from the van seemed to fade into the surrounding darkness. Emmett saw nothing. The four Children stood silently, each tense with their arms twitching at their sides as if prepared to react to something, and the scene was disquieting enough that he had to look behind him once to see if anything stalked them in the darkness.

Despite the pain inherent with any movement, Emmett quickly hurried up to join them. No one was speaking, but it was the first time that he did not see Keiran turning his ear up as if listening intently to the night. They simply stood in the road, transfixed by something that apparently only they could see.

A faint hissing sound rattled in the wind as one of Amala's black serpents licked at the air behind her. Emmett felt a swirl of movement behind him just as the hawk circled down and landed gently on Rhiannon's shoulders.

"Do you remember what I told you about ghosts, Emmett?" Keiran asked.

"Sure."

Keiran turned to look at him, and when he did Emmett saw his expression and understood the gravity of what was happening, even if he did not know exactly what was happening.

"Show him," Rhiannon said.

Keiran took two fingers and touched them gently to the back of Emmett's neck. He produced a low hum muffled by the cold wind moving through the trees. Emmett felt his eyes watering, harried by some dense irritation, and he blinked several times.

The world seemed to upend itself, the sky becoming the ground and the trees turning upside down. Staggering with his hand over his head, he blinked again, and his vision quickly righted. Only now, the forest around him took on a preternatural glow, the darkness focusing brilliantly with thousands of sparkling stars overhead, and millions of points of impressive lights twinkling around him.

Keiran was looking at him, nodding as if to confirm that

something had changed. Every element of Keiran's features came shockingly into focus. Out of the corner of his eye, Emmett saw Rhiannon watching him, her red hair now with his new vision a waterfall of rolling fire.

He realized that Keiran was still touching his neck and was mouthing something to him. Focusing beyond the brilliant palette of visual sensation, he willed himself to listen. Emmett found that there was no sound but for a soft rushing. He swallowed heavily, listening for his own heartbeat but finding only the endless wind.

Looking directly ahead, Emmett saw points of light crossing the roadway in a procession of white brilliance. The lights seemed to be passing across in a soft dusting of sifted flour, the tiny, individual points of light almost powdery and seemingly weightless as if they drifted along on wind that carried them.

What am I looking at?

Keiran withdrew his touch, and Emmett felt the world turn upside down once more, the saturation of bold light exploding in his vision and returning to a dull, aching darkness as he opened and shut his eyes several more times. With a disconcerting lightheadedness, Emmett steadied himself with Keiran's shoulder, shaking his head a few times before finding that the night had returned to normal.

"The restless dead," Keiran indicated.

"And a haunted forest is a big deal?" he asked as he coughed again.

Keiran shook his head with a grave expression communicated by his eyes. "If a soul is unable to let go, it's because it remains tethered to this world. Fixed. Unable to move."

"So what are they doing?" Emmett asked.

"Fleeing," Rhiannon and Oliver both answered at the same moment. Their eyes met briefly before turning back to the invisible spectacle.

"Why would a ghost flee?" Emmett asked.

The Children shared a mutual, blanched expression before Amala answered him. "Out of fear, Emmett. They are afraid."

He was certain that no answer would comfort him, and despite everything that Keiran had warned him countless times before, Emmett could not stop from asking. "Of what? The Black Hounds?"

Keiran blinked as Oliver turned to look at him. Emmett immediately regretted saying anything as Oliver leaned over and stared at Keiran.

"Few things can frighten the spirits of the dead; only those things that are ancient, strange—the aberrant and weird things that have been displaced from the natural order of creation," Rhiannon said.

"The Old Ones," Amala said plainly. As if everyone else had been thinking it but not wanting to say it for fear that it might make it true.

Emmett was so close to the Archivist, and once again he faced the presence of something beyond his understanding or any of their abilities. Keiran stared ahead without making eye contact with him, but Emmett knew what had to be going through his mind: the image of the Hag coming once again for Emmett, the only child, the boy born under the Light of Arthur and pursued by Death.

"The area that the Archivist identified is about ten miles up ahead," Amala said almost conversationally, as if focusing all of them gave them the strength to see beyond their situation. "We will continue there so Emmett can be healed."

"And the spirits?" Oliver asked rhetorically, motioning with one hand at the invisible procession.

Amala looked directly at Emmett without turning to face the

others. Her eyes softened as she looked at him, her face awash in a silent determination that instantly communicated everything he wanted to hear. Everything would be okay. She would make certain of that.

"Let the dead remain dead. Life is for the living. The Archivist awaits Emmett."

CHAPTER 27

Several miles ahead, an unmarked side road turned down into a valley. It ended at an unremarkable wooden cabin not large enough to fit more than three rooms. Its single door and window faced out over a shimmering lake whose glassy waters reflected the moon overhead.

Emmett felt the intensity of the approaching moment as they exited the van. He watched the two Bards slowly circling the area, both with closed eyes listening to the forest. Rhiannon walked over to Amala, who stood mutely staring at the cabin.

"Are you okay?" she whispered, bringing her hand up to the side of her face. "I know this place holds memories for you."

"No longer," Amala said stoically, turning as Oliver spoke.

"There is *something* out there. Do you hear it?"

Amala and Rhiannon narrowed their eyes, both searching the forest's darkness.

"Aye. It's about—"

"—five hundred yards north," Keiran and Oliver said at the same time.

Oliver's head snapped around to where Emmett was standing, and a second later Keiran did the same thing. They both stared at something in the trees beyond Emmett, and both cocked their heads to the side as they listened.

"It's changed direction—"

"—at least three hundred and fifty yards due south," Keiran finished.

Again, both Bards spun toward a sound only they could hear, listening to a distant point, facing away from Emmett. "Now it's in the east—"

"No, it's in the west!" Oliver corrected as they both spun around.

Amala stepped toward Emmett as Rhiannon, too, drew closer to him. Amala's serpents hissed and uncoiled from around her shoulder, winding down her arms. The Druids each raised their arms above their hips as if expecting an attack. With their sparkling eyes widening, both stared into the obscuring forest for signs of attack.

Before Emmett could say anything, a twig snapped sharply in the distance. Amala reacted before Emmett could even process what was happening, feeling the strength of her grip on his arm as she bore him almost aloft in the air. With a backward stumble, Emmett managed to twist around before diving to the ground, with Amala's form crouched over him defensively.

"Stay down!"

Rhiannon's arms spun outward, an iron stave the length of her body now twirling in her hands above her head even as the hawk circled above. Keiran had dashed for Amala and Emmett as Oliver fell to a crouching position like a cat waiting to pounce. Both Bards' eyes closed and turned their ears up to the night as they strained to hear the smallest of movements.

Keiran was standing guard with Amala over Emmett as Rhiannon slowly circled them and Oliver stood a few yards away still listening for the unseen presence. Emmett was so winded from the pain of being thrown to the hard ground that he had to struggle just to speak.

"The Archivist?" Emmett managed to ask.

"Until we know for certain, Emmett, we must assume otherwise," Keiran said.

Another twig snapped. Another. Then another. As if something were charging toward them.

"From the north, two hundred yards," Oliver said as he spun in place to face the direction from where the sound was coming. As one, the others turned, though Amala's serpents continued to pivot in the air to watch behind her.

Suddenly, the direction of the sound shifted, and now it sounded as if the running was coming from another direction.

"From the west, one hundred yards," Keiran noted, and again they all moved in preparation.

"Eighty yards."

"Sixty."

"Defensive positions. Now!" Amala commanded.

Again, the running was now coming from a different approach. "East now, fifty yards," Oliver called out. Emmett felt Amala place one hand onto the back of his shoulder and squeeze firmly as she crouched low over his prone body.

The sound of the hurtling form in the forest changed direction again, and this time it was so close that neither Bard had to call it out for all four of them to turn as one to face it. The sound ended suddenly, and they all collectively held their breath.

Something flew out of the forest, hurtling through the air faster than any human could run on the ground and faster than any bird could fly. Emmett had only a moment to catch a glimpse of it as the form landed on the ground a dozen yards from him and fell into a graceful tumble before uncoiling upward and bursting into motion directly for him.

Oliver had already loosed a deafening roar of sound at the

figure, but its movement through the air was so fast that it had avoided it entirely. Rhiannon's body was a blur of motion as she spun around several times and brought her stave around again and again. The form tumbled low and then broke into a run so fast that it easily avoided her attacks, as if Rhiannon's stave chased the form's shadow.

Amala did not move from standing guard over Emmett, and he saw Keiran step in front of them with his arms spread wide open as he unleashed a heavy, forceful bellow that rolled directly over the form. It spun forward on the ground in a tumble before unfolding back up and sprinting around him.

Oliver turned around and pierced the night with several short, abrupt notes that singed the air. The figure ran wide in a semi-circle around the group, jumping up several feet into the air and propelling itself over several low-hanging branches from trees on the periphery of the forest. Oliver's notes crashed into the trees and splintered them easily, Rhiannon's powerful swings felling large trees and upending smaller ones. Through it all, the form escaped unharmed, so fast and agile it was.

"What the bloody hell is it?" Keiran managed to ask before taking another deep breath and unleashing a strident note that produced an invisible force that missed the form by several yards as it leapt through the trees.

"Where is the Archivist?" Rhiannon responded, watching the figure disappear into the forest before hurtling out of the trees again and bounding directly for them.

Oliver loosed another series of notes that the figure deftly leapt over before twisting and contorting through the wide slashes of Rhiannon's diving hawk. The figure was within reach of Keiran when he extended his open palm outward and bellowed deeply. Its speed was too great for the eyes to track, the figure seeming to pirouette and contort around him.

The figure was so close to Emmett that he could feel the rush of wind as it seemed to swim through the air. Amala stood her ground, sweeping her serpents at a spot where the figure had once been. The figure dove underneath her so fast that she did not have time to recover the motion, and she was as easily off her feet as if the ocean had knocked her from the beach.

Emmett spun over onto his back, struggling to get up despite the stranglehold the Rot had on his body. The figure loomed over him wild, formless, and insubstantial. Emmett's vision was already blurring, and he could not tell if it was from the slow suffocation of the Rot, or the figure that was now atop him on the ground, having so easily defeated his four guardians.

Dizzy with effort, in a distant corner of his mind, he recognized that he was taking his final breath. The darkness of the grave subsumed his vision as human hands pressed down on his chest.

And then there was only black.

He was surrounded by emptiness. The beginning of everything that came after. If life were a canvas upon which the people and experiences and everything learned or known is drawn, then this was the material from which the canvas was made.

Emmett heard a voice: urgent, and with less confidence than before. "Follow me."

The nothingness coalesced with a whirling of colors and forms as Emmett's consciousness transfixed onto a shaping substance within the chaos. Soon, his mind saw a world form beneath him, a vast plateau of green fields dotted with trees and shrubs that swayed soundlessly in a placid breeze. A wide, shimmering river of blue and white wound across the flat pastures of grasses as small animals grazed at the water's edge.

Emmett felt the dizzying movement of color as the ground rushed up toward him, his consciousness plummeting from the cloudless sky. As he drew closer, the animals took shape, their varying stripes and patterns sharpening in focus. Proud racks of horned antlers craned above the tall grasses as large, bristled hides moved just beneath the river's surface. Mighty tusks of pristine ivory were raised with trumpeted calls from long trunks.

His consciousness focused at a wide-reaching tree in the distance. Its massive, swollen trunk sported thick branches that tapered at their ends like giant, unearthed roots, spreading majestically outward with a dark green canopy of leaves and laden with large, bulbous gourds of fragrant fruit.

Before the canopy of the grand tree sat a lion, whose pensive eyes were cast along the distant horizon as a gentle breeze softly ruffled his brilliant and majestic mane. Seated underneath the tree just behind the lion in the canopy's wide-reaching shadow sat a lone woman with her back to the engorged trunk. Her dark, aged skin folded over on itself with a plump, homely face that brightened with wide jowls and a bemused reflection in her eyes. They sparkled with the preoccupied expression of distant stars that have seen the coming and going of countless, untold eons.

Emmett felt his consciousness drawn toward the figure, the waving grasses almost parting as he sped toward it. As he drew closer, he saw other animals standing near the figure in groups—gray gorillas, several tending young babies while lone silverbacks with shocks of white fur running along their backs paced in the distance. Elephants and giraffes grazed along the perimeter.

He felt himself slow to within a few yards of the figure. Though distinctive in form, the definition of her face was shrouded by the tree's shadow. Only the heavy lines that surrounded her starry eyes could be seen. An aged hand reached out to stroke one of the infant gorillas near her, which responded approvingly with a wide yawn of teeth as it settled against her hand.

"Am I dead? Are you God?"

The voice tickled his mind with a laugh that was full of the wonder and joy of an infant, the attentiveness and devotion of a mother, and the wisdom and patience of an old woman. The voice touched his consciousness like a waft of air carrying a soft whisper.

"Neither."

Emmett recognized the peace that spread through his mind and the world around him. It was the voice he had heard before in his previous visions; an ageless, genderless voice that spoke to him from an imperceptible distance with the intimacy and immediacy of someone embracing his spirit.

"Archivist?"

"Indeed, I am here. I have been waiting for you."

At once, every single emotion he had experienced since the Underdweller's attack—fear, anger, frustration, anxiety, confusion, appreciation, camaraderie, joy, love—all swelled through him at once like a symphony reaching a climactic crescendo of sound. He felt everything acutely and specifically, as if every moment had been leading to that moment, right then. The Archivist.

"Can you heal me?"

"Do you wish it?"

"Yes!" Emmett exclaimed in his mind, wanting finally to be free of the gnawing pain of the Rot coursing through his body, penetrating his organs and claiming his body for itself. He wanted to be cleansed of the decaying flesh. He wanted to be free of the nausea and the discomfort that he felt whenever the Revenants were nearby. Most of all, he wanted to free Keiran and Amala of their duty, the burden they carried to protect him. The burden that he saw in their eyes when they looked at him and only by their faith in their Elder held out hope that they would reach her in time.

Emmett expected to feel water washing over him or warmth passing over his skin. He expected the Archivist to reach for him and touch him, *or direct some kind of light or sound at him. Yet none of those things happened. He felt no difference. Indeed, he did not feel or see that he had a body at all. And so he only knew that he had been healed when he felt the Archivist's voice tickling his awareness.*

"It is done. And yet, it is just beginning. You sense this, don't you?"

"You say that as if I'm special in some way."

"Strength is often not measureable until it has been sufficiently tested."

"I have the gift of the Mara, don't I? I'm a Dreamer."

"You are the last one who will see things that the others cannot; things that must be seen in your age. When the people of your age can no longer see, then death becomes an end rather than a beginning."

Emmett had been preparing himself to hear that he was entirely unremarkable and that there was nothing special about him. He wasn't sure what to say now that he knew the opposite was true.

"I'm the Waking Dreamer."

The Archivist's eyes twinkled under the shadow of the mighty tree, and though some of her features remained hidden, Emmett thought he could almost see the crinkling of her face from an unseen smile.

"It would appear that you are."

"What does that mean? Who am I really?"

"Who do you think you are?"

Had Emmett his body, he would have shrugged. Only weeks before, the question would have seemed meaningless. His name was Emmett Jonathan Brennan. He was nearly eighteen years old. He had no family or home. He was just a name and an age.

"You are quite more than a name. You may not realize your impact until you see another person give their life for you."

Emmett saw Keiran's face smiling at him. That Cheshire cat grin that seemed so amused by Emmett's dry sarcasm and endless film references. He saw Amala's face visiting him each night in his dreams, telling him he would one day save her even though it had been her up until this moment who had been saving him.

"Keiran and Amala were ready to give their lives for me. How do I even begin to deserve something like that?"

"When you no longer have to ask, then you will have earned it."

Emmett thought of the attack in the forest. His anxiety for his friends rolled outward from his awareness, upsetting the graceful animals around the great tree. The lion shook his mane heavily, the gorillas pounded their fists on the ground, and the elephants trumpeted nervously.

The Archivist cooed the animals, and soon all were settled.

Emmett saw that a glassy image had formed in the air. He saw himself lying on the ground with the large figure hovering over him. All was frozen in time: Oliver and Keiran lunging toward the figure as Rhiannon and Amala prepared to strike. Nothing was happening in that moment, though it still appeared as if they were in danger.

"That is my Attendant."

Emmett thought of Dr. Hazrat's Attendant, young Eitan, and he willed his awareness to look deeper into the image suspended in the air. Whereas young Eitan was petite, cultured, well mannered, and appropriately manicured, the Archivist's Attendant was the farthest concept from human civilization.

"Not the warmest welcome, really."

He saw that the form crouched over him was actually a woman: wild, untamed hair snarled with leaves and twigs caught in unkempt tufts, with layers of furs or skins woven together covering her body. She looked like someone who lived entirely in the wild, her face hidden mostly by her overgrown hair and her brown eyes alight with a feral sort of fire.

She was clearly powerful. Emmett could remember now how she moved through the air with speed that outpaced even the Druids and Bards, who themselves moved with alacrity far greater than he had ever seen another human capable of. Yet the Attendant had not attacked any of them, deftly avoiding their attacks to finally reach Emmett, which had immediately pushed his awareness into this communion with the Archivist.

"Next time just say hello and save everyone the bother of fighting."

"Her posture was not due to your presence."

Emmett recalled the procession of spirits fleeing through the forest. Again, he felt the heavy burden as he understood that his friends still were in danger.

"It's an Old One, isn't it? The Hag has come for me."

"Not the Hag, Emmett. It is time that you finally remember."

The Archivist raised a hand pointed at his head. Suddenly, Emmett's mind reeled under the weight of memories that raced to the surface. He was watching the moments following his birth, staring up into the green luna moths fluttering about the Archivist's face. Amala the child was holding him, staring down at him. She was trembling now, frightened by the red eyes that had come for Emmett. The Grinning Man was searching for Emmett, the Waking Dreamer. It was not yet time. Then the Archivist named The Grinning Man just as Keiran named the Hag, and he was gone. Only to torment his mother in the hospital, searching for Emmett, until finally she died.

"He came for me!"

"The Grinning Man is the harbinger of the Waking Dreamer, the final Mara of this age. The Grinning Man will take you, Emmett. And his Master will finally kill all the Children of the Earth."

The shadow cast by the tree overhead widened, and a coldness he had not felt blew through him. His mind focused upward to see a sky swollen suddenly with dark storm clouds like black shadows that stretched across the horizon. Emmett felt a tenseness pulse through the area as animals shifted nervously, many bounding away into the grasses as great winds whipped along.

Emmett's mind was finally pulling all of the pieces together.

"Amala knew I was the Waking Dreamer all along."

"You are intertwined, as you always have been."

Emmett thought of her Companion, Keiran, and he saw the Archivist nod.

"So is Keiran. Their journey is the Waking Dreamer's journey."

"Which is what? What am I supposed to do?"

"It has already begun, and it begins tonight. The Master sends The Grinning Man for you, and for the Children you will face him."

"Who is the Master? Who is this patron?"

"The Rugged Mountain. The Unremarkable Man. He is the Second and is chief amongst the Old Ones. He is the true darkness of the world."

Already Emmett saw that the great shadow overhead had darkened the valley and swallowed the suspended image in the air.

"Banish The Grinning Man, Emmett. Then go to the Lady Karina with Keiran and Amala. Your journey is theirs, too. It always has been, and it always will be. There is something important in Noronha for you next to learn."

Emmett felt the urgency of the moment as his consciousness began to fold in on itself, his mind racing with a tangle of half-formed questions.

"What about Silvan Dea? Your Grove has been destroyed. What do they do?"

The Archivist seemed to sigh with the feathery touch of her consciousness on his own.

"Let the dead remain dead, Emmett."

Before Emmett could respond, he felt himself plummeting backward into a black void bereft of color or sound. With shocking awareness, sensation and feeling shot through his limbs like electricity, and his watery eyes opened to a starry, crisp night.

CHAPTER 28

As he opened his eyes, Emmett felt the soft tickling of something touching his nose. Hair. No. A leaf? A leaf wound in hair. His eyes struggled to focus, and as darkness separated, he saw a face half-hidden by a mass of unkempt, wild hair staring silently at him.

The Archivist's Attendant.

The world responded as if it had been paused, and there was a sudden rush of movement as the two Druids and Bards who obviously did not know her identity and thought she was attacking Emmett leapt with a flurry of coordinated attacks.

Amala's swinging serpents were the first to reach her, and though the Attendant did not move off of Emmett, she ducked to the side just as Rhiannon brought her iron stave down across a spot where the Attendant's head had been only moments before. Oliver and Keiran followed with bellowing attacks of concussive sound that the Attendant dodged as she rolled away and scuttled across the ground on hands and knees before bounding up to the limbs of a tree nearly twenty feet overhead.

Emmett's mind started into action as he jumped up with his hands above him and bolted in the path of the Archivist's Attendant between the attacking Children.

"Wait! Stop! She's the Archivist's Attendant!"

As one, all four paused mid-attack, and had he not seen the look of utter disbelief in Keiran's eyes he might have forgotten that he was standing so easily on his own, waving his hands wildly in a pattern that should have been painful.

"Emmett?" Amala asked tentatively, her hand reaching out toward him as if to see if he were truly standing on his own.

Emmett looked down at his chest as he pulled his coat aside. He knew what was happening before he saw it, but he had to see it with his own eyes. Ripping apart the buttons on his shirt under his coat, he exposed his skin to the damp Appalachian air. His pale skin was still mottled and black with the Rot's disease. He knew something had changed, because the suffocating tightness and throbbing pain was completely gone.

Amala reached him first, staring at his exposed chest. She raised a finger toward the Rot. When her finger grazed the edge near the center of his torso, the blackened skin seemed to crumble away like a fine dusting of soot. With a clean breeze rich with pine, the Rot's final remnants blew away from his torso to reveal healed flesh that was whole, pink, and supple.

"Praise her," Rhiannon breathlessly whispered as she lowered her stave and fell to her knees.

"She did it," Amala whispered, kneading her fingers along Emmett's chest and feeling his heartbeat. "She said you would make it."

"Brilliant!" Keiran said, and Emmett saw that tears had come to his eyes. Even Oliver was nodding to Emmett with an expression of satisfaction.

Emmett felt a moment's reprieve, wishing he could embrace each of them. He wanted to take Amala into his arms and celebrate the life that had nearly been taken from him. He wanted to scream out into the night with the freedom that he had from the Rot.

But he could not. They did not have time.

Purpose and knowing, the kind of confidence Emmett had never known before, suddenly focused him. He walked toward the Attendant. Amala and Rhiannon were behind him, along with Keiran, and Oliver seemed to be standing a respectful but noticeable distance back.

"Attendant?" Emmett called out, unsure how to properly address her. "Can you come down here, please?"

Emmett watched as she tilted her head, silently staring at him crouched on the large tree limb high above them. Her motions were feral, primal, and Emmett wondered if she could even understand what he was saying to her.

As if in response, she leapt down, falling easily within feet of them on her hands and feet like a feline. Her face arched up and her eyes regarded Emmett beneath the mass and tangle of hair.

"How long has she been in the wilderness?" Keiran asked.

"I thought you were dead," Rhiannon whispered. She drew close with obvious familiarity, but the feral, unrecognizing look in the Attendant's eye caused her to slowly back away.

"Not dead," the Attendant croaked as if she had not spoken for years.

Emmett was beginning to understand everything now. How, he could not say. But things that the Archivist had said were beginning to make greater sense.

"You've been in hiding, haven't you? You've been waiting?"

The Attendant nodded, and Emmett knew without saying aloud that the Attendant had been waiting for him. To serve as the conduit to the Archivist, the Elder who for reasons known only to her could not be present for what was coming.

"He's coming now, isn't he?" In a distant part of his mind, Emmett was confused that the question had come not from the

Attendant, but from Amala standing beside him. As his mind raced through Ellie's story and the Archivist's visions, the meaning of his childhood dreams suddenly became clear.

The Grinning Man was coming for Emmett.

Something crashed into the van, a violent and brutal shock of force that blew it apart and sent burning metal careening in all directions with a plume of fire into the air. They were thrown outward, and somehow, instinctively, Emmett threw his hands over his face as he tumbled like a rag doll through the air and was showered in an explosion of shattered glass. Emmett felt the wind pushed from his lungs as he slammed into a distant tree and fell backward onto the ground, his vision a blur of blinking lights.

Several moments of unimaginable pain passed before Emmett felt something touching his head. He fell forward limply into a pair of strong arms that dragged him through piercing wreckage into a chilling, foggy air that assaulted his exposed skin. His eyes swam into bleary focus, feeling dull pain throughout his body that was crisscrossed by interlacing cuts from broken glass along the ground. He coughed dryly, unable to stop himself as he continued to violently heave for air. Though the Rot was free from his body finally, everywhere he ached from the van's explosion.

He heard a commotion several yards from him. He saw the Attendant, her arms cut badly with deep wounds running down her face, dragging Amala away from the burning wreckage and dropping her next to Keiran's motionless body on the ground next to Emmett. Emmett could not tell Keiran or Amala's condition, but he saw in the Attendant's stagger that she, too, was badly injured.

Oliver lay unmoving on the ground far away from them, having been thrown in the opposite direction. Rhiannon, too, was crumpled in a heap some distance from him. Burning into the

Appalachian night, the van's fire blazed from its torn engine as flaming rubber and smoking, smoldering metal combined with a toxic cloud of burning oil to blanket the area in a suffocating haze.

Something in the air demanded Emmett's attention. He felt it presently. It was grave and oppressive like an immense weight. The hair on his arms stood on end, and Emmett felt something crushing against his ears. There were painfully low sounds reverberating within his mind like a bellow from the deepest point in the earth, gathering strength as it echoed up an impossibly long tunnel.

Emmett clawed at his ears, fearing he might go mad from the sound. He searched the area for the source and saw nothing but the burning van. Whatever *it* was, it felt both maddeningly distant and somehow all around him, charging the air with a sort of electricity that could alight a thousand fires if given the dry kindling to do so.

The Attendant was crouched low to the ground like a wild cat, and though she did not move, her eyes darted around as she seemed to sense the presence. She stood upright suddenly, and with great, visible effort, turned around in wide, sweeping circles. Blood dripped down from her wild hair as her eyes seemed to almost swim in and out of focus.

"Show yourself," she growled as if she were still finding how to speak.

The Attendant was answered with a deep booming sound that was the crashing of waves against unyielding cliffs. There was mocking laughter whose breadth nearly made Emmett's ears bleed. They popped again under the enormous pressure, and as he feebly tried to cover his ears with his hands, he strained to see where the laughter came from.

Across from them near the empty cabin, a fog was rolling

toward them. Curtains of fog folded over each other in thick layers as the fog grew heavy and low to the ground, soon covering much of the cabin as it stalked toward where the van had exploded.

Suddenly, the living whorls of fog parted, and a tall figure stepped forward from the darkness itself of the forest beyond. Standing taller than any of them, it was covered entirely in shadow as the fog itself whirled in tendrils covering most of its features. Yet clearly through the mists and shadows, pouring itself into a shape from the fog itself, Emmett saw a pair of glowing red eyes staring from the fog, eyes that lacked any white or black to separate the swimming color of blood that preternaturally illuminated the darkness. Below the eyes was a wide, grinning mouth.

Emmett saw Ellie and his mother in his mind as their living nightmare, The Grinning Man, stepped forth from shadow.

The Attendant still had not moved, her head tilting back and forth as if assessing The Grinning Man. Emmett did not know what her powers and strengths were versus the Old One. She was certainly more powerful than four Bards and Druids, which meant that if she could not defeat the creature, none of them could.

He heard a moaning next to him and saw Amala beginning to slowly stir, struggling to lift her head.

The unnatural rows of white teeth seemed to chatter as the creature laughed again. It was scornful, hateful laughter as if it delighted in the suffering of a mother weeping over the loss of her own child. It abhorred all manner of life; indeed, it loathed and reviled all of them. It laughed cruelly at the fear it engendered in them from which it drew and wielded its great power.

Emmett and Amala both ground their teeth and clutched their hands over their ears. The laughter was maddening, penetrating

Emmett's mind and forcing its way through him as if it would literally tear him apart.

A Bard's call, at once plaintive and pleading with the tenor notes of a mourning lament, dimly reached over the cacophonous laughter, suffusing Emmett with momentary courage. He looked over, expecting to see Keiran struggling to hold his note, lifting his voice to channel energy and strength to his friends. But Keiran was still collapsed in an unmoving slump beside Amala.

Oliver staggered up to his knees as he bellowed over The Grinning Man's laughter. Struggling to stand just at the edge of the rolling fog, his hands were spread wide as he channeled the core of his being into a desperate, final song; a healing song that had already roused Rhiannon from her stupor and was beginning to stir Keiran, too.

The figure's laughter ceased long enough for its red eyes to cast their preternatural glow toward Oliver. A single, gloved hand rose out of the mist and made a sort of shooing gesture with two fingers in Oliver's direction. At once, an invisible force lifted Oliver easily into the air and sent him flying backward a dozen yards away, slamming him against a tree and crashing down to the ground motionless.

"No!" Rhiannon screamed. With stave in hand and her hawk circling overhead, she exploded into a flurry of motion that Emmett's eyes could scarcely follow. Sprinting forward, she was steps from the figure before it raised its gloved hand again and made the same gesture, sending Rhiannon hurtling backward into the air before she landed in a heap of charred metal.

The laughter was elevated now as the figure glided forward on the rolling fog. Amala was fighting bravely to stand but was still unable to do so. Emmett struggled to right himself, to resist or to fight for his friends' lives. The creature was coming for him, and too often already these people had bravely stepped in front of him to defend him, giving their lives to protect someone that they had barely known. If it meant his own death, he would die trying to save his friends, to call out with some power or do something.

"No," the Attendant growled finally as the creature came within yards of them. The fog surrounding it continued to billow and swirl as if alive and responsive to the being that it enshrouded. The rows of bone-white teeth trembled again under its maddening laughter.

A voice intruded into their minds. It was a sound of parents raping their own children. The words burrowed painfully beneath his skin like maggots, as if carved into his skull with a dull, rusty blade wielded by a madman who delighted in the suffering that he caused.

Stand aside, monkey.

"No," the Attendant repeated with greater force in her feral voice.

The Waking Dreamer shall now serve his Master.

"No." It was not the Attendant's voice this time. It was Emmett's.

Emmett forced himself to his knees, grinding his teeth against the pain. The Grinning Man's mouth turned sideways as if evaluating Emmett for the first time.

Little baby boy, you still stink of your mommy's insides. I can smell them on the wind. Perhaps you would permit me a taste.

Emmett remembered the terror in his mother's face staring into the corner of her hospital room. He saw the child Amala trembling as she held Emmett in her arms in the abandoned basement.

The meddler will no longer deny me.

The Attendant leapt through the air at the figure, landing atop him just as a pair of gloved hands reached up from the fog and snatched both of her arms. Both struggled as the ground beneath them trembled with the force of their combined powers.

"Emmett?" a voice weakly called out. Amala was struggling to lift her head, beckoning Emmett to her. He knelt beside her, cradling her head in his hands just as she had once held him in her arms. He lowered his head to her so that her hand was touching the side of his face.

"You told me he would return for us and you would banish him."

"When?" Emmett asked.

"In *my* life's dreams," she answered, the light in her amber eyes growing dim.

Emmett felt panic as he watched life drain from her face. He was neither an Elder nor a Bard, commanded no measure of power to summon and wield.

"How?" he pleaded. "How do I banish him?"

She raised a hand to his face and cupped his cheek. "Look at the sky, Emmett."

The last piece of his life's mystery fell finally into place. The painting. The dream. The words. He knew what he had to do.

Completing finally what he had never done in countless dreams, Emmett raised his hands and placed his open palm to hers just as Keiran had done at Silvan Dea.

"I know the words," Emmett said before laying Amala back down.

He looked over at the fighting, and he saw that the Attendant was losing. The Grinning Man had her nearly pinned to the ground, pummeling her with rage against all life. The Old One was coming for Emmett just as the Hag had come for him. Emmett was the only one who could defeat him.

He saw Keiran, near death, lying on the ground. His heart swelled with righteous anger, looking to each of the four who

had defended him: Oliver and Rhiannon, once Companions separated by dogma yet reunited briefly to ensure he was healed;
Keiran Glendower, the Bard who protected Emmett as if he were
his brother; and Amala, the Druid who had told him she would
return for him and had.

There were other faces in his mind. Emmett saw Emaline
Carmichael and Derrick Williams, people who had somehow
found purpose in the face of great loss and tragedy. He saw the
Children who rose to defend Silvan Dea, an attack that Emmett
now understood was for him. He saw Ellie Brooks, who unlike
Emaline and Derrick had been consumed by her pain and sought
freedom offered by the dark, unknown Master.

Then the other faces in his mind receded, and Emmett saw
his mother. The mother he had never known. The mother who
studied art history and had been slowly driven mad carrying
him. The mother whose unborn child had plagued her dreams
with the same cryptic words that, in desperation and madness,
she had defaced her favorite painting with. The mother who was
made to forget his birth and yet could not forget that she had
once carried a child within her. The mother who was haunted by
The Grinning Man and driven to despair and finally death.

Their faces all flashed in his mind's eye. Their lives had been
given so that he might live.

For this moment.

For moments yet to come.

For the Children of the Earth.

Emmett Jonathan Brennan stood.

"Bezaliel," he called loudly.

The Grinning Man's gloved hands paused mid-swing, the
Attendant near death. The red eyes turned up to stare at Emmett.

*Your Master awaits you, Waking Dreamer. You will attend the
Rugged Mountain and watch the Children burn.*

"You will leave this place and never return," Emmett said.

Laughter erupted in their minds. *You cannot banish me, child. I am Old as the unknown universe is old. I exist as the profligate and depraved fetishists who seek power exist. I am beyond the whoring meddler as I am beyond you.*

"I am telling you to leave this world," Emmett repeated, his voice nearly shouting.

You have inherited the meddler's weakness. I would dine on each layer of your skin if you did not belong to the Master. I may not kill you, but I can taste your despair. You will watch as I kill these monkeys. They can die like your mother did, desperate and pathetic. Dead like the rotting corpse of Silvan Dea. Futile, meaningless death will visit all those you care for.

"They died to protect me!" Emmett roared, seeing their faces in his mind again. "Their lives have meaning because I live! I live *for* them! I know the words, because I've been weighed and found worthy. 'All this from year to year forever and ever and ever like the bottomless sea and the endless rivers that lead to it.' That means they live on within me! It's for them that I name you, Bezaliel, and tell you to leave this world and never return!"

The sky rumbled as if a star had been rent in two. A shaft of silvery light poured down from overhead from some distant, unseen point in the night's sky, encircling The Grinning Man in a beam of the purest light that Emmett had ever seen.

The Grinning Man threw its gloved hands before its face, its wide mouth thrown open in an expression of unmitigated pain. A horrible sound filled with the voices of countless people, old and young, male and female, some cursing, others crying, erupted in Emmett's mind.

The Old One struggled under the weight of the light, stepping back from the cone of brightness enshrouding it and seemingly willing the fog to cover and protect it. The Attendant, barely moving on the ground, grabbed onto whatever body it hid in the mists. She somehow held tightly to him as the silvery light burned through him.

Emmett felt The Grinning Man's scream reach far into his mind, far beyond any point that he knew existed. It ravaged the corners of his memory and bade distant echoes of memories he did not recognize. He felt as if his heart might explode in his chest, the scream peaking like a wail that could never end unless it consumed all in its wake.

The scream reached a cacophonous, painful pitch, and The Grinning Man burst in a violent explosion of dark nothingness that seemed to stun the entire forest. Emmett felt himself rocked backward before a searing wave of heat passed over him. The wave's force cleared the unnatural fog, and with a single breeze all cleared away and disappeared into the night.

Fading a moment later, the beam of light disappeared, plunging the valley back into darkness. The Grinning Man and the Archivist's Attendant were gone. The empty cabin overlooking the lake was aglow with the low flames that continued to burn from the smoldering wreckage.

Emmett coughed against the smoke, his body aching from the explosion. He felt Amala stirring beside him, heard her forced breathing as she hissed against the pain of hundreds of small wounds all along the length of her body. Oliver and Rhiannon were unmoving and grievously wounded. Keiran was immobile, too.

Part of him wanted to give in to the pain and permit him the ease of unconsciousness.

Let someone else rouse the others.

Let someone else drag the wounded from this place.

Let someone else be the hero.

It was a distant voice that Emmett never heard again. Emmett stood with shaky, uncertain knees like a newly birthed foal and permitted himself a moment's pause for assurance of his footing before checking if his friends were still alive.

CHAPTER 29

Emmett quickly checked each of the four and was thankful they all were breathing, though Oliver only barely. Seeing that Amala was already struggling to rouse herself, he focused on tending to her first.

Kneeling beside her crumpled body, Emmett could not reconcile the image of her battered form amid the wreckage surrounding him. In the dreams of his youth and when he had finally met her in the Blackwater River State Forest, she had possessed a physical grace and uncompromising poise. She had touched him while he lay on the ground with the same care she had held him with moments after his birth.

Now she lay in his arms, damaged and injured in ways he could not imagine, and Emmett noted the symmetry of the moment as he now comforted her in a dark, cold forest many miles from his home. There was a time once when he would have understood the moment's meaning within the context of some movie. The former Emmett. The child Emmett.

Lifting her head slightly, he cradled her neck underneath his arm as he looked down into her face, searching it for some hope of recovery. She had seemed to exert her last strength to remind him of the words in his mother's painting. He did not move her, afraid that he might injure her more, and seeing that no wounds were severely bleeding, understood that it was all he could do to wait. The others lay immobile, and Emmett could only pace his own racing pulse by timing his breathing to hers, as if he could almost breathe for her.

"Amala," Emmett whispered as she continued to struggle opening her eyes. "It's me. It's Emmett. I need you to wake up. Please. I need your help."

She swallowed hard and pushed her eyes completely open, and for a moment they sparkled in the darkness as if they had been closed for years. Her hand grabbed on to Emmett's arm firmly, and she inhaled deeply as she tried to sit up.

"Whoa, hey now. Take it easy," Emmett cooed as he continued to support her body with his own. Amala shook her head and blinked her eyes several times before pushing herself up on her own knees.

"Is he gone?" she all but whispered through several gasping coughs. "You banished him?"

Still kneeling beside her, Emmett kept a watchful arm just behind her back in case she lost consciousness or fell backward. "He's gone."

She turned around slightly and put one hand on the ground as if to steady herself, her head hanging low as she closed her eyes and coughed several more times.

"The others?"

"Breathing but barely. I need your help."

Emmett steadied her as she moved between them, first to Keiran, and then to Rhiannon, and finally to Oliver, whom she agreed appeared to be in the worst condition.

Despite her injuries, Amala helped Emmett carry the three down toward the lake's edge, using the fresh water to wash away the glass from their wounds and comfort each of them until they awoke. It was silent, focused work.

Kneeling on the ground, Amala cradled Keiran's head in her hands as she brushed his blond hair away from his closed eyes. Emmett knelt beside Rhiannon and Oliver, occupying himself by continuing to wash or remove glass from their exposed skin. He watched Amala's careful movements of her hands over Keiran's body, checking and rechecking for open wounds, and all the while staring at him with an expression that silently articulated the most intimate, private emotions the Companions shared.

With all that had transpired, Emmett felt that familiar pang in his heart. The Archivist's words, though, echoed in his mind. He could not know how their journeys were intertwined, yet he needed only to remember Amala holding him in her arms to know that she cared intimately for Emmett, too.

Amala touched her forehead to Keiran's. In the silent winter twilight and above the soft sound of the lake's ripples along the pebble shoreline, Emmett heard her whispering delicate words into Keiran's ear. Emmett could not discern the words she spoke, yet when she finished she lifted her head up and held one hand to his jaw.

Keiran awoke quickly only moments later, his eyes opening as he groaned. Lifting his hand to touch Amala's, he managed a strained smile as his eyes continued to flutter, and Amala brushed her hand through his hair again as he inhaled deeply.

"And I, you," he said. Amala only nodded, and then she looked to Emmett who was still standing a respectful, emotional distance away.

"Emmett, join us, please," Amala said quietly, and Emmett stepped over Rhiannon and Oliver to kneel alongside Keiran opposite Amala.

"All right?" Keiran managed to say with a croak in his voice, the color slowly returning to his pale cheeks.

He looked dangerously frail to Emmett, more than at any other point in their long journey already. This was his sentinel—his brother—and never before did Emmett recognize how very human he was, how easily he, too, could succumb to death in the defense of Emmett's life.

Emmett felt the words lost in his throat, and he could not bring himself to say everything that he needed to say. Emmett began to understand the Archivist's words: *You may not realize your impact until you see another person give their life for you.*

"You look crackin', mate." Keiran grinned, and Emmett's insides buoyed with relief upon seeing joy once again returning to his face.

"You look horrible," Emmett said. "If you don't get up, I'm going to take a picture and upload it to every site I can find."

"You bloody won't," Keiran laughed with several rasping coughs.

"Let's help Keiran up, Emmett, so he can tend to himself and the others."

Keiran felt unstable in their arms as he shuddered under his own sweet melodies, healing himself only enough to stand properly and focus on rousing Oliver and then Rhiannon to a semblance of awareness. Emmett was certain that their internal injuries must have been severe, the external bruising on various places of their bodies already turning dark purple on their skin.

Oliver awoke next. Emmett assumed that because his injuries were so severe and Keiran's strength was so greatly weakened that Keiran had only enough energy left to tend superficially to their wounds. Oliver said nothing when his eyes opened and, seeing Rhiannon lying with hastily applied bandages and the other three in states of injury, too, seemed to understand immediately the moment's triage and struggled to rise and assist Keiran.

Another fifteen minutes passed as Keiran's songs were joined with Oliver's, strained and muted though they were. Rhiannon rose finally, her waterfall of red curls matted to her porcelain skin with sweat, dried blood, and debris still tangled in her hair. Her green eyes had lost much of the Druidic sparkle. She watched with a satisfied expression as her Wisdom swooped down from a tree and nudged the side of her cheek.

With Rhiannon now awake and both Keiran and Oliver seeming to finish their ministrations, Amala stepped into their circle and spoke. "The Archivist's Attendant gave her life, banishing The Grinning Man. Now that Emmett is healed, we will leave here."

Emmett watched each of them, in turn, look from Amala to Emmett. Though Keiran looked on him with an expression of profound appreciation, and Rhiannon's was one of contemplation, Oliver's countenance was as guarded and cautious as anything Emmett had ever experienced before. He did not make direct eye contact with Emmett, nor did his posture denote anything he might be thinking.

"We will remove any evidence from the van. Then we'll hike back toward the main highway and find a ride out of the mountains and to an airport. We are in agreement?" Amala said more than asked.

Keiran and Rhiannon both said yes, and Oliver merely nodded once without comment. Emmett knew by their expressions that Amala was avoiding the most critical issue: an Old One had come for Emmett.

As the moonlight danced along the water, the van's glowing embers began to die. The natural world displayed its usual resiliency as the forest slowly returned to its winter chorus as if nothing had disturbed it. With the first sounds of hooting owls, the expressions on the four Children subtlety shifted to comfort. Emmett imagined how they must experience it, Bards with their ears and Druids with their eyes. It was the night's songs, nature's songs. The Song of Creation.

Amala explained to Emmett when they began their long walk back out of the mountains that the cabin had been abandoned for many years and no one lived for many miles to have witnessed what happened. She never explained how she knew or what her connection to the area was, but it was a sign of Emmett's true fatigue that he did not ask.

The walk down the mountain was blessedly silent. Even Keiran was quiet as he walked just behind Emmett with Amala leading. Even now, after Emmett was finally healed, the pair still guarded him. Oliver and Rhiannon maintained a noticeable distance from each other. Emmett would notice Rhiannon watching Oliver, and when he would follow her eyes to Oliver, he would notice that Oliver had been staring cautiously at him.

There was no question in Emmett's mind that Oliver was already now recounting everything that Emmett had ever said or done in his presence, reconsidering Keiran's actions in light of everything that had happened.

Then there was Omar Hazrat. He had all but implied his own suspicions when he had questioned Emmett. News would soon reach him from Oliver that Emmett had been attacked by The Grinning Man, if he did not know already through his visions of the Mara or had not known all along.

When they finally reached the main highway just before dawn, Emmett began to see cars that they could flag down. Keiran was approaching the shoulder to wave at a passing motorist just as Oliver turned to Emmett specifically and confirmed everything Emmett had been expecting.

"Emmett, what did the Hag say to you when you met her outside the train?" Oliver pointedly asked, drawing a confused look from Rhiannon as she looked to Keiran for silent explanation.

Emmett saw Keiran turning around from the highway shoulder to look from Amala to him, and Emmett did not need to look into his eyes to know what he was thinking. "We already knew an Old One was present at the train attack."

Emmett knew that there was no point in lying to Oliver, so he spoke plainly. "Nonsense, mostly. Isn't that the way of beings like that?"

"And now The Grinning Man. What did he say into *your* mind?"

Emmett saw Keiran take a step away from the road and toward Emmett, perhaps to physically come between them in an effort to shield him.

Oliver had his back to the three of them, so he could not see that Amala held her hand up to stop Keiran, shaking her head briefly without looking back at Emmett. Rhiannon, too, was watching the interplay between them as she absently stroked the copper-headed hawk perched on her shoulder.

"Does it matter? Does evil need a motive to *be* evil?" Emmett asked rhetorically.

Oliver's eyes narrowed. Emmett saw the suspicion, and the mistrust.

"So why would something so *old* come for you? Twice now, you have encountered the Old Ones. Who, exactly, are you? Why are the Old Ones so interested in Emmett Brennan?"

As one they all turned to stare at Emmett.

Emmett searched himself for a peace that could quell the uneasiness that comes from the emotional vacuum left by unanswered questions. In searching, Emmett's mind spread out before him a verdant plain of tall, waving grasses; a mighty tree that offered shade from the hot sun overhead; a proud lion that watched over gorillas, antelope, elephants, and infants that suckled from their mothers; and whispers from an ageless, genderless presence that sat among them.

Her words came unbidden to his mind once again: *It has already begun, and it begins tonight.*

Emmett watched a car drive by on the lone highway as they stood in the shadow of the forest's edge. The four awaited his response. In his mind, Emmett could see a dismembered hand floating above his head, pointing to words written on a wall. Only now, though, Emmett knew what the words were and finally understood them.

"Anyone can be special. Anyone can be the hero that chooses to do great things. After everything I've seen, I *have* to believe that. That makes me a threat to them even on a normal day. And I don't even know what the hell normal is anymore. That's why it doesn't surprise me that evil would come for me. Now that I know what's out there, I'm coming for it."

Keiran and Amala only smiled. Nothing in what he said had changed how they saw him. They already *knew* Emmett. It was Emmett who had not yet known himself.

Oliver nodded with a restrained look of circumspection that told Emmett that there would be many conversations between Oliver and Omar Hazrat. The Lighthouse would further investigate who Emmett Brennan truly was.

"And so it is, brother. I take my leave of you and return home," Oliver said as he turned to Keiran. He clasped Keiran on the shoulder with a detached, almost formal air. He nodded at Amala, too, before turning and walking away, presumably to some distance from them before attempting to gain a ride from the rare passing motorist. Rhiannon's expression was an obvious hurt which briefly showed before she regained her composure and smiled.

"The Archivist was right about you," Rhiannon said, unexpectedly embracing Emmett. She then touched his cheek and smiled. "You have your mother's eyes." Emmett felt the lump in the back of his throat, and he did his best to swallow it.

"Are you coming with us?" Amala asked.

Rhiannon released Emmett and stepped back from him. "You don't need me now that you have your Companion. What an interesting little trio the three of you will make," she added, looking between them.

"Would be better with you, Red," Keiran smiled.

"My journey lies elsewhere. But I'll be seeing you soon enough."

"Where are you going?" Amala asked.

"I am not the first Druid to lose her Companion, nor the first to still hear him in her mind at moments of his intense pleasure." She turned away from them to look at the forest as she spoke. "Our young Emmett was right, sister. We need only quiet ourselves to hear the Song in our hearts and allow it to sustain us. The time will come when I commune and find the peace that I once had. The Archivist has more for me to do. But if you have need of me, you need only send a calling. I will always come to you."

Rhiannon stepped away and headed for the forest, turning around once to speak to Amala. "I am very proud of you, Amala. Despite all that has happened between us, I am thankful each day for Oliver Gray ... for without him, I never would have found you."

Before Amala could respond, Rhiannon turned and walked directly into the trees, her hawk turning its head to watch the trio standing together beside a dark, empty highway.

Amala looked down at the ground, her hair falling into her face. Keiran put a hand on her shoulder, and she reached up to touch it with her own.

It was Emmett who broke the initial silence. "Once we get to

328

somewhere *safe*," he began, motioning with his head in the direction Oliver had walked and presumably could still hear them, "we'll discuss everything *else*. Okay?"

Amala's answer was a sudden and tight embrace. Emmett felt her soft skin against his as she held to him.

Emmett saw Keiran staring at him, watching his response. There was no jealousy in his eyes. Emmett allowed himself only a moment's hesitation before bringing his own arms around her, finally holding the woman of his dreams with nothing between them.

Keiran smiled and placed his hand on the back of Emmett's neck, firm and comforting with a brotherly love that did not require words to express or convey. It was all that Emmett could do to fully return Amala's embrace and turn his head toward Keiran, silently mouthing the words he was certain that Keiran already knew.

For the first time in his life, Emmett felt complete, connected to *this* world. He finally understood what joy was—intoxicating and boundless to the expectations and limitations of the mundane world. Overwhelmed by his joy, Emmett did not notice the Hag standing in the distant trees watching them. Or the other Old Ones in the forest—powerful, fearsome beings of eons past whose names had been long since forgotten to myth and legend—who had all come to silently bear witness to The Grinning Man's eternal banishment at the hands of the apocalyptic Waking Dreamer.

CHAPTER 30

A heavy, laden sleep overtook Emmett as their plane's ascent breeched the dawn's stretch of clouds to cross the morning horizon. It was the first time that he fell asleep without any effort. No visions or cryptic dreams came to him in his first true sleep since being healed of the Rot the day before.

He continued to sleep and think of the spiraling world around him as their plane descended and the cabin lights turned on with the usual warning spiels. Keiran roused him with a nudge and a plastic cup of ice water. It was almost stinging in its temperature, forcing his eyes open with a suddenness that was actually refreshing. He was awake fully, perhaps for the first time in weeks. For the first time, indeed, in his life.

It was this new life that his mind immediately focused on. Shaken though they all were, Amala had found a measure of comfort in the Archivist's instructions. Keiran, of course, accepted her confidence as his own, bounding about with the same jovial charm that Emmett had experienced when waking in Silvan Dea in Portland.

Emmett found that even now, on occasion his hand would absently trail the renewed flesh along his neck and chest where the Rot had once been, feeling the odd twitch or spasm as a shadow of the pain that had sorely snaked along his torso. Healed though he was and returned to some form of obscurity from those who had once pursued him, Emmett seemed nevertheless accepting of the Archivist's plain issuance: that his journey was only just beginning, and it was their journey, too. He was important in ways he did not fully *understand* and yet somehow *understood*.

For what final purpose he could not say, and yet without knowing the finality of it all, he nonetheless felt a stirring pride, a desire to live a life whose purpose was greater than his abilities. It was a longing that challenged him, the voice of a kindly old man present in his thoughts: *I try my best. I don't know if it's good enough, but it's all I can do. Someday soon, I'll be going home to be with my wife and daughter, and if I can measure up halfway to the lives they led, I'll feel okay about standing in their shadow.*

Purpose swelled in his heart, fed by passion that burned in his soul. It was a thirst that could only be sated by living, truly living. It wasn't in movies or work or the everyday life. True living was inconvenient. It necessitated effort. It was found in the moments when breathing required deliberate focus. It derived from purpose when lives were robbed of joy, and yet somehow, quite inexplicably and beyond what anyone believed was possible, it persevered and survived with meaning and intention.

Life finally felt as if it had to be *earned* before it could be truly experienced … where life, for all its hidden mysteries and wonders, was intrinsically *alien*.

"All right?" Keiran nudged Emmett just as Amala was leaning across the aisle and appearing to check to see if their seatbelts were both fastened.

"Yeah," Emmett said as he rubbed his eyes again. Lost in introspection, Emmett had not been listening to Keiran talking to him about their first plans once they landed. The pilot was wishing them a Happy Holidays just as the flight crew began to inspect the cabin in preparation for landing.

"So we're in agreement, then? Take care of the particularities and then a spot of shopping before we fly out, aye?" He was leaning toward Emmett in a hushed whisper, and he knew that this meant that Keiran wanted Emmett's agreement before telling Amala, for it was likely that she would not approve otherwise.

Keiran loved Amala; that much was obvious. Emmett evoked in Keiran a childlike playfulness like a brother conspiring with his younger sibling to play some practical joke. That Amala seemed to regard their interaction with passivity rather than irritation encouraged Keiran all the more. Only Emmett would see that when Keiran had his back to Amala, she would look down with the briefest smirk to herself that Emmett was uncertain if she intended for him to see or not.

"If we're flying to Brazil, I daresay a basic trundle of goods would be in order, don't you? I'm not suggesting a full wardrobe, mind you, but a proper selection at the very least, mate. You agree with me that a few hours for shopping would be beneficial, yes? Because I think Amala would appreciate hearing you agree with me on this point. You'll tell her, Em, yes?"

Emmett never ceased to be amazed at Keiran's own boundless enthusiasm. He had overhead Nancy calling him "Em" over the phone and had adopted it himself ever since. It was a testament of who Keiran had become to Emmett that the nickname no longer bothered him.

He had called Nancy from the local airport the three had caught a ride to. Amala purchased a disposable cell phone for him, and Emmett had blocked the call so Nancy would not see he was not calling from Ormond Beach. He told her how he was settled quite comfortably with a job and an apartment and the promise of schooling in the spring and all other manner of things that Nancy found both reassuring and placating.

The call was the first step in what Amala referred to as the Sundering, the process of separating oneself from the world and truly embracing the Song. The Sundering meant that a new Druid or Bard would say good-bye to their former life and experience a rebirth, with new awareness and openness to unknown possibilities. Amala was firm that Emmett would undergo the Sundering, Annie not having fully done so, which led to her death. Amala wouldn't have that happen again. Not to Emmett.

That the Archivist had not explicitly stated that Emmett was to be made a Bard but rather that his journey was now one with Amala and Keiran's satisfied Amala that he would be made a member of Silvan Dea, a Grove that, if all others were dead, would still exist and survive in them. That Amala said this to Emmett with the same pride and conviction as Keiran's proclamation to the Hag made Emmett swell with even greater conviction.

She began to explain the process almost immediately as they waited for Keiran to flag down a passing truck out on that highway in the Appalachian Mountains. Amala had looked at him with an expression of warmth and pride as they stood together in the silent dawning hours of a crisp December morning.

"You will need to say good-bye to everything that composed your life, Emmett: family, friends, places. Everything that defined who you once were must be removed. Your presence puts them in danger now."

"So where do we begin?" Emmett had asked as he saw Keiran waving at them, for a motorist had pulled onto the shoulder.

"You tell me," she said with a smile.

He heard Derrick in his mind. *I do miss that beautiful smile of hers.*

Emmett answered without having to pause for thought. He

knew where he had to go to begin his journey, their journey. Had he been alone in the world, nothing could have caused him to return. With Keiran and Amala now, Emmett knew there was nothing that he could not face. For he was never truly alone, after all.

"Detroit," he answered just as Keiran called out for them to hurry and get in the waiting vehicle. "There's one person I need to say good-bye to."

As their plane taxied into the terminal, a gray, overcast morning welcomed Emmett back to Detroit. As they deplaned, Keiran insisted to Amala that he considered it to be utterly barbaric and cruel—"quite uncivilized," he repeated three times—to force Emmett to begin the Sundering without proper attire before their journey. Only when she finally agreed did Keiran stop insisting that the outing was quite appropriate and reasonable for Emmett's sake.

None took notice of the trio that seemed to glide with ease down the concourse; alert and vigilant the amber-eyed beauty, confident and jovial the angular-faced young man, and bemused and windswept the seemingly fragile boy who had faced death more than once and bested it each time.

The harsh, fluorescent lights and monotonous announcements of the airport terminal washed the throngs of travelers in a sea of noise. The noise and light caused Keiran to flinch and Amala to don sunglasses. Perhaps he had always been sensitive to it, or perhaps something else had changed in him already, but Emmett found himself flinching, too.

They took a taxi from the airport out onto the twisting, clogged arteries. When they arrived at the Renaissance Center on Keiran's insistence, an amused Emmett and Amala tagged behind as Keiran abandoned all pretense that they were there for Emmett and hurried between designer shops with the excitement of a child on Christmas morning. The air was filled with the haunting chorus of "What Child Is This," and all around Emmett was the flurry of last-minute shoppers hurrying for gifts for Christmas Eve parties later that evening.

"An entirely new wardrobe for a Brazilian New Year, yes? Oh, nothing flashy, I promise. Something appropriate for the climate," Keiran said. "The fact is that we have no idea what grand adventures we have before us now that our pair has become a trio. I think at least two dozen or so different outfits with some seasonably appropriate accessories would be required."

"Emmett and I will leave you here if you insist on bringing that much, Keiran," Amala said, her dark features able to convey an appropriate degree of seriousness despite the minor smile that she tried to hide on her face.

"Oh, honestly, I'm only thinking of Emmett. The boy would spend his life in denim if permitted. I think not, Amala. We could be down in Brazil for months. We could even be there for *Carnaval*. Oh, we must take him if we are still down there, Amala! He would positively love it!"

"I'm picturing Keiran shirtless on a float in silver glitter paint," Emmett said.

"Perhaps gold, thank you," Keiran deadpanned.

"I think you're forgetting that ever since that last little episode—"

"I knew you'd bring that up again, Amala. Every time you mention it. How many times must I apologize for that?" Keiran interrupted.

"—you are banned from ever stepping foot in Rio again. If you do, you can find yourself a new Companion," Amala laughed as Keiran waved dismissively at her.

"Oh, it doesn't matter because everyone knows that the true fun is in Bahia, anyway. You can be as stodgy and insufferable as you wish so long as you stay at home. I can take Emmett with me and we'll have a grand time."

"Don't think you won't regret that," Amala warned Emmett with a smile. "If you value your sleep at all."

"The insomniac worried about sleep? Really?" Emmett snarked, to which Amala laughed.

"Ignore her. Remind me, Em, to take you to this gorgeous little eatery that overlooks the Bay of All Saints down in Salvador. This wonderful woman I know makes the most incredible *vatapá* you will ever have in your life. Marvelous blend of shrimp, coconut milk, and African palm oil. It's quite immense, really. Otherworldly. Pure heaven, mate."

Keiran bounded into another clothing store and set the staff into motion with his presence. Emmett was already thinking of Emaline Carmichael as Amala leaned toward him with a whisper. "He has little old women in practically every city on every continent," she said seriously with a raised eyebrow that made Emmett laugh.

They joined him in the store, and Emmett listened as Keiran continued to promise to show him all the best of wherever they traveled: the sorts of hidden, tucked-away gems that only people who valued the local culture could truly experience or appreciate. Amala spent most of her time teasing him as he alternated between acting emotionally wounded or completely unaffected.

Emmett enjoyed the casualness that they shared now that the pressing need of curing Emmett of the Rot or alerting Silvan Dea of an impending attack was passed.

After Amala stopped for morning drinks for the three of them, Keiran continued to lead them to different boutique stores throughout the morning. Always it was the same experience.

Emmett and Amala would sit quietly on a bench and watch as he bounded through the store, reminding them often that he was there for them, of course, sorting through various outfits arranged and brought to him by the attentive store clerks. That he was the center of attention of every store's employees was enough to make both Amala and Emmett chuckle as he turned heads wherever they went.

"Honestly, I don't know how you do it," Emmett had said as they sat together watching him admire the cut of a new pair of slacks in a full-length mirror.

"You know that he doesn't even see it, right?" Amala asked as she sipped from her chai tea. "How affected they all are by him?" Keiran was joining in a conversation with a mother and teenage daughter who were shopping for some special event, offering his much-desired sensibility to their decision-making process. That Keiran seemed able to convince the young daughter that she would be quite a bit more attractive in a more conservative ensemble, to the mother's delight, made Emmett laugh out loud.

Emmett sipped his own hot chocolate with mint as he watched how Keiran smiled and laughed so freely with the strangers around him, so completely comfortable and confident in his own skin. *So* unlike Emmett. Before now, at least.

"And it doesn't bother you?"

"You mean do I get jealous?" Amala looked at him. She was wearing her brown hair down this morning, and its full length draped elegantly around her neck and framed her petal-shaped face so perfectly with her wide amber eyes that glittered from the surrounding light though hidden from curious onlookers by a pair of sunglasses.

"What you two have as Companions goes well beyond special. It wouldn't be unreasonable if you were protective of it, you know?"

"It's not quite like that, Emmett," she smiled, sipping again from her tea. "Words are so awfully imprecise, and that one is perhaps the most imprecise of them all."

"'A word means what you choose it to mean,'" Emmett said, bringing his hot chocolate up to his face and enjoying its sweet steam as it tickled his nose.

"Companions are chosen by our Elders. Often it is a bonding borne of practicality. If there is a new Druid or Bard in a Grove, the Elder selects someone of a similar temperament, and perhaps only due to availability. Siblings are usually joined as Companions. It is far more a relationship of sensibility and sometimes expediency."

"Keiran spoke of it with so much more—"

"Passion? Intensity?"

"Yeah."

"Love in all its various forms isn't forbidden by *ikkibu*. We celebrate it. Some believe that Companions cannot experience the truest strength of bonding unless they *are* in love. Others think differently."

"And you?"

Amala closed her lips and swallowed slowly. "I love him, Emmett. How could I not? He would give his life for me a thousand times and never once ask for anything from me in return. He would devote himself to filling my life with laughter and joy and that boyish grin of his. You know what I'm talking about, don't you?"

Emmett nodded immediately. "I do."

She looked wistfully at him as he walked between racks of clothes and gestured excitedly at new outfits brought to him by the store's clerks. "I would absolutely do the same for him. Without question. But could I love him in *that* way? Could I let

338

him love *me* in that way? No. There will always be a part of me that I could never give him."

Emmett saw the flash of something conflicted in her eyes, and he instinctively looked away to respect whatever struggle was there. That she could experience it for that briefest moment in Emmett's presence told of vulnerability and trust that he knew was not easily granted.

Emmett looked down and cleared his throat. He wanted to say it ever since they had left the Appalachian Mountains. Perhaps ever since she had come for him on Prince Edward Island. There had never been a moment to tell her, though, before now.

"Amala, I want to thank you," he said simply, unable to make eye contact. "For saving my life. For everything."

Placing her hand on his, she smiled and raised her tea. "You can make it up to me by keeping Keiran entertained when he gets all excited about going out. I could use the rest."

The panging feeling of jealousy was gone. Sitting beside the woman who had held him at birth and populated his life's dreams felt comfortable and familiar now. Neither had discussed what Emmett had learned from the Archivist's vision of Amala and how that might relate to Keiran being her Companion. Nor had Emmett asked how Amala had dreamed of him, too, as he had dreamed of her.

Emmett knew that eventually they must deal with it. But not today.

"Deal," Emmett smiled, watching Keiran waving at them as he purchased his latest selections.

Several hours later and with new luggage for all three of them to hold their new wardrobes, they took another taxi away from the urban center and toward the inner city. Amala and Keiran sat with respectful silence, their postures of reverence like mourners at a wake. When they arrived at the abandoned hotel, Amala paid for the driver to wait while they went inside.

Emmett said nothing as he stepped over broken glass and syringes. He sighed when he turned the corner and entered the boiler room of his birth. It looked the same as it did in the memory of his birth the Archivist had shown him.

He stood in silence for several minutes, wondering to himself what he needed to do to say good-bye.

As if to guide him, or simply to support him as he found his own path, he felt Keiran's firm grasp on his shoulder and Amala's reassuring hand along the small of his back. Silently, they stood with him, and their presence in that moment of grief released a burden weighing on him ever since he had finally seen what his mother had suffered for him.

I guess I should say good-bye. He had never known his mother, of course; only now did he know something of her from the dreams of his youth. He spent his childhood avoiding an orphan's isolation with the magic promised in film—distant shores where islands hid the secrets of mythical beasts and ancient peoples; stars and planets and galaxies that teemed with life undiscovered; places traveled to in the remote past and the far-off future. And somewhere amid this great fascination, his mother had once lived.

But she had not. She had become pregnant with the Waking Dreamer, the last Mara to bear the visions of the Chief of the Old Ones. The Rugged Mountain. The Unremarkable Man. The unborn infant whispered in his dreams for nine months, driving his mother mad with visions she could not endure and the same words repeated over and over until finally she scrawled them across a reproduction of her favorite painting hanging in her apartment.

Madness touched her mind. There was no room for ghosts that fled through forests; or living dwellings of stone grown so high in the mountains that they touched the very clouds in the sky; or castles that breeched the coast in the cold, stormy north; or monsters that stalked the land; or men whose voices could change winter winds to summer breezes; or women who communed with animals and shared in the infusion of power; of companions who would fight and die to save the life of a stranger.

There was no room for that kind of world. There was no room for that kind of life. The promise of adventure that Emmett had instinctively sought was the adventure his mother had been denied. Because of him.

A tear lapsed heavily onto his cheek, and he shuddered with a faltering gasp, overwhelmed with self-awareness. He bit down on the inside of his cheek, tensing against pain and the bitter tang on his lips.

Then Emmett was crying. He did not know when it began, but when he recognized it fully, it became a heavy sobbing. He felt his grief overtake him, wounded so profoundly that he could not stop himself from experiencing it nakedly in front of his friends. Shoulders sagging, he gasped several times through the tears, feeling Keiran and Amala hold firmly to him through the shuddering pain.

He was crying for his mother; for the Children of Silvan Dea; for the passengers aboard the train; for those whose lives had been taken because of the Waking Dreamer. Whether by chance or fate, Emmett had found purpose in a grand adventure that promised both joy and sorrow and was intertwined with so many deaths.

For several minutes, he cried into his trembling hands. When the tears had run dry and he thought he could cry no more, the emptiness within him seemed to fold inward. It turned in on itself in different ways until it grew smaller, focused, and finally was a distant point beyond his immediate perception. The images of so much death faded from his immediate memory: his mother, alone in her hospital; Paulo and Sebastian's corpses; the frightened passengers who fled helplessly into the night from the burning wreckage of the train; the Attendant who looked to him in the moments before her death; even the cold look of Ellie's face as he killed her with his own hands.

As he steadied his breathing, Emmett found the grief somehow manageable.

Amala and Keiran stood with him in the silence, bearing witness to its passing. They understood his grief, in their own way, and their solidarity gave him the strength to begin letting go.

"It's time," he whispered softly, uncertain who the message was meant for.

The present roar of traffic coming through the roof's holes died away with a heavy, mourning melody. Emmett did not look up, his eyes closing with a final tear as he felt Keiran's song pass through him. It dulled the noise of the world. Its somber tone conveyed the mourning within his heart. He felt the notes pass through him, effortless and light underneath his arms as if it meant to lift him into the sky, far beyond the world below.

"A paean," Emmett nodded.

"We honor a life that has passed as a new one begins today," Amala whispered.

"And on my birthday."

"It is your rebirth," Amala said.

Keiran's notes finally softened. Emmett turned away from the place on the ground where he had been born to face both of them. He did not know where his new life would take him, but he understood that he would not face it alone.

"You ready, mate?" Keiran asked.

Ready for what, exactly? For his new life? To follow Amala and Keiran headlong into the darkness? He had been ready for it since before he knew it was even possible. He had been searching for it the moment he got into his car and began driving for Florida—for answers, purpose, and adventures that ended in rabbit holes. He was ready for a life that had to be *earned*. Truly, he had always been ready.

"I'm afraid," he answered honestly.

"Then you see clearer than most," Amala responded as Keiran stepped behind her. "There is nothing more powerful than when you recognize that you are inadequate for the journey before you."

"That's when you know you're new life begins," Keiran added.

Emmett heard the Archivist's warning in his mind. He thought of the Old Ones and remembered the Hag's stare and her Black Hounds. He felt the brush of ineffable power from the Revenants that had pursued him; dark and wicked magiks summoned by people whose unknown motives were fueled by some mysterious Master who was already pursuing him. For the Master *knew* Emmett as the Hag knew him. And he was coming for him.

It has already begun, and it begins tonight, Emmett repeated to himself.

Soon is right now.

"I'm ready. Let's do this."

Photo by Beverly Guhl

Joshua Elijah Alexander loves veering off the main road in search of abandoned mines, dense bogs, and other ghost-infested settings for future stories. He is an ardent devotee of esotery, sarcastic fringeheads, and jam. Especially jam. He currently lives in Austin, Texas, with near-term plans for lunar relocation, weather permitting. He encourages fans to connect with him online where his attention can be caught with discussion of cryptids or ginger-infused confections. Or ginger cryptids.

authorJEA.com

www.ingramcontent.com/pod-product-compliance
Lightning Source LLC
Chambersburg PA
CBHW020328180626
46812CB00001B/90